# Strike
# Price

## L.A. Starks

Nemaha Ridge Publishing
Group, LLC

Cover photo courtesy Can Stock Photo at CanStockPhoto.com.
Cover design courtesy HarveyStanbrough.com.
Interior design by Lisa Smith and Nemaha Ridge Publishing
Group, LLC.

This is a work of fiction and is produced from the author's
imagination. People, places and things mentioned in this novel
are used in a fictional manner.

ISBN:      978-0-9911107-0-4

Visit the author on the web at lastarksbooks.com

First print edition published by L&L
Dreamspell, 2013. Second print
edition published by Nemaha Ridge
Publishing Group, LLC, 2014.
Printed in the United States of America

*Note from the author:*

*The people described in this book are fictional. I do not purport to represent any actual security systems, companies, places, or events. All errors are mine.*

*Dedicated to the memory of
Linda Lewis: geologist,
artist, sister.*

⚮

*"There is nothing hidden, except to
be disclosed; nor is anything secret,
except to come to light."*
—Mark 4:22-23

# One

*Vancouver, Downtown Eastside*
*Mid-August, Thursday morning*

If the seventh circle of hell existed on earth, the southwest corner of Main and Hastings was its zip code. To stand in one of North America's most fetid basements, a place nicknamed Pain and Wasting, was to see hopelessness at its most pathetic, horror at its most unredeemable. It was no mistake I was to meet the enforcer here. I had been told he was Chechen.

Main and Hastings warned of the living death I would endure if I didn't accept the terms I had been offered. But the Chechen, or whoever he was, didn't know I'd been suckled on abandonment and neglect.

The squat Chechen was easy to identify, the only healthy-looking person for blocks.

We stepped over a bundle of urine-soaked rags hiding some loser on the nod, walked around feces, and avoided dozens of orange-tipped syringes dotting the sidewalk.

The square-headed man spoke matter-of-factly. "This. Or worse."

"I've seen worse." That wasn't strictly true. In Iraq, there was no separating friend from foe. None in my squad could determine who was hiding explosives in a belt, under a blouse, or in a baby carriage. Yet the Iraqis were vital, full of plans, ripe with love and hatred.

These zombie husks, as desiccated as eighty-year-olds, were tracked and scabbed from cocaine, heroin, and meth. A knot to our left scoured the sidewalk for cans to recycle.

Rain pelted cardboard boxes the heartless called condos, softening them until they collapsed on the oblivious occupants inside.

We wouldn't be overheard. If someone did report us, it would be dismissed as a stoned-out hallucination. If the slightest thing went wrong, I would leave here with broken fingers, a sliced-off ear, a shot-up knee.

We passed boarded-up storefronts and drug deals, a woman skinnier than a runway model and a man with his hand in her shorts, a transgendered woman kissing another something-or-other, two men leaning against a wall, their hands hidden. One lacked all of his teeth. The arms of the second were covered in bruises and speed bumps.

Each looked at me, beseeching. Not to be saved, only to be saved for the moment. Money for the next score. High by ten a.m.

The Chechen grabbed my arm with a muscleman's grip. "If we trust you to do this thing, you good for it?"

I nodded.

"Then we help finish your problem." He drew out the last word, rolling it on his tongue.

I doubted I would ever finish with him or our boss. They had pulled me into a sticky web of payback, keeping me thrashing until time to devour me.

I missed my platoon, though it had been a while since I'd seen them. Somebody would have had the right joke to put this fucked-up place in perspective. More likely, someone would have told us to leave this hellhole and hit clothing-optional Wreck Beach. Let's see if anyone can really rock it in old Van.

I waved away crack smoke, trying not to inhale.

The effects from last night's booze slowed me, or I would have seen what was coming. The enforcer dropped two steps behind me. In a heartbeat there was a gun muzzle at the base of my skull.

A drug deal gone bad, that's all anyone would think when they found my body. Curious skeletons drifted closer, ready to scavenge.

"We give you four weeks," the enforcer whispered.

When the muzzle was gone, so was the Chechen.

# Two

*Dallas, Texas/Tulsa, Oklahoma*
*Thursday afternoon-Friday morning*

"*Rumor travels faster, but it don't stay put as long as truth.*"
—*Will Rogers*

Lynn Dayton, TriCoast's executive vice president of US refining, took off her jacket. She tied blonde hair in a ponytail and
tossed basketballs at one of the five goals in her office, a blue-
gray aerie forty-five floors above the street. Swish. *Should I
worry about this surprise one-on-one meeting with the boss?*
"The only way you'll be Dirk Nowitzki is if you're..."
"Reincarnated as Dirk Nowitzki," she said, completing
Mike Emerson's sentence as he took a chair. She masked her
concern with a casual tone. "Gotta dream, don't I?"
Despite sitting directly across from her, Mike's eyes didn't
meet hers. "Hope your dream is to go to Oklahoma."
"What about our appointment to review your Congressional
testimony on gasoline prices? The most important issue going,
according to you and every media group in the country."
"Claude's got me prepped," he said, referring to TriCoast's
French-born public relations manager. He ticked off on his fingers. "First, the Cherokee Investment Group wants to buy the
Tulsa refinery and supply contracts. They already own many of
the gasoline and diesel stations we supply in eastern Oklahoma.

They want to put in their own guy, but isn't your refinery manager ready to retire anyway? Second, the Saudis are asking. Third, so is an Asian consortium. A UK company wants to bid, too."

Lynn felt her face redden. "Whoa! How can you think of dealing away my refinery and my people without talking to me first? When did this happen? Why haven't I heard about it?"

"I'm talking to you now. There's no deal because the bankers just called me. You saw what the Seminoles invested when they bought the Hard Rock chain."

"Almost a billion bucks." She was annoyed, even as she realized Mike could have kept the secret even longer than he had.

"The Cherokees have the same kind of money and they want to diversify beyond casinos. Besides, Midwestern refineries have become unusually profitable with all the North Dakota and Canadian oil. It's a once-in-lifetime chance to sell." He looked out of one of her glass curtain walls, then back at her, ready as a bulldog.

"And we're the target?" Lynn asked.

"Target is not the word I would use. Look, I know the Tulsa refinery is special to you—hell, you're in love with all of 'em— but you heard the board: our shareholders depend on us to find projects that optimize returns. You keep saying we need to spend money on more-efficient fuel technologies. And by the way, we're still paying for the refinery you had us buy in Houston. You told me you had your eye on another metal mountain in Illinois, right? How do you think we finance these expansions?" He stopped to catch his breath.

Lynn said, "It's true that the Tulsa refinery has become more profitable with all the oil being produced in Canada and the US, even Oklahoma, which many people thought was played out. The whole country is producing more oil than it has in years and it all has to be refined. In short, it's a *terrible* time to sell that refinery. I don't think you're giving my people there the chance they deserve."

"Lynn, the bankers came to me, not vice versa. But we'll be strung up by our shareholders' lawyers, and rightly so, if we don't consider these big bids."

"How big?"

"A billion three."

She felt a jolt in her spine. A billion three was twice the last valuation of the Tulsa refinery. But that valuation had been done a while ago. She recovered enough to say, "I told you it was profitable. But don't you think the banks whispered that number into bidders' ears after they toted up the fees they wanted? Are we going to let our company be picked over every time someone sees a shiny refinery or hot-shit oilfield of ours they like?" She didn't want Mike to see her confusion and suspicion at the high offer.

"As for these bidders, ask your ex-husband."

"Keith?"

"The same. His fund is backing the Cherokee group."

*Crap. Just what I don't need.* "The exploration and production division gets ten times the cash I do."

"First time I've heard of not wanting to sell something for more than twice what it's worth," Mike said.

"The accountants' valuation is out of date. The Tulsa refinery is worth a lot more now. That I can prove."

"You don't have to. These bids do the talking."

"What does Sara think?" Sara Levin was TriCoast's chief financial officer.

"We could use the money for more drilling."

"So much for female solidarity," Lynn replied.

"You're attached to these chunks of steel, aren't you?" His eyes bored into hers.

"Of course. We all are." But it was true that both the refinery and the rolling forests of eastern Oklahoma claimed her heart. A north-south dry line near Interstate 35 bisected the state. East was green. West was a flat, austere plain. Selling the Tulsa refinery meant she'd have fewer reasons to return to the lush hills near which she'd grown up. She hated conceding but was boxed in for now. "Preston Li should go with me," she said, referring to her division's resident statistical genius.

Mike shifted in his chair. "And you need to include Riley Stevens." He held up his hand. "Yes, you've given him severance notice. It's a favor to Burl Travis, his friend on TriCoast's board. Someone you need on your side."

"Jeez, Mike, could you make this a bigger pain? Riley won't help."

As if she'd voiced agreement instead of anger, he said, "So you're going to Tulsa. You're acquainted with the area, right?"

*If I don't take this on, someone else will jump all over it while the wedding planner has me picking out tablecloths. Hell, Dad doesn't care about the color of the napkins. I just want him to live long enough to get to know Cy's children. They'll be my stepchildren, his only grandchildren.*

"Spent six years in Tulsa when I was a kid."

Mike shrugged: his signal to get on with it.

As they drove from the Tulsa airport to the refinery, Riley Stevens settled in the passenger seat. "I told Burl including me would be worth your while. You've got buyers who'll pay a premium price for that junk heap. It's just a collection of ancient metal. And I'm glad you stopped here before the European holiday."

*Does freaking everyone have my schedule?* After Tulsa, Lynn was traveling to Paris to negotiate with the Saudis, and on to London to meet another bidder, North Seas Resources.

Although she'd put Riley in charge of special projects—corporate-speak for "find yourself another job fast"—she hadn't expected him to produce much. She'd never seen him work so hard, but she'd been clear he still only had two months left with TriCoast. If he stopped hitting on the young women around him, Riley could be a good hire for the next company.

Lynn laughed as she steered the rented Camry across the Arkansas River on I-244. "Look, Riley, Tulsa is an up-to-spec refinery processing a hundred thousand barrels a day." She smiled.

"Hardly a bunch of junk and I don't want to sell it."

Riley touched her arm to get her attention. "You won't get another offer like these."

"On the contrary. The Brazilians or the Chinese could call me next week." *Well, they wouldn't call me, a female EVP.* Their bankers would do what they'd already done—call Mike, male and CEO. She kept a sigh to herself.

The moment Mike had told her CIG, the Cherokee Investment Group, had offered to buy TriCoast's Tulsa refinery for $1.3 billion she knew no sane director would turn it down. Feeling proprietary because she was ultimately in charge of this "collection of ancient metal" as Riley put it, didn't change the size of their offer, nor the fact that three others wanted it. So the refinery was in play. Reality was biting, no matter what she wished.

To her left, a sunrise slashed pink. The sky dripped Monet hues, layers of blue, white and orange.

"Mike tells me I'm coming with you to Europe."

She stopped herself from swearing. Riley was the last person she needed stomping through delicate talks with the Saudis, the Asians, and her counterparts at North Seas Resources. She felt her ears glowing. Not only would he interfere but Riley would report everything back to his buddy on the TriCoast board, a director who could shred Lynn's career with a few well-placed telephone calls.

"You okay? Your ears are kind of red." Riley's tone was nonchalant.

"You'll need to get up to speed for the European meetings," Lynn said.

"I'm sure you can tell me what I need to know."

*Two lousy months, Riley Stevens, and you'll be so gone from my life!*

They turned down an asphalt road with dirt shoulders, waited behind tanker trucks, and wheeled left to park in front of a white, flat-roofed, one-story office.

Inside, refinery manager Gene Blahunka offered doughnuts

and coffee from a side table, then introduced two people from CIG: tribal elder Jesse Drum and hefty Jimmy Deerinwater, an accountant. He also introduced Pete Whitehawk, who was missing one finger and whose traditional banker's suit stopped at his bolo tie.

"Hope you haven't been waiting long," Lynn said.

"About thirty minutes. No problem," Gene replied.

"Pete's company may invest with us," Jesse said. "He's already managing some of the tribe's money. Born-and-bred Cherokee who grew up around here, then spent time in New York making big bucks. Used to work in the oil fields, too."

"And I hear you're partners with my ex-husband," Lynn said. *Might as well get it out in the open.*

Pete nodded modestly. "We've done deals together. I'm glad to be back here. I live in Tulsa now." His handshake was firm and dry. She guessed that underneath the suit and bolo tie was the physique of a tennis pro.

Gene's eyes were red and shadowed by dark bags. She took his hand. "How're you feeling?"

He waved away her concern. "The sale has been keeping me up nights. Guess I never really thought it would happen."

When she'd first met him and remarked on his last name, he'd explained spelling Blahunka every day of his life had taught him patience. He'd retained some of his upper Midwestern accent, honed by his extended Polish family and was able to turn one word, "Sure," into so many syllables it was a sentence by itself. "Shoooooooor."

Her engineering manager, Preston Li, had also arrived. Preston was a focused, reliable member of her staff.

Lynn said, "Let's give these gentlemen the tour, shall we?"

She climbed into a white refinery truck with Jesse while Preston squired the other three men in a larger, four-door Tundra. After crossing the road and driving through the security gate, Lynn directed Gene to the first place she expected the CIG buyers would want to visit—the new, seven-story hydrotreating tower.

Standing in harsh summer light near valves at the base of the tower, Gene gestured toward a truck-mounted telescopic crane. Its operator was using a grapple hook to unload lengths of heavy pipe. "We're diversifying our blendstocks so we can use even more heavy oil from Canadian tar sands and the good, light North Dakota crude washing down here in waves."

Pride touched Gene's voice. Although medium-sized and remote from the Gulf Coast, this refinery was up-to-date and technologically flawless. Lynn was surprised when the grinding of the crane sounded louder. From the corner of her eye, she saw it creeping toward them, clutching an immense pipe.

*If it drops....* "Move back, folks." She eased them toward the road.

Gene shouted at the driver to stop, his voice lost in the roar of the massive machine.

Then they all yelled.

"Run!" Lynn shouted, as the crane rolled toward them, its driver seemingly oblivious. A reflective sunshade pulled across the front window of the cab blocked their view of him.

All but Gene ran. He leapt onto the slow-moving crane and clambered up into its cabin. Suddenly a siren sounded and the crane stopped.

Gene leaned out of the cab and shouted down, "Call security! Tom Martin's dead!"

# Three

*Tulsa*
*Friday afternoon*

Despite the expert CPR the refinery's volunteer firefighters gave the driver, EMTs verified the crane operator's death from an apparent heart attack. Lynn felt another punch in her gut. The driver, Tom Martin, shared a first name with her father, Tom Dayton. Her father, who would soon follow Tom Martin to the grave.

The Cherokee investors left after offering condolences. Riley promised to wait for the medical examiner. Gene called Tom's minister, who agreed to meet them at the Martins' house so they could notify his wife in person.

As she guided their car through Tulsa streets, Lynn's heart sank. This was the worst part of her job. Fortunately it was rare, but once was too often.

The asphalt became patchier as they wound through the narrow streets west of the Arkansas River. Single-story Craftsman bungalows with tapered columns and big porches showed the area's origins in 1920s wealth. Nearby Glenpool had been the site of the first major Oklahoma oil discovery. The Tulsa refineries on the Arkansas River were built soon after.

Their Camry stood out on a street full of old Expeditions and Suburbans. After she parked the car they waited on a cracked, brownish sidewalk, its 1946 cement contractor's stamp still visible.

She wished she could rewind the day, wished desperately they'd been able to save Tom Martin.

A small, white sedan pulled up, and a man with a nose as flat as a hockey goalie's stepped out, adjusting his white clerical collar. Lynn and Gene introduced themselves.

Tom's wife cautiously opened her front door. "Gene? Reverend? Whatcha doing here in the middle of the day? Is Tom all right?"

Gene shook his head. "I have bad news. Tom seemed fine when I saw him early this morning, but he collapsed a little while ago. Medics think it was a heart attack. I'm afraid he didn't make it."

Her face seemed to fold in on itself. "Oh no. That's not possible!" She sobbed. "No! You have the wrong house!"

"Mrs. Martin, let's go inside." The minister turned to Lynn and Gene. "Could you please wait out here?" He put his arms around Tom's wife and she stumbled against his support.

When the door closed behind them, Gene sat on a rusted lawn chair. "Tom told me he just had his physical. I wouldn't remember except the doctor told him he had the EKG of a teenager. He looked so pleased when he said it."

"Medical problems get missed." She thought of her mother's bone cancer, hiding and growing for years before the symptoms exploded into view. When they did—unexplained fractures and nonstop pain—it was too late.

The screen creaked open and the minister motioned them inside.

They sat on folding chairs around a tiled mosaic coffee table. Mrs. Martin looked at them without seeing. The minister took their cards and placed them on the table.

"Mrs. Martin, I work with Gene," Lynn said.

"You're the one selling the refinery, aren't you? Tom said you'll have every damn nationality in the world traipsing through. Asians, Arabs, Englishmen, even the Cherokees from down the road, made so much damn money with their casinos. Tom's been worried sick about his job. The stress of the sale killed him!

He's dead and it's *your fault,* lady!" She leaned across the table and grabbed Lynn's shoulders.

The minister and Gene moved next to Tom's wife and lifted her arms from Lynn. The woman bent her head. "You couldn't possibly understand how much I loved him!"

Lynn thought of her fiancé Cy Derett, his children Matt and Marika, and of her father gasping for each shallow breath his emphysema allowed. "I do understand."

# Four

*Berlin*
*Saturday*

In the last weekend warm enough for sunbathing, throngs of men and a few women lay facedown in Berlin's vast Tiergarten Park. Fair-skinned sunbathers prided themselves on their deliberate recklessness of exposing skin to sun naked of sun block, or anything else. The air was crystalline, the blue of the sky infinite.

A cell phone rang and one of the bodies rolled over, wrapped a bath towel around his waist, and answered. Gernot Insel's chest was smooth-shaven and glistening. Hair dark, green eyes close-set, his features showed his Austrian heritage.

His clients were legitimate businesspeople representing governments, organizations, funds, or companies who wanted information not easily found on the Internet or through normal channels. Often, they wanted more.

The rows of slick bodies around him increased the risk he would be overheard. The park was too quiet for this conversation. He told the client he would return the call.

Insel dressed, carefully wiped the phone, strode a kilometer to Strasse Des 17 Juni, and hailed a taxi. He bent as if to tie his shoe and slid the phone in front of one of the taxi's rear tires. He listened as they pulled away and was satisfied to hear the crunch.

Insel's driver sailed east, staying away from the bicycle lane with its beautiful young women pedaling clunky commuter bicycles. He turned past crowds of tourists and buses at the Brandenburg gate. Berlin was changing—change was its essence—yet the blocky, preserved buildings and museums of East Berlin remained, dour impediments. *All capitals are the same anachronistic tributes to the past,* Insel thought, *full of museums and little else.*

He wondered if the foreigners pouring money into Berlin had seen the city beyond its government-funded Potsdamer Platz vibrancy. Brash but sophisticated, Berlin was rebuilding itself, starting with its well-supported government center. Sponsors' names were omnipresent—DeutscheBank, DeutscheBahn, Starbucks, Dunkin' Donuts. But the city, like the country, struggled to combine its long-separated east and west halves. Berlin officials were reluctant to cut subsidies to the three opera houses, two zoos, and six housing authorities, so the city strained financially. Reunification costs had been followed by the burden of supporting entire other countries in the European Union. Thus, the massive Sony Center and film museum were the exception; graffiti marked walls in the rest of the city. Even Sony had sold off ownership of its center, though it had kept the name.

Nominally Insel was Austrian, but he traveled around the world. His office and favorite house were in Vienna; here he kept a suite reserved at the Mandala Hotel. His irrational attachment to Vienna aside, the glittering condo he owned on Canada's Vancouver waterfront was a better investment. Indeed, the client who had just phoned had leased it a few days last week for a substantial sum.

The driver maneuvered south on Ebertstrasse, slowing for more tourists—these shaken and grim—leaving the undulating maze of crypts that was the Monument to the Murdered Jews. One of the older American tourists Insel had met insisted the monument belonged a few blocks over, on the front lawn of the Reichstag, as a reminder to German lawmakers. In America, he'd said, every president and congressman in the nation's capital could see headstones of the thousands buried in Arlington Cemetery.

Insel had shrugged. Guilt, piles of it, was everywhere. Though some of his best friends were Americans, in the eyes of many of them, Germans should be swallowing guilt *mit alle mahlzeit,* with every meal.

Near Potsdamer Platz, foreigners stepped back and forth across the double row of cobblestones striping the wall's former location, saying, "East, West, East, West."

It was a good story, happier than the war, the horror of which had left a fifty-year hole in Germany's history. He Who Could Not Be Named became It That Could Not Be Named. The practical side of the eraser taken to history was to avoid marking places where neo-Nazis could create shrines.

In the current cultural mythology, tearing down the wall brought the Germans more benefit and security than when the wall meandered through the city. Even Checkpoint Charlie was as commercialized as a Bavarian castle.

Gernot assessed the bicycle lane as he exited the cab, stepping back when a velotaxi charged past, its driver pedaling hard while the young girl and older man he carried sat forward, looking around eagerly. He heard the girl say in English, "Berlin will be something to tell my classmates about. They've all been to New York, Paris, Rome, and London, but not here." She seemed too earnest to dismiss as yet another spoiled, over-traveled child. Yet at her pace, she'd be seeking more dangerous experience within a few years.

Neither Interpol nor any other European, American, or Asian security agency had evidence against him. As a precaution, though, he'd started charging more for London assignments—too many security cameras. And, most of his assignments were legitimate.

The angular, urban design of the Mandala Hotel was the perfection Berlin could be—hip, restless, urban, compact, and well-engineered.

Only a few groceries remained in the suite's refrigerator. He'd asked the staff to get wine and a few of the thousand types of sausage sold at eight-story KaDeWe.

In the suite's bedroom he switched the television channel to the music video station Viva in time to hear a replay of the song "Emanuela" by the band, Fettes Brot. He hummed the refrain,"lass die finger von Emanuela"—"keep your hands off Emanuela"—and relished the soft warmth of the goose-down duvet he pulled over his feet. He picked up another cell phone and returned his client's call.

The client had a new project. Although he would not be given much time, it was sufficiently intriguing. His fee was non-negotiable. Those who couldn't afford his multi-million-euro retainer didn't telephone.

At the end of the conversation, he called to cancel his KaDeWe grocery order, called another contact about certain supplies he would need shipped, and began to pack.

# Five

> *"Even if you're on the right track, you'll get run over if you just sit there."* —*Will Rogers*

Gene Blahunka answered his phone, listened, and said, "Send her through." When he hung up he said, "Crap. She's here."

"Who?" Lynn asked. She and Preston had been talking to Gene about who would replace him when he retired.

"Neliah Jefferson, the medical examiner's investigator. She's here about Tom Martin's death. Lynn, Preston, would you answer her questions with me?"

"Sure, if you think we can help. Need to check with Tyree?" she asked, referring to TriCoast's general counsel.

"I already did, earlier. He's fine with you two sitting in."

"So you planned our meeting on refinery personnel knowing Jefferson would show up?" *Wish you'd given us more notice.*

"You saw what happened to Tom. You visited his wife with me."

When the knock came, Gene opened his office door to an African-American woman taller than Lynn's five-foot-nine. The woman's black pantsuit had kept its press despite the August heat.

"Investigator Jefferson, this is Lynn Dayton, our executive

executive vice president of refining and Preston Li, engineering manager, both from our corporate office."

Jefferson sat in one of Gene's brown leather chairs and drew open a tablet computer. "I'm sorry to hear about Tom's death. The medics thought it was a heart attack or stroke."

"Maybe heat stress?" Gene said, a little too quickly. "Although people here who are terminally ill usually die at the beginning of summer to save themselves the trouble of four hot months." His laugh sounded nervous.

Lynn thought of her father gasping for each breath and hated Gene's honesty. Her father's doctor expected him to live another two to eight months but the only part of the range Lynn had heard was "eight months."

The investigator stared at Gene, then said, "I've spoken on the phone with his wife and seen his medical records. His wife said his recent physical was nearly perfect. Didn't smoke. No diabetes. She doesn't understand it."

"Me, either," Gene said. "He underwent all the training. Everyone here participates in a weekly safety drill, so if something went wrong mechanically in the cab, he knew what to do."

Jefferson's face didn't change. "Explain what you saw."

As Neliah Jefferson listened to Gene recount the refinery tour with the potential Cherokee Nation buyers, she glanced at Lynn and Preston for confirmation.

"Cherokee," Neliah said. "Three years in a row we faced Sequoyah High School team for the girls' state basketball championship. We only beat them once. Any of you play basketball?"

"Yes," Lynn said.

"Long time ago the traditional three," Gene said, "football, basketball, and baseball."

Preston's face was unreadable. When he didn't answer, the investigator went on. "Gene, how did you discover Tom?"

"The crane was rolling toward us. We tried to get his attention but of course we couldn't."

"Gene climbed up into the cab," Lynn said. "He stopped the

crane. No question he prevented injuries and saved lives." She turned to Gene. "I'm still amazed when I think about it."

"What happened next?" Jefferson asked.

"We isolated the loader. I was the only one who went into the cab, but he was dead by the time I got to him." Gene's face sagged. "His skin was cool to the touch."

Inspector Jefferson looked up sharply. "So no one else actually saw Tom?"

Seemingly unaware of what she was suggesting, Gene said, "No, not until the medics arrived. It was horrible. Who'd want to look at a dead man?"

Jefferson made a note, closed her laptop, and gave Gene a printed form. "Could you write me a brief statement of what happened?"

Gene looked at Lynn and she nodded. They waited as he sat and wrote for several minutes, then handed over the form.

"Thanks. This is just routine. We need it for our files." Neliah Jefferson put her hands together in front of her mouth as if she were praying. "From what I've heard, you run a safe operation." She paused as if waiting for one of them to disagree.

"We try." Gene tapped a pencil. Lynn recognized one of his signals of impatience. "I'll walk you out if you're ready."

Preston waited to speak until Gene returned. Lynn started when Preston slapped the table. "Of all the administrative bullshit! What a waste of time!"

Usually she could count on Preston's calm, so his eruption was surprising. "You don't sound like yourself. Why are you so upset?"

He didn't answer.

Oklahoma's first burst of wealth was nearly a century old and much evidence of it was still standing. The mansions—great heaps of brick that had never been scooped from their foundations by storms or bulldozers—survived. A few were bed and breakfasts; others were museums.

Yet Oklahoma remained defined by its oceans of wind, some

of which became tornadoes, others merely violent storms.

At the state's base was a changing patchwork of fortunes from the numerous Native American tribes who'd been forced to make homes here. More than thirty tribes still headquartered in Oklahoma. Not just the Five Civilized Tribes, as they were labeled, but many smaller nations had been resettled at the muzzles of rifles: Kaws, Otoes and Missourias, Poncas, Tonkawas, Pawnees. Even the Nez Perce lived in Oklahoma for a time.

In the 1990s, after decades of decline, tribal casinos brought recovery to the state and more importantly, to the tribes themselves. The first of Lynn's meetings with the groups bidding for the refinery was in Tahlequah, the Cherokee headquarters fifty-five miles southeast of Tulsa. The Cherokees were the least-experienced bidders and Tahlequah the least-glamorous of the three locations they would visit.

*But I prefer Bakersfield and Amarillo to Milan and Paris,* Lynn thought. *Must be a character defect.*

Rolling through downtown Tulsa for the hour-long drive to Tahlequah, Gene pointed to the Boston Avenue Methodist Church. Its elaborate, crenellated design was another of Tulsa's well-regarded Art Deco buildings, and its past included a bishop who had covered up the gay half of his life until his death from AIDs.

"Lovely church and part of the city's beautiful architecture, but I still think of ol' Finis when I see the church," Gene said.

As the houses thinned out, Lynn pointed to a kite, flying way up in the sky. The figure holding it was far away.

"Must be seven hundred and fifty feet along the hypotenuse," Gene said.

"Pythagoras. Don't remind me," Lynn replied, thinking of the Parisian devotee who had almost killed her and her sister.

"Kites and windmills. They're all this Oklahoma wind is good for," Gene said.

Until they were out of sight of it, Lynn watched the kite embrace the wind. She wished she herself could fly with its crazy, zigzag freedom.

Oklahoma and Creek Nation license plates on passing cars gave way to Cherokee Nation and United Keetoowah Band (UKB) license plates. The UKB plates were captioned, *Honoring Our Ancestors*. Gene explained the UKB was a Cherokee band about a twentieth the size of the larger western Cherokees and one that emphasized a more traditional restriction to full-bloods. The third and final band, he said, were the eastern Cherokees still living in North Carolina, descendents of those who had evaded capture.

"When you were growing up, they named it the Trail of Tears. Today it's called the Removal," Gene said.

"For a Chicagoan you've absorbed a bunch of Oklahoma history."

"When ya live in the middle of it, it's hard not to."

As he drove, Lynn thought ahead to their destination. The meeting at the W. W. Keeler tribal complex would be large. Too large, really. Besides the two of them, they were meeting Preston Li, her engineering manager; Riley Stevens, the executive on his way out who was helping with the project; and one of Preston's junior planning analysts, Greg Sutton. Greg was another of the youngsters TriCoast recruited each year. According to Preston, he was hard-edged, brilliant, and just barely politic enough to keep his tattoos covered.

Jesse Drum, the senior Cherokee Lynn had met the day Tom died, had said he would bring several members of the tribe with him, as well as Jimmy Deerinwater, the tribe's accountant. Pete Whitehawk, Jesse's friend who ran a fund that would be co-investing with the CIG, would sit in. A Cherokee translator would record the meeting.

Lynn thought the final person in the group, Pete Whitehawk's partner, was the most problematic. He was Keith McConaugh, her ex-husband.

She hadn't seen him since they'd walked to separate cars from an Orleans Parish courthouse five years ago. It couldn't be anything but bad luck, Lynn figured, to have to deal with her ex-husband just before her wedding to Cy.

Thinking about those plans made her stomach churn. Lynn wanted to get married while her father could still physically attend the ceremony, but the planner had talked Cy into a much larger wedding than Lynn had wanted. Yet she was reluctant to nix Cy's wish for a big celebration.

Cy's kids, two-year-old Matt and seven-year-old Marika, would be bubbly with childhood impatience at a ceremony. Nor could Lynn's frail father spend much time away from his house and his now-constant nursing care. *If Cy's trying to please his extended family with a large wedding, we need to talk about it further,* she concluded. In a single, selfish moment, Lynn wished her mother was alive to help her. The thought brought her back to Gene. "Gene, thank you. I can't say it enough. Climbing up and stopping that crane took courage."

He blushed, then shrugged. "Part of the job."

"Everyone should do their job as well as you."

Although the turnpike was featureless, this part of Oklahoma was hilly, a geologic prelude to the Ozark Mountains.

The low-slung brick building harmonized so well with its surroundings that Gene drove past twice before identifying it as the tribal complex. Once inside, they were directed to a small room where the others were waiting. She was glad to see Riley, Preston, and Greg had already arrived.

*Keith,* she thought again. *He's probably fat, gray, and wrinkled.*

He wasn't.

He faced away from her. His arms were tight in his sleeves. His back was broader, as if he'd spent time in a gym. *He's finally doing something besides 12-ounce curls.* Then she thought, *I loved you once.*

But his long nights of drinking had erased her passion for him.

Still, when he turned, for a moment there was Keith and no one else in the room. She caught her breath and ducked her head so he wouldn't see her reaction. He'd gotten better-looking, if that were possible—slimmer, darker, and no doubt with the same boyish tentativeness that could yield to a surprised or wicked smile. *I'm not going to feel this way just because he was great in bed. I'm engaged to the finest man in the world, with wonderful children.*

Her ex-husband exuded pure sexual heat, and she was the only woman in the room to receive it.

Riley looked at Keith, then whispered to Lynn, "Think you can work with your former hottie?"

"Yes, of course."

"You might start by unclenching your jaw." His voice was soft, with more than his usual diplomacy.

When Keith shook her hand and touched her shoulder, she felt another bolt of unwelcome desire. She remembered why she'd married him.

He nodded at her, his eyes flicking down to her shoes and back up. For a few seconds she wished she'd worn clothing that better displayed her physique, the body he'd ultimately ignored in favor of barstools.

Then it was over and she could breathe again.

❦

"I'll be frank," Lynn told the Cherokee group when she got up to speak. "I lived six years in Tulsa when I was growing up, so this refinery means more to me than it should. However, the offers for it, yours and others, also make clear its value.

"I'll turn this meeting over to Gene Blahunka, the refinery's general manager. Let me tell you a little about his background first." Lynn described Gene's thirty years of experience, his expertise, and his focus on safety and environmental issues. She concluded, "He's the right general manager for this refinery. Unfortunately, Gene is retiring soon. So I'm urging all buyers to make him an offer he can't refuse to help train his replacement."

She smiled at Gene, and felt satisfied she'd made as strong a case as she could for him. He would keep all his current benefits in any sale, but she wanted the buyers to fully appreciate him.

Gene spoke for a few minutes about the refinery's equipment

specifications and projects underway. He then introduced Greg Sutton, the young analyst. Greg gave more detail about the refinery's sales and operating profit.

Greg also described the oil supply for the refinery—Canadian crude from Alberta, Bakken crude from North Dakota, home-grown Mississippi Lime crude from nearby counties, and a full range of flavors from the giant Cushing storage tanks a few dozen miles away.

Riley's description of nearby refining competitors was better than Lynn had expected. He noted the other two refineries in Tulsa, and that Darby Oil operated a third refinery a hundred and fifty miles away in a little town called Ponca City.

Pete tugged on his bolo tie. "If this is so profitable for you, why are you selling it?"

*Ouch.* "Our first obligation is maximizing value to our shareholders. Although we see considerable worth in this refinery, others see even more, particularly with the increase in Midcontinent oil production and the shortage of refining capacity here to handle it."

Keith threw her a softball. "What's the refinery's safety record?"

"One of our contractors, Tom Martin, died yesterday from an apparent heart attack. He was our first fatality in three years and first serious injury in two."

"Heart attack work-related?" Keith's voice was sterner.

"No."

Pete asked, "All your environmental permits in order?"

"Yes."

Questions continued from the Cherokees, Pete, Jimmy, Jesse, and Keith.

When Jesse suggested they adjourn to eat, he mentioned a nearby restaurant, a small, low-priced place with a salad bar, and waitresses who could serve everything else. Lynn hoped it would feature food for which the tribe was famous: fry bread, *kanuchi*—hickory nut soup—and wild onions with eggs. But the choices were lackluster. When her pot roast arrived, it was dry and covered with anemic pellets of garlic. She noticed others picking at gritty macaroni and cheese, limp salads, and greasy fried chicken, except for Jesse and Riley, who ordered seconds.

The pies on display sported ancient crusts and too-solid meringues. Lynn was reminded of the joke about what a shame it would be to eat the pie—it had been there so long it would be like eating an old friend. The rest of the group developed a sudden interest in their soft drinks, coffees, and rolls.

◈

I assumed the meeting would be a waste of time and it was; however, it allowed me to evaluate the flaws of everyone in the room. When my turn came to speak, I played the part expected of me, as I had for years.

It seemed unplanned that we would pick the restaurant we did, but it was inevitable since groups from the Council House frequently ate there, more to talk than to eat, since the food was execrable. I saw my chance with one of those who had been asking questions, the one with the potential to give me the most trouble before I could complete my plans. The bad food gave me additional cover. It would take weeks or months before anyone figured out what had happened and who had done it. I'd be gone by then.

If I had a conscience, I'd regret the trouble I was leaving behind, but conscience was an inconvenience I had never possessed. Besides, I figured there was an equal amount of troublemaking and do-gooding in the world. Someone had to create the trouble for the do-gooders to stay employed. So in the end, I was doing good by creating trouble.

I almost laughed.

# Six

*Tahlequah*
*Saturday evening*

After another long day in the stifling brick council house he should have felt ecstatic at finally achieving freedom. Freedom to drive alone, late at night.

Shocked by the stab of a stomach cramp, Jimmy Deerinwater swerved off State Highway 51. He jerked the wheel of his Suzuki Reno just in time to steer away from a rollover into the mucky bottomland fifteen feet below. He steadied the car and stopped on the shoulder near a huddle of bur oaks west of Gar Creek. Then he opened his door and threw up.

He spit a few times to clear his mouth and felt for the bottle of water he kept in the car. Maybe the rain that had threatened all day would finally start and wash away the thin, acrid puddle of vomit.

He'd had many late-night meetings with the Cherokee Investment Group. Today was different; they'd had an hours-long diligence session with TriCoast executives. Jimmy had familiarized himself with the accounting statements for the refinery, the stations, and the supply contracts. CIG was considering buying TriCoast's Tulsa refinery and a group of fifty nearby gasoline stations.

He wiped his damp face. The relief from vomiting brought dread of more nausea.

He had almost reached the easy part of the Tahlequah-to-Tulsa drive. The Muskogee Turnpike was only a mile or so away. He hoped he would feel well enough in the morning to go to his daytime job as a pipeline company accountant.

Maybe the nausea would pass if he waited. Jimmy leaned back to clear his head. Fulfilling a promise to his father, he advised the Cherokee Nation, including council member Jesse Drum, on its investments. He prepared budgets and audited revenues and expenses from the nation's casinos. He reviewed all of CIG's investments to be sure they were fiscally sound. And if there were any irregularities, he was the first called to investigate. *Which reminds me . . .* While he was sitting on the side of the road waiting to see if he would feel better, he wrote out the questions on trading positions the Commodities Futures Trading Commission, or CFTC, had been asking. His first question was who had originated the trades. The second was why the trades hadn't been documented.

Another wave of cramps squeezed his stomach. Not as vise-like as the last one.

His promise to his father meant sometimes driving over a hundred miles several times a week. Recently he'd been learning more about tribal experience with oil and gas. He'd gone west to Pawhuska to speak to Osage elders, who had vast, sometimes tragic, experiences with oil royalties. He'd driven to Oklahoma City to meet representatives from the Chickasaw Nation, who talked about living near large oil and gas drill-sites. If CIG could buy this refinery and the stations, it would be a profitable tie-in with their casinos. He'd studied the statistics. Most casino customers drove themselves in their personal cars rather than arriving by bus.

That tall, blonde TriCoast woman had not named the other bidders, but Jimmy had deduced their identities. One was Sansei, an Asian refining consortium about which he could learn little. One was a sovereign wealth spin-off from Saudi Aramco, looking to find another home for Aramco's crude and a profitable investment. A third was an English company, North Seas Resources. First-class competition, no slackers among them.

He wiped sweat from his forehead with the sleeve of his jacket and felt warning acid in his throat. He leaned out and threw up again. He found his cell phone and called Jesse. No answer. "Jesse, it's Jimmy. I'm feeling really sick and I need a ride, or at least someone to follow me. Call me back when you get this message."

He flushed his mouth with water and spit it out but he still couldn't get rid of the sharp stench of vomit. If he concentrated on something else, maybe he'd feel better.

Today he'd met Keith McConaugh, an Anglo investor, and Pete Whitehawk, a friend of Jesse's who'd made it big on Wall Street and had done a few deals with CIG before. Keith and Pete's fund was called Adela, the Cherokee word for "money." He formed the symbols in his mind, DSW, *ah-day-lah*.

Jimmy trusted them. Keith was an outsider but looked like a decent man who knew the business. Pete won him over when he described how his now-deceased father had been a member of the United Keetoowah Band of Cherokees. Adela, Pete told him, had grown by investing in small companies, buying them when the owners' children didn't want to take them over, and then profitably reselling them later. It sounded like a good business.

Acid scorched his throat again, but it receded. He still felt light-headed, as if he'd been drinking.

Headlights shone in his rearview mirror as a car rolled to a stop behind him, gravel crunching.

"You okay?" It was dark-haired Keith with the action-hero features and big wallet. "We're headed the same direction. Recognized your car."

"Flu or something I ate."

"Let me follow you home," the man insisted. "Or can I call someone to get you?"

Jimmy turned away from him and retched again. Nothing came up but he felt better. "I'm only a half hour from home. I called Jesse, but now I think I can handle it."

"I'll follow. I can stop as often as you need to."

Jimmy nodded. *Couldn't hurt.*

He eased the Reno back onto the road, accelerating smoothly. He adjusted his mirror but couldn't lessen the glare from Keith's car. Every light around him was blinding. He squinted, his eyelids nearly closed to protect his eyes. A few drops of rain splashed on his car.

A Pike Pass mounted on his windshield allowed him to drive onto the Wagoner-Coweta ramp without stopping and he merged onto the Muskogee Turnpike.

He heard a distant bleat of a car horn and forced himself to check the rearview mirror. Keith's car wasn't there. Had he imagined talking to Keith? *No, he's probably stuck at the turnpike hutch.*

Another horn blew. It was deafening. He yanked the wheel out of its leftward drift toward a speeding sedan. Lightning forked a few miles ahead.

The blackjack trees and purple coneflowers were almost out of sight. Soon he'd be home in his Tulsa apartment. He had to concentrate. He couldn't lose control.

The accelerator rode down under his foot and the speedometer clocked ninety miles an hour before he noticed. He couldn't believe how fast he was going. *Something must be wrong with the speedometer.*

He felt himself slipping away again and looked up when he heard the left rear tire grind into the pavement. He crunched the brakes, but they wouldn't engage. The Suzuki slid back and forth, right-angling across the lane, then swinging back a hundred and eighty degrees.

When he looked up, the Reno's hood was aimed at the concrete stanchions of the overpass. Jimmy Deerinwater tried to jerk the steering wheel to avoid the collision but his arms wouldn't move.

# Seven

*Tahlequah*
*Saturday evening, a half-hour earlier*

## ᏚᏣᏡᎤᎫ ᎤᏈᏍᏘᏓ ᎥᎬ ᎠᏣᎬᎱ ᏣᏴᏴᏘ

Galohisdi ulisduida gesv aquadelohosa, wagiyvtlvi.
*When I found out the door was open, I went in.*

When Keith walked Lynn and Gene to the parking lot, Lynn was grateful Gene hung back to talk to others.

"It's good to see you. You look better than ever." Keith took her hands, then let them drop.

"You, too." She hoped he didn't notice the quaver in her voice.

"Less drinking, more snowboarding."

"Good." *I sound condescending.* She wondered what music he liked now. When they'd been married, he'd played country-western with lyrics like "drink by drink, I'm taking the bar exam."

"I heard you're getting married."

"Soon. You?"

"Not likely. Not many around like you. Who's the lucky guy? And how's your father?"

*A little late, Keith...or more likely, it's the usual BS.* But she said, "You'll find someone." She didn't add, *if you're sober.* The resurfacing bitterness, mixed with surprise that he'd remembered her ill father, took more energy than she wanted to give.

"I met Cy at a fundraising luncheon. He's a lawyer, two kids, lost his wife when she was killed by a drunk driver."

Keith winced. He'd never killed anyone while driving drunk, but he'd had many close calls.

"My father's...the same." She couldn't acknowledge how much he'd worsened since the last time she'd seen Keith. She looked at Gene, waved him over. "Gene, you met Keith, my ex-husband. Although I'll say it feels weird to be across the table from him, he's one of the best negotiators around, so beware." She couldn't help but think how little he'd left her after the divorce. It was one of many factors that had goaded her into getting an MBA.

Gene looked at him. "Glad to meetcha. You're an investor on this deal with CIG?" Gene kicked at the tires of his green Malibu.

"Jesse at CIG brought me and Pete in. We've done other deals with them," Keith said.

"Jimmy made a good presentation, especially when he talked about how the refinery and the casinos fit together." Lynn scanned the asphalt lot. "Where is Jimmy, anyway?"

"He left a few minutes ago," Keith said. "He didn't look good."

"Maybe we should leave, too," Lynn said.

Keith gave her a quick, side-armed hug. Nothing like the lingering, full-body ones she remembered. "I'll see you again, soon."

As they exited the parking lot Gene said, "In a hurry to leave, were you?"

She laughed. "Was it obvious? But don't let him fool you. That 'little company' of his and Pete's is a couple billion dollars."

"Yow." Turning right instead of left, he said, "Highway 62 is fast, but it's longer. Let's take 51."

They wound through downtown Tahlequah with its 1920s-era buildings and graceful Cherokee script on every sign.

Gene pointed out that the bank and stores  were named in both English and Cherokee.

"How cool is that. Glad they have the English translations though," she said.

"What's the story with Keith, anyway?"

Mindful that everything she disclosed would be reported throughout TriCoast, Lynn described how she'd met Keith, his quick proposal, and their short marriage. "A few years into it, it was clear he'd always rather be talking to a bartender than me." She didn't explain that she'd called the divorce lawyer the day after her miscarriage, when he was five days into a supposed two-day hunting trip. "He's still handsome, for sure. Looks like he's been off the booze a while."

Once on the turnpike to Tulsa, Gene said, "You don't know his personal life, yet you know he's got billions to invest."

"He has a bunch of friends who couldn't wait to tell me how successful he'd become. I'm glad for him." She was, she realized.

"By the way, thanks for the boost back there." He interrupted himself to say, "Hey buddy. Any lane will do."

They watched the unpredictable car in front of them and tried to avoid crashing into it. Gene flashed his lights to get the driver's attention, but there was no response. Instead, the car slowed to fifty, wove across the center line three more times, then sped up so fast it was soon out of sight.

"Was that a Suzuki?"

"Yep. If Jimmy's behind the wheel, his secret life is a wanna-be stunt car driver," Gene said.

"Whoever it is will kill himself, or someone else. We can't catch up with him, but maybe the highway patrol can." Lynn pulled out her cell phone and called the highway patrol's emergency number.

"Might take them a while. This area gets thin coverage from the county," Gene said.

She hoped the driver would be found and stopped. "Do we have a cell phone number for Jimmy?"

Gene shook his head.

Lynn called Jesse and Keith for Jimmy's phone number. Neither one answered. *I'll try again once we get to the hotel.*

She thought about how much she appreciated Gene's solid calm and what his concerns in the sale were likely to be. "We should be able to get you at least a multi-year consulting contract."

"Sounds good. Is that Jimmy's car again?"

The Suzuki changed lanes a hundred yards in front of them. Smoke puffed from the left rear tire and the little car swung back and forth.

"Jesus Christ!" Gene said.

"The bridge!"

The little car t-boned the concrete bridge crossing the turn-pike.

The hollow bang of the collision penetrated her senses.

"Call 911! I'll see if I can get him out," Gene said.

She dialed 911, described the location, and asked for an ambulance.

Gene pulled onto the left shoulder. They got out and ran to the twisted black Suzuki. "It's Jimmy!" Gene yelled.

She could see that although the airbags had inflated, Jimmy Deerinwater had slipped sideways between the door and the steering column. His head was bleeding against the window.

The driver's side of the car was mashed against the concrete and the passenger's side door was locked.

Gene said, "There's a tire tool in my trunk. Get it!"

She ran back to Gene's car and pulled the keys from the ignition. Fingers trembling, she found the trunk release, popped it, and grasped the heavy iron bar.

As she started back toward Gene, she heard the loud whoosh of the Suzuki exploding. The force of the explosion knocked Gene down, and the little car was swallowed in flames.

Fighting every instinct that told her to run away, she dropped the iron bar and ran toward the heat.

Flames screeched hotter than she could stand. Gene's arms were up in front of his face, but he wasn't moving. She knelt, grabbed his body, and pulled him away from the blast furnace the burning car had become.

He weighed two hundred pounds—he'd told her so—but now he felt no heavier than a pile of wet clothes. She dragged him behind his car and felt his pulse. It was rapid and weak, but he was breathing.

She stood up and grabbed the iron bar, readying herself to pull Jimmy to safety. With another whoosh of flame and the sound of glass exploding, the smoke turned black. The Suzuki's tires had caught fire and its windows had shattered.

An ambulance screamed up. EMTs jumped out and ran toward her.

She pointed to the burning car. "He lost control, ran into the bridge. He's still in the car." A sob climbed into her throat.

The EMTs raced toward the burning car. Lynn was amazed they could get so close to the heat. The redheaded medic unlocked the passenger door through the heat-shattered window and swung it open. Somehow they were able to get Jimmy out. Even from a distance she could see his body was badly burned.

Flames hissed as they hauled Jimmy back behind Gene's car. "No pulse!"

The EMTS worked steadily but couldn't restart Jimmy's heart.

"Is he...dead?" Lynn asked.

One of the medics pulled on a red lock of hair that was now black. "I'm afraid so. All we can do is transport him. A doctor at the ER will make it official." He sounded calm, but sorrowful.

She closed her eyes. *He was so badly burned.* No one could have survived that. She forced herself to think of the charming, competent, alive young man Jimmy had been just a few hours ago. His family needed to be told. *But I'm not the one to tell them.*

One of the EMTs ran back to the ambulance and called for fire units. The redheaded medic took Gene's vital signs. "Tell me about this man. Is he your husband?"

"No. He works with me. Gene . . . Gene Blahunka." She took a deep breath but her hands still trembled. "We were driving back to Tulsa from a meeting in Tahlequah. Jimmy was at the meeting, too. He was driving crazy."

"You the one who put in the first 911 call?"

"Yes. I was afraid he'd crash into someone."

"Guess we're lucky it was some*thing* instead of someone. The highway patrol was going to intercept him a few miles down the road. Here, hold your friend's hands."

The red-haired EMT brought back oxygen, water, and other supplies. She gave him details as he tended Gene.

Gene's eyes opened, and then everything seemed to happen at once. Two volunteer fire trucks and two highway patrol cars rolled up.

Gene was unable to hear for another half an hour, so Lynn answered the officers' questions.

"What did you notice before the collision?"

"Three things. He was driving erratically. Had been since we saw him east of here, on highway 51."

"Did you see him drink today?"

"No. I wasn't with him all day, but when I was, he didn't." Almost under her breath, she generalized, "He's an accountant, so no surprise he doesn't drink."

"Plenty of accountants do. Wine to go with the books they cook," one medic said.

When even Gene smiled at the gag, she felt the first pinpricks of hope he would recover.

"So you said three things. What were the other two?"

"His tire blew out. Left rear. Made the loss of control even worse."

"And?"

"And he wasn't slowing down. I'd think he'd have slammed on the brakes. Though someone said he looked sick when he left."

"You've named four things."

"Right. Maybe he was out of it, or in a rush to get home."

The firefighters hosed down the burned metal that had been

Jimmy's car, while the highway patrol directed traffic around the wreck.

Accident scene investigators arrived. Lynn answered their questions, too. Seeing they would be there for a while measuring, photographing, and interviewing, Lynn called Jesse Drum. This time he answered. When she told him the news, his voice became so soft that at first she thought she'd lost the connection. Jesse promised to tell Jimmy's parents in person.

On the advice of the EMTs, Gene was loaded into their ambulance. Lynn called his wife. "Gene's fine, but he's being taken for observation to Hillcrest Medical Center. I'll drive his car there. Come and meet us. Once he's been checked over, you can drive him home."

She gave the cell phone to Gene. She knew his hearing hadn't completely recovered when he shouted into it, "I'M FINE, HONEY. REALLY."

Later that night in the lobby of the hospital, she gave Gene's car keys to his wife and prepared to catch a cab to her own hotel. He held his wife's arm and leaned onto a cane. "I owe you one, Lynn," he said.

She hugged him tight.

# Eight

*Tulsa/Paris*
*Sunday*

> *"The quickest way to double your money is to fold it*
> *over and put it back in your wallet."* —*Will Rogers*

She savored the freedom to run.

Lynn would make calls later, then leave for Paris. TriCoast's board had booked one of its corporate jets to fly its executives to the meeting with the Saudis, the second group of potential buyers. *That we have use of a jet shows how eager the board is to sell the refinery.* Despite the full schedule, she hoped she would have time to see her sister, Ceil, who was still living in Paris.

She groaned at the prospect of Riley accompanying her. Although he was attending at the request of one of the directors, she didn't trust his diplomacy. The Saudis had already had a US consulting company verify the operations of the Tulsa refinery; however, she and other TriCoast executives needed to answer further questions face-to-face. A second important reason for the trip was to discuss continued Saudi oil for all of the company's five refineries. Their ten percent of TriCoast's oil supply, which measured in billions of dollars a year, was key to TriCoast's operations.

Lynn's bluff-top hotel overlooked the Arkansas River. Hills gave the city texture—its east-side streets sloped to the river's bank. Yet its highways begrudged the existence of modern cars. With their sharp turns, lack of signage, and too-short on-ramps, they had been designed for fewer, slower, vehicles.

The names of the streets evoked other cities. Tulsa's 1920s aspirations could be found in avenues called Denver, Boulder, Cincinnati, Detroit, Harvard, and Yale.

The silver columns of Lynn's refinery and two others like it framed the west side, across the quarter-mile of river. The blinking cell towers of Lookout Mountain stood behind.

Of all of Oklahoma's tribes, only the Osage, who lived in the next county west, had retained mineral rights. But those rights carried their own tragedies. Shortly after non-Osage men married Osage women, the new brides turned up dead. So many were killed during the 1920s that the Osage Tribal Council brought in a just-created agency, the Federal Bureau of Investigation. The FBI found and prosecuted the most egregious killer, William Hale, and his accomplices.

Lynn had grown up hearing those stories. Seeing the city's architectural legacy reminded her of them. She crossed the street into River Park and settled into a fast pace.

The Arkansas River flowed high and muddy. From Colorado elevations, the river played down near Dodge City and Wichita, Kansas, then on to central Oklahoma, where its drainage basin was the entire northeastern corner of the state. Near Tahlequah and Muskogee, where she'd been yesterday, the river had been made navigable to larger ships by the US Army Corps of Engineers, and so morphed from river to the formidably-named McClellan-Kerr Arkansas River Navigation System.

She ran past pink rental bikes sponsored by St. Francis Hospital and waved to a park officer patrolling in a golf cart. Her feet landed comfortably at each step; the asphalt path had more give than the concrete streets on which she usually ran. She turned onto the wooden pedestrian-biking bridge that crossed the river. The rush of the water became so loud it was hard to hear anything else.

One sign read *Light will flash if water is rising.* The light was flashing. From the bridge the power of the river was evident: thousands of gallons pillowing over the shallow-water dam, hurtling downstream. The sandy-muddy water swirled in a rhythmic flow, strong enough to drown anyone and send a body far away in minutes. She tried to shake the morbid thought, but was reminded of Tom's and Jimmy's deaths. *Was it a coincidence Gene was nearby both times?*

Moisture from the river air condensed on her sweat. She startled when two runners she hadn't heard came from behind and passed her, their arms swinging in rhythm.

The wooden bridge creaked and shifted under her quick steps. On the west side pier she saw early-morning fishermen and heard train whistles. A man reined in his snarling dog as she passed. She felt welcome stretches in her quadriceps and glute muscles.

Back across the bridge, she waited at an intersection to leave River Park. The light changed green in her direction and she stepped off the curb, assuming the oncoming Denali would stop.

It didn't. As the SUV bore down on her, she tried to make eye contact. But with the driver's mirrored sunglasses and cap pulled low, she couldn't.

The bass thumping from the SUV drowned her shouts.

She accelerated and leapt up on the curb across the street. The SUV roared so close behind her she felt the hot breeze off the metal.

"You idiot! What are you doing?"

The Denali backed up. It came at her again, over the curb. She ran up the steep hill with as much strength as if she hadn't just run seven miles.

The truck accelerated up the hill after her.

She swerved left toward a tree and tripped over its roots, landing hard on her hands. Beyond her, up the hill, were more bushes.

She tried to push to her feet, but her wrist was throbbing. Finally she got her balance. The hill was so steep the Denali lost traction. It skidded into a tree trunk three feet behind her with a bang.

Lynn scrambled up higher to the cover of the bushes. The SUV circled, then screeched down the hill. It slammed onto the street and sped away.

She memorized a few letters of the license plate, shocked at how close she'd been to becoming a sack of broken bones. *Or worse . . .*

Back at the hotel, she needed both of her shaking hands to open the door to her room. Her adrenaline-soaked body continued to shake and a chill settled in her spine.

She felt her sore wrist and rang the hotelkeeper for ice.

Lynn called her boss, Mike Emerson, and security chief Mark Shepherd to tell them about the incident. Shepherd agreed to speak with one of his Tulsa police friends. Then he said, "Get a full-time bodyguard. Now. I have several candidates."

"I have so little privacy already."

"Privacy won't do you any good if you're dead. Don't forget your recent Paris adventure with Guillard. That high-society jerkwad would have killed both you and your sister. And yes, we've confirmed he was using your sister to get to you."

Mike was even blunter. "When your contract comes up for renewal the board and I will require you to have round-the-clock protection. Just start it now. And don't take it personally. I'm requiring it for everyone, myself included."

*Don't take it personally.* That was the Emerson she knew.

After a shower, she made more phone calls and replied to e-mail and texts. Gene Blahunka felt sore, but he was walking around, she learned. The Tulsa medical examiner would not release reports on Tom or Jimmy for several days.

She packed ice in a plastic bag and wound it around her wrist.

Lynn called Jesse Drum, the Cherokee Nation executive they'd spoken with yesterday. His conversation with Jimmy's family about the young man's death had been difficult, he said. She fought memories of yesterday's horrific accident. *Too much, too close together.* Doubts crept in. *Could the attempt on me, Tom Martin's death, and Jimmy's accident be connected?*

The ice wasn't enough to relieve the fiery sting in her wrist. She looked up 24-hour urgent care clinics and drove to one nearby.

Downtown Tulsa church bells sounded while she examined budgets for TriCoast's refineries and waited to be called in. She would soon be asking the board for over a hundred million dollars for safety, environmental, and upgrade projects. The amount was nothing compared to the tens of billions of dollars required for oil to supply the refineries. Although much of the oil was TriCoast's own, piped in from offshore, shipped in from around the world, or traded with other producers, two or three billion dollars' worth was purchased from others. *Like the Saudis I'll be seeing. Of course they're interested in the Tulsa refinery,* Lynn thought. They often looked for American and Chinese homes, or joint ventures, for their production.

Pushing the board for more refinery money than they'd budgeted would be a challenge. David Jenkins, both colleague and rival when it came to slices of the TriCoast budget pie, was also asking for a sizable increase. He'd said, "At these meetings I gotta put my dick on the table." She'd laughed and knew he would use the same words with the board.

"Why the rush on this French meeting?" Cy asked when she called him. "And why am I getting the calls from the wedding planner instead of you?"

"We're trying to get agreement ahead of Ramadan," she said, "though I'm not sure that will happen. As for the calls, doesn't the wedding involve both of us?"

"I don't know anything about flowers."

"Me either. But I'll call her back." She decided to tell him later about today's near-calamity and about her mixed feelings in negotiating with her ex-husband, after she'd had time to think about both.

"So what's this about a Ramadan deadline? Because all business in the Middle East stops for a month?" Cy asked. She heard hope in his voice.

"It slows. Everything has to be done after sundown. People who are fasting can't focus during the day and they're not in the best mood, either."

"In my neighborhood, the noticeable holidays are the Jewish ones." Although not Orthodox himself, Cy lived in an observant neighborhood. For north Dallas, that made it a walker-friendly district, or *eruv,* as she'd learned to call the area within the marked boundaries. Severely-dressed synagogue members traveled by foot from sundown Friday to sundown Saturday.

In the background Cy's daughter, Marika, said, "Dad, when are we swimming? Let's go right now."

He laughed. "You can hear what we're doing next."

"Sounds like fun. Can we swim when I get back to Dallas?"

"Depends. When are you back?"

"Next weekend. I can't wait to see you."

"That's two of us."

Lynn's final call before returning to TriCoast business was to her father. He sounded the same as a few days earlier, but worse than a few months ago. The strain of breathing due to his emphysema was taxing his heart, his doctor had told Lynn.

She kept the conversation short, and promised to text and e-mail him if she saw Ceil in Paris. *My arm doesn't hurt much. It can't. Too many people depend on me.*

She was called into an examining room. "We'll be able to tell you more when the swelling goes down. Come back day after tomorrow for an X-ray."

She shook her head. "Can't do it. I'm leaving tonight for a European business meeting."

The doctor stood. "Well, if the first thing you can think of is hopping onto a plane, your wrist is probably sprained, not broken.

If you change your mind, go see a doctor once you arrive."

He splinted her wrist and showed her how to adjust the laces and Velcro to bind it. "Keep this on for a week."

That evening, she gingerly shook hands with the pilots flying them from Tulsa to Paris. They would stop in Washington long enough to collect TriCoast CEO Mike Emerson and board director Burl Travis.

Riley settled in the seat behind Lynn. "What do you think of Greg?"

"Don't know him. He seems expert," Lynn said.

"He's just a spreadsheet with balls. Or in his case, without."

"What do you mean?"

"Unmarried, in his late 20s. Draw your own conclusions."

"Not everyone has your track record of marital success."

"Ouch." He laughed at her reference to his two failed marriages.

The jet's engines roared beneath her. She opened a book Jesse had loaned her, Teresa Miller's memoir about growing up in Tahlequah, and adjusted her iPod. Cy had teased her when he learned she still listened to Coldplay. "But I like it."

"You'll like what I download even more," he promised.

"I always do," she said, laughing.

She fell asleep to "Clocks'" cascading piano and lyrics.

When they touched down in Washington, she awoke.

Another stress nightmare. She'd dreamt of rushing to her own wedding in a giant tanker truck, one running out of gas. When she arrived at the church she saw other women dressed in white. Bride substitutes.

She shook her head, as happy as she'd ever been to talk to Mike and Burl.

# Nine

> *"See what will happen if you don't stop biting your
> fingernails?"* —*Will Rogers, to his niece on seeing the*
> Venus de Milo

Their Mercedes driver halted at the turn onto Boissy d'Anglas, his way blocked by a massive metal cylinder, a bollard the size of a small car. Two sub-machinegun-carrying police officers also protected the intersection. After the driver explained their destination and showed his credentials, one officer put aside his weapon to push the button that lowered the cylinder. Their black car, first of two in the TriCoast caravan, rolled through, keeping to the left. The right-hand side of the street was blockaded with steel interlocking barricades.

"Do I really have to walk five steps behind all of you?" Lynn asked Mike Emerson.

He shifted in the leather seat. "Would you prefer to skip this meeting with a prince who controls some of the largest oil super-provinces in the world?"

She shook her head, then adjusted the hijab covering her blonde hair. She wrapped her splinted arm with a billowy tunic sleeve.

Next to her, Henry Vandervoost said, "Ms. Dayton is a distraction. As always." Vandervoost was Lynn's counterpart in charge of European and Asian refining, and her constant nemesis. He'd arrived by train from Rotterdam the previous day.

"And Vandervoost, you're helpful, as always," Lynn countered.

"You convinced me to bring you to this meeting," Mike said. "Your career and those of women in the oil industry hang on its success. Not worried, are you?" His voice had a joking tone, but Lynn could tell he was rethinking his decision to include her.

Women, even one like Lynn who ran five refineries, seldom met for business with Middle Eastern princes. Claude Durand, TriCoast's public relations director and a Frenchman well-acquainted with Saudi culture, had prepped the TriCoast executives, spending extra time with her and Riley.

After the police and blockade experience was repeated at the other end of rue Boissy d'Anglas, the two drivers parked in front of the Hotel Crillon, aligning their cars with the others at the entrance. Bristling, black Mercedes sedans were all pointed outward, ready to scream away with their passengers at a moment's notice.

Lynn had hoped TriCoast's CFO, Sara Levin, would attend, but Sara had declined. "Much as I'd love to shop Paris, no point in starting World War III the minute they hear my last name," she said. "We want this to be successful."

*So instead of Sara, we get Riley. Bad trade.*

The appointment had been arranged by one of TriCoast's directors, an oil-pump CEO named Burl Travis. Burl had insisted his buddy, Riley Stevens, attend. Both were now exiting the second car.

Riley Stevens was the walking harassment lawsuit Lynn had wanted to terminate ever since she'd heard his offensive comments herself. He had arrived at TriCoast as part of Lynn's Centennial refinery acquisition a few months before, and had been the only unfixable part of the bargain. TriCoast's human resources department had already documented enough complaints that Lynn and TriCoast's general counsel had started the severance countdown.

But Burl Travis had a different idea. Although the world was changing, crude oil was still purchased from outside the United

States, he'd said, and TriCoast had to make its suppliers comfortable. Riley was available and the Saudis, the Venezuelans, and others wouldn't have the same difficulty dealing with him, a man, as they would with Lynn. "The feminine mistake" was what Burl Travis called Lynn, though only once within her earshot.

*So there it is. Burl is ready to hand over the EVP position, for which I've almost literally given my life, to slimeball Riley Stevens.*

Mike and the other directors held Burl off, but even they were frank with Lynn about her gender as an issue in certain oil-rich countries.

As they grouped together in front of the Crillon, Mike said, "The Saudis can sell to any company—hell, any *country*, in the world. And we need this production from them."

"A lot of folks can't take the Saudi high-sulfur crude, but we can," Lynn countered.

"Then let's show the shareholders those tens of millions of dollars for sulfur upgrading were well spent," Mike said. "And by the way, the Indian and Chinese governments are sending representatives to see the prince later today."

"We were fortunate to get an appointment between Fajr and Dhuhr prayers," Burl Travis said. "This is probably the last chance to talk business for a while."

"What do you mean? It's the middle of the day," Riley said.

"The Muslim weekend starts Thursday," Burl answered. "Not much can be scheduled between midday prayer and five in the evening. And with Ramadan coming up, there will barely be any business done for a month."

"Fruitcake schedule." Riley's voice slid to inaudible as Mike glared at him, but Burl gave him an indulgent smile. It appeared that, under stress, Riley had forgotten all of Claude's preparation.

When they climbed the stairs, Lynn gathered her skirt to avoid tripping. Like Claude had suggested, she'd chosen a formal yellow blouse covering her elbows and collarbone, topped by an even more concealing dark blue tunic falling past her hips, and finished with a matching ankle-length skirt. She wore a pale blue scarf that hid most of her hair. *As long as I don't have to inspect a catalytic cracker or escape an AK-47-toting madman I can bear hobbling skirts a few hours.*

Their appointment was in Le Salon des Batailles. The reference to battles seemed appropriate. When Claude briefed them, he'd said the salon itself was a designated historical monument.

Riley turned around and looked at her, tucking in his shirt where his beach ball of a belly had escaped. "Maybe you should get down on bended knee. You're pretty desperate for more oil, right? Or is that pretty and desperate?" Riley winked. "He's a prince. Maybe he needs another wife."

Lynn kept her hand behind her back so he wouldn't see her clenched fist. Punching him wouldn't make a good impression.

"Remember, Lynn, you follow me into the room," Mike said. "I don't hold the door for you."

She and Mike had rehearsed this and many other variations from American manners. By Islamic custom, men were to be afforded no provocative rear views of their female counterparts.

Mike stopped their group of five plus two security officers at the entrance to the salon. He offered the traditional greeting of peace, "As-salam alaikum." They waited a few anxious seconds. If the prince did not reply, it meant they were unwelcome. If so, they would have to delay until the following week to ask for another meeting.

From within the room a voice replied, "Wa alaikum as-salam. And upon you be peace."

Inside the door, twenty-foot coffered ceilings and large windows let in the sunlight and framed the view of the Place de la Concorde. Gold leaf detailed the room, and the parquet floor gleamed. The luxury of the salon reinforced the seriousness of the negotiation. For a brief second Lynn wished her father, a former oil pipeline inspector, could be at her side.

The prince and his aides wore suits that, even to Lynn's untrained eye, looked unusually well-tailored. Vandervoost was the only one of the TriCoast group whose attire came close. *The rest of us might as well have dressed in dark closets.*

The TriCoast men in front of her shook hands, starting with the prince, who was first in a line of three. Lynn tried to memorize the appearance of each man without staring.

When it came to her turn, she inclined her head. "Your Highness." She kept her right hand at her side, expecting he wouldn't shake it. To her surprise he offered his, though he did not touch her shoulder as he had with the men. Above his salt-and-pepper mustache and through his fashionable, rimless glasses, his dark eyes appeared intelligent but weary, as if he'd seen everything the world had to offer. He wore a black suit, not traditional robes, stooping a little as if his back hurt.

The prince invited them to be seated. Each man found a place until, like a nightmare version of musical chairs, the only spot left for Lynn was on the sofa next to the prince. He spread his arm across the back of the sofa—he no more wanted her there than she wanted to sit there. Mike jumped up and offered his seat while a TriCoast security guard dragged in a chair.

Another man brought coffee in the hotel's trademark silver service; Lynn smelled cardamom. All took the thimble-sized cups they were offered.

Claude had warned them this was a critical familiarization meeting so business could proceed later. Lynn quelled her impatience to leap into the technical explanations she was ready to provide.

Mike spoke with the prince at length about their last discussion, conferences they'd both attended, and the progress of refinery expansions. Their dialogue was interrupted only by the sound of Riley moving his chair a few inches out of the circle. Finally, Mike turned to her. "Your Highness, I included our US refining executive vice president, Ms. Lynn Dayton, in this meeting, so she can talk about the refining improvements we have underway."

Lynn displayed a few charts, charts the planning department had spent hours translating into Arabic. "These will guide us through the discussion. The keyword at the bottom will get you the podcast we prepared, which covers all of these same points."

The aide sitting next to the prince smiled and turned his hand outward, displaying his own silver iPod.

"Your Highness, you and others have voiced your concern about sufficient US oil refining capacity. TriCoast Energy has 1.7 million barrels per day. We just finished connecting the former Centennial operation to our major Ship Channel refinery. Because of additional hydrotreating upgrades we've made, we can refine your Zuluf crude, as well as Ghawar crude, in eighty-five percent of our capacity."

The prince nodded. A man standing beside him made a note.

Riley pulled additional charts from his briefcase and started to hand them to the prince with his left hand. "I believe we agreed I would speak about our other locations."

Lynn looked in horror at him. *No, Riley!*

The prince put up his hand in a stop gesture, refusing to take the charts Riley extended.

Mike grabbed the papers from Riley.

*Is Riley so overwrought he's forgotten Claude's rules?* By Arabic custom, the left hand was considered unclean.

Riley appeared to realize his mistake. He blurted an apology and said, "Your Highness, your wife? How is she? I mean they? Your many families?"

Burl's reaction was low-key but instantaneous. "Riley, Lynn, we have more efficiency and environmental graphs for the prince. Lisa was trying to send them from Houston when we had to leave the hotel. Could you go see if they've arrived?"

Burl's close friendship with Riley had apparently vanished. His stare at Lynn implied something more direct than his easygoing words: *Get Riley the hell out of here.*

Lynn kept as still as she could. It took all her willpower not to shake her head. Burl had never mentioned graphs. She was being penalized for Riley's blunders.

Gripping her skirt firmly, she glared at Riley until he flinched.

They got up to leave. The blood thumped in her ears, then almost exploded when she heard Vandervoost's smooth voice take over—and mangle—her presentation.

It was enough to cause her to forget Riley was supposed to precede her out of the door. Their collision turned everyone's heads.

She wished she could slam the door behind them.

Once outside on the rue de Rivoli, Lynn spun to face the chubby executive. She'd already put him on notice to find a new job. Burl and Mike had assigned him to this project over her protest, which only made her angrier. "Did you leave your brain on the company jet? What were you thinking, using your left hand? I can't believe I got shoved out of that meeting, for which I've prepared the last two months, to herd you around because you decided to act like an idiot."

He shook his melon head, his face a map of chagrin. "Those boys got way too close to me. Did you see the tall one? Right in my face. Made me nervous. Didn't do it to you since you're a woman." He spat out the last word.

She sighed, counting the weeks until his special project assignment was over and he'd be out of TriCoast. The pounding in her head receded slightly and she pulled up to her full five-foot-nine. "You have to keep cool in any situation. We're not just talking to your neighbor-down-the-street landowners about drilling rights."

"I can't let another man stand or sit that close to me."

She sighed again. "You can put up with it for another few minutes. Let's get back now, since the mythical charts won't be arriving."

They were admitted as Vandervoost was finishing her presentation.

Riley gave a slight shake of his head. Burl said to the prince, "I apologize. The materials aren't here yet."

"We must dismiss for Dhuhr prayers. We look forward to seeing you tonight." He turned to Lynn and held out his right hand, which was speckled with age spots. "A pleasure to meet you, although it was too brief. I am sorry to hear from Mr. Travis you won't be attending tonight."

"But…" *Burl Travis is a goddamn jerk.* She could attend. Burl had excluded her while she was babysitting Riley, then announced it to the prince. But Burl's words were final. To argue in front of the prince would cause everyone to lose face.

One of the prince's men ushered them to the door.

In front of the Crillon, Lynn fought to keep her voice low. "I'm so angry I could spit nails. Burl, why did you shut me out?"

"Your presence bothered the prince."

Mike shook his head. "I don't think so."

The director's response was a chuckle. Then he said, "Henry, impressive presentation. I liked the Arabic translation. Good idea."

"It's fortunate my planning group was able to come up with those charts and translations," Lynn said. *And fortunate for Burl this tunic doesn't have a gun belt.*

The only sign Burl gave was a glance flicked in her direction. "If Riley isn't a match for Lynn's position, you might consider consolidating all the refining businesses under Henry."

Lynn stretched out a deep cramp in her leg, the kind she experienced only with extreme stress. When she spoke, she kept her voice steady. "That doesn't make sense."

"You're getting married," Burl said. "We have to cover our bases if you decide to play house."

She gritted her teeth. "I have no plans to retire."

After the others left in the first Mercedes, Mike and Lynn climbed into the second. She had seldom seen him look so uncomfortable. *Damn right you ought to be uncomfortable, Mike Emerson,* she thought as she ripped off her scarf. "Burl and Riley are out of control."

"Your face is red. Lynn, you're in charge of valuable plants, so everyone wants a piece of them. Burl can only make suggestions. Remember, he got us this introduction."

"He's undercutting me."

"There'll be more opportunities to meet the prince." Mike

was trying to sound soothing. "Why don't you prepare for the meeting with Sansei tomorrow?"

She pulled fiercely on one long sleeve. The cotton fabric tore. "Why didn't you stand up for me?"

He shrugged. "I had no choice. I don't have to tell you the kingdom is a major source of oil. Forget tonight. Have dinner with your sister. Charge it as business. After London, we're flying on to Washington to meet with Homeland Security. Seems they have concerns about the Tulsa refinery, too."

At the hotel, Lynn called her sister.

"So you did get a free evening, like you said you might in your e-mail. I was hoping you would."

"Ceil, there's no one I'd rather see right now, or any time, than you. Let's get dinner."

"How about Chez Flottes?"

"Float? Like seafood?" Lynn puzzled over the French pronunciation.

"F-L-O-T-T-E-S. It's close to the Louvre, the food's good, and it's not far from you. I'll make the reservation. I'm sending a 360 view to your phone right now."

Lynn shed the concealing clothes, along with her hope of securing an additional fifty-five million barrels a year of crude oil for her refineries.

# Ten

*Paris*
*Tuesday evening*

*"The only time people dislike gossip is when you gossip
about them." —Will Rogers*

Mark Shepherd, chief of TriCoast security, insisted on accompanying her when he learned she wouldn't be joining the prince
and the other executives. "I don't need to remind you what happened the last time you were in Paris with your sister." The decision had been final once Mark learned several of the prince's
bodyguards would be present when the prince and other TriCoast
executives ate at Crillon's Les Ambassadeurs.

Embracing Ceil in front of the hotel felt to Lynn like the sun's
warmth in winter. She introduced her sister to Mark. Ceil smiled
when he promised to keep them in sight but out of earshot.

"So you rate a bodyguard now?" Ceil studied him for a moment. "He's hot."

"He's married with four kids, in case you're asking."

Ceil laughed. "Anyone's an improvement on Robert." Robert
Guillard, an established member of France's governmental elite,
had turned out to be a terrorist. Lynn had saved her sister from
Robert's attempt to kill her.

Her sister's willingness to joke about the danger she'd survived gave Lynn a rush of relief. *Maybe she's moving past the
trauma of the rape Guillard ordered inflicted on her.*

Ceil asked, "What happened to your arm?" She guided Lynn along the narrow sidewalk on rue Cambon, past tiny Smart cars. To Lynn's eye the cars were a third the size of the sedans and SUVs jousting in Dallas traffic, or the Denali whose driver had tried to run her down.

The Smarts were as bright as Christmas ornaments and about as big.

"Just a sprain. I'm due to take the splint off soon."

Once they arrived, Ceil pointed out their seats on the sidewalk. Somehow there was enough room for passers-by to squeeze around them, and even for Mark to find a table a few meters away.

When Lynn explained the events of the afternoon, Ceil interjected several ranchers' epithets, then said, "How's Dad?"

"Same, and Dr. Renfro doesn't have any suggestions," Lynn said. "I think he should get another doctor but he doesn't want to talk about it. Now Dad thinks he'll come up with something on the Internet."

Ceil shifted in her chair and looked dubious. "Maybe, but I believe he has only a few months left, just like the doctor said. When will you accept that?"

"If I accept it, it means I stop trying to help him. I think there are still solutions." A sob caught in her throat.

Ceil grimaced. "Maybe it's his time to go."

"How can you say that?" Lynn choked. "How can you give up?"

"I'm not giving up. Just make sure you know what he wants."

"I see him. He's not ready to die."

"Have you asked him? He may be ready to 'go gentle into that good night.' When Mom got to the end of her life, I was there and she needed to hear it was okay to let go."

"You're too pessimistic. He seems cheerful."

"Good. And I'm glad you're around to take care of him," Ceil said.

"I am, but not enough. What's ever enough?"

"How are Cy, the kids, and the wedding planning?"

"Cy's good, so are his kids. The wedding planning, less so. Eight weeks away and it's still unorganized. Cy wants a bigger, more formal event than I do. On top of that, one of the people I'm negotiating with right now is Keith. Of course, everyone is watching me."

"What's that like? Is he still cute?"

Lynn sighed. "I wish he wasn't, but he is. I'd be lying if I said otherwise. But all I have to do is remember how he treated me during our marriage. Cy is more honest, fewer secrets, and he doesn't drink like a fish. Though it looks like Keith might have slowed down on the alcohol."

"So I'll keep my ticket to fly over for the wedding," Ceil said.

"Hell yes. I can't believe it's so soon. Invitations are out. Cy's arranged the church. I'm supposed to be handling the reception. There are a thousand details left." Lynn changed the subject. "So, tell me why we're sitting outside."

Ceil explained that in many Parisian restaurants, the non-smoking interior was tourist Siberia, blocked from even a glimpse of the intriguing street scene. "And not everyone out here smokes."

"But you still do."

Ceil didn't answer.

Lynn decided to drop the subject. Chez Flottes was north of Place de la Concorde. Ceil reminded her that the area was originally named Place Louis XV until Napoleon renamed it Place de la Révolution. During the eponymous revolution, she explained, it was the site of over a thousand beheadings, including that of Louis the XVI.

*I can name two men I'd like to behead.*

Did the striking white Obelisk of Luxor, a gift from Egypt in 1836 taking the place of the guillotine, transform anything? Lynn wondered. How about the multiple name changes? Now the square was Place de la Concorde. Do an obelisk and a pacific title smooth over the past? Is a killing field ever drained of its blood?

When the waiter named a few house specialties, Lynn's reaction was immediate. "Steak tartare? Non, merci." She asked for a few minutes to look at the menu.

"We had a meeting with the prince also," Ceil said.

"You did?"

"I work for the International Energy Agency. Remember?"

"But I heard the Saudis weren't talking to the IEA. The key question: what did you wear?"

"The prince is touching all his bases before Ramadan. They're finally responding to our complaints about their unreliable statistics. Oh, what I wore? Probably the same as you—a jilbab. It's similar to a long coat, like an abaya but more elegant. Cost me a month's salary, but I'll be wearing it often."

"What did the Saudis tell you?" Saudi Arabian officials were famously secretive about the operations of their giant oilfields.

"I can't give you anything nonpublic. But I can tell you what I posted on the IEA website today. They admitted their drilling techniques at the Zuluf fields aren't as effective as they'd hoped. Oil production is down."

Lynn kept her eyes level. *Yup, a percentage of the Zuluf production is what they want to sell and you want to buy. Sounds like it's a shrinking number.* "What else?"

"One aide suggested the best crude source is still the giant, Ghawar, the field where they have the most production."

Ceil ordered for both of them: country wine, roast chicken, and potatoes aligot.

"Aligot?"

"Whipped with garlic, butter, cream, and cheese."

"Comfort food."

"The last time you were here you saved my life," Ceil said. "It's my turn."

<hr>

The Austrian's assignment was low-key for now. He didn't need the silenced Glock he carried inside his coat but he wouldn't have left Hotel Le Bristol without it. To the staff at the hotel, he was another rich man—as indeed he was—in Paris for an investors' conference.

He cursed when he realized the woman had split off from one of the two groups he was monitoring in Paris.

His initial instructions were to watch the TriCoast officials. If possible, he was to disrupt three of the bidding groups so they'd drop out. It had been left to him, a creative free-lancer, to choose the form the disruptions would take. He decided to start with a direct approach.

Through the busy streets of the first arrondisement, he trailed the blond woman and a younger look-alike he guessed to be her sister. He recognized Mark Shepherd a few feet behind them. Mark was making no effort to conceal his mission of keeping the women under surveillance. *Not unpleasant duty, either,* the Austrian mused.

When he walked past their street-side table, they were leaning toward one another. He heard rapid English and thought about how easy it was to follow the Americans. They were trusting. In their country, few public security cameras existed. In London a person could easily be caught on CCTV cameras. After a while, he decided that even though the blonde woman had a guard, since she was not with the TriCoast group she must be of little importance. He circled back to the Intercontinental and waited for the American men. They soon appeared. The weather was mild enough that the men wore suit jackets but not coats.

They returned to the Crillon nearby and were met by the prince's bodyguards. The prince must have arranged dinner within so as not to leave its confines. He had no chance entering unnoticed. He would not have the open shot he wanted.

He walked about a hundred meters and turned the corner to a sidewalk cafe. He recalled the prince's bodyguards looked trim and athletic. *Very trim. No bulletproof vests.*

A few hours later, he waited out of sight of the entrance to the Crillon. With the mild weather, dozens of people crowding the sidewalks, and the guards' lack of body armor, he'd decided on another, equally-effective disruption. He only needed to frighten the Saudis out of doing business with TriCoast for three months.

A tight cordon of bodyguards surrounded the prince as he walked his American guests out of the Crillon.

The Austrian fired one precise shot into the head of the guard closest to him. By the time his body hit the sidewalk the Austrian had vanished into the crowd of terrified onlookers.

# Eleven

*Paris*
*Tuesday, late night-Wednesday morning*

Lynn rolled over to answer her buzzing cell phone.

"Thank God you're okay!"

After a few sleep-stunned seconds, she recognized Mike's voice and looked at the time. "Why are you calling me?" She couldn't resist adding, "Stag party break up?"

"Good thing you weren't there. Wish I hadn't been." He took a breath. "When we left the restaurant just now, one of the prince's bodyguards was shot and killed. Right in front of us."

"That's awful! You're fine? Burl, Henry, Riley okay?"

"Yeah. But I talked to Mark Shepherd and he doesn't want us meeting with Sansei tomorrow. Given your experience with them here in Paris, he thinks they could have been behind the shooting."

A few months earlier Lynn and Ceil had been caught in the crossfire at Paris' Sacre Coeur between a Sansei operative and a man they learned was not only an elite French official but also a saboteur. Afterward, Lynn had been debriefed by FBI agent Jim Cutler and TriCoast's security chief, Mark Shepherd.

"Why would Sansei be involved?"

"He thinks it's more than coincidental."

"That interferes with our ability to do business. If he's worried about security, he can add more people tomorrow."

"We'll talk about it then."

"Mike? I'm really glad none of you were hurt."

"Thanks." He hung up.

What she hadn't mentioned was her gut frustration that the Saudis would likely break off all discussions with TriCoast, not only for the refinery, but for oil supply, or any other deal. Getting them back to the table would take a masterstroke. *Guess we'll find out if Burl is worth his juice.*

As Lynn rubbed her eyes, she wondered about the killer. *Is it Sansei? Is it an unhappy Saudi ex-pat? Is someone or some group genuinely trying to scare the Saudis away from TriCoast, and vice versa? If so who, and why?*

She adjusted the splint on her wrist.

She decided to call Josh Rosen, a New York trader with whom she'd attended business school. She'd helped him get a job working for Sara Levin at TriCoast, but after a few years he'd moved on to Kodiak, in New York. His insights were always fresh, though Sara had once described the hyperkinetic Josh as someone who could only relax when he was awake. Rosen moved, thought, and talked at lightning pace.

"Rosen." His heavily-accented voice reminded her of their countless meetings during finance study sessions.

"Josh, it's Lynn Dayton."

"Lynn! My dear! How are you?"

"Good. You?"

"Not so good. You remember my uncle? Dead. Prostate cancer. We sat shiva for him last week."

During long afternoons, Josh had entertained Lynn's working group with stories of his uncle that always started with: "You think I have an accent? My uncle, when he came to America…" and always ended by illustrating a difference between the United States and Josh's family's native Russia.

"You must miss him."

"At least he left us stories. But what brings your delightful voice to my telephone?"

"I'm in Paris."

"Same mail codes as Dallas if I recall. More civilized."

"So you think. I'm calling about the Russian trading groups who sell oil. All I know is the Russians have broken every contract we've ever made with them. It's not always clear who's in charge—the president, the prime minister, or the oligarchs. But we may have to talk to them in the next few days about supply. Hell, we're talking to everyone. I wondered if you can give me some insight."

"They're creative, paranoid, and vicious. My father's side of the family anyway. So why are you dealing with them? Oh yeah, crude baby crude. Where are you meeting them?"

"London," she said, glad her father's family was so completely unlike Josh's.

"Better there than Russia. Even in London, assume you'll be taped and followed. And you already know any deal is subject to change at the whim of the government."

"Happens with most governments, we've learned. But we're looking at a simple purchase."

"Simple is good. Lynn, you're not meeting with any journalists?"

"No."

"So you might make it back alive."

"Grim."

"Realistic. Now Lynn, quid pro quo. You and Sara keep us in mind for options, risk products. The head fred at Kodiak has clamped down, so I have to meet with ninety-five auditors to make sure we're following regulations, but we're still in business."

"We're working on something where we might need you. We'll bring you in the loop if we can."

After she talked to Josh, she paged through a bookmarked site on Versailles. It was the closest she would get to seeing it this trip. After thwarting Robert Guillard's attempted kidnapping of her sister and the gun battle in which he was killed during her last trip to Paris, Lynn and her sister had concluded their time together at Versailles. They had rowed its Grand Canal and talked about Guillard's murderous plans.

Daylight came too quickly. In an e-mail message from Gene Blahunka he asked her to call him immediately.

It was the middle of the night in Tulsa. "Gene, I got your message."

"The ME investigator, Neliah Jefferson, called me," Gene said. "She asked who provided our doughnuts the day Tom died. Told her we get them from the shop down the street, always have. When I asked why, she said it appears Tom Martin had been poisoned. Not necessarily from the doughnuts. Could have gotten something on his skin, in through a cut. The ME's office is testing everything from the crane's cab to see if they can identify it. Said whatever it was caused muscle paralysis and cardiac failure. Worst part is even if we'd found Tom earlier, he likely wouldn't have been able to speak."

*So Tom's death was even worse than it seemed.* "That's terrible! Gene, have the inspectors check everything and everyone who was around Tom that day."

"Already doing it. So Tom's wife was telling us something important when she said his last physical showed no heart problems."

"The ME isn't sure it was the doughnuts, right? Did anything show up in his stomach?"

Gene sighed. "No." Once again, she remembered Gene had been the last to see Tom, although his scream at finding Tom dead had seemed genuine.

She called her sister, apologized for waking her, and explained that one of the prince's bodyguards had been shot. "The Saudi ambassador, Saudi police, and French police are all over it."

"Your security chief—that handsome man I saw last night—is in touch with Interpol, too, I'd bet. I've met a woman who works there—we always have foreign heads of oil countries through here—and you want her on the case. Her name's Simone Tierney. She's in the headquarters office in Lyon."

"Thanks, Ceil. One of the best parts of the wedding will be

having you back in Dallas for a few days."

"As long as you don't plan it for one of those hundred-degree scorchers."

At breakfast Lynn joined three of the TriCoast men at La Verrière. They looked like they hadn't slept. "Tough night."

Mark Shepherd ran his hand over his bald head. "We didn't finish answering questions until four hours ago."

"Where are Burl and Riley?" Lynn asked. *Probably busy screwing up someone else's career.*

Mike Emerson shifted in the upholstered red chair. "They're sleeping in. By the way, except for getting shot at, you didn't miss much in the way of real negotiation last night." He leaned toward her and said, "Like I told you, we decided to ax the Sansei meeting today. We're getting negative vibes from our U.S. government contacts. We'll fly on to London instead." When she opened her mouth to protest, he said, "It's unanimous."

The warmth of sympathy mixed with the chill of incredulity. "No, it *wasn't* unanimous. I didn't participate. Are you taking over my responsibility for supplying our refineries with crude? Do I need to remind you we're looking for over a million barrels every single day?"

Henry Vandervoost shoved a scone in his mouth. Mark cut a piece of tea bread in half and shook his head. "You can't buy crude oil if you're dead."

Mike signaled the waiter to bring her a cup of coffee and said, "Lynn, cut us a break. We know your history with Sansei. They even make you nervous, which is saying a lot. And you've been telling me their focus was on selling us gasoline, which we don't need, instead of crude oil, which we do. If the feds aren't going to approve a sale, we're wasting our time meeting with them."

"We'll lose face. Worse, *they'll* lose face. We can't dump the meeting." She chewed through two entire croissants before she realized how fast she was eating. *Stress.*

"We spoke to them last night. They understand our concerns." Mark's head flushed red all the way past his ears.

"Did we at least reschedule with them?"

"They were able to switch their other meetings, so they aren't inconvenienced. Once we determine who was really behind the bodyguard's murder and confirm Sansei wasn't involved in any way, we can set up a new meeting."

"Did you change the London plans?"

"Our meetings there are the same. We'll just leave here later. But there's something else I meant to tell you," Mike said. "Mark wants one-on-one security in London. One of his MI-5 contacts has recommended bodyguards for you and Henry. Burl and Riley are returning to the States today."

*If I clicked my heels together three times would they leave even sooner?*

After Henry excused himself to pack, Lynn said, "Two other things we need to discuss. My sister mentioned Simone Tierney as one of the best at Interpol."

"I know the name. She's got a good rep," Mark Shepherd said.

"And Tom Martin, the man who died in Tulsa, did not have a heart attack. He was poisoned."

"Why haven't I heard about this?" Mark asked.

"I just found out a few minutes ago," Lynn said.

Mike Emerson sighed. "Does trouble follow us more than it used to?" He looked at Lynn. "Or did you drop a bad-luck magnet on us?"

# Twelve

*Tahlequah/London*
*Wednesday*

*"Diplomacy is the art of saying 'Nice doggie' until you can find a rock." —Will Rogers*

"The BIA (Bureau of Indian Affairs, part of the US Interior Department) manages 56 million acres of land on behalf of 315 tribes and more than 300,000 individuals; royalties from the lands generate more than $1 billion annually. But in 1996, a group of Indians led by Elouise Cobell, a member of the Blackfeet Tribe in Montana, sued the Interior Department, claiming mismanagement and malfeasance over more than a century had cost Indian landowners at least $10 billion." *—Native America Press/Ojibwe News*

When the telephone rang, Cherokee Investment Group head Jesse Drum clicked down the volume on his computer. Steady chants from a Native Voices program rolled from the speakers.

"Jesse, how're things?"

*Why was Billy calling?* Billy was the BIA's new deputy assistant secretary for economic development. Jesse rubbed his eyes and looked away from the numbers on his screen. "Osiyo."

"Hello to you. How's the casino expansion?"

Jesse smiled. Everyone wanted credit for the newest hotel the Cherokee Nation had erected near one of its casinos. "More people coming into Oklahoma from Arkansas and staying the weekend, just like we figured."

"Good. What else is going on?"

*Not like Billy to be inquisitive, but maybe it's part of his new job.* He needed to talk to Billy Perry anyway. "We're looking at buying a refinery and gas stations. Need 'em for our casinos. We have private capital lined up and a seller."

"Refinery and gas stations? Jesse, you're begging for heartaches or a rip-off. The last thing the BIA wants is some tribe investing in oil and gas," Billy's response sounded prepared.

"We're not some tribe," Jesse said. "We're a large nation with many successful businesses."

"If it's not on your land, why mess with it? Or if you have to, then spread the risk and bring in some other tribes. And we need to see the environmental permits." Billy coughed.

"Billy, you and I go way back, but since when did you turn into the EPA? We're big enough to handle this business ourselves. We've got a backer, Adela. Adding another tribe makes it needlessly complicated."

"Adela? As in 'money'?" Billy coughed again.

"Yes. We can improve this refinery, especially if we increase gas station throughput. Last week you told me, and I quote, 'Tribal economic self-determination is part of the BIA's mission.' In the same conversation you said you liked the Citizen Potawatomis diversifying so they don't rely just on casinos."

"You already have other businesses."

"I don't call manufacturing plants, a few C-stores and smoke shops enough diversification," Jesse said. A flute sound wandered from his computer speakers, spinning into a slow vibrato.

"Build on what you know."

"We are. This fits with our other businesses."

"Running a refinery is not the same as running a casino. You'll be taking orders from OSHA and a hundred other agencies." Billy's voice had a harsher note.

Same old *u-yo*, garbage. He's jealous we'd be talking to someone in Washington besides him, Jesse thought. "Billy, somebody's
been sitting here, probably in this very building, hearing the same
thing from the BIA for the last hundred and fifty years, sure as
*hi-yv-wi-ya-dv*." Without thinking, he'd lapsed into Cherokee,
his words reminding Billy he was Indian.

"Yes, we're both Indians. So why not another casino?"

"We'll build another one eventually. But there's a limit. State
of Oklahoma won't do a compact with us for the Class III Las
Vegas machines. So we'll never be as rich as those tiny bands with
their slot banks. Man, my college profs never mentioned those
little three-person tribes."

"Indian gaming is a good thing."

"When the money goes to Indians. Not some *a-ni-da-lo-ni-
ge*, like the Malaysians," Jesse said.

"Well, keep pushing the state government. Your casino tax
revenue is makin' 'em see the light. Tell me about your equity
source."

Jesse could almost see Billy hunched over his computer, ready
to take notes. Pete and Keith would get a call from Billy this
morning. "Like I said, Adela, which means Pete Whitehawk and
Keith McConaugh. You know Whitehawk, local boy made good,
friend of mine. And through him I've worked with Keith before."

"Is Keith red or white?" Billy wasn't talking skin color. In the
1700s and 1800s the "red council" was a tribe's war government,
usually made up of younger men, warriors. The "white council" was its peace government, made up of older men. The white
council's rule came first, but in times of war, it ceded authority
to the red government. Thus a "red" was a warrior, a "white" a
wise elder. Red also referred to men who were noble and brave.
There was no higher compliment than to be called a red man.

"More red than white," Jesse said.

"Say, what do you hear about the Chilocco reunion? I'll never
know how you survived that hellhole." Billy sighed.

"Boarding schools. Another winning BIA idea, Billy. But

Chilocco was good for me," Jesse grinned at the memories of pranks he had masterminded, and looked outside to the Tahlequah town square. Brown leaves skittered on the bare sidewalk near the huge, inlaid seven-pointed star.

The drummers on the Internet radio show sped up their rhythm. Jesse could almost see a fancy dancer keeping time. "You know we don't need your approval for this acquisition."

"How much money do you get from us?"

"Are you threatening?"

"No, just a question."

No matter what Billy said, Jesse felt squeezed. The feds, the state, no one really wanted the Cherokees on their own. *Hell, the feds even abolished our government for seventy years,* Jesse thought.

Billy was speaking. "Don't the casinos fund your arts exhibit every year? And pay for health care services? So why do you want to buy an old refinery?"

"Oil prices are down again, so gasoline margins are up."

"I still don't like it." Billy hung up. He'd never given Jesse a real reason why it wasn't a good idea. Jesse suspected he didn't like the idea of refineries because it hadn't been his idea, because Billy didn't really like new ideas in general, nor complex ones in particular.

The drumbeat now was repetitive instead of reassuring, and the tune was much too traditional.

⁂

*London, afternoon*

"Overseas travel is a pain. My anchor's draggin'." Mike looked even worse than he sounded.

Lynn agreed. "Forget 'seize the day.' Try 'erase the day.'" She felt betrayed by her lagged body, which kept trying to pull her back to US central daylight time. Every morning since she'd left Tulsa she'd had to fight not to go back to sleep. The interruption last night made her feel even worse.

Henry Vandervoost appeared more relaxed. "You are still contending with the time change. I am not."

Henry noted that the part of London's financial district through which they were walking had been the site of a Roman gladiator arena. "Maybe the blood's less literal now, but it still does run in the streets from time to time."

"Henry, you made a joke! We should meet with you in Europe more often," Lynn said.

"This is much more civilized than those ridiculous video-conference calls," he replied. "Of course we rotate them so that everyone takes turns suffering, but I hate trying to talk business at two in the morning."

She expected North Seas Resources' offices to be more richly furnished than TriCoast's, but found it hard to ignore the company's even more stringent level of security. At one door she removed her padded splint so it could be x-rayed separately.

*North Seas is probably having similar trouble ignoring TriCoast's bodyguards.* One each for Lynn, Mike, and Henry were spread in front and behind.

Fingerprint readers secured most doors; when they passed an open one she saw the furniture in the rooms was a mix, a Hepplewhite sideboard inlaid with mahogany next to a pressboard conference table. *Yup, oil's a volatile business. Looks like they bought the Hepplewhite when they were making money and the pressboard when they were losing it.* When the company escort took over, the bodyguards followed to wait nearby.

North Seas vice president Nigel Wold folded his pink *Financial Times* and shook hands first with Henry Vandervoost. Henry introduced Nigel to Lynn and Mike, explaining he and Nigel often met at European energy conferences.

"Ah, Henry, Mike. You'll like this story," Wold said. "We just bought this little seismic company. We kept the owner in place to run it, like we always do. So this owner, a Scotsman, his every other word was 'fuck.' Finally one day he asked me, 'Nigel do I swear too much?' Know what I told him? 'Fuck, no.'"

Lynn laughed. "I've met a lot like him."

Another woman joined them, and Wold introduced her as Helena Farber. Her dark brown hair was pulled back so completely it almost appeared she was bald. Her long black skirt was equally severe. Only her silk blouse suggested ease.

"Let's get right to it, shall we?" Nigel said. "Helena here is one of our more senior project managers. We'd like her to run due diligence on this refinery. Due diligence before the purchase is always a good idea, eh?"

Wold had spoken as if he knew the full story of Lynn's Centennial Refinery purchase, and the insider damage that had followed. *But we did a thorough review. No one could have figured out the Centennial's marketing VP's treachery in advance, nor known he'd already turned into a mercenary for a French saboteur.*

Wold continued. "She has fifteen years of experience and has, I must say, kept us out of some bad scrapes. Investments later going sour, and so forth."

Lynn caught Mike's dubious look. It appeared the first order of business once Helena arrived in Tulsa would be to suit her up in more practical clothes, including steel-toed boots.

"North Seas Resources hasn't made an offer yet on the Tulsa refinery. Aren't you jumping the gun?" Lynn asked.

"Such a delightful American expression. So cowboy. Or should I say, cowgirl." Wold's smile looked practiced.

"So here's the anti-cowboy. The Cherokee Investment Group has already offered in excess of a billion dollars," Mike said.

"Measuring cocks, are we?" Wold's smile had disappeared.

"Not at all. We're suggesting you're wasting your time, and Helena's, if you're not serious about an offer," Lynn said.

Helena spoke up. "We are serious. We've pulled capital away from Russia. Nasty thing when your 50-50 partner takes over your business."

"Sounds like Venezuela, where the contract gets rewritten while soldiers stand with AK-47s at your head," Mike said.

"Few people are building grassroots refineries," Helena said. "From the *outside* your refinery looks attractive to us."

Despite Lynn's first doubts about Helena's expertise, she found the woman's confidence winning. North Seas Resources had a reputation for deep-voiced executives with Hollywood-square jaws and Wharton MBAs who mouthed the occasional profanity for oil-field cred. Wold fit the type. Either Helena was the exception that proved the rule or the company was changing.

"Once you've signed the confidentiality agreements, why don't you plan on staying a week or two in Tulsa? I'll tell the refinery manager, Gene Blahunka, to show you around." Lynn gave Helena Gene's contact data. "Can you drive on the right?"

"Most of my projects are outside of England. In fact, it's no secret we have a Midwestern refinery on the market. Would you consider a trade?"

Lynn's heartbeat quickened. *Of course! The North Dakota oil field could help supply it, too.*

As if reading those very thoughts, Mike shook his head. "Lynn, you just had us buy a refinery in Houston."

She smiled at him. "Don't rule out a trade. I can run an additional refinery."

Vandervoost frowned. She'd hit a sore spot because Vandervoost believed she already had too much responsibility.

"Right," said Wold. "So, it sounds as if our little circle jerk can end."

Helena turned to him. "We know you're only speaking for yourself, Nigel, but save your boorish metaphors for the pub."

Wold was unfazed. "Thank you, Helena, for reminding me we would like to host the three of you at dinner... at a pub."

Lynn blinked back an eye roll at the thought of another two hours with Nigel Wold. Mike said, "Excellent. We'd like to join you."

After they left the office, Helena and Nigel guided them through a maze of financial district streets so narrow they could barely accommodate a motorcycle. Helena had to warn them several times to look right instead of left when stepping off curbs to cross the street. Lynn felt fatigue wash over her.

Despite a meal of roast lamb and Stilton cheese at The George & Vulture, a Dickensian pub in the middle of the maze, Lynn's opinion of Nigel Wold did not improve. Fortunately, Helena regaled the group with stories about the peccadilloes of English royalty past and present, including meetings of the bawdy, satirical Hellfire Club upstairs from where they were eating. "We English, and Europeans," she nodded toward Henry, who was from the Netherlands, "can hold grudges for centuries."

Later that evening, Lynn pulled Mike aside. "You need to talk to Burl Travis. The Saudis will be superstitious about meeting with us after the murder of the prince's bodyguard. But we have to keep the lines open. If Burl really has the magic touch with them, I want to see him use it."

"I'll talk to him tomorrow. It *will* require magic to convince the Saudis to talk to us again anytime soon."

Lynn wondered if there was there a connection between Burl, Henry, Riley or, worst of all, Mike, and the bodyguard killer or killers.

⁂

Gernot Insel had both clients and targets in London. Some were there for personal safety, some for financial safety, some both. All claimed the need to diversify—to spread their billions from the UK to Dubai to China to North America.

He completed a few meetings before joining the client who had just hired him, one of the many with a London office.

When Insel was ushered in, the client—medium in build, with wide-set eyes and wavy hair—closed the door and directed Insel to chairs at a glass-topped table.

"Congratulations on Paris." The Chechen spoke English although it was not a native language for either of them.

"I did not expect to get close to the prince and I could not. Nor would killing him really serve the objective. We want him frightened but still in control," Insel said.

The client made further payment arrangements and handed him a piece of paper with suggested locations and targets.

Insel nodded, handed it back, and the client fed the paper into a shredder.

"You have the discretion to research operations and to recruit or kill whomever necessary," the client said, "as long as you accomplish the final objective. We prefer only one bidder."

"Good." Insel leaned back in his chair.

"I suggest you learn as much as you can about the habits of people at TriCoast and those at North Seas involved in the Tulsa refinery purchase."

"Tulsa. Strange name. Like so many in the United States it seems to be derived from the country's indigenous peoples."

The client showed him to the door. "Staying unnoticed at your next destinations will be more difficult than avoiding London's cameras."

Insel stopped back at his hotel, dyed his brown hair blond, added glasses and dental inserts, and changed his clothes to some even more nondescript, and then went on to a vantage point near the main door of North Seas Resources' offices. From there he saw the group go in.

He'd traveled London's streets many times before this client had requested he tail the two Americans and one Dutchman. He kept out of sight of the bodyguards the three had added. The additional obstacles had resulted from his Parisian success.

He followed a larger group later from North Seas to The George and Vulture. From prior assignments he knew The George and Vulture was a favorite of Nigel's, located in a warren of alleys so small they were seldom shown on any map.

With the rain and his disguise, it was easy to stay hidden; he hoisted a black umbrella like the hundreds around him. Still,

England's MI5 and MI6 and London's omnipresent CCTV cameras couldn't be underestimated.

Insel had, in fact, discussed doing reconnaissance work at North Seas Resources, but wasn't employed by them at present. *Just as well.* He preferred not to work both sides of the same street. Though if one felt no loyalty, there was no loyalty to divide.

# Thirteen

*London*
*Thursday*

Still half asleep, Lynn reached out in the dark, trying to recall her location. *Last night? Blood. No, the blood was on stage.* After a few drinks, Nigel and Helena insisted on taking their TriCoast guests to see *Macbeth* at the National Theater. Lynn remembered one of Shakespeare's addresses was "Muggles" Lane and laughed when she thought about how Cy's daughter, a Harry Potter reader, would get wide-eyed when she heard.

She opened blackout shades to pale light and tugged her wrist splint back into position, wondering again who had tried to crush her in Tulsa with an SUV. *Seems like weeks ago, but I'm stuck with this splint for three more days.*

She pulled sweats from her suitcase. On Nigel's advice, they were staying in large Mayfair apartments. Despite the wealth of the surroundings, one bathroom offered hot water but no cold. Near the hall doorway, sensors misfired so badly the heating and cooling operated simultaneously.

She lingered for a moment, putting off the first hard mile as she studied the ornate room. Medallions had been carved into the marble mantle and columns of the nonworking fireplace. The sitting room glowed burnt orange and cream, offset by magenta carpet. Everything was patterned, from the ceiling moldings to the door lintels to the red and silver pillows. Even the light fixtures were mini-chandeliers.

The embellishment matched Nigel's formality and Helena's reticence. More than any weather report, the heavy fabrics testified to London's damp cold.

But today's weather was a welcome sixty-five degrees, perfect for running.

Lynn mapped a route southwest through Hyde Park. She was tempted to go alone but relented and called her newly-assigned bodyguard, Cheryl Wilkins. A Louisiana native, she had just joined TriCoast after serving in Iraq and the Coast Guard.

Cheryl greeted her outside. Once past the congestion of Park Lane, branching paths offered many choices. Lynn suggested a loop past Serpentine Pond and into Kensington Gardens. Cheryl kept pace and directed Lynn away from the road traversing the middle of the park.

Her calf and hamstring muscles unwound, which felt so good she found herself anticipating her next run. After four miles on verdant, open paths, they crossed Hyde Park Corner and jogged on Piccadilly along the north side of St. James's Park, stopping finally at a Pret convenience store to buy yogurt and crackers.

⁂

The bodyguards nixed riding in the Tube, so Henry, Lynn, and Mike took taxis to TriCoast's regional London office. Henry introduced them in three large meetings to a few hundred of his employees. Mike spoke to each group. Henry was careful to also introduce Lynn and Mike to a half-dozen of his high-fliers, young men and women she would soon see at TriCoast's Dallas headquarters on fast-track assignments, many of whom she might want to bring into her own division. For now, she was glad Greg, the tattooed analyst, was working with her on the Oklahoma refinery sale.

Afterward, Henry showed them to empty offices. Lynn sank into an oversized leather chair, pulled out her phone and responded to voice, e-mail, and text messages from her refineries in New Jersey, south Louisiana, Houston, Tulsa, and California.

Vandervoost and the three bodyguards joined Lynn and Mike as they left TriCoast's London office. The bodyguards required them to again split into three individual taxis for the ride to Mayfair. Since the taxi driver could hear her if she called, she texted Mike instead.

*You think asking the Russians to sell us crude is worth the time? The news I get is their exports are spoken for.*

He replied, *The President suggested it. Diplomatic courtesy.*

⁂

Amanda Parsifal was careful to keep her online identity separate from her real one. She'd developed a following for her research into energy prices, updated frequently on Internet sites and in daily blog posts. Her insight into the timing of oil and gas shipments led to the usual speculation she was sleeping with her information sources.

Sometimes she wished relationships were so easy. Instead, she had three occasional boyfriends at the sort-of interested stage. She'd had sex with none of them yet.

Her sources had competing axes to grind, so together they gave her a whole picture. One source in particular, had been detailed in his whispers about drastic OPEC and Mexican oil decline rates.

Amanda didn't hear her cell phone ring the first time. She looked out the window of her Southwark flat across the Thames River to the City, the financial center of London. The established analysts there outwardly bristled at her guerilla research, but several of them were among her most loyal subscribers.

She was sitting in front of her screen correlating a computer model to account for differences between officially-stated reserves in two Middle Eastern countries and what their actual production numbers told her about the size of the reserves. She smiled. *Does everyone have to exaggerate size?*

She'd been getting so many complaints from those countries' statisticians she knew her model was accurate. Among her growing group of followers, several had begun paying for more detailed analysis. *Money in the bank, the real breakthrough,* Amanda thought, as she typed in a larger number for European gas reserves.

She jumped up from her computer at the second chime of her cell phone.

"Flowers here for you," said the doorman when she answered. "Shall I sign for them?"

She flipped on her security camera, which gave her a view of the lobby and the doorman. *A large bouquet of roses. Old-fashioned. Intriguing.* "Thank you, Nash. I'll sign for them myself."

She turned off her alarm system, unlocked the door, and went downstairs where the doorman was waiting with the flower deliveryman. He was pleasantly good-looking, another GQ wannabe. But her attention was on the big spray of two dozen red roses.

With a grin, the doorman asked, "Serious boyfriend?"

"Maybe, more than I expected." She wondered who had sent them, pleased that her romantic life might be improving, too. *Fuck you bloody Oxbridge,* she thought. *I'm surviving and thriving, despite your refusal to admit me.* She buried her nose in the blooms. Their smell was delicious. She sneezed.

Once back in her flat, Amanda opened the card accompanying the roses. She was amused to see that the man with whom she'd gone to the theater last night had sent them. He hadn't seemed especially keen on her. She sniffed the roses again and placed them in a vase next to her computer. Then she swung long, graceful legs under her desk and turned back to the screen. She sneezed a few more times.

❦

Insel had trailed Lynn Dayton on her run through Hyde Park early in the morning. Her bodyguard kept her away from autos, bicyclists, and most other runners. That was acceptable. He had determined he needed Lynn alive and healthy for a while.

Another of Insel's clients had decided Amanda Parsifal's blog was closing in on the truth too often, making several senior officials uncomfortable.

Insel was to silence her in whichever way he thought was best. This was his favorite assignment because the client dictated only the result. Insel was to choose the time, place, and method. The client had doubled the usual fee. It was all the more delicious because he himself had been the recent source feeding Amanda's newest, exact calculations on the country's poorly-performing oil wells.

He'd learned her address two months earlier. Southwark was strangely appropriate. For its entire history, everything new and risqué in London had originated there, on the south side of the Thames. The least-reputable and best entertainments, prostitutes, and theater troupes—including Shakespeare's—had located in Southwark.

Indeed, the mythical Crossed Bones graveyard had been found and excavated nearby. True to the rumors, Crossed Bones was a burial ground containing hundreds of bones and bodies of prostitutes.

The evidence of the city's rough past had shocked respectable London more than it ever would him; prostitution was legal in Germany. There the biggest concern was air pollution from customers' autos. To combat it, some women preferred their patrons arrive by bicycle.

Since Insel was in London, he decided to complete the Parsifal assignment. It was a shame he wouldn't be around for the very end.

◈

Amanda became weaker. She had trouble breathing. She vomited. The second day she made an appointment to see a doctor. She stopped posting. When she texted the man whose name was on the card with the roses, he told her he hadn't sent them.

She woke up the night of the second day, unable to breathe. By two a.m., her computer was permanently dark.

The neighbors called police when they noticed a smell a week later.

Amanda's landlord let the police into her flat. The stench, nothing like a bouquet of roses, was overpowering.

Done on an accelerated schedule, Amanda Parsifal's autopsy would show she'd suffered ricin poisoning.

Scotland Yard found the powder on the dead roses.

And when the investigation was complete, the man whose name was on the gift card would have a solid alibi. The doorman would not remember much about the flower deliveryman. The hard drive of Amanda's computer would be analyzed but yield no information. It would be discovered CCTV cameras had captured unidentifiable images of Amanda Parsifal's assassin, a blond man wearing glasses and a Yankees baseball cap. He was one of thousands, and he had disappeared.

✿

Russia and Saudi Arabia alternated places as the world's leading oil producing country, depending on how much production the Saudis closed in any given week. This week, Russia was leading.

Lynn's taxi took her on Curzon past Riyad Bank. The Qatari Embassy was not far away in Knightsbridge; Lynn had visited it earlier. She remembered what Josh Rosen had told her to expect of the Russians. *Creative, paranoid, and vicious. Like many people with whom I've negotiated.*

She met Mike when he stepped from the taxi behind hers at an anonymous Mayfair building. Once they were buzzed in, their bodyguards—Mark Shepherd, Cheryl Wilkins, and Vandervoost's guard—closed around them. Unlike the North Seas offices, the guards would stay in the same room with them while they talked to the Russians.

The men the TriCoast executives met could have stepped from a Nebraska farm and walked through a Lands End catalog. They wore khakis and gray polo shirts with upturned collars. Their serious, close-set eyes were narrowed to slits as if they'd spent many polar summer days without sunglasses. Square foreheads were interrupted by widows' peaks of dark hair. Departing from the Lands End image were their well-sculpted biceps. They smelled pleasantly of cologne.

They didn't appear to mind the bodyguards. They'd brought two of their own and a slight woman who appeared to be their translator.

The bodyguards sized one another up. *All beefy friends here,*

Lynn thought. Even Cheryl seemed to have added heft and grown a few inches taller.

The meeting was short and more successful than Lynn had hoped. She and Vandervoost secured a couple of million-barrel cargoes of Russian export blend, each enough to run one of their smaller refineries for five days. Since the Russian traders often blended down, providing crude of worse quality than contracted, Lynn negotiated a provision to deduct payment for anything worse than 1.2% sulfur and 32 API gravity, or density.

The Russians announced lunch at Scott's. She grinned at the sly selection. The seafood restaurant was famous for its appearance in Cold War novels.

Once they arrived, Lynn admired its marble floor mosaic and oak-paneled walls, but was put off by menu choices of blood pudding, blood sausage, quail, and pigeon, until she spotted fish entrees. She noticed Mike, too, neglected the blood and bird dishes for steak and onion pie with bashed neeps. When they ate, the sea bream and squid were as fresh as if they'd been swimming a few hours ago.

After a few drinks, Lynn and Mike said good-bye to their hosts. Mark and Cheryl rejoined them as they left the restaurant for a flight to Washington. Vandervoost and the now-jollier Russians stayed behind at Scott's, appearing to have just started a long afternoon of shaken-not-stirreds.

# Fourteen

*Washington, D.C.*
*Friday*

*"Nothing you can't spell will ever work."* —*Will Rogers*

Lynn relished her sleep on TriCoast's private jet as it flew from London to Washington Thursday afternoon. She woke as the jet landed and, with Mike, stumbled through customs at what her body protested was one a.m. London time. Later, in the lobby of Foggy Bottom's Melrose Hotel, they headed to their separate rooms. She couldn't remember the last time a bed had looked so welcoming.

❧

In Lyon, France, Simone Tierney sat slumped in a bunker-like building, door closed to her office. Simone's actions, graceful but full of coiled energy, suggested those of a panther. She tapped a finger against her screen. The assassination of the Saudi prince's bodyguard appeared to be the work of a mercenary. *Not a religious zealot with a bomb up his ass,* she thought.

Only three dozen men in the world, and even fewer women, could have completed it. The Paris police had requested her involvement. So had Mark Shepherd, TriCoast's head of security. Most curiously, Simone had also heard from acquaintance and friend Ceil Dayton. They had met when Simone interviewed her about her relationship with Parisian dreamer-gone-bad Robert Guillard. As confirmed by Shepherd,

Ceil's sister's colleagues had coincidentally been meeting with the Saudi prince at the time his guard was assassinated. So if the stakes were the trillion-dollar global oil business, there were many who would find it worth hiring an assassin. *Too many.*

⚬✦⚬

The next morning Lynn and Mike convened young TriCoast Washington analysts and then split up for a day of meetings with White House staffers, senators, representatives, and officials at an alphabet soup of regulatory agencies, Congressional committees, and lobbyists. To each, she explained TriCoast's oil supply security as well as her refineries' environmental and safety compliance.

Late in the afternoon she greeted Mike at the Treasury building. They rode together to the Department of Homeland Security.

"How'd your meetings go?" he asked.

"I'll give you more detail after this one," Lynn said. She didn't want to lose concentration. "Feels like 11 p.m. London time to me. I finally got synchronized yesterday, just in time for our return."

Cheryl drove them south across Douglas Bridge to Martin Luther King, Jr. Boulevard. Streets wound in circles or met at odd angles. Even ace driver Cheryl had to rely on the car's GPS system.

"The analysts forwarded the bios of the folks we're meeting." Lynn tightened her leather jacket against the chill leaking through the sedan's windows and braced her arm on the armrest to avoid sliding into Mike. Cheryl turned a corner toward what had been the west campus of St. Elizabeth's Hospital and was now the headquarters of the DHS. The converted hospital overlooked the junction of the Potomac and Anacostia Rivers.

After a few minutes, they were ushered into a plain conference room and met by the secretary herself. She introduced two men and a woman, undersecretaries from the Office of Intelligence and Analysis, the Office of Operations Coordination, and the National Protection Programs Directorate.

The director faced them. "Refineries are automatic security

issues. I asked you here because I want to recommend a simple deal between TriCoast as seller and the Cherokee Nation as the buyer. We have word you're considering other bidders. For national security purposes, we're not prepared to permit a sale of your refinery to Sansei."

"Can you explain?" Lynn asked, buying time. She didn't know which she found more surprising: that the Secretary knew the identities of the potential bidders, that she would order TriCoast to drop a bidder, or her relief at not having to do business with the company whose operatives nearly made Lynn and her sister collateral casualties when they killed Robert Guillard.

The Secretary went on as if Lynn had not asked a question. "I hear that in addition to Sansei and the Cherokee Investment Group, your other potential buyers are the Saudis and North Seas Resources. While we wouldn't object, we wouldn't feel good about ownership of American assets in those hands."

"But we're obligated to take the best offer," Lynn replied. "Our board of directors won't stand for anything less."

"In the case of national security they would," the Secretary said.

"You don't think Oklahoma's a safe place?" Mike asked. "It's in the middle of nowhere."

"It's my job to assume any place in the United States could be targeted. Remember April 19, 1995? Do you suppose those people going to work in the Murrah Building in Oklahoma City were worried? It only took two local nut jobs to blow the place down."

Lynn decided to be conciliatory. "Here's one option. If the Cherokee Nation is the top bidder, we sell our Tulsa refinery to them and they obtain additional financial backing from Adela. We win because we can continue to invest in optimizing gasoline production, buying crude supply, and developing new fuel technologies. The Cherokees diversify their investments and get gasoline and diesel for the stations they own at their casino developments. However, you know I am bound by my fiduciary obligation to our company's shareholders to consider all bids."

The Secretary's expression was unreadable. "You have to accept that this country's international and internal security requirements may overrule your company shareholders. Both Federal Trade Commission and DHS approval of the buyer will be required."

# Fifteen

*Dallas*
*Saturday*

> *"My ancestors didn't come over on the Mayflower,*
> *but they were there to meet the boat." —Will Rogers*

Outside of her father's East Dallas gingerbread cottage, Cy had installed handsome landscaping—buffalo grass, yuccas, tall rudbeckias with thimble-like centers, yellow primrose, and Mexican feather grass. Everything was low-effort and low-water, important since her father couldn't walk much.

She kissed Cy. "Is it just a daydream we're getting married?" she whispered. "I feel so lucky."

He smiled and stroked her cheek, then pulled away from her to rescue two-year-old Matt as he leaned toward the yucca spikes. It was another example of the parental mind reading she hadn't yet mastered.

Once inside the compact house, Cy and Lynn listened to the sounds of Matt and Marika playing, prepared to interrupt their conversation with Lynn's father if the children made too much noise, or worse, not enough.

For issues like future oil supply, Lynn engaged several outside consultants, as well as her own planning staff. But for corporate politics she valued her father's perspective. *Which I won't have much longer.* She massaged her arm, relieved to have the splint off at last.

Since the subject of the Tulsa refinery had first come up at work, she'd talked to him about it occasionally. She described her latest experiences with the Cherokee Investment Group, the Saudis, and North Seas Resources. "Selling the Tulsa refinery is depressing. I hate to lose the hardware."

"Please...for me," her father said. "Sell to Jesse...relative... saved my life."

Lynn was positive she hadn't understood him. He always spoke softly now and his emphysema-induced shortness of breath meant broken phrases.

"Whoa. Sell to Jesse Drum? Dad, you of all people know I'm legally obligated to consider all the bids, not just his."

Her father shrugged, a response she hadn't expected.

"And anyway, what do you mean Jesse Drum's a relative and saved your life?"

"Everyone... Oklahoma."

He wasn't making sense. He shook his head, the oxygen tube swaying. "All Indian...me...you," he said, pointing at himself and then Lynn.

Lynn stared at him. Brown hair, green eyes.

"Little bit...Cherokee... Eighth. You're half that..."

Lynn laughed. "Can't be. Daytons are the usual European salad. English, German, Scots-Irish, some French thrown in. Maybe that's why Ceil loves Paris so much."

"Having Indian blood wasn't something one spoke about when your father was growing up," Cy said. "I heard about it in cases during law school. Displaying your heritage, if it was the wrong one, would get you shut out of neighborhoods and businesses."

"Too different . . . looked down . . . but Jesse . . . saved me," her father insisted.

"What?" Her surprise overcame her caution. She wanted to hear what had to be an amazing narrative. But with his shortness of breath, he couldn't tell it.

As if he read her mind, he shook his head. "Too much."

"What about your computer, Dad? Could you write it and send it to me?"

He waited so long she thought he was going to refuse. Finally, he nodded.

"Two questions in the meantime. First, how are you and I related to Jesse?"

He started to speak, and gasped for air instead. "Complicated."

She nodded reluctantly. "Let's try the second question. How did he save you?"

Instead of answering immediately, he moved the oxygen tube out of the way, rolled up a sleeve, and showed a triangular white scar on his forearm. He'd never explained how he got it. "Snake...I never...paid back."

She had to refuse his request that she sell the Tulsa refinery to the Cherokees without considering the other bidders. She couldn't have his old debt to Jesse, whatever it was, upending her career and her professional reputation for the very job that afforded his care. Lynn lasered her eyes into her father's. It might be the last thing she could do for him, to somehow repay this debt to Jesse, whatever it was. But maybe not in the way he wanted.

Her father motioned toward a photo album.

Cy filled in the silence. "Mike's asked you to complete the sale of the Tulsa refinery. The Cherokee Nation is one of the bidders and you're already talking to them. You told me they control a multimillion-dollar budget and several times as much in tribal assets."

"It's hard to dive into yet another culture I don't know. I had enough problems with the French. And legally I can't give them preference over the other bidders." As she spoke, she recalled that the DHS expected her to do just that. It was almost as if her father and the DHS Secretary were reading from the same script, although for different reasons. Then she wondered where the Cherokees, Keith, and Pete were getting the $1.3 billion they were bidding for the refinery. *Is it real money?*

Her father opened the album to a picture of two men with their arms around each other. The picture was labeled in her mother's clear hand: *Oklahoma to Vietnam, 1965*. In her father's youth he had been straight, tall, skinny even. The other man's resemblance to the older Jesse Drum was unmistakable.

They gathered Matt and Marika and walked outside. Cy said, "I know this puts more stress on you, and God knows you have enough. But you should take care of your father's wish. It may be his last."

"Even if I don't know what it is? Even if I have to slow down the wedding plans, Cy?" She dug the toe of her shoe into the Mexican feather grass.

He put his arm around her shoulder. "We'll have plenty of time to celebrate. It's true my family is asking for a big wedding. It's just that everyone wants to meet you."

She'd seen the pictures of Cy's wedding to his first wife, a beautiful woman who, from Cy's stories, had been a wonderful mother and wife. *I don't have to measure up. We don't have to have sixteen bridesmaids and groomsmen. But it has to happen soon. I want Dad to know Matt and Marika, the only grandchildren he'll have before he dies.*

They drove to Cy's house. After his children were distracted with a new video game, Lynn and Cy enjoyed a half-hour to themselves and all her concerns receded.

Returning to her house, she saw in the mirror an imprint of Cy's fingers where he had gripped her back. She smiled and began to do everything necessary after a week away. The worry about negotiating with her ex-husband shrank to small, dark pile she shoved into a far corner of her mind.

She checked her phone for e-mail messages and was surprised at the length of the one from her father. He started bluntly.

*I am an eighth Cherokee. Your mother had no Indian blood so you're one-sixteenth. I don't have many stories of my Indian relatives except this. When I was eight my parents said there was someone I had to meet. A great-grandmother. My father had often gone to see her, always before without us. He wouldn't take us because he told us we couldn't sit still that long.*

Her father was successful and Lynn knew Cy was right. It was partly because he hid his Indian heritage. For three hundred years, some people had believed Indian blood was bad blood.

*We drove a ways from Tulsa not too far to Claremore. When I saw the small white house and met the tiny wrinkled brown woman inside I knew why my father hadn't brought us before. I also knew I would be bored. She held my hands. They were dry and smelled of onions. Her house was like any old person's house.*

*At one point the old woman looked me in the eyes and told me she grew up near Will Rogers' house. I wasn't interested. Years later I learned more about Will. Especially after his name was plastered all over the place including the Oklahoma City airport.*

*I resigned myself to an afternoon of kicking my brother and hoping the strange old woman might have soda stashed in her refrigerator.*

*Before long, six or seven other kids showed up. They were even browner than my great-grandmother. They made fun of my and my brother's white skin but invited us to play in her back yard. They showed us the handholds on her pecan tree and the two holes they'd dug and how high the dog next door jumped on the fence.*

*One of the boys was about my age. His name was Jesse. He told me he would beat me at basketball and Cherokee marbles. I told him I was a good basketball player but didn't know what Cherokee marbles was.*

*He explained it. Instead of regular marbles you used big ones the size of pool balls. He told me it was played on a field longer than my great-grandmother's back yard. We were supposed to dig five holes about ten yards apart then roll the marbles from one to the next. You could knock out your opponents' marbles and the first one to finish the course won. So it was like the shoot-out marble games I used to play with croquet or pool sort of thrown in.*

*We found a wooden hoop and nailed it to the pecan tree. One of them brought a ball and we shot it through the hoop.*

*"Are you related to me?" I was snotty then like many eight-year-olds. We had friends in Tulsa who thought family bloodlines were important. I'd picked up their attitude. I told him that's my great-grandmother in there.*

*"Mine too," Jesse said.*

*"Then how come I don't look like an Indian?"*

*"Stupid. My parents don't look like yours."*

*My great-grandmother never did produce those sodas I was hoping for but after a while she invited us in for a doughnut-looking thing with powdered sugar. She called it fry bread.*

*I'm telling you this because I never went back. It's all I know about your Cherokee heritage. My great-grandmother died a few months later and my parents said I was too young to go to the funeral.*

*Then when I started my first job inspecting pipes I was assigned to the area around Sho-Vel-Tum.*

Lynn whistled to herself. Sho-Vel-Tum was one of the largest oil fields in Oklahoma and still in the top fifty US fields.

*So I was living in Ardmore. Jesse got my address somehow. He was stationed at Fort Sill about a hundred miles away.*

*We got together a few times. It was good to see family. We went out drinking one night. That was a bigger deal than you think because it's damned hard to find a liquor store in Oklahoma.*

Those liquor laws hadn't changed much, she thought.

*We were driving west of Lawton. Jesse asked what I did. When I told him he said the Osage had been into oil too and it had brought them a lot of trouble but he thought maybe the Cherokees ought to invest if they ever had the money. Show-off that I was I drove him away from the highway to a big gravel pad. There was a bunch of pipe manifolds where the pipes came to the surface.*

*So we're out in the middle of nowhere, which is almost always where I worked. I figured I'd demonstrate how we measured pipe wear.*

*We parked and got out of my truck. The pad's sort of lit up but not underneath the pipes. It was night and some of the lights were out.*

*We left the radio on and the wind was blowing like hell, which is why I didn't hear the rattle.*

*Next thing I feel the most goddamn awful sting on my arm where I showed you. A rattler bit me and clamped on.*

*I hollered and couldn't shake him loose. Jesse yanked the snake off and damned near took my arm with it. He killed it with a brick. Then he took his knife and carved out around the bite. I was yelling the whole time. He got me tourniqueted and drove my truck to the emergency room in Lawton. They said if I'd gotten there any later I'd have lost my arm or died.*

*Jesse stayed with me until he had to report back to the base. Someone gave him a ride. Not long after, he shipped out to Asia. Kept re-enlisting. I sent him what I could but I could never make it up to him for saving my life. That's what you have to do. Sell them that refinery. Help him provide for his people. Our people.*

Lynn sat back. He'd never written anything so lengthy. *But he's nearing the end of his life, and he's getting ready to die. Still, I can't do what he's asking. Not without jumping through a lot of approval hoops first, and that's only if the Cherokees are the high bidder. Maybe it's just as well the DHS is pushing the same agenda.*

She e-mailed back, "Dad, I'm so glad you told me about how we're related to Jesse. What a story."

Jesse Drum had saved her father's life. It was a blood debt she had to repay somehow, and soon, before her father died.

# Sixteen

*Dallas/Tulsa*
*Sunday, Labor Day weekend*

> *"Don't gamble; take all your savings and buy some good stock*
> *and hold it till it goes up, then sell it. If it don't go up, don't buy it."*
> —*Will Rogers*

It still surprised Lynn to see her father's oxygen tank and the thin plastic tube running up his nose. His chest was the only large part of him that remained. He'd been a big man before his illness, so large his co-workers nicknamed him Big Tom. But his body had shrunk until he was so insubstantial the most vital part of him was his memory.

She sat with him in the late morning while he slept. When he was first diagnosed, she'd researched his condition furiously. She still hoped lung reduction surgery could give him several more years. But the experience of talking to the doctors who had treated her mother's bone cancer was stuck in her mind. When they'd finally told her nothing else could be done, Lynn learned the stages of grief were not always sequential. Sometimes they all happened at once.

After Hermosa, the woman Lynn had hired to care for Big Tom, arrived, Lynn exchanged updates.

He woke.

"I read what you wrote and it's amazing," she said. "I've been thinking about Jesse. I will repay him, somehow. I don't know if it will be by selling TriCoast's refinery to the Cherokee Nation. I can't guarantee that, but I will figure something out. Take care, Dad. I love you." She hugged him gingerly, then left his East Dallas cottage for Cy's house.

She'd promised Cy she would watch his kids while he shopped for groceries. The wedding planner had agreed to stop by.

She laughed at a highway billboard as she drove toward Cy's house. The advertisement for the Dallas Gun & Knife Show noted, without irony, that blood donations could be given in the parking lot during the show. It didn't mention whether donations were voluntary.

Another succession of billboards for the Choctaw casino a hundred miles away read: *The DNA test came back negative. Luck changes. Strike while you're hot.*

She thought of the Cherokee Investment Group's readiness to buy her Tulsa refinery. She'd be talking to other TriCoast executives in a few hours about the sale.

When Lynn arrived, Cy met her in the driveway. "Did you talk to your father again?"

"He sent me an amazing e-mail, explained his ancestry and how Jesse really had saved his life."

"Literally?"

"Yes, from a rattlesnake bite."

"You're kidding!"

She shook her head.

"Wouldn't it be interesting to have all your ancestors together in one room, say the ones from five or six generations back?" he asked.

"Mine would be fighting one another within ten minutes."

Seven-year-old Marika ran up to her. "Did you know a frog could vomit out its stomach? How cool is that!"

"Very cool." Lynn tried not to picture it.

As if the frog fact had reminded him, Cy said, "Remember, no calamari hors d'oeuvres."

"No deep-fried rubber bands?" She smiled at him.

She found Matt helping Marika fill water balloons. The two-year-old, with long baby eyelashes, threw the sloshing balloons on the ground and giggled as they splattered. Lynn felt her heart fill and said a silent prayer of thanks to Matt's biological mother.

Cy kissed her and left in his cream-colored Volvo.

Soon, the door of a BMW shut. The wedding planner had arrived.

The woman was a prototypically thin, blonde, well-kept Dallas woman, a friend of Mike's whom he'd recommended when Lynn had wished aloud that her mother was still alive. Lynn had meant to indicate she missed everything about her mother. Instead, Mike thought she was talking about the wedding and suggested she delegate the planning to a friend of his. It has seemed a good idea at the time.

*It* was *a good idea, if only the planner would stop delegating back to me.* The few hours Lynn could spare were less than the weeks the planner expected her to spend. The planner seemed more accustomed to dealing with women like some of those in Cy's neighborhood who enjoyed arranging special events.

The planner was cheerful and organized. *Too bad she's not a refinery turnaround chief. She'd have contractors toeing the line and delivering on schedule.*

Still, Lynn and Cy had begun calling her the WP, or the Whippet. During the last week while Lynn was in London and Paris, she'd received fifteen texts and e-mails from the Whippet, each overloaded with exclamation marks. From the urgent tone of the messages it seemed they'd be lucky to offer their guest anything more than crackers and water.

The wedding planner walked up with as much energy as Marika. "Honey, even my own car reminds me to exercise."

"You have a workout video instead of a GPS screen?"

"The little blinking light that says 'ABS.'"

"Automatic braking system," Lynn said.

"Oh, right."

"I need to keep an eye on the kids."

The Whippet looked at Matt and Marika warily. They returned the stare.

"Been a long time since we talked," she said to Lynn in a voice intended to summon guilt. Then the questions came rapid-fire. "Location still the backyard of your father's house?"

"Yes."

"So no problems reserving it."

Lynn thought, *Surely it's my imagination that the Whippet just sneered.*

"Have you chosen a florist yet?"

"No."

"Rings?"

"No."

"Tent rented?"

"Can you?"

"Of course. What size?" The Whippet prepared to enter a number in her cell phone.

"I won't know until the RSVPs come back."

"Guess."

"A hundred."

Marika came up and looked solemnly at both of them. "Lynn should I tell her about how the frog can vomit out its stomach? You said you thought it was cool."

Lynn shook her head at Marika. She was relieved to see the Whippet was unfazed.

Matt gagged. Lynn raced over to him. "What do you have in your mouth?"

He coughed. Lynn reached into his mouth. Her fingers found

a wad of paper squirreled where his molars would later grow. As she scooped it out, she felt his bite, first deep in her spine, then a few seconds later in her finger.

"Ow!" Lynn tossed the wet wad of paper in the trash. "Matt, where did you get this?"

He pointed to the garage floor.

"Is he okay? Honey, I know all about the promises parents make to God when their children are hurt or sick. Mine are grown, but I remember." The Whippet smiled sympathetically and looked back at her list. "Caterer?"

Her mind was still on Matt's choking. She reeled at the split-second attentiveness needed to be a parent, then took a deep breath to wrench her attention back to the Whippet. "I've made some calls."

The Whippet's answering frown was so deep it could have scared away an entire herd of Matt's favorite dinosaurs. "Get your caterer. I'll e-mail you a list of my suggestions. Now, you have your dress?"

"I've been looking for it." The answer seemed to mollify the Whippet.

"Maybe you should think about scaling this back." She turned and began walking to her car.

"I thought that's what we already agreed to do," Lynn said.

"Talk to your fiancé. You two must not be communicating. And I mean," the woman winced as she spoke, "bare bones. Minimalist. Ferns instead of orchids, for example."

"Absolutely." Out of the corner of her eye, Lynn saw Matt toddling behind the Whippet. "No, Matt! Watch out!"

Too late. Matt threw his water balloon to the ground. It broke and splashed up onto the woman's suit.

"I'm sorry," Lynn said. "He's fast." She picked Matt up and shook her head at him.

"No problem." But the woman's smile was tight at the edges. Then she concluded with a statement Lynn herself had used with underperforming employees. "Think about whether you really want to continue with this."

"You mean I shouldn't get married?"

The planner got into her BMW. Lynn thought about the flashing yellow 'ABS' light and sure enough, the woman pulled in her stomach.

The Whippet's smile didn't reach her eyes. "I mean whether or not it's the best use of your time and money to engage me to help you organize your wedding, something you clearly need someone to do."

After she left, Lynn lifted Matt up, hugged him, and said, "Looks like it's crackers and water for us, buddy. We better talk to your dad, though. I think he's got bigger plans."

"Dad!" Matt grinned.

David Jenkins, the exploration and production EVP for the Americas—North and South—wanted to meet in his office. Lynn was amused by his trophies from oil drilling contractors, trophies and awards TriCoast had essentially purchased with its business. There were plaques for what was once the deepest Gulf of Mexico well; for heaviest platform set, over ten thousand tons; and longest horizontal frack job in Oklahoma. Deepest, heaviest, longest; a theme here, she thought. But it was the divisional trophy for most days without a safety incident that gave her a pang. She remembered the lives lost in TriCoast refineries and elsewhere—including very nearly her sister's—to a French saboteur with mercenaries inside TriCoast. She'd been the first to suspect sabotage when others thought accidents were afoot. But being right didn't bring anyone back to life.

The biggest trophy was not inside David Jenkins' office but the view out of his window west toward Fort Worth. One could still see a few rigs poking into the Barnett Shale, the first of the new, enormous, unconventionally-drilled gas formations. Drillers had even located gas at DFW airport.

Through David's foresight, TriCoast owned positions in several valuable oil and gas shales. In his office, the view of the rigs did all the talking.

So it was not the best place for Lynn to negotiate an increase in her division's budget at the expense of his.

Sara Levin was already seated at David's conference table. "Lynn, you *have* to hear my new theme song. Everyone at TriCoast is singing it to me." She played "Strapped for Cash," by Fountains of Wayne on her cell phone.

David Jenkins grinned in appreciation. His face was hawklike and silver hair winged back from his forehead. His arms were sunburned; despite his executive position he spent as much time in the field as possible. When the song finished, he drank coffee and looked at the cardboard cup appreciatively. "Did I ever tell you about visiting this Houston pipeline company? They had a brand spanking new building—beautiful place—to show how much money they were making. Every conference room had china coffee cups. Now, you get us old oil-and-gas men in there, we don't know what to do with china. Can't tell you how many of 'em I heard ask for Styrofoam cups instead."

"Got a contract yet on the Tulsa refinery?" Sara asked.

"You'd have seen it if I did," Lynn said.

"We have to know what you're getting for it before we can talk about the rest of your budget," Sara insisted. She clicked to spreadsheets on her laptop.

Lynn said, "David, it's rare I get to see you face-to-face. I'm on a scramble meeting with the Saudis, the Russians, and soon the Canadians to find oil for my refineries. Still, I'm getting a lot of supply proposals from right here in the US with all the new oil production. It's made the Tulsa refinery more valuable, even though folks here want to sell it." She nodded at Sara. "So, how much onshore production are you looking at next year, especially from the Bakken?" She was referring to a monster oil field in North Dakota and Montana that had been revived with horizontal drilling and fracturing.

"In the US, we see a thirty percent increase, which is phenomenal. We're not close to meeting the needs for all your refineries, though."

Lynn nodded. TriCoast's five refineries required 1.7 million barrels of crude oil a day, every day, but its own US oil production could only supply about a third of that.

Lynn had promised Jesse she would visit Tahlequah during the four-day Cherokee National Holiday. She rose, shook hands, and left for her Tulsa flight to arrive for the last day of the celebration.

I returned to my mother's house occasionally, mainly to see if she died yet. She was healthy despite, or more likely because of, her mean temper. I wasn't welcome, nor did I especially want to see her. But she was familiar, like a scar.

I was thinking about the Chechen's time limit as I walked up the crumbling cement steps. I had paid off the mortgage to this 1920s brown brick house after my stepfather succumbed to heart disease. One thought flashed through my mind: the wrong half of the couple died.

She greeted me at the door, looking out at my car. "Haven't made your nut yet? Oh, I forgot, you don't have any nuts." That's Mom.

"I brought you chocolate and fruit."

She let the fruit fall to the floor and unwrapped the candy. "Dark or milk chocolate?"

"Dark, Mom, the only kind you're supposed to eat."

"Dammit, can't you get anything right?" She put the candy aside.

"I did get it right. This is the kind you're supposed to eat." *Is that smell what I think it is?* "Are you taking baths?"

A sly look came into my mother's eyes. "Every time I can get a man into the shower with me."

In other words, no.

"Have you flushed the toilet recently?" I went into the bathroom. After flushing, I scrubbed the toilet, the sink, and the bathtub with the chlorine bleach I'd brought the last time I was here. She was getting worse, although she'd been cruel before the dementia started, really for my entire life. *Time to move her into a home.*

From the hall, my mother told me about a meal she'd eaten sixty years ago, down to details about the amount of salt and number of eggs in the meat loaf. She watched me clean but didn't offer to help. She acted as if I were cleaning up after another person entirely.

Her viciousness hadn't changed. But until five years ago, there'd been someone there to apologize and to clean up. Someone else for her to abuse. I figured my stepfather had a foot in heaven before he ever left earth.

I wished again I'd known my biological father. He'd been killed in the Vietnam War. That's what I'd been told, anyway. I would have liked to compare notes with him, Hamburger Hill to Baghdad, mano-a-mano.

I washed my hands with hot, soapy water for five minutes. She slumped in her chair, like a button had been pushed. The television roared in the next room. *How the hell could I move her out, sell the house?* She'd leave claw marks an inch deep.

I tore off paper towels and dusted shelves I'd missed last time.

As if she were reading my mind, she said, "Why don't you set me up in a fancy place instead of this dump? You got so much money. Or do you? You never could negotiate your way out of a paper bag."

"Love you, too, Mom."

"Look at you, cleaning up after me like a woman."

*If I strangled her, how much would she fight?* I'd killed and would again. But that was a different exercise, merely removing obstacles. None of my family and only a few of my friends had ever become obstacles.

I ticked off a few in my mind, reviewing the way I'd killed each. I attempt variety, when I have the time.

The refinery death was at the request of the Chechen. The

Chechen demanded a "death of distraction," something to keep everyone's attention on the hazards of working in a refinery, and off of his and my activities, to give us the time we needed. He hadn't pinpointed a target, so as I intended, it was his bad luck the crane operator manhandled the doughnuts onto which I'd dropped grains of a very deadly, homegrown poison.

Jimmy Deerinwater, however, was specific. He had started asking intrusive questions. It would be a while before all I'd done there would be discovered. Or maybe it wouldn't ever be discovered, since Jimmy was barbecued.

Lynn Dayton was physically attractive and so worth keeping around. However, she hadn't been as helpful as I expected. And a few others were starting to become obstacles.

I decided to stay until nightfall. My mother fell asleep around dusk. I kept the lights off so she wouldn't wake and resume her cackling. I felt my way to the kitchen, pulled a glass from the cupboard, filled it with water, and started to drink.

Something rough brushed against my lips. I put the glass down, ran to the just-cleaned bathroom and rinsed my mouth, trying to wash away the impersonal kiss of a cockroach.

# Seventeen

*Tahlequah*
*Monday, Labor Day*

Cars and trucks inundated the highways leading to Tahlequah. Most bore white and blue Cherokee Nation license plates.

"It's been like this for three days," Jesse told Lynn, satisfaction in his voice. He explained the Cherokees celebrated their national holiday each year on Labor Day weekend since 1953 to honor the signing of the Cherokee Constitution in 1839. "It brings out the spirit of *ga-du-gi*, working together for the community. For older people and people who can't get here, we stream it online."

"A hundred thousand people," Carla Fourkiller added. "Parades, fireworks, the youth choir. We have every craft and competition you can imagine."

Riley sidled up to the Cherokee accountant. "I can think of a few." He winked.

Carla frowned.

Lynn sighed. Riley continued to be a walking legal liability. She didn't want to lose the Cherokees as a bidder for the refinery because Riley offended their new head accountant. She again experienced the sorrow and mystery of Jimmy Deerinwater's death.

A large group clustered around Jesse Drum: Pete Whitehawk, Gene Blahunka and Lynn's ex-husband Keith McConaugh joined Lynn, Carla, and Riley. Cheryl Wilkins, Lynn's bodyguard, scanned the crowd. Lynn noticed Keith was quiet. *He looks sick, or more likely hung over,* she thought grimly.

"We have a school for seventh through twelfth graders, Sequoyah High School." Jesse waved toward a big building adorned with a seven-pointed star and Cherokee script on one side. Then he pointed to the gym. "We call this *Tsu-Na-Ne-Lo-Di*, which translates to 'place where they play.' Usually at least one or two of the high school teams wins a state championship. Our athletes sign with college teams and some even go to the pros."

"I played basketball against Sequoyah High girls," Lynn said. "They were incredible athletes."

"We announce our games in Cherokee as well as English," Carla added. As they walked around the gym, she said, "We also host traditional games like Cherokee marbles, a cornstalk shoot, a blowgun competition, a stickball tournament, and," she narrowed her eyes and addressed Riley, "hatchet throwing."

Before Riley could reply, Lynn asked, "Where can we see those?"

Jesse had arranged a van. Lynn's bodyguard drove them through the crowds to a field on the west side of the tribal complex. Lynn noticed even the stop signs were bilingual. ᏙᏧᎾᏓᏟᎥᏏ

"How do you say that?" she asked Jesse.

"*A-leh-wi-s-di-ha,*" he replied. "I spoke Cherokee, not English, until I was in the second grade. A few of our council members are fluent. We have people everywhere who take the language in our online classes—even overseas in Ireland, Germany, and Greece."

"I served in Germany," Carla said. "The Germans were always curious about me. Guess they thought I hunted buffalo in my free time."

Pete laughed. "Almost everyone I know, and their fathers and sometimes their mothers, served in the military. Tribal tradition. Ironic that we join the army that defeated us."

"We're warriors, and we fought to a damn draw." Jesse shrugged. "We had the veterans' reception two nights ago. You should have been here."

"That must have been some powwow," Riley said.

"It was a very moving event. Lots of injuries, these wars. As for the powwow, we had one of those, but it was later."

Riley slapped him on the shoulder. "Didn't insult your religion, did I?"

Jesse kept a straight face. "Powwows are more social than religious. We honor our high school graduates, Pulitzer Prize winners, Oklahoma state poet laureates, people like that."

"Of course," Riley said quickly.

Lynn smelled the hickory nuts and hog fries being sold at nearby stands.

Waving toward a field further away where about twenty men and women were running, Jesse said, "But *a-ne-jo-di,* or stickball, can be part of a religious ceremony. We play it before a stomp dance."

"Sounds like my kind of dance," Gene said.

"It looks like lacrosse, but the women don't have sticks," Lynn noted.

"They use their hands to catch the ball," Jesse said. "Originally women weren't even allowed to play. Only the most athletic men participated. *A-ne-jo-di* was a battle training game or played to settle disputes between communities."

Pete explained the teams hit or threw the ball at a target, often a wooden fish, mounted on top of a tall pole.

"And historically, the most important player wasn't even on the field," Jesse said.

"What do you mean?" Gene asked.

"The key competitor for each team was its medicine man."

Crowds of people surged and ebbed around Lynn. She heard a choir singing in the vowel-rich Cherokee language.

A hundred-foot-long field off to one side was marked with five holes each about two inches in diameter. The holes were roughly ten yards apart and shaped in an L. Several people on the field took turns tossing their own billiard balls toward the holes and knocking others out of the way, like hopscotch or pool.

A nearby sign read ꝹꙄꙆ꜠ꙋꙉ.

"Cherokee marbles?" Lynn asked Jesse.

He nodded. "We've been playing it for over twelve hundred years. How did you know?"

"My father told me all about it." She motioned him aside, away from the others and spoke in a low voice. "I know who you are, and I think you know who I am. Turns out we're related. And more important, you saved my father's life. My father is Tom Dayton."

Jesse stared at the ground and didn't answer.

"I'm deeply grateful to you."

He nodded.

Riley interrupted with a shout. "You're engaged, you got your ex right here, and you're whispering sweet nothings in Jesse Drum's ears. Lynn Dayton, you are a piece of…something."

"Riley, shut the hell up. You have no idea what you're talking about." She kept herself from adding, *as usual*.

Carla interrupted to point to two foot-thick, three-foot-long walls of dried cornstalks a hundred yards apart. She explained to the TriCoast visitors that the cornstalk shoot began when Cherokee hunters and warriors competed with their bows and arrows to see who could shoot most accurately.

Across the field, another competition was going on. At first, Lynn thought the teen-agers were holding reedy instruments, but she realized the competitors were using six-foot blowguns to launch darts at a target twenty yards away.

She and Cheryl walked toward the competitors, followed by the others.

"A blowgun. Cool!" Her bodyguard's enthusiasm was evident. "I saw one in a shop, but it was loaded with a toothpick of a dart. Wouldn't do much damage."

"We don't sell the traditional darts to outsiders," Jesse said. "The ones we use are heavier and sharper, and about fourteen inches long. Blow darts preceded bows and arrows."

"Sure," Carla said. "I've used them to kill squirrels and rats." She glanced at Riley. "I'd be happy to demonstrate for you."

Riley shook his head. "I believe you."

After one of the competitors launched a dart in a perfect arc, Cheryl asked if she could hold the tube. "Bamboo?" She turned the six-foot-long polished tube in her hand.

"River cane. We collect it early in the spring, and ream it out with a red-hot rod to get rid of the membrane. We make the darts from bois d'arc wood and thistle down. Use it for competitions like this or to kill rodents mainly. Poison on the dart makes it a weapon, but then you can't eat what you kill."

Cheryl handed put the tube back to the teen-ager. "Quieter than a .22, for sure."

An old woman with wiry gray hair sat alone off to the side. Despite the crowded fields, Lynn noticed the woman was given a wide berth.

"She tells traditional stories," Pete said.

"I'd like to hear one," Riley responded.

Carla shook her head. "She only tells bad ones. They're worse than slasher movies."

"Then we better cuddle up," Riley replied. Lynn shook her head at him and mouthed *No.*

"Maybe our guests should have the full cultural experience." Jesse approached the old woman and spoke quietly with her.

She looked at him sharply. After a while she began to speak in Cherokee. She stopped every few sentences while Jesse translated.

*The Cherokee have many kinds of witches. The worst are the Raven Moackers. They are old and wrinkled from all the lives they've stolen.*

*If someone is sick, Raven Mockers go. They fly with their arms out like wings. They make a noise like a storm wind, and you can see their sparks. When they dive, they screech like a raven. If you hear the sound, it means someone is about to die.*

*Raven Mockers may appear at the dying person's house. Without a medicine person watching who can drive them off, they all go inside since they're invisible. Raven Mockers torment the sick person to death. The man's friends around him don't see the Raven Mockers. They think the sick man is just fighting for his breath.*

*No wonder Dad's emphysema scares him sometimes,* Lynn thought. *I wonder if he ever heard this story.* The woman continued talking and the Jesse translated faster.

*After the person is dead, the witches take out his heart and eat it. This lets them add to their lives however many years they have taken from his life.*

*No one can see them. There is no scar where they have removed the heart but if the friends of the dead man look, they find no heart in the body.*

*If a medicine person with the right medicine stays with the sick person, the witches are afraid to enter, for when one of them has been recognized he dies in a week. When friends of a sick man know he is dying, they ask a medicine person to guard the body until burial. Witches don't steal the hearts after burial.*

Lynn thought of the similarity to the horror in Edgar Allen Poe's "The Telltale Heart" and his poem, "The Raven." She wondered whether Jesse had picked this story to warn Riley to stay away from Carla. She glanced at Riley.

The color had left his face.

# Eighteen

*Tahlequah/Tulsa*
*Monday evening, Labor Day*

*"Gonna set my watch back to it 'cause you know I've been through it...Livin' on Tulsa time." —Danny Flowers, songwriter for Don Williams*

As the TriCoast group prepared to return to Tulsa, Carla Fourkiller pulled Lynn aside. "Did the Raven Mocker story bother Riley?"

"Maybe so," Lynn said, glancing at Riley's still-drained face. "And you? How's your transition going? Poor Jimmy Deerinwater. Did he leave you any information?"

"Yes. I can see where he was in his spreadsheets. He also left notes, but some he wrote in Cherokee. My language skills aren't good and I don't know who to trust to translate it."

Lynn tried not to react visibly. She didn't want the others to realize Carla was telling her a surprising secret. "What about..." She nodded toward Jesse Drum.

Carla shrugged. "I need someone outside this group. And hey, can you get Riley to tone it down? Sounds geeky, but the Cherokee Nation wins awards every year for our good financial systems. I don't want to mess up Jimmy's work because I have to waste time fighting off a lech."

"I'll do what I can."

When they rejoined the group, Pete Whitehawk was speaking

casually, but he looked at Riley. "I've found there's an inverse correlation between the number of women a man sleeps with once he's married and how much I can trust him in a business deal."

Riley laughed. "Pete, if that's your criterion, I'm surprised you do business with anyone. But I forget. You have dogs instead of girlfriends."

Pete grinned. "Sure. Mammal closeness without romantic complications. Only problem with kissing a dog is you get biscuit breath."

Gene, Lynn, and Riley drove west from Tahlequah toward the turnpike, leaving behind the blue and white license-plated trucks of the Cherokee Nation. When they passed Fort Gibson, Gene said, "If I was Cherokee, I wouldn't like any town with 'fort' in its name."

When they swerved to avoid a road gator—a big, ragged strip of blown-out truck tire—Lynn thought about Jimmy's accident and what Carla had said. She wondered if Carla would find a translator she could trust.

A horse farm sign noted *Standing at stud: Lost Opportunity.* Riley laughed. "Story of my life."

As they neared Tulsa, a highway billboard split its space, advertising a church on one half and a casino on the other.

They soon saw the casino, a development the size of a large shopping mall. Its parking aprons spread in several directions. The lots, packed to the edges with end-of-holiday celebrants, were themselves advertisements. The casino building was at least three hundred thousand square feet. Three hotels, a golf course, and two gasoline stations flanked one side. Further away, a pawn shop's neon sign glowed white. A clutch of bulldozers and road graders alongside a new roadbed suggested more construction. The development even had its own water supply.

"Look at all of those cars!" Lynn said. The parking lot brimmed with buses, campers, pick-up trucks, work vans, and sedans, all needing fuel. *No wonder Jesse wants to buy a refinery.*

Gene said, "You can even play slots at the gas stations. Place like this employs thousands of people. It's ironic the tribes are feeding Anglo vices right back to us—smoking, drinking, and gambling. In fact, a few of the smaller tribes like the Tonkawas want to move their casinos off their own lands. They don't want the customers in their home villages. The money goes to support schools, hospitals, arts, and tribal health, so it's a double-edged sword. The jobs and financial support are vital. But with the casino right there, temptations increase."

"Do you suppose that's why Jesse and the Cherokee Nation are trying to diversify their industries?" Lynn asked.

"Yup." Then Gene added, "I like the Cherokee National Holiday, but I can't let a day go without at least stopping at the refinery."

"Sounds good. I'll have Preston meet us there." Preston hadn't joined them on the trip to Tahlequah. When he answered his cell phone, she heard noise in the background. "Sorry to bother you, but we're going to the refinery. If you have the new hydrotreater proposal ready, we could show it to Gene."

Preston sounded weary at first, distracted, but then his voice was stronger. "What? Oh, yeah. I'll meet you there. Sorry. I need more sleep."

*Why is getting enough sleep a problem for you now?* Lynn wondered.

As they drove toward the TriCoast refinery, Lynn saw the familiar groups of metal columns. The three refineries along the river were a peculiar mix of suburb and industry. Roads carved through the trees led away from the river and the refineries up to Lookout Mountain. Given the chance, the trees appeared ready to take back the land.

Razor wire topped the refinery's fence. A road where trucks had driven for decades—ever since the Oklahoma fields had been discovered—fronted the development. The always-on gas flare marked one boundary. A few white tanks stood apart, the TriCoast logo showing discreetly on one. Little houses sat directly across from the refinery gates on a street without curbs or shoulders.

It seemed like a place where a pipefitter, machinist, or boiler-maker would always find work. Yet most plants weathered layoffs every few years. Lynn had helped make the final choices during the latest round. At euphemistically-named "outplacement meetings" she'd seen crumpled faces and heard the accusations in dozens of pleading questions. *A bad time. Why does my division always take the brunt of layoffs?*

They stepped into one of numerous trailers hunkered in a group, temporary housing that had become permanent. Three men and a woman were sitting at a table.

"What are you playing?" Lynn shut the door.

"Liar's poker. Find your favorite bill," Preston said.

"Don't have it." Some of her colleagues kept bills with a row of sevens, or other number combinations, just for this purpose.

Preston's appearance shocked her. He slumped, and his unwashed hair clung in wads over his red-rimmed eyes. He shrugged. "I haven't had a chance to check in at the hotel yet."

"There were plenty of rooms when I arrived. When did you get to Tulsa?"

"Last night."

She tried not to let her mouth drop open. There was only one place he could have been: the casino.

When Gene joined them, she covered for Preston. "Don't let Preston's absent-minded-professor-look fool you. When he first came to work, I asked him to measure and reduce furnace energy use. Catch was, he had no direct authority to make changes. He started sending out furnace efficiency reports. The reports caused operators to compete with one another. The end result was we cut energy use on the furnaces by ten percent. First of many successful assignments he's overseen."

To the others, she said, "Selling the refinery is not a given. We need to go ahead with the projects we have on the schedule. If we do sell it, we want it to be in the best possible shape anyway, because most of the same folks will still be working here." She looked at Gene. "Including you, I hope."

"We'll see," he said, without conviction. He turned to Preston, brightening. "You see the operating logs. We're so good we could show the devil himself how to manage hell."

Then an edge sharpened Gene's voice. He sat forward, hands clasped between his knees. "Preston, this refinery is my baby. I work here, eat here, think about it when I'm driving home, and dream about it when I sleep. If you fat-finger a spreadsheet or make a design mistake, me and my folks have to live with it for years, no matter who buys it." He sat back. "We want the right iron in place."

Lynn was nodding. She knew just what Gene meant.

Preston pulled out blueprints and a laptop. "I hear you. Got a few cartoons." His illustrations showed the configuration of pipes, towers, pumps, and exchangers starting upstream of the desulfurizer and going downstream to the cat cracker, reformers, coker, and light ends separator. "My group based these suggestions on our last discussion. But why don't we start with what you want?"

"You need to look at pump sizing throughout the unit, especially at the cat pretreater," Gene said. "You also need to help us recalculate condenser and exchanger duty. I know we need at least a couple new heat exchangers."

Preston wrote while Gene spoke, then said, "I've based this all on the three-year strip," referring to the three-year futures prices for oil and gasoline.

"And not just any elderly pole-dancer, either," Riley added with a smirk.

⁋

There was no reason for her to awaken at two-thirty a.m. Cy had described his sleepless-night worries about his kids. This felt similar.

If she could have rolled over and gone back to sleep, she would have. Unbidden, an image of Preston's slump came to her. When she got up and looked out at the hotel's parking lot, she couldn't see his car.

She texted him. No reply.

Pulling one of the hotel's scratchy robes around her and pocketing her room cardkey, she went and knocked on his door. A light was on, but as she expected, no one answered. She remembered his red eyes.

*I'm not his mother.* But she knocked on her guard's hotel room door, right next to her own. "Cheryl, wake up."

Cheryl opened the door, already dressed in a T-shirt and jeans. "Come in. What's wrong?" She went around turning on lamps.

Lynn stepped inside a room so neat it appeared Cheryl wasn't even staying there. "Preston's gone and his car isn't in the lot. He told us he was going back to the casino last night. I'm afraid something happened to him."

"Has happened or is happening? You think he's still there?" Cheryl asked.

"He's not in his room. Usually I can raise him by texting, but tonight he's not responding. Considering what happened to Jimmy Deerinwater and Tom Martin—and me—I'm worried. I'd trust Preston with my life. I have, in fact. He helped save me and several others when Jay tried to take down the Centennial refinery."

"The way I heard it, you saved yourself from that asshole."

"No time to argue. Let's find Preston."

"I'll drive."

Lynn returned to her room, changed into khakis and a fleece jacket, and met Cheryl at the parking lot. She was exhausted.

Cheryl zipped up her coat and summarized, "So, Preston was here twenty-four hours before he checked in. You said he almost botched his presentation to Gene, and he won't or can't reply to your text. Lynn, you take risks, make billion-dollar bets because you have to. That's your job. Gamblers bet on anything. They're driven by the thrill, not by an analysis of how much they'll lose."

"But he's so smart, so analytical. He can dissect odds better than anyone. You're suspicious because he was playing liar's poker? Lots of people do. Sometimes to settle the check at lunch."

"It can be part of the pattern."

A north crosswind pushed against the car as they traveled

several miles east on I-244 from the hotel toward the casino. Lynn noticed how hard Cheryl had to steer against being swept into the next lane. Even when a tornado was not spawning, the Oklahoma wind could gust twenty or thirty miles an hour. This one was fierce enough to tear off chunks of billboards.

"Does he always gamble this much?" Cheryl asked and braked quickly to avoid another car rocketing in on the too-short entrance ramp.

"Whatever he's been doing before, he's kept it from interfering with his job."

"Are you sure? I've seen many people who overestimated how much they could handle—scotch, whores, gambling, you name it."

"He's focused. He can code faster than anyone."

"Sounds like an addictive geek to me."

Lynn bristled at this characterization of her long-time colleague, then wondered sadly if the 'addictive' part was so true it was finally interfering with Preston's wizard-like abilities.

Even from a mile away, she could see the casino was busier at three in the morning than during the day. Now, pick-ups, vans, and campers spilled past the overflow lots. A surprisingly cold north wind knifed through her and she wished she'd worn an extra sweatshirt and gloves for their quarter-mile walk to the front door.

They dodged around buses clogging the drop-off lanes. Valets ran back from parking cars to steady lines of new customers.

"Look at this place at three a.m.," Lynn said. "Lot of people stretching out Labor Day weekend a few more hours, I guess."

The first sensation she had on entering was warmth. Incredible, cozy warmth.

When they took off their coats, Lynn was surprised to see Cheryl was not carrying. Cheryl noticed her glance. "Metal detectors everywhere and I don't want to slow us down by getting approval from security. They're well-prepared here. Everyone working for the casino is watching for out-of-control assholes. If Preston is one, they may have already tossed him."

"Let's split up and see if we can find him, first. I'll meet you back here," Lynn said.

Cheryl frowned. "You don't get it. They hired me to protect *you*, not him."

The black-walled casino was cavernous, its main illumination from thousands of video games. It was like a continuous party, or several big parties, with themes from Mardi Gras to Soul Train, palace to circus.

The next thing she noticed were cash machines and small bars in every nook. The bars featured coffee and tea as well as beer and liquor. The floor was laid out in regiments of video slot machines interspersed with poker tables. All beckoned, with the sounds and lights of payoffs, and hosts like Bourbon Street barkers.

Several casually-dressed people, lit by their video poker screens, melded into them as if they'd been there through several meals. Numerals, especially lucky sevens, festooned everything. Lynn found them strangely calming and realized Preston would, too.

A gray-jacketed guard stopped their progress into the carpeted game room. "The high-limit tables are in the next concourse."

"We're looking for a middle-aged Asian man."

Gray Jacket shook his head. "Tonight you could be describing any of a thousand people."

Lynn pulled out her cell phone and found Preston's picture. "This man."

He studied the photo. "I'll go with you."

Although she passed a bakery and a barbeque serving dozens, she couldn't smell any food odors. Instead, cigarette smoke scratched her throat, its taste coating her tongue and reminding her of her father and her sister. Her father had given up smoking after years but had still been struck by emphysema. Yet the air was fresher than could be expected, especially given all the smoking. *Good ventilation and recirculation. Wonder who their system supplier is.* The thought was automatic, involuntary, and one Preston would have understood.

Every machine was lit, every poker table crowded. Floor-walkers and guards squeezed through the throngs. Jesse and Cheryl were right about full employment. She, Cheryl, and the guards seemed to be the only ones walking. Everyone else was still, sitting in front of machines or gathered around dealers near the felt blackjack tables.

Lynn looked at her cell phone display for the time. Three-thirty.

When they finally found Preston, he wasn't at a genial game of Texas Hold 'Em. He was motionless in front of one of the video screens, watching sevens fly past.

"Preston, I'm worried about you. We have an eight a.m. meeting. Today," Lynn said.

He didn't turn to glance back, or even act surprised to see them. "I'll be there."

"You've been drinking."

"Imagine that. It's a casino."

"Why?"

"Makes me feel better."

"Preston, let's go back to the hotel. We'll drive and you can pick up your car later today."

"I'm almost finished." His words slurred. "I pay my bills. Never miss work."

Cheryl said, "Preston, the only way to beat this is to go back to Dallas."

Gray Jacket turned surly. "Are these women harassing you?"

*Well-prepared is right*, Lynn thought. *Well-prepared to keep the sucker money from leaving.*

"No. They're okay."

Cheryl and Lynn gently pulled Preston away from the screen. Lynn's heart sank when she saw how he stumbled. *If he can't function at a refinery located in the middle of a bunch of casinos, he's not doing himself, me, or TriCoast any good.*

"Preston, I'm referring you to…" Lynn started.

"I know. EAP," Preston said, using the acronym for TriCoast's employee assistance program.

"You have to fix this. It's interfering with your work. Preston," Lynn felt her eyes fill with tears, "don't make me let you go."

By the time they walked him through the biting wind to the car, it was four a.m. Lynn called Mark Shepherd and explained what was happening. Cheryl drove. Preston slumped in the back seat. Despite the casino's superb ventilation, Lynn could smell smoke in her clothes.

"Tell me what flight he's on," Mark said. "I'll meet him, make sure he's okay."

"Thanks. How's everything else?"

"We have a missing person in your neck of the woods. Gene said his distillation foreman clocked in but never clocked out. Nobody on his crew can find him. Likely he just took off early or has a girlfriend stashed somewhere we'll find out about when she decides to sue. But it's the other possibilities I'm worried about."

"Me, too."

"I've reported him missing. Is Cheryl with you?"

"Of course."

"Keep it that way. I want her at your side."

When she got off the phone, she looked in the rearview mirror at Preston's dark hair. He was staring out the window. *Preston's been stressed before. Why did he snap this time?*

As if he'd read her mind, he sat up and said, "Did you know one of my cousins died in the Murrah bombing in Oklahoma City? I keep trying to forget it but now that I'm in Oklahoma, I'm reminded of it every minute. So sure, I've been to several of the casinos around town. You have no idea how much temptation I've already resisted. Tonight they didn't limit me. Every time I was ready to walk away, they gave me more house credit."

"Because you'd already been such a good customer?" Lynn couldn't mask her bitterness. She'd liked and respected Preston all the years she'd known him. He was a valuable colleague, but more, he was a good friend.

⁂

The Chechen, or whatever he was, told me other bidders needed to be scared off. I understood. Occasional accidents and disappearances can spook people, wreck deals.

It isn't often I get a twofer. Well, one and a half. The first was easy. I'd studied his background and saw his face when casinos were mentioned. I arranged with one of the casino owners to give him a high credit limit to keep him playing. Second man? In the words of the boss woman or her Asian engineer I sidetracked, "What's the root cause analysis?"

I'll tell you what it is. Guy falls into thirty, forty tons of sulfuric acid, he gets digested.

He'll probably never be found. If someone suspects what happened, there won't be much for the medical examiner to do. They won't find a body, not even a ring.

# Nineteen

*Tulsa/Washington D.C.-to-*
*Tulsa Tuesday*

"Certain numbers play an important role in the ceremonies of the Cherokee. The numbers four and seven repeatedly occur in myths, stories and ceremonies. Four represents all the familiar forces, also represented in the four cardinal directions. These cardinal directions are east, west, north and south. The number seven represents the seven clans of the Cherokee, and is also associated with directions. In addition to the four cardinal directions, three others exist. Up (the Upper World), down (the Lower World) and center (where we live, and where 'you' always are)." —Cherokee.org

When the sun began to rise just a few hours later, she called Preston's wife. Gently, Lynn explained his breakdown and arranged for her to meet him in Dallas.

Gene and Cheryl joined her to take Preston to the Tulsa airport. Preston and his wife would then consult with TriCoast's general counsel and its head of human resources. They had already agreed with Lynn to suggest counseling, or even an intensive intervention.

Helena Farber was due to arrive from England, after connecting through New York and Chicago, to evaluate the refinery for North Seas Resources. Lynn, Cheryl, and Gene planned to wait at the airport for her once they'd seen Preston to his flight.

She also called Mike Emerson. He was worried, but reassuring. "Treatment will be the best thing."

"I hope so. I miss him already," she said. "Mike, while I have you on the phone, has Burl made in any progress in getting the Saudis to agree to talk to us again?"

"He said they're moving in the right direction, although it's likely that, for safety's sake, we'd have to send a whole new team."

"I want to try."

"Well, since you weren't with us at the dinner, maybe they would accept you. Who else do you suggest?"

"Reese Spencer is on senior advisor status." Reese, a former mentor Lynn had hired, was about to complete the combination of the Centennial refinery with TriCoast's second Houston refinery. He would no longer be needed for Centennial's day-to-day management.

"Reese, yeah. The more I know him, the more I like him." That was reassuring; Mike had originally been against bringing Reese, an outsider, in to run a TriCoast refinery.

When she and Gene said good-bye to Preston at the security checkpoint, Lynn felt even more desolate. Preston had been consistent, reliable, a sounding board, an innovative thinker. *Did I push him too hard?* He'd claimed Murrah bombing memories, but had she been expecting too much from him in the past few months? He'd been with her when they'd nearly been poisoned in a lab by hydrogen sulfide. He'd helped her corner one of the refinery sabotage perpetrators in Houston.

She pointed to a Starbucks where they could wait for Helena's flight. All three of them ordered the daily drip, black.

"Preston's out-of-control gambling is not your fault, or anyone's," Gene said, as if reading her mind.

"How could I have overlooked it?"

"You didn't. Lots of people gamble, and it doesn't conflict with their work," Cheryl said. "Preston's an adult. You had to assume he could take care of himself."

Gene nodded. "Otherwise you'd spend all your energy worrying about the habits of the five thousand people who report to you."

"But how long will it take him to recover? What if he doesn't?"

"If he wasn't fundamentally solid, you wouldn't have hired him fifteen years ago." Gene stirred a few grains of brown sugar into his coffee.

"And I've always been able to rely on him. Who can possibly take his place?"

"The work will have to be done without him," Cheryl said, more harshly than Lynn would have liked.

"No one is as quick and accurate as he is." She drank her coffee, craving its warm kick. She wished she could tell Gene and Cheryl everything: her anxiety about her upcoming wedding, the tension of seeing her ex-husband, her struggles with Burl Travis on the board, her concerns about getting enough crude oil for Tulsa and the other refineries.

*But dammit, Gene works for me and Cheryl might as well. They can't be my sounding boards on everything.*

As much as she liked and wanted to confide in both of them, their business relationship was not one of equals. Gene, in particular, relied on her to run interference so he could do his job.

"So let's talk about Helena's Tulsa schedule," Lynn said.

⁓

They waited outside the security gate nearest her flight.

"Riley has offered to take her to dinner tonight," Gene said. When Lynn winced, he added, "Your planning analyst, Greg Sutton, and I will go with them."

Helena was as severely dressed as when Lynn had met her in London. "I've had quite the tour of U.S. airports," Helena said. "Can't wait to unpack for a while. This place I'm staying—the Mayo—it's good, is it not? I'm quite positive it does not measure up to the London Ritz, but it will have to do."

Lynn introduced Helena to Gene Blahunka and Cheryl Wilkins. Gene's glance conveyed just how annoying he expected Helena would be.

"I did read a bit about Tulsa," Helena said. "You must show me these John Duncan Forsyth houses. Doesn't appear he was an especially talented architect. It's curious someone who was merely a Scotsman with airs found so many clients here."

Gene coughed. "Yes, we like the Forsyth houses. You'll get a tour this evening if you want."

"Will we see buffalo? Cowboys?"

"More of a drive than I was planning, Helena." And then, Lynn saw a teasing sparkle in Gene's eyes. "Of course, to really fit in here, the rites of passage are learning to shoot rifles and teach Sunday school."

Lynn was relieved at Helena's laugh. "Then it appears I will not 'fit in,' as you say."

Gene offered to bring the car around while Lynn, Cheryl, and Helena retrieved Helena's luggage. Without waiting for an answer, he hurried off.

A mischievous grin lit Helena's face."Could we see a tornado? Like the Wizard of Oz?"

"Anything's possible. It's true, we're close to Kansas, about seventy miles," Lynn answered.

"That's close?" Helena said. After they picked up her three large suitcases, she said, "I'm still not used to all the driving required in your country. It's so much easier to walk, or ride a train, or the Tube. London to Paris on the Eurostar is only two hours and fifteen minutes."

"Oklahoma is larger than England," Lynn said cautiously. "And it's spread out, so driving's easier. In Texas and Alaska, the best way to get between cities is to fly."

Helena shuddered. "No, thank you. I have had quite enough of airports for a few days."

⁂

Jesse settled into a seat across from Carla in the private jet. Keith had offered their company's plane, a leased eight-passenger Citation Excel, so the two Cherokee Nation officials could make the trip to Washington, D.C. from Tahlequah and back in a day.

Jesse had demurred at first, but Keith and Pete had insisted. "We're business partners. It'll save you time, which is good for all of us."

So they'd made a courtesy call on Billy Perry, deputy for economic development at the Bureau of Indian Affairs. Jesse and Carla explained their progress in bidding for the Tulsa refinery. To Jesse, Billy seemed more at ease than he had during their recent phone call, something he attributed to Carla's expert, pleasant analysis of the deal's benefits.

"And our success will open the door for other tribes," Jesse concluded.

"Without specifying, there are others here in Washington who want this deal to happen, so keep me in the flow," Billy said.

"Who?" Carla asked.

"I'm not at liberty to say."

"How about a hint?" Carla asked.

"People very senior in the administration."

In another meeting, the deputy Homeland Security chief had asked blunt questions about the Cherokees' ability to keep the refinery secure. He seemed satisfied with their answers.

At the moment Jesse was amused to see Carla marvel over the jet's luxurious gray leather seats and wool carpet.

While they flew, he considered what he'd heard and read about the blonde woman, Lynn Dayton. Did she truly speak for her company, as former chief Wilma Mankiller had for the Cherokees, or was she simply a nice woman sent to persuade them, with bigger guns arriving later if he didn't agree? In his dealings with casino operators he'd met many attractive, persuasive women who turned out to have no authority.

This woman was more like the sharp-edged New York bankers with whom he negotiated. But their niceness—indeed, the exquisite correctness of many people around him—meant money leaving Cherokee Nation coffers if he was careless.

A painful memory snagged in his mind. After the tragedy of

his friend's death, he had done as much as he could for his friend's son until the boy became a young man. And unlike Jesse himself, the boy had not been shipped off to Chilocco or another Indian school. He thought of the successful man the boy had become.

In the 1970s Jesse Drum had loved to party. Party like there was no tomorrow. Party like the ship's come in, from Saudi Arabia to the Gulf of Mexico all the way back up the Arkansas River to Tulsa. Oklahoma boomed in the fresh year of 1974, with oil at forty dollars a barrel and good times everywhere. You didn't have to be smart, or rich, or educated. Just lucky. Even fifty-year-old wells squeezing out a few barrels a day made money. Horsehead pumps sucked furiously, as if it were the 1920s again, when the young state had soared the first time and the Osage Indians were the richest people on earth.

It was a time before AIDs—or at least people talking about it—and before Indian casinos. All of Jesse's friends and relatives were as poor as the dirt around their houses.

After the Vietnam war, after his friend had died—he wouldn't think about that night—he met his friend's widow. He first noticed her at a drillsite, a patch of ground with a clanking, towering new rig, penetrating a zone they knew would be productive. The dusty roughnecks on the rig talked about her with the same words. *Drill down. Penetrate. Pay zone.* She had stylish-messy blond hair and teetering high heels, higher than any mortal should walk in.

So when she walked from the Pontiac to the drillsite trailer, the admiration was constant. "Hey baby… What's your number… I'll take orders from you…Hey sweet thing…"

And when she came back out of the trailer, more than a few of them looked at their watches. They figured no one, even the boss, was that fast.

She turned and gave them all a smile. "You get to Tulsa-town, come see me. I'm at Manchester's most nights."

Later they did. Why out of all of them, she picked him, Jesse never knew. Maybe because he'd been a close friend of her now-dead husband.

"Don't be shy just because I'm a widow. Haven't seen you in a while." She stuck her hand out. She was a modern woman. *And so damn good-looking.*

Jesse circled around her. Those white legs couldn't be any longer or trimmer, her breasts any tighter, and she had an ass that could crack a walnut.

"Do you work for Quentin Drilling?"

"Part-time receptionist."

Weeks after they started dating, he met her son one night when they stopped by her house. Two small terriers barked at him. A dark-haired, brown-skinned boy lay on the floor. He ate peanut butter from a jar as he watched television.

"See you later, kiddo," she said.

"'Bye Mama."

"Shouldn't we take him with us?" Jesse asked. "He's awfully young to be here alone."

"He'll be fine. Can't wait till he turns twenty-one. Then I'll always have a date." She laughed merrily.

Jesse felt sick. Manchester's seemed grimier than usual. Jesse saw her home. When the boy asked Jesse to help him change, he realized the five-year-old still wore diapers. He also noticed the boy's blistered bottom.

The widow's nonchalance over her son stunned him, but he figured despite growing up at an Indian school and fighting in a war across the ocean, maybe he'd been too sheltered.

One night he waited outside her house for her to return. He could hear the television inside, and saw her son watching it. Jesse didn't have a key and didn't want to break in and scare the child. But when the boy jumped back from the television and sobbed, "Mama, Mama!" as if his heart was breaking, Jesse's chest went hollow.

She finally stumbled up the driveway, saw him, and said,

"You here for a quickie? My back's not good now, and I'm coming down off poppers." Once inside, she fell onto the sofa, snoring.

"Mama! Mama, look what I made!" the boy shouted. He put a drawing next to her face but she didn't wake. Then to Jesse, he said, "Are you one of my uncles?"

Jesse put the boy onto a low mattress covered with stained sheets and a knotty blanket the boy said was his. He carried the widow to her bed, then fell asleep on the sofa.

The next morning, he found the stink and mess of the apartment horrifying. Neither the boy nor the two terriers were trained. How could his friend not have seen the woman's craziness? How could he have missed it himself?

When she emerged from the bedroom, all she said was, "Jesse...I need help and the boy's not old enough to take care of me." The reversal—her assumption her kindergarten-aged son should care for her instead of the opposite—scared him because he remembered his own lonely childhood.

"Do you have family? Or friends who could help you?" Jesse asked. He put a used diaper in the trash and cleaned up dog shit.

"They won't have anything to do with me. He's half-white, half-Indian. His daddy is one of those guys I was with. I don't know which one. When he grows up I'll see who he looks like." She laughed. "I know, your friend married me because I was pregnant. I am pretty sure it's his."

She cried for a while after Tulsa's child protective services took the boy. Within a few days, she returned to complaining about her menstrual cramps and her toe fungus, oblivious to her son's life. Jesse wasn't ready to adopt the boy. But he stayed watchful and as involved as the boy's relatives would allow.

The woman was still alive somewhere, maybe in Tulsa. He hadn't seen her since a month after they'd taken the boy. . . His thoughts returned to the present.

From the window of the private jet, Jesse watched the countryside unroll below him. They were crossing the forested Ozark Mountains. The rise and fall of the earth—here, the bosom of

Mother Earth. *Like Carla's chest.* She was so young, but her looks at him were not *usdi,* a baby's. Something else to puzzle through. He couldn't ask her out as long as she worked for him. And from the strange behavior of Riley Stevens, it appeared he'd have competition.

Up here, thousands of feet above the ground, you couldn't smell the chicken farms.

The Ozarks folded into good, strong eastern Oklahoma hills, an echo of the Appalachians, a rebuke to the craggy newness of the Rockies. The hills and valley could hold secrets in their winding trails for generations as easily as the booby-trapped and tunneled mountains of Vietnam.

Often they were simple secrets. People went into the hills and never came out, dying as hermits up in the hollows. But sometimes they were darker secrets, and the Oklahoma hills hid those just as well.

# Twenty

*Eastern Oklahoma*
*Wednesday*

"The number seven also represents the height of purity and sacredness, a difficult level to attain. In olden times, it was believed that only the owl and cougar had attained this level. The pine, cedar, spruce, holly and laurel also attained this level. They play a very important role in Cherokee ceremonies. Cedar is the most sacred of all, and the distinguishing colors of red and white set it off from all others. The wood from the tree is considered very sacred, and in ancient days, was used to carry the honored dead." —Cherokee.org, Cherokee Nation website

"Who wants to ride the river?" Pete asked, stretching back in his chair and flexing his hands.

"Canoe? The water's too chilly. Let's shoot a few rounds of golf," Jesse said.

"I have work," Lynn responded.

"Oh, come on," Keith urged. "Pete and I will let you in on our secrets, how we make so much money."

"Pete will have to tell me, because I'm not paddling a canoe with you," Lynn said. The last time she had canoed with Keith was the breaking point of their marriage. Indeed, it seemed the last canoe trip with Keith was their marriage, condensed. However much she could feel herself attracted to him, replaying those memories chilled her back to reason every time. *Am I making a mistake marrying Cy? Will marriage and stepchildren wreck the magic we have together now?*

"We'll be fine, unless someone hits a downed tree," Jesse said. "We could put in at Sparrow Hawk Loop." He had warmed to spending time with some of the tribe's financial backers.

TriCoast's general counsel might worry Lynn was favoring one bidder over another. But Sansei and the Saudis weren't here now. She, Gene, and Riley had spent the day educating Helena from North Seas Resources, the third bidder.

Even if the company's general counsel objected, Lynn knew her own boss and the chief financial officer would be pleased at the due diligence. They, too, wanted to know how Pete and Keith made money, or if they did.

"We'll golf in a few days, Jesse," Pete suggested. "But today the river isn't crowded."

"Indians in canoes. What a cliché," Riley said.

"I suppose." Jesse frowned. "But around here the Illinois River is prime entertainment."

The last time Lynn asked her father's doctor how long her father had left, the doctor had responded by putting his fingers a few inches apart. So Lynn kept her cell phone always on and with her. Each time she felt it vibrate her breath shut down to hollow puffs until she checked the caller's name. *Will I feel the phone over the jostle of the river?*

"What if we tip over?" Carla asked. "The water's cold."

"We won't," Jesse said. "Besides, we all can swim, right?" He was staring at Riley, who looked uneasy.

"I'm game," Carla said. "Riley—you?"

"Will you warm me up after I fall in?"

She shook her head. "But I'll bring extra blankets."

They agreed to change clothes and gather at the float rental dock Jesse's friend owned. Lynn put her cell phone into a pocket closed with Velcro, and got into the car that the tattooed analyst,

Greg, was driving. When Lynn's bodyguard learned their plans, she insisted on accompanying them.

"You're stuck to her like a wet blanket," Riley said.

"And I'm just as much fun, right?" Cheryl laughed.

"Hey, you carry?" Riley asked her.

"Glock 19, nine millimeter."

Riley circled around her. "How come I don't see it on you?"

"That's the point. Jackass shoulder holster," Cheryl said.

"You don't like the shoulder holster?"

She smiled. "No, that's just the name of it."

The nine of them—Lynn, Cheryl, Greg, Riley, Carla, Pete, Keith, Gene, and Jesse—made a three-car caravan. Lynn asked Greg to stop at a convenience store so she could buy beer.

Hearing a song by anorexic Karen Carpenter wafting through the store made Lynn cringe at the irony of using too-skinny Karen to promote buying groceries. The cashier rang up four six-packs and pushed them across the Formica wood-grain counter.

"You can tell a person by his or her music," Greg said when Lynn and Cheryl rejoined him in the car. The young analyst plugged his iPod into the car's phone jack.

They heard a song in German with a marching beat. The only word she could understand was "Emanuela." The next song came out as a breathy, restless plea from the singer, "All the things you said, all the things you said."

"Russian group, T.A.T.U. You'd never know they were Russian, would you?"

"You like music," Cheryl said.

"No disrespect to the woman carrying the gun, but duh. Most of my friends want to be musicians."

"You?" Lynn asked.

"Promise you won't tell," Greg grinned as he turned the car back onto the road. "Wait, promise you *will* tell."

"Sure." Lynn was curious.

"An actuary."

"Seriously?"

"What do you think?"

She shook her head.

"Yeah. Way serious. They're like accounting geeks on steroids. I could tell you how likely it is one of our refineries will be hit by a hurricane, stuff like that."

"After hours hobby?" Cheryl asked.

"It should be what Lynn wants me to do at work." The song ended and another one started. In German. Greg saw her surprised look and laughed. "It means 'through the monsoon.'"

Lynn liked the plaintive melody. While Greg drove, she answered e-mails, texts, and calls and tried to keep the memory of the last canoe trip from her mind. But it kept intruding. It had sealed the fate of her first marriage . . .

Increasingly, Keith claimed Lynn wasn't spending enough time with him. So when he made the dream of a perfect day sound tantalizing, as he always could, she agreed to an afternoon canoeing on Bayou St. John in New Orleans with their friends. She would meet them at the bayou after she returned Saturday morning from a trip to an offshore drilling platform.

When she parked on the street near the bayou, she saw he'd remembered everything: not only the canoes and the paddles, but the life jackets, bottled water, snacks, and dry clothing. Then she saw what he'd hidden from her. He unpacked three 56-quart coolers. Ice and six-packs of Dixie beer filled each one. An empty plastic ring already looped onto the side of one cooler.

"You bought for everyone, right?" she'd asked him, unable to stop herself.

"Sure, darlin'. Everyone who wants one," he'd said. He looked so happy she didn't speak further. She was nagging. It's what he always said. Maybe he would mature, she thought, if they had a baby. She hadn't told him because she wanted to wait another few weeks to be certain. A baby. What a change a baby would bring them. Scary, but wonderful.

He'd insisted on taking the stern to control the canoe's

direction, even though she was the more experienced canoeist.

With his wayward paddling, they drifted from one side of the bayou to the other. She said nothing, trying to adapt her bow strokes to give them direction while he dragged an oar in the water at the back. Steering from the front took three times the energy of steering from the stern. Within minutes her arms were sore.

She could smell the stagnant water along the banks. A few ancient mansions graced one side of the bayou, vast City Park, the other. As they zigzagged, she saw both more closely than she wanted.

He refused her offers to change positions or change canoes with the others. Most of the six-member group were people she supervised. A knockdown, drag-out with Keith on a sweltering August afternoon would be bountiful fodder for the next three weeks in the cubes. She was trapped, able only to put on a pleasant expression and wait for the afternoon to end.

Then they approached a bridge a few feet above the level of the bayou.

"Let's switch, Keith."

"No. I can handle it."

It was an old bridge, four car-widths across. Just one narrow stretch of water underneath had enough clearance between the tops of their heads and the bridge struts.

Keith's approach, with her strong-armed corrections from the bow, was fine. But once underneath, in the darkness, they lost momentum.

"Damn. I gotta piss, bad." Keith started paddling furiously.

The canoe slid sideways, then turned left out of the narrow lane of safe passage. She could still feel the rude concussion when her head smacked against the solid iron struts. Doctors would later tell her she'd loosened four teeth.

"Keith, stop paddling!" She'd yanked a cooler out of the way and slipped down into the bottom of the canoe, cradling her head, unable to see, or paddle, while he golly-geed and drifted back and forth another five minutes before they cleared the bridge.

Her friends gasped when they saw her. One took her to Tulane University Hospital where she was stitched and ordered to stay overnight. The nurses attending her took extra precautions when she told them she might be pregnant.

She cried when she woke up in the hospital that night with blood everywhere. One nurse hugged her and held her hands, while others changed her sheets and clothes. "I'm so sorry to tell you this, but I think you understand what's happened."

Lynn nodded, sobbing. A miscarriage.

Keith had been too drunk to visit her. By the time she was released, he'd left for a two-day hunting trip that somehow required him to be gone for five days and included numerous bar stops.

She rented an apartment and called a divorce lawyer. She returned to their house only once to pick up clothes, a computer, and the few other things she'd accumulated during their few years together. Like the canoe, their marriage had drifted to a cheerless end.

No, she definitely wouldn't get into a canoe with Keith. She only hoped buying beer today hadn't been a mistake.

# Twenty-One

*Northern Oklahoma/Lyon, France*
*Wednesday*

They arrived at a livery—really a shed with soft drinks and snacks—near Comb's Bridge.

A sunburned woman in her sixties pointed out four canoes to Jesse. "It will take you about three hours from here to where you're getting out. You can barely make it before dark. Take the Royalex Prospectors."

Jesse and the owner each grabbed a canoe from the rack, lifted it onto their knees, put their fingers on the gunwales, then flipped and hoisted the canoes above their shoulders. Like big fiberglass capes, the bows reached above their heads, the sterns angled down behind them. Jesse and the woman each kept the ninety-pound canoes balanced on their shoulders.

Lynn whistled. "Those look heavy."

"Easy, once you know what you're doing. Trick is balancing and keeping the bow high." Jesse's voice echoed into the belly of the canoe as he walked down to the gravel bar. Reversing the motion of the pick-up, he and the owner slid the canoes halfway into the water. Lynn could see well-developed deltoid muscles through the back of the sixty-year-old woman's knit shirt. *No surprise there.*

Jesse and Keith repeated the trip with two additional canoes.

"Life jackets?" Lynn asked, hoping her voice sounded strong, wondering if her upper-body workouts had been sufficient should she need to mimic their lift-and-carry. She passed yellow and orange vests to the others and tightened her own straps.

"It'll be quiet today. Weekends in the summer you can't see the river, so many canoes and rafts. Arlie," Jesse nodded at the owner, "told me since last weekend was Labor Day *and* the Cherokee National Holiday weekend they had eight hundred people out here. Good for us in Tahlequah," he said, the coffers of the nation seemingly always worrying him.

"Riley, have you and Lynn canoed?" Pete asked.

"Yeah," he said. Lynn nodded.

"You take the stern, and I'll take the bow," Pete said to Lynn.

"Good," Lynn said. More than good. Perfect. The stern paddler controlled the canoe. The bow paddler provided the power and the spotting. Her weightlifting notwithstanding and his missing finger aside, Pete's shoulders and forearms looked like he could supply more power than she could. In other canoes, Jesse, Gene, and Carla opted for stern positions while Riley, Greg, and Keith took the bows.

"I'll take the middle," Cheryl said to Lynn.

Lynn looked at Pete and shrugged. "She makes the rules for stuff like this. I'm still getting used to it. We can rotate off with Cheryl if one of us gets tired."

Before they launched their canoes, Gene pulled Lynn and Cheryl aside. "My distillation foreman is still missing. Mark and I reported it to the Tulsa PD. He was doing routine checks on the sulfur treating units. That's apparently the last time he was seen. We've combed the refinery but no sign."

"That's terrible! I'm so sorry to hear it. Have you been in touch with his family?" Lynn asked.

"We have, and so have the Tulsa police. No word."

⚬⚬⚬

Despite the late hour in Lyon, France, Simone Tierney was still at her desk. She read the bulletin from MI-5 about the ricin-on-roses poisoning of UK citizen Amanda Parsifal. The CCTV video they'd attached of the flower delivery courier displayed a man, or a woman who carried herself like a man.

Simone listed the facts of the two cases—Amanda Parsifal and the Saudi bodyguard. Different countries, different killing techniques. The only characteristic they shared was the level of professionalism, and the fact that Amanda, too, had been employed in the oil business. Who was the killer, and for whom did he, or they, work?

⁂

Once underway, Pete turned and talked to Cheryl and Lynn over his shoulder. "Since I moved back from New York, I've been out here on weekends. This time of year the river's at its lowest level, so the rapids are easy, Class II or even Class I. Flow's about four hundred cubic feet a second. When I was on it in April and May, it was much rougher. The river's volume of water was four times what it is now so it was much faster and more turbulent."

He pointed out downed trees with submerged branches. Lynn J-stroked the heavy, commercial canoe away from them.

"There's a cheerful sign," Cheryl said. *People have been paralyzed diving from this bridge.*

Gene pulled his canoe up beside theirs and pointed backward. "Now if this was still water, instead of flowing, those branches would be a perfect place for noodling."

"Gene, catfish-grabbing is something I haven't thought about for a long time." One of her relatives hunted catfish by finding a likely hole, wading into the muddy waters or even diving beneath them, and sticking a hand into what he hoped was a catfish lair. When a catfish bit down on his hand, he'd pull it out. Most of the fish were medium-sized but a few were thirty pounds. She'd heard stories of fifty-pounders.

"Hey, it's all official now. Car dealers, Walmart, even oil companies when they're looking for new employees, sponsor the tournament in July. And the rules specify bare hands only."

"So we missed the tournament?" She tried hard not to sound relieved.

"I've got perfect places, one bank under some tree roots and another near an old broken-up highway. I'll enter you in next year's tournament."

"Tell me when it is," she said. *I'll have an urgent meeting in Montana then.*

"This river here, you're better off fishing for small mouth bass anyway," Gene said.

She looked ahead to Riley, afraid he'd blustered—lied, even— about his paddling prowess. Instead, she saw his canoe glide ahead in a straight line, no side-to-side zigzagging that would mark a novice. *Could it be he was showing off for Carla in the canoe behind?* His bright, engaged smile and glances back at Carla gave Lynn the answer.

Finding a center channel deep enough proved more difficult than she expected. The smell of the river at its low point was as strong as a compost pit. Exposed roots and branches rotted in the late afternoon sun.

"Do you mind telling us what happened to your finger?" Cheryl asked.

Pete stopped paddling and turned around to look at them again. "Like Will Rogers said, 'There are three kinds of men, the one that learns by reading, the few who learn by observation and the rest who have to pee on the electric fence for themselves.' Afraid I'm a pee-on-the-fence guy. I had a rig accident on a summer job. Got my finger caught between some pipe and casing on a rig deck while I was trying to direct the pipe downhole. Sucker was spinning, I was moving it into position and *whap!* My finger was gone."

Lynn flinched. "Then what?"

"I yelled. Someone pulled me away. The crime of it was, they couldn't retrieve my finger. It just shot down the hole with the drill pipe. So now it's buried under the Gulf of Mexico."

"Sorry," Lynn said.

"Don't be. From what I hear the well's still a good producer."

He turned back around and resumed paddling. Cheryl looked

at Lynn, and Lynn saw the Louisiana native's expression change briefly as if she were appraising the honesty of his story.

Riley's and Jesse's canoe pulled even with them. "Jesse tells me the river has water moccasins," Riley said.

Jesse added, "They like still water the best. Anyway, doesn't matter if you get bit, most places here your cell phone won't work, so you're screwed. And if you get stuck in quicksand, it's even worse."

*Another parade-of-horribles test,* Lynn thought. *They want to see how I react.* "Keep it up, boys. You'll get a scream out of me yet."

"The only dangers I'm worried about are human," Jesse said. "Occasionally someone finds a meth lab with a bunch of toothless crazies guarding it."

"So I'm really glad we have Cheryl with us," Lynn replied.

She was reassured to see Riley paddled when Jesse told him, didn't stand up in the canoe, and didn't go rigid when they plowed through rapids. After a half hour, they got stuck in an inlet and had to drag the canoe over a gravel bar. Another time they hung up in tree roots. But Riley backed them out adeptly without spinning, and Jesse, likely the superior canoeist, remained gracious.

In tranquil water near the verge, mosquitoes skated. After Jesse's warnings, every willow branch looked to Lynn as if a snake was resting on it, waiting to drop onto her shoulders.

In her canoe, Pete as bowman read the river. He pointed toward dark-water deeper channels and directed them away from the lighter-colored water, which meant rocks right below the surface.

She heard the rushing sound of more rapids ahead and spoke above it. "You lured me out here with a promise about telling me your company's secrets," she said.

"Pillow! Go right!" Pete pulled hard on his paddle.

Cheryl added her strong paddling and Lynn steered sharp J-strokes.

A pillow was a smooth sheen of water, often only a few inches deep, running over a big rock close to the surface. To cross directly through a pillow usually meant getting stuck on the rock below.

Pete indicated constriction waves, whitecaps formed by water rushing between two rocks. An evening mist rose from the river. At its low level, it continued to smell of wet root balls. Lynn appreciated the glass-smooth water and tried not to be anxious that the high, brushy banks isolated them.

Her hands were blistering. She loosened her grip and weariness from the last two hours cascaded through her arms, upper body and abdominal muscles. She thought of the Whippet responding to the ABS signal in her car and smiled.

Pete turned around. "It's calm ahead, so let me answer your question. Cheryl, you can listen in and determine if you think I'm telling the truth."

Lynn was motionless. *It's like he read our minds.*

"Lynn, your ex-husband and I have contacts among small business owners. We go to capital conferences, meet a lot of people. Hasn't he told you about this?"

Lynn shook her head. "We haven't talked much since the divorce. No need to."

"Many of these owners—mostly men, a few women—are in their seventies and eighties. They're good, religious people. In fact, it happens that most of the ones we work with are teetotalers."

*So Keith can't wow them with his drinking prowess.*

"They have trouble letting go of the companies they started, think they'll live forever. But if they get ill and there's no one they want to sell to and no heirs who want to run it, we buy it from them. We fix the company up, then resell it."

"Like a real estate investor?" Lynn asked.

He smiled. "Yeah. A lot of these companies need rehabbing—new operating and accounting systems. So we install them."

She'd wanted to ask him another question for several days and this seemed to be the chance. "What about Jesse? How long have you known him?"

He shrugged, his back to them and said over his shoulder, "Forever, I think."

They slid down a watery chute, bordered on one side by a high bluff. When they rounded a bend, they heard shouting.

"What are you doing? Get away!" Carla yelled.

Carla and Keith were kneeling in their canoe, swinging their paddles. A few yards away a man with stringy brown hair and a dirt-caked denim shirt splashed through waist-deep water toward them, waving a handgun.

"You're on private property, bitches," the man shouted. He fired into the air and the sound echoed down the river.

"We're on the river, not your property! Dammit, now we're stuck!" Keith shouted back.

Cheryl pulled out her gun, aimed it at the stringy-haired man, and without hesitating, fired a shot in his direction. "Get the fuck away from here *now.*"

Lynn had no doubt Cheryl's next bullet would be lethal. Apparently the meth man, or whoever he was, believed so, too. He backed slowly through the river, looked around for a tree branch to lever himself out onto the bank. "Just saying you're close to private property." Then he turned and ran, his clothes sloshing water.

Distracted by the man, Carla and Keith had allowed their canoe to slip sideways against a line of rocks. Carla jumped into the water as high as her elbows and got downstream of the canoe, trying to pry it off the rocks.

Keith slipped and the canoe tipped toward the current. Then he slid out. He tried to grab coolers as they floated downstream.

Suddenly the canoe turned completely sideways, open to the current. River water gushed in, filling it. The force of hundreds of gallons a second pushed the canoe even harder against the rocks. Carla was wedged in open water between the canoe and the rocks, still trying to dislodge it.

"Carla, get away! The canoe's going to wrap around you!" Lynn shouted.

If Carla didn't get upstream of the canoe, she would be pinned between the hundreds of pounds of water pressure pushing the canoe from one side, and the rocks on the other side. Human bones were no match for such a vise.

Lynn, Pete, and Cheryl tied their own canoe to a tree and ran as well as they could through the shallow parts of the river. Lynn lost her footing amid the strong current and deep holes in the flint riverbed.

"My life jacket's caught!" Carla screamed.

"Take it off!" Lynn shouted.

The fiberglass skin of the canoe started to groan. Keith, Lynn, Cheryl, and Pete grabbed the gunwales and tried to pull it away from Carla. If it slipped farther, it would crush her ribs.

Carla unstrapped her life jacket and tried to move away from between the big boulders and the canoe.

She fell. Her foot seemed to be jammed in the sharp flint rocks of the riverbed, like Lynn's had been.

The fiberglass canoe bent and screeched.

Lynn and Cheryl lifted Carla up and away from the canoe just as it loosened and slammed into the rocks where Carla's body had been a half-second earlier.

"Are you okay?" Cheryl asked her.

Carla sobbed, but nodded.

Lynn and Pete pushed on the bow while Keith and Cheryl pulled on the stern to extricate the canoe, wedged between the grip of the current and the wall of big rocks. Lynn felt as if she was trying to move a mountain.

Finally it slid free, half-filled with water. Pete guided it to a gravel bar. Carla's teeth were chattering. Everything belonging to Carla and Keith was gone or soaked, including their extra clothes.

"I think my clothes will fit you," Lynn said.

Carla took them and walked behind the trees to change.

Lynn found her cell phone. As Jesse had warned, she couldn't get a signal.

"Carla, sure you're okay?" Keith repeated when she returned wearing dry clothes.

"Yeah. Freaked out, though. Who was that man?"

"Must have been one of the meth lab crazies Jesse was talk-ing about," Pete said.

"I thought we were dead!" Carla said, and looked at Cheryl. "Thank God you were with us, Cheryl."

"I'm not totally surprised to see a meth guy, but these days a lot of them make it in smaller batches instead of some lab hid-den in the country," Cheryl said.

Lynn nodded. Her clothes were wet, too. She was realiz-ing how cold the river water was, even though it was only early September. She toweled off and Cheryl gave her a jacket.

The two men also appeared chilled.

"Can you guys split clothes, so Keith has something dry to wear?"

"You can have my extra shirt. It's probably too big for you, though," Pete said.

"Like hell it is," Keith replied.

And with that exchange, Lynn knew they were all right.

As she thought about it more, the appearance of what must have been a meth lab guard surprised Lynn. She was glad she and Pete had been close behind Carla and Keith. She was especially grateful Cheryl had been with them. Then she wondered whether or not he'd also threatened the two lead canoes. She hadn't heard or seen anything that would suggest it.

She wondered why the man had come after them today, and apparently Carla specifically. Dozens of paddlers rode this stretch of river. Today was even quieter than the weekend; anyone fearful of being discovered should have been worried a few days ago, yet the owner of the canoe livery had reported no problems. Even to-day it appeared Gene, Jesse, Greg, and Riley had passed the spot fifteen minutes earlier without incident.

*Did he think Carla was a good target because she appeared to be the weakest?*

Something else was troubling her, too. Lynn replayed events in her mind but couldn't identify the thing that had been even more startling than the appearance of the attacker.

# Twenty-Two

*Los Angeles*
*Thursday*

Lynn had been asked by Claude Durand, TriCoast's French-born public relations vice president, to appear on a Los Angeles talk show. "It will enhance the TriCoast brand," Claude said. His hands formed an invisible banner. "The corporation, with a human face."

"Why can't the face be yours?"

"You're in operations, you're an executive, and you're photogenic. In addition you're a woman, like most who watch the show."

"I'd rather be home with my fiancé and his kids," Lynn had replied to no avail.

During the flight from Tulsa to Los Angeles, she read the preparatory messages Claude had sent. She'd scrubbed the scent of river water from her hair and skin but kept visualizing the crazed man.

She and Cheryl had reported the attack to Mark Shepherd, TriCoast's security chief. Carla had also reported it to the tribal police. Mark responded with alarm, saying he would alert the Tulsa police and the county sheriff. He ended his message to Lynn with, *And keep Cheryl in your sight every waking moment. She has my orders to be on you like paint.*

At the airport, she and Cheryl met the limousine driver arranged by the talk show producers. An hour later, they drove by the spindly Miro sculpture on the studio's plaza. Skateboarders were crisscrossing in front of it.

The closed windows of the limo didn't buffer the shouts of protestors in front of the studio. Claude had correctly predicted their vehemence.

She understood their frustration. She'd grown up with every purchase examined, measured, and delayed as long as possible. For years she had never looked at silk or linen clothes because she couldn't afford them. When gasoline or heat became more expensive, something else had to be cut from the family budget.

The noise diminished as the limo driver pulled into an unmarked entrance on a side street. Claude met them inside and the show's assistant producer pointed out the green room. Lynn fought her jumpy stomach while a sound tech made final adjustments to her mike.

"Weren't you the one who suggested to the board all this openness was a good idea?" she asked Claude.

"*Oui*. And seeing you puts a face—a beautiful one—to concerns about high energy prices."

"Same thing you said to Mike before he went on the air in New York?"

"*Mais oui*. And you saw how successful he was." On the show TriCoast's CEO had displayed his usual even temper and sense of humor. His assistant had fielded several proposals the next week, explaining to each caller that yes, Mike was happily married.

"Everyone will watch to see how you handle it. No pressure." The corners of his mouth turned up in a rare smile. He'd told her French men didn't smile.

"Pressure. I'd rather be handling a superheated steam valve."

She wondered whether it would be worse if she goofed up, lost her temper, and got two million hits on YouTube for making a fool of herself, or if no one watched at all.

The show's host was friendlier than Lynn expected, emphasizing Lynn's up-by-her-bootstraps personal history and only once bringing up the old news about her status as a woman in a male-dominated industry. Then it was time for questions.

"Do you support plug-in hybrids?" asked a bearded young man in loafers and a Ford gimme cap.

"Yes. One of the most important things we can do is diversify our energy supplies, both different sources for oil and different kinds of energy altogether. Plug-in electric hybrids give us a wider variety of sources since electricity is produced from coal, natural gas, nuclear, and renewables."

"Why are we still using so much oil?"

"Oil's energy-dense, so it delivers many more BTUs per barrel, or miles per gallon, than anything else. While electricity is good, a lot of energy is lost between the primary fuel, like natural gas, and your electrical outlets." The studio lights were hot. She wondered if she could will herself not to sweat.

"Why don't you invest your profits in green start-up companies?"

This she'd expected. "Our shareholders rely on us to help them pay for their retirement and other personal goals. So we look for ventures we think will be profitable in places where we have expertise. If we spend money on an unprofitable project just because it's green, we violate our legal responsibilities to our stockholders, which probably include many of you, either directly or indirectly."

After several more questions, an assistant producer held up a thirty-second time check.

"Did you fly to L. A. in a company jet?"

She looked at the host and smiled. "I flew commercial. Seat 14A."

"Why are we talking to you instead of the CEO? Doesn't he care about these issues?"

"If you'd like to see a video of CEO Mike Emerson's interview last week, it's online."

After the host thanked her and broke for a commercial, Claude and Cheryl met her. "Excellente!" the Frenchman said. Outside, they opened the doors to the waiting limousine.

Suddenly, a familiar-smelling bottle whizzed past her, in the direction of the Miro sculpture. "Here's what your gasoline's good for!" a protestor yelled.

Others screamed and ran before the glass shattered.

The Molotov cocktail fireballed the base of the sculpture, scorching the bottom half and sending real flames almost to the height of Miro's sun.

Cheryl grabbed Lynn, another guard grabbed Claude, and everyone hustled back inside the production studio.

A security guard wrestled the bomb thrower to the ground.

"We'll call for an armored limo," Cheryl said.

# Twenty-Three

*North Dakota*
*Friday*

Gernot Insel was satisfied with the flash protest he'd arranged in Los Angeles. The Molotov cocktail had been poetic: gasoline for a gasoline producer.

He reported the progress to his client. His client had paid, urging him to move faster. The sale of the TriCoast refinery had to be made, and there was only one acceptable buyer. Others must be discouraged from bidding or else, they had to be removed.

But more potential buyers kept appearing. Neither he nor his client had expected such interest. That's what had brought him to Williston, North Dakota, to the dreariest land he had ever seen.

Because the town was so small, Insel had the same challenge in avoiding detection as with London's cameras. However, with thousands of new oilfield workers, many transient, there was less need of a complete disguise. So far, no one had questioned his cover as a petroleum engineer evaluating reserves and making contacts at a regional conference. In his drives around town, the office of his target, Nordval Oil Company, had been easy to spot, a new four-story building springing out of the hilly plains.

After the Los Angeles interview, and time spent with the LAPD describing the Molotov cocktail incident, Lynn had requested one of TriCoast's private planes for her and Cheryl.

Although Allegiant Air flew nonstop to Bismarck and Fargo from LAX, its schedule did not match hers.

She was excited. A few miles underneath the remote North Dakota and Montana grasses lay the biggest oil deposit found in the continental United States in the last sixty years. Although the Bakken had actually been discovered in the 1950s, only with the recent horizontal drilling and multistage fracturing techniques—honed within a few miles of TriCoast's headquarters—had it been possible to drill the oil profitably. The production fed optimism in the frigid area, not least from state officials as they counted new jobs and tax revenue. Oil-field suppliers, like those of pre-fabricated housing in Idaho, had ramped up their manufacturing also.

Before leaving, she had asked the pilot if they could fly a few circles around McKenzie and Montrail counties once they were over western North Dakota. He'd put in for the route adjustment.

She pulled up the video TriCoast's exploration VP had made. It was filled with maps and graphs, but his excitement was clear by his emphatic tone: "...puts North Dakota's crude oil production ahead of Alaska's and second only to Texas... 4.3 billion barrels recoverable according to the USGS, some operators suggest as much as twenty billion barrels, on par with Alaska's Kuparak... total reserve is upwards of four hundred billion barrels... challenges include keeping rigs running in weather with wind chills of 50 degrees below zero, but we will draw on our Alaskan and Russian experience."

Lynn drummed her fingers. While TriCoast was producing a moderate volume of Bakken oil, about fifty thousand barrels a day, other companies had leapt ahead. They were the people with whom she wanted to speak. One of the biggest producers was tiny Nordval Oil Company, run by Dag Nordval.

Oil from the Middle Bakken and Three Forks formations in North Dakota, Montana, and Saskatchewan had grown so much she could readily contract for another sixty to seventy thousand barrels a day. Although seventy thousand barrels was only four percent of what she needed to feed the hungry maws of her five refineries every day, the oil was high-quality 41-gravity sweet, or light and low-sulfur, thus inexpensive to refine. It cost less than most other crudes to make it into higher-valued gasoline, jet fuel, and diesel.

If this were an ordinary oil purchase, part of Lynn's never-ending hunt for new sources, she would have handled it alone. Because of Nordval's interest in buying the Tulsa refinery, she had arranged for Gene Blahunka and Greg Sutton, the young corporate analyst with the barely-hidden tattoos, to meet her. Cheryl made four and they'd been beyond lucky to get rooms at the Candlewood Suites Williston. Usually the Candlewood, and every other motel, apartment, house, or structure with a roof and four walls, was booked for months. Tent cities and RV parks had sprung up to accommodate those without a permanent roof over their heads.

The pilot told her their route change had been approved. He signaled when they crossed the border from Montana. She looked out the jet's window. Fleets of pumping trucks, flatbeds of fracturing equipment, and wells were everywhere.

All of the CEOs she would talk to at this conference produced oil from these burgeoning fields. Most were ready to do straightforward sales, particularly since she had transportation capacity on rail cars and pipelines. But Dag Nordval, CEO of Nordval Oil Company, was holding out for more. In TriCoast's Tulsa refinery, he saw a secure, long-term home for his production of sixty thousand barrels a day of oil. He'd proposed a joint venture to buy half of TriCoast's refinery in exchange for his supply.

Lynn sighed. More good domestic crude was being produced now than had been for years, but she needed so much oil she had to include Nordval's proposal as a potential buyer for the refinery.

At the conference reception, Lynn greeted Gene and Greg.

They split in three directions, each talking to different landmen, scouts, and production engineers for the fifty or so companies in attendance. Cheryl stayed near Lynn.

After picking an appetizer of bite-sized Swedish pancakes with lingonberries, she introduced herself to one craggy-faced man, a CEO who had started as a rancher until he'd followed the example of the companies drilling in the land around his.

"I saw your interview," he said. "Looked you up. You spent time in Chicago. So did I."

"I commuted to the University of Chicago weekend business program," Lynn said.

"How'd you like it?"

"The weather's the same as here: hard and cold. Kind of like the economic realities they teach. Competition and survival of the fittest makes sense when the wind chill is eighty below."

He chuckled. "When it's that cold, you don't waste words. You notice we don't have asphalt roads? Hell, the temperature swings from a hundred and ten in the summer to forty below in January. Asphalt wouldn't last a year. Everything's concrete but damn, it's so busy here, we need more of it, just like we need more of everything. I get caught in a damn five-mile truck back-up at least once a week."

The reception's buffet featured local German and Norwegian specialties, another way to draw the line between insiders and outsiders, she realized, like serving calf fries in Texas. She was glad to have Chicago native Gene here. But even he shied away from the smelly *lutefisk*, lye-treated fish. Other dishes were hearty: warm, filling food for the many bitterly cold months of winter, like *knoepla* soup—chicken soup with dumplings—*lefse*, a flat bread made of mashed potatoes served with butter and sugar; *fleischkuekle*, a deep-fried entrée of ground beef covered in dough and served with chips and a pickle; and at the end of the table, pie-like *kuchen* and chokecherry strudel.

After the reception, Cheryl drove Lynn, Gene, and Greg to Nordval's offices. Similar to much of the business district for this town of over twenty-five thousand, it was near the airport.

"Couldn't decide whether I ought to delay our meeting. I got a guy coming in after you, a petroleum engineer. I need him more than I need you." Dag Nordval, the man behind the booming voice, was easily six-foot-five. His red hair was flecked with gray. He shook their hands. Then at Nordval's request, Cheryl excused herself to wait outside his office. "Your gun makes me nervous, lady. Like if I make the wrong offer you'll shoot me."

"Hasn't happened yet," Lynn said, and laughed.

"Well anyway, yup, I'm Norwegian, Lutheran to boot. Grew up around here. The Norwegians at Statoil took me for one of them when I worked there and it sure helps now when I want to lease land from my neighbors."

*Whoa!* Lynn thought, looking at Gene. Nordval had the same Midwestern accent, even lengthening 'sure' into a sentence, just as Gene did, "shooooooooor."

"Any relation to Nordquist, the guy who discovered the Bakken?" Gene asked.

He grinned. "Maybe, if I looked back a hundred years."

"What's your total production?" Lynn asked. When he answered, she wished she had asked the question differently.

"Our Bakken and Middle Fork 2, 3, and 4 bench well results are de-risking our acreage and showing thirty-day rates above our model," Nordval said. "There's over a fifty percent upside to our conservative twenty-one dollar a share three-P. The next few months will see four material wells that could de-risk up to three hundred more locations and put us in play for large-cap E&Ps looking for oily exposure. Our biggest NAV impact will be acceleration."

Gene frowned. "English, please?"

Nordval smiled and spoke slowly. "We have good wells that will prove up even more of our acreage, so we can put more assets on the books. We perform better than other companies because we can drill faster—acceleration. We've been told we may become a takeover target by bigger companies who are interested in our reserves. Like you."

Then the man's smile disappeared and he leaned forward.

"Now, how do I know you're not sniffing around to buy my company? Maybe you're trying to grab my leases."

"Dag, we're not interested in your leases," Lynn said. "I'm looking for 1.7 million barrels of oil a day to refine. My suppliers are all over the world. We'd like to do business with you, even to the point of discussing a joint venture on our Tulsa refinery."

Nordval rocked forward on his elbows. "Bet you can't *give* that thing away, with the EPA and whatnot hassling you."

"On the contrary, with the new domestic production from here all the way south to Texas and east to Ohio, people are really interested in finding homes for it nearby. Refineries like ours have become much more valuable. We have strong bids," she said. "How about you? Can you verify the quality of your oil? Your ability to supply fifty thousand barrels a day, not just tomorrow, but five or ten years from now?"

A shadow passed over his face. "Nordval Oil has one of the best lease positions up here. We're at sixty thousand and we'll get to eighty thousand barrels a day next year."

*Now we're talking.* "We have pipeline and rail capacity to get the oil to Tulsa. Do you?"

The smile was back. "I've got space locked up on trains in case the new pipeline doesn't get built soon. I'm already moving my production to Cushing." Nordval was talking about the massive oil terminal forty miles west of Tulsa. It was a pipeline crossroads for the country, with eighty million barrels of oil storage. On a map, Cushing was the center of a dense star, radiating crude oil in and out to the rest of the US.

"What role do you see for Nordval in running the Tulsa refinery?" Lynn asked, hoping he would say 'silent partner.'

"We'd want to participate in all decisions, maybe get you to teach us about the refining business."

*Damn.* She was distracted by the sight of green lightning illuminating snowflakes that had begun to fall.

He noticed her glance. "Weird if you're not used to it. It's snow lightning. Sometimes we get it with snow or hail. Little early in the season, but it's happened before."

She smiled, to ease the conversation. "Our Texas live oaks would be dead oaks with as much snow as you get here." She turned and looked at him. "Dag, I'll be honest. You don't have the conceit I often see with oil-finders. They think all they have to do is discover the oil, and to hell with the market. But you're smart enough to see beyond thirty-day production rates to realize people don't buy oil. They buy what we make from it.

"But refining is complicated. You can't learn it in your spare time like trying to lower your golf handicap. And you can't run a refinery from a thousand miles away. If that's your expectation, you'll be disappointed."

He shook his head. "I've read about it. The refining industry loses money most quarters. I can do better. Hell, I'll build my own refinery right here."

Gene's face reddened. "TriCoast's refining business doesn't lose money. Not my refinery."

With a glance at Gene, Lynn said, "Building a refinery is expensive, complex, and the local market is not big enough to be worthwhile." She didn't mention the several refineries already in Minnesota, Illinois, Montana, and even here in North Dakota. *No point in advertising my competition.*

Dag squinted. "Fair enough." He stood, looming over Gene. "Would I have say in who runs the refinery?"

Gene, Lynn and Greg stood, too. Lynn smiled and shook Dag's hand and said, "No. Not a chance. But we'll meet you back here in an hour. We'd like to buy you dinner at the country club, and tell you about Gene's operation. Can you rough out a term sheet for your offer? Something about how you can guarantee fifty thousand barrels of day for a joint interest in the Tulsa refinery?"

As Cheryl joined them and they stepped out of the building, Lynn noticed the sky was already darkening toward sunset, casting long, liquid shadows over the road. The air sparkled as tiny crystals continued falling. Despite the gloom, she could see Gene's red face.

"Man's a Northern-baked idiot."

"He has a good position and he's trying to leverage it," Lynn said. "You'd do the same. How about if we take a break at the hotel for a half-hour, then drive around town—see the grain elevator and other wonders. We can pick him up back here and have a decent dinner, check out Williston's wine supply."

⁂

Gernot Insel had not expected Dag Nordval would be so tall. It would mean a slight change in plans. However, the office setup still accommodated him.

"Jerry Havard, welcome, welcome," Nordval said when Insel entered, using the alias Insel had provided. "Hope you had no problems getting here."

"No, none."

"Impressive resume the headhunter sent. Can I offer you something to drink?"

"No, but thank you. Your assistant left already?" Insel had experience using the never-say-quit American work ethic as a cover, and it would simplify his plans if the woman didn't return.

"Well, she's got a couple of kids to take care of. How about you, Jerry?"

"Divorced with no children, I'm afraid."

"So that's why you're free to move here. Sometimes the wives think Williston is too remote. Say, why'd you leave Petronas?" Nordval asked, referring to the Malaysian national oil company.

"Not enough juice. I understand you offer participation?" Insel had expected a small, busy company like Nordval's would not check his references until after the interview. By then it wouldn't matter.

"We do. Good man who slogs through the winter here, finds reserves to get Nordval Oil on the map ought to get more than just a salary. So you'd get a one percent override, after expenses."

"I brought a flash drive. It has some of my work on it." Insel pulled it out of his briefcase and handed it to Nordval.

"Good." Nordval inserted the drive into his computer. "Which files?"

"I'll show you." Insel got up from his chair and stepped behind

Nordval. The gun lay flat against the small of his back, underneath his jacket. "Look in the file labeled 'Nigeria.'"

Nordval clicked open the file. "Wait a minute, Jerry. I thought you—"

Before he could finish the sentence, Insel gripped the Glock, visualized the approximate location of Nordval's cerebellum behind all the red hair, and fired. After Nordval slumped forward, Insel sat him up again, and fired another round through his heart. He grabbed the bottle of mid-level scotch, took a drink, and put the bottle in his briefcase. Then he wiped every surface he'd touched, retrieved the flash drive from the computer, and left as Nordval's blood continued to pool.

After a shower and a quick drive to see the commemoration of Lewis' and Clark's campsite and Sakakawea Reservoir, Lynn, Gene, Cheryl, and Greg returned to Nordval Oil Company's headquarters. They punched in the after-hours code he'd given them, a glass security door opened, and they rode the elevator to the fourth floor office.

"Hope he likes steak. Seems to be the only menu entrée here," Greg said.

Dag Nordval's office door was closed. Light shone under it.

Cheryl's knock echoed down the hall. No one answered.

"Is the door locked?" Gene asked.

Lynn tried it, and it swung open. She covered her mouth mid-scream, then gripped Greg's and Gene's arms.

"Get out of here!" Cheryl yelled. "Don't touch anything!"

Dag Nordval was slumped over his desk, a red puddle under his chair. A long, sticky thread of blood coursed from the back of his head, through his red beard, and onto his desk in a plate-sized pool of thick, congealed Jell-O.

# Twenty-Four

*North Dakota/Dallas*
*Saturday*

Williston police officers began questioning the four TriCoast employees Friday night, but on the advice of Cheryl and Tyree Bickham, TriCoast's general counsel, they declined to answer until Tyree and Mark Shepherd, TriCoast's security chief, arrived early Saturday morning.

"They said it was only two shots, heart and head," Lynn told Mark when they met for breakfast. "Dag's cell phone and wallet weren't taken."

"Sounds like a professional hit, not a pissed-off husband," Mark responded.

Cheryl nodded.

"There was so much blood," Lynn said.

"Head wounds bleed like crazy."

By mid-morning Cheryl, Gene, Lynn, and Greg returned to the Williston police department with Mark and Tyree, wrestler-turned-lawyer.

Their fingerprints in Nordval's office and the coincidence of their appointment to the time of his apparent murder prompted numerous questions until Lynn remembered Nordval's comment about meeting a job candidate. Following extensive interrogation, with several interruptions from Tyree, the officers had them write down everything they remembered. Mark and Tyree noted the names and phone numbers of the officers.

When Lynn and her co-workers returned to their hotel, a ghostly snow fog had closed in.

"I'm exhausted. I barely slept, and it wasn't just because of the truck noise," Lynn told Mark. Gene and the others had returned to their rooms, allowing her to speak more freely with him.

"I'm bringing in the FBI. I want Cheryl with you as much as possible."

"Who from the FBI? And I need privacy. She's already with me most of the time. I can't have her living in my house, unless she can help with the wedding plans."

"Jim Cutler. Cheryl *is* helping you with the wedding plans. She's keeping you alive. But no, she doesn't have to move in with you. Not yet, anyway."

"As long as Cutler listens to me this time," she said. A few months ago, when she'd been suspicious that apparent refinery accidents were really sabotage, Cutler hadn't believed her.

"You have cred with him now."

The fog cleared early in the afternoon. A few minutes after the corporate jet took off from Williston, she slept until they touched down in Tulsa to drop off Gene.

When the plane landed in Dallas in the late afternoon, she, Cheryl, and Greg said good-bye to one another and the pilots.

At her house she dropped her luggage, pushed a week's worth of mail to the side, then changed into shorts and a T-shirt. Three miles into her run on the White Rock Lake path, she didn't expect to see her father's pulmonologist. But when they both stopped for water at one of the fountains, she re-introduced herself to a doctor she'd seen many times with her father.

He was her height, intense eyes focused right on hers. His legs were striped with black hair matted by sweat to his skin.

"Yes, of course I remember your father. Let's run this last mile together. Looks like you can keep up."

*Typical runner's bluntness.* "I appreciate the care you've given him."

"I wish there was more we could do for him. Ready?"

"Let's go." She wondered if he would tell her anything op-timistic.

"One option is a lung transplant, but he's too frail to be high on the list and a group of cystic fibrosis kids are above him. He's stopped smoking and is on oxygen, two of the best things he could be doing. He's already lived more than four years since the diagnosis, well above average."

*Seems like he's trying to placate me.* She increased her pace. "But he's deteriorating. Can't he get lung reduction surgery?" Her breath came harder, and not just due to the faster pace.

Instead of answering, the doctor shook his head.

Lynn said, "He doesn't panic, but he won't eat much because then he can't breathe. Even chewing tires him out. He can hardly get up and walk." She heard pleading in her voice.

"I know. Take a deep breath and hold it as long as you can. Then try to take another one. That's all the breath your father has."

She followed his instructions, and her lungs burned. She slowed a few steps when she finally exhaled and gasped, "It feels like I'm drowning."

He sped up the pace. "Most emphysema patients can only exhale twenty to forty percent of the air normal for people their age. A healthy person's lungs contain many tiny alveoli. Their to-tal surface area is huge, so oxygen can get into the blood easily. You're an engineer. You understand surface area."

"Yes, though I'm usually talking heat exchangers, not lungs." She pushed floppy stray hair behind her ears and wiped her face with a bandana.

The doctor was breathing easily. "In people who smoke, lungs change. Walls separating the alveoli break down, so air spaces combine to make larger, but fewer, air sacs." He looked at her to see if she understood.

She nodded and they rounded a corner. "Go on."

"The total surface area of these air sacs is much smaller than the surface area of the original alveoli. The lungs transfer less oxygen to the bloodstream, so he gets short of breath. His lungs have also lost elasticity, which is important in keeping airways open. More patients die from cardiovascular causes, stroke, and coronary heart disease than from respiratory causes."

Being slammed with the bitter news made her feel as if she'd strapped twenty-pound weights onto each of her legs. She tried to breathe more deeply, and felt tears moistening her eyes.

The marker to their right indicated a half mile. *Not much time left running with the doctor.* "Why can't he get lung reduction surgery? I understand it helps." She asked him again because she wanted his honest answer. She'd read the surgery could triple the exhale volume of air, giving relief to patients like her father.

The backwater on their left was populated by ugly white-and-black turkeys that were somehow able to swim.

"We only do the surgery on patients we think..." he paused for a deep breath as they pounded over the bridge, "...will survive. I'm sorry."

It was if he'd pushed her over the bridge into the reeking water with the ugly birds. "Is there anything we can do?"

The sweaty doctor shook his head. "The disease is throughout his lungs, not concentrated in the upper lobes. His odds are the worst."

Leaving him, she walked slowly up the hill back to her house. *Goddamn. It's foolish to think I'll find hope on a White Rock Lake running path. But Dad has to live a few more years. I know he likes Marika and Matt. I want them to know him and love him as a grandfather.*

⁂

After showering and exchanging dirty clothes for clean ones at the laundry, Lynn called her father's cell phone. Hermosa, her father's caregiver, answered and said he would likely be awake in another half hour.

*What will I do with Hermosa when—*

Lynn's phone rang.

Cy said, "We're swimming this evening. Are you coming over?"

"Absolutely. But I'm going by Dad's house first."

Her father's house was a few blocks from hers. Hermosa had left the front door unlocked for her. The air conditioner blew cold. Cool air reduced humidity, which helped him breathe. Lynn found the sweater she kept in his hall closet.

She got a glass of water in the kitchen and returned to the living room to help Hermosa position her father's wheelchair and oxygen tank. For a few minutes he continued to breathe hard from the move, the tube taped to his nose fluttering with the effort.

Lynn hugged him. His straining rib cage reminded her of the conversation with his doctor.

Hermosa retreated to her own bedroom to give them privacy.

"Your sister?" he asked, using as few words as he could.

"I saw Ceil in Paris. We had dinner together. She's well." *No point in telling him about being excluded from the work dinner, or what had happened to the bodyguard.* There was only so much bad news he could absorb. In some ways she measured her words as much as he did.

"And yes, I've talked to Jesse. The Cherokees are still in the game to buy the refinery. In fact, I just got back from North Dakota. There's more oil there we can use to supply it." She tried to sound upbeat. She also wouldn't talk about discovering Dag Nordval's dead body.

"Need surf—" His question broke off into a cough.

"Surfactant? Drag reducer? We will. I haven't talked to the pipeline guys yet about it," she said. Her father had worked on pipeline inspections around the country. Despite having no formal classes he had learned a lot of engineering. Drag reducer was sometimes injected into oil to lessen its friction and so allow it to flow faster in pipelines.

He smiled. "I need surf—"

It was if he knew she'd talked to his doctor. His body was feeble but his mind was quick. "You mean for your lungs?"

He nodded. Another problem he faced was the loss of his body's own biological surfactant in his lungs, something that acted like a lubricant to minimize friction. Although he had medicines to help, the absence of surfactant meant his alveoli stuck together, tearing them even more.

"When I'm up in Tulsa, I think about the old days of the oil business," she said, trying to distract him. "Glenn Pool must have been quite a find." She was referring to Oklahoma's first big oil discovery.

"Finally, Cushing."

She nodded, and stared at his cuticles. They were blue from not enough oxygen. His fingers had clubbed at the tips, like spoons, another symptom of his slow suffocation.

"Yes, Cushing's the heart. My colleagues at NYMEX always talk about it," she said. *Is he ready to die? Does he want to?* It didn't seem like it, but she couldn't bring herself to ask him. *Not today.*

Cushing was the center of an oil pipeliner's universe. Its millions of barrels of storage tanks sprouted pipelines to all parts of the country. Her father had spent months there working on projects, one reason for his long posting to Tulsa. Cushing had become even more important as a storage and transit hub with the increased oil production in several nearby states.

His head fell forward as he slept. Lynn eased the warm plastic of his oxygen tube to one side and kissed him good-bye, then spoke to Hermosa.

She drove the five miles to Cy's house. They had decided she'd move in with him after the wedding, and sell her place. Eventually they would buy another house together once the kids—*they'll be my kids*, she thought fondly—had become accustomed to her more constant presence in their lives.

But, she would be further away from her father. When he died, she'd be faced with selling not one, but two, houses. Three, if she and Cy built and moved.

She thought about the afternoon ahead. When married to

Keith, she'd had two painful miscarriages. She and Cy wanted children. While she couldn't wait long, she wanted a few months to settle in with him, Matt, and Marika, and for her father to feel the joy of the bigger family. In the meantime, her hours with Cy's children had been sudden immersion into the pleasure of parenting offset by the tension of constant alertness, as well as the challenges of finding common interests with a two- and a seven-year-old.

Still, when she swung open the gate to Cy's backyard and saw the pool, it was a glimpse of paradise. Cy was standing in the shallow end, catching little Matt as he jumped off the steps. Marika splashed nearby, diving as effortlessly as a dolphin.

Cy turned to her and grinned. "I figure Matt has fifteen minutes before we make another trip to the bathroom."

"I'm really glad to see you," Lynn said. *And Cy, I love you but I hope Matt gets potty-trained before I move in.*

As if he read her mind, Cy said, "Takes boys until they're three, so the Mattman is on schedule."

"Is he still in the loaders-and-dump trucks phase this week?" Lynn asked, citing Matt's interest in all things construction-related.

"Now it's dinosaurs, based on the books he's picking."

Lynn looked at Marika and smiled. "What's next, Marika?"

"Animals with sharp teeth!" she shouted. "Legos! Then the best of all, horses!" She grabbed a water gun and aimed it at Lynn.

"My hint to change clothes."

When she returned, Cy signaled his approval of her bikini with applause. Marika shouted, "Lynn, you look adorable!"

"You are too sweet," Lynn said. *Marika is a great salesgirl for motherhood . . . today, anyway.*

Matt rotated his arms to make big splashes. "Lynn, look! I'm a compeller."

She laughed. "I know a lot of people just like that."

Cy hugged him. "You mean a *propeller?*"

"Yeah," the two-year-old announced.

Lynn moved into deeper water, her toes barely touching bottom, still facing Cy and Matt on the steps. Suddenly, she was grabbed from behind, an arm around her neck and a hand over her eyes.

"Guess who?" the seven-year-old girl shouted.

She tried not to lose control when the girl climbed onto her shoulders, pushing Lynn under the water. She twisted away from the lock of the girl's knees around her head, swam to the surface, and gulped air, letting the panic of being trapped underwater flow away. Then she turned to Marika and said, "Please don't do that. You could hurt someone."

The pain in the seven-year-old's eyes was immediate. "Did I scare you? I'm sorry."

Cy glared at his daughter, but Lynn shook her head at him. "She had an instinctive reaction, but it's a dangerous one."

"People do it to me in the hallway at school," Marika said, her mouth still turned down in a frown. "We always try to guess who it is. Usually I can tell by how sweaty their hands are."

"Not in the pool, Marika," Cy said.

"Okay, I promise."

Next to Cy, Matt tripped on a diving bar and slipped underwater. Cy hoisted him up and the two-year-old started to cry.

Cy grinned at Lynn. "Did I say swimming was relaxing?"

"It's like being a brand new firefighter," she said. "Long periods of waiting punctuated by moments of terror."

Finally everyone calmed. She snapped goggles onto her head and swam to the hot tub, where water sluiced into the pool. The cascade was a smooth, clear wave, an unbroken ribbon. She put her hand into its silken uniformity. Then diving under, she watched the cascade hit the surface and launch wedges of iridescent, pearly bubbles. Each was perfectly formed, yet the patterns varied.

Lynn floated up and glanced at Cy playing with Matt and talking to Marika. She was glad to be spending the night.

# Twenty-Five

*Dallas/Lyon/Tahlequah*
*Sunday*

> *"We don't know what we want, but we are ready to*
> *bite somebody to get it." —Will Rogers*

The perfect evening with Cy had ended with urgent lovemaking. Before they fell asleep, he held her and said, "I can't wait to get married."

But even that wasn't enough to dislodge a persistent nightmare. Lynn saw her mother, emaciated, face contorted with pain from the last stages of cancer. Day after day, her sister had fed and bathed their mother as their mother willed herself not to cry out. Waking from her dream it seemed to Lynn she could still hear her sister talking softly to their mother, as slowly as one would to a baby.

The dream always prompted the question of what more she could do for her father. She had no answer this morning, only the doctor's grim words from yesterday. She sighed, then tickled Cy's toes to wake him for the few seconds it would take to deliver her message. "I promised Mike we'd run together. Then I have to meet security guys for breakfast and the board has scheduled a late-morning meeting, even though it's Sunday and some of them don't like to miss church. I'll be back in four or five hours. Love you."

"Love you, too," he said, and rolled over. When her boss, Mike Emerson, had requested she run with him, it surprised her because Mike was, at best, a leisurely runner. Any time she could get with him was important, but she was anxious about a one-on-one in a venue where he would already be physically uncomfortable. *Have I offended Burl Travis more than usual? Did he convince the board that no woman would be effective negotiating with the Saudis and so none fit the executive vice president's job? Will the board tell me to leave my job the same way I put Riley on notice? If so, how will I afford Dad's care?*

Although it was September, the days hadn't cooled enough to run later than nine in the morning. They were to meet at the Cooper Aerobics Center, founded by Kenneth Cooper, father of aerobics. The 30-acre center shared boundaries with the eruv of a nearby Orthodox neighborhood.

Cy had convinced her to join the Cooper since it was near his house. "You're already part of the sweaty set. Make it official," he'd said. It seemed part of his plan to settle the where-to-live question by persuading her to move in with him. On nights she stayed over, the Cooper was convenient, particularly once Cy bought her a bicycle. He'd picked a sleek racing Trek and had the tires coated to resist flats.

She rode streets quieter than those of her dense East Dallas neighborhood and navigated a hectic crossing at Preston Road. She met Mike and the bodyguards in the Cooper's parking lot, their start and finish point. The bodyguards had cleared the route, which included an overlap for a few miles with a fund-raiser 5K run. It was a gentle course and she would take it slow for Mike, another reason she'd exercised vigorously yesterday.

She was surprised the thickset CEO initially kept up with her. She wasn't surprised at the easy stride of their security guards. Mike's was a man who looked like he'd won a few boxing matches. Cheryl appeared as steady and refreshed as she had the afternoon before when they'd split up at the airport.

The guards ran a few discreet yards behind them.

They were soon in a crowd of people on the 5K route. She'd planned this part of the run for the motivational pace and the spectators' humorous support.

Sure enough, one man held up a sign reading, *If you can't be a good example, be a horrible warning.*

Another man offered *Free mouth-to-mouth resuscitation (ladies only)*, while a woman held a sign that read *Run faster. They're almost out of beer at the finish line.*

Mike was still chortling when she said, "I'm doing a strider. I'll be back."

"Not another one," he groaned. "I won't even try to keep up this time. My legs aren't as long as yours." She waved to her bodyguard and dashed ahead through a gap in the crowd. Head up, legs pumping, she ran as fast as she could until she couldn't open her mouth wide enough for air. Forty, eighty, a hundred yards. Crowds seemed to close in on her, jarring her elbows. And…stop. She turned and jogged slowly back toward Mike. Cheryl shook her head at Lynn. "Please don't do that again."

"You…don't…know…how good it feels," Lynn said, her breath slowing.

As they cleared the crowd and turned away from the 5K route, Mike looked down at the heart monitor readout on his wrist. "One-sixty. Not bad for me… Glad you talked me into buying this monitor. But seems you're always talking me into buying something… Only last time it was two hundred twenty-five million for the Centennial refinery."

"Well worth it."

"Even if you…almost got yourself…killed over it." Mike was gasping.

"So if you're worried, why didn't you have Sara's group sell the Tulsa refinery instead of me? She'd put a price-earnings ratio on her own mother if necessary. And make her mother feel good about it." Lynn considered Sara tough, fair-minded, and just bloodless enough. In other words, perfect for the job of TriCoast chief financial officer.

Then she noticed Mike was wheezing like her father on a bad emphysema day.

"Selling the refinery will be...growth experience... Stop running. I have to...walk," he gasped.

She stopped and turned to face him. "Mike, do I have to lay out my résumé? I'm thirty-eight, EVP of domestic refining for TriCoast, dedicated my life to the company, and as you just recalled, almost got killed for it a few months ago. I don't *need* a growth experience."

"You do if you want my job." He mopped his forehead with the sleeve of his sweatshirt.

"Me? Me for CEO?" The shock was sudden. "You're awfully young to think of retiring, aren't you? Or are you throwing me a bone after the disastrous meeting with the prince?"

"I wouldn't have risked it if I didn't think you could wind up as CEO, Lynn."

"I'm honored you think so. But in a crowd with Burl, Riley, and Vandervoost, you were a cheering squad of one, and a whispering cheerleader at that. Besides, I'd never get the board's support."

"Don't underestimate yourself or your support. Now, for the bad news. You have to keep Riley on the project."

"After his performance with the prince? The roadblocks he threw? His cultural flat-footedness? He hasn't done well getting along with Jesse Drum and the Cherokees, either. You're kidding, right?"

Mike shook his head.

"Having Riley on the job is worse than having no one. I figured he'd be busy with headhunters looking for a job. Too bad Burl Travis is offering him a platform to screw my career." Mike was breathing hard, so Lynn kept talking. "Riley's only been at TriCoast a few months since the merger with Centennial and he's already put himself on thin ice with too many of my employees.

Young women, mainly. Some of them are your and my future best players. We need their skills, not their lawsuits."

She wanted to run ahead again to separate herself from the unpleasant news about Riley. Sweat trickled to a new place on her neck.

"I noticed you already recruited one of our younger analysts."

"I really need him since I've lost Preston for a while." She hadn't seen Preston since she'd put him on a plane to Dallas to get help for his gambling. He was in a treatment center that didn't allow visitors.

Mike nodded in sympathy.

She stole a glance at her own heart monitor. *Down to a hundred. Not a vigorous workout.*

He opened his mouth to speak, but she shook her head. "I'll have the Tulsa refinery bids ready for the board within two weeks."

"Lynn-"

"Know why? Because I have crude supply negotiations coming up, and a wedding to plan."

⁂

Simone Tierney would never consider working at her office on the weekend. That was a habit for stressed-out Americans. But among all of her Interpol cases, the one that seemed to link Amanda Parsifal and the Saudi bodyguard occupied her mind, as she sautéed mushrooms and braised veal.

Lyon's fall weather was crisp and rainy. She'd spoken with Cutler, a brash, stubborn, but insightful FBI agent with whom she'd consulted before. He told her about Dag Nordval's apparent murder and the Molotov cocktail thrown at Lynn Dayton in Los Angeles.

Simone discounted the gasoline bomb: it was showy and amateurish. Any number of groups could have done it.

But Nordval's death was troubling, and she noticed TriCoast civilians had been nearby, just as with the Saudi bodyguard. *Different ones, though.* She had spoken to Mark Shepherd, then looked into their backgrounds. Lynn had speeding tickets, Riley Stevens and Mike Emerson had sealed divorce judgments, the others similar minor offenses. She also knew from Ceil about Lynn and her sister's encounter with Robert Guillard in Paris, and how they'd almost been collateral casualties. *Was the killing of the Saudi bodyguard, which also occurred in Paris, somehow linked to the followers of Robert Guillard?* But they weren't sophisticated with weapons.

*What about Lynn's bodyguard, Cheryl Wilkins?* Simone was certain Mark had screened her, but even more seemed to be happening around Lynn Dayton now that Cheryl was there. Was Cheryl ensuring herself job security by arranging the encounters? The woman's background seemed solid—served in Iraq, then the Coast Guard. Yet a few months ago one of TriCoast's security guards had helped plot to sabotage Ship Channel refineries. *Maybe Mark's screening was poor.*

Shepherd had told her that Riley Stevens was on notice to leave TriCoast. Tierney sighed as she poured herself a glass of wine. None of them showed the requisite sophistication with weapons or poisons. If anything, they seemed *un peu naïve* about the dangers that accompanied the worldwide trade of oil, in which the stakes could be the rise and fall of entire countries.

⁕

Jesse felt his eyebrows bunching together as he typed a report for the BIA. It would go to the chief and the tribal council first. Next year's budget would be over half a billion dollars. Most of it came from the casinos; some of it would go back into CIG's businesses, and most of it into health and social services for tribal members. *No wonder so many imposters keep trying to claim Cherokee citizenship*, he thought.

Carla was sitting across from him, ready to explain the numbers as she finished charts summarizing the totals. Although still new to the job, she'd picked up the routine with no hesitation or error after Jimmy Deerinwater's death.

She must have been thinking about her predecessor, too, because she asked, "Hear any more about Jimmy? Driving drunk wasn't like him."

Jesse shook his head. "No coroner's report yet. Another week or so, I've been told."

She adjusted her glasses. "He and I went to Sequoyah High School. He was ahead of me a few years, though. I've been by to see his family."

Jesse stopped and looked at her. "How are they?"

She shook her head. "They're so broken up they can barely talk. He was the oldest son and he'd made good."

He nodded. "Same as when I went to see them." He resumed typing on the computer's keyboard. "You've been an auditor, right? You like the Adela investors, Pete and Keith? Think they're good for the money they promised?"

"Yes, I was an auditor, but auditors spot-check."

"What do you mean?" Jesse tried not to stare at the brilliant luster of Carla's hair, focusing on her eyes instead.

She used her fingers to tick off, "One, we rely on them to give us the correct numbers; two, we can't actually see much of the information—it's remote from us; three, they're biased—so is everyone—because they want their numbers to look good; four, there's so much data. She tapped her thumb to make the final point. "Five, some of the transactions are complex."

He shrugged. "No offense, but you're giving me auditor CYA. What do you really think?"

"Pete and Keith gave me stats on their other projects. They get a sweet rate of return, fifty percent or more," she said. "But helping us buy this refinery doesn't match their usual business model."

He stopped typing and looked at her. "How so?"

"This is a big, capital-intensive project. Refineries suck up the dough because they have to operate at such large volumes. Keith and Pete usually buy into small, one-owner companies. They cut costs and improve efficiencies, then sell the companies and pocket hefty profits. They don't stay in for the long haul or commit big dollars for upgrades."

"Maybe they're changing their business model."

"Maybe." She sounded dubious.

He looked up again to see her smiling at him. He wanted to touch her face. By her expression, she seemed to want that, too.

Instead he sighed and looked down, paralyzed. She was doing good work. He remembered how vehemently she had complained of Riley's advances. He couldn't afford to lose her by scaring her off with a harassment concern, real or imagined. If she did like him—an image of her unbuttoning her blouse flashed through his mind—surely there was another job she could take so he wasn't her boss.

*But if the feeling was mutual, would it really be harassment?* He sighed. It was all too complicated.

"You okay? What's on your mind?"

He jumped a little. "The budget. Operating expenses for the new casino and hospital were higher than I expected."

She shut down her computer. "I just sent you the graphs. We're ready to talk to the council. See you tomorrow."

"No canoeing planned, right?" he asked, referring to her near-drowning a few days earlier.

"Don't worry. I won't get into another canoe until after we make these presentations." She smiled at him again, packed up her laptop, and left.

He watched her from the window. *Probably finds Pete or Keith or another young man much more attractive than me. Hell, I served with Pete's father in the Vietnam War.* It was one of many reasons he'd given Pete and Keith a hearing when, like so many others, they wanted to invest with the Cherokee Nation.

# Twenty-Six

*Dallas/Chicago*
*Sunday*

> *"One of the cardinal sins in warfare is losing contact*
> *with the enemy." —US Army Colonel Paul Hughes*

After the run with Mike Emerson—a slow jog really—Lynn met Mark Shepherd and Jim Cutler for breakfast at Barbec's, near the south end of White Rock Lake. From their athletic builds, it was apparent Mark and Jim seldom indulged themselves as they were this morning: beer batter biscuits with a side of gravy.

"Best biscuits in the world," Jim said between bites, "and I've spent time in Georgia, Alabama, and Mississippi, so I know."

"They're nothing that about five thousand crunches won't make up for," Mark said.

"And worth every one," Lynn replied, wiping her lips. She had ordered eggs and one biscuit, which she ate a few bites at a time. Both men had already eaten three biscuits each.

They kept their voices low. With a few prompts from Mark, Lynn told Cutler about finding Dag Nordval.

"Have you heard of a woman named Amanda Parsifal?" Cutler asked.

"I've seen her newsletters, though not in the last week or so. Why?"

"As we discussed, I brought in Simone Tierney with Interpol

after the prince's bodyguard was assassinated in Paris. Tierney mentioned the name. Woman was poisoned with ricin."

Lynn grimaced. "That's awful!"

"Lynn," Jim said, "if there's one thing I learned about you the last time we talked, it's that you're either paranoid or observant."

"Is that a question?" Lynn felt her cheeks flame.

"Why don't you tell me everything else that's been happening, even if it doesn't seem connected." Cutler stirred his coffee.

"I'll jump in here," Mark said. "We don't have complete reports back from the medical examiner yet, but first there was Tom Martin at the Tulsa refinery. When we were in Paris, you told us Gene had been notified by the ME's office that he was poisoned. Turns out he died from aphaxia—he stopped breathing."

"What else do you know now?" Lynn asked.

"It appears to have been brought on by batrachotoxin," Mark replied.

"The word toxin has a bad sound to it." Lynn frowned.

"Batrachotoxin blocks neuromuscular transmission," Cutler explained. "It paralyzes muscles, including the ones needed for breathing."

"That's horrible! And it doesn't sound like something I'd find in a drugstore."

"No, you have to grow it," Mark said. "That is, grow the poison dart frog that's the source. And be practically a surgeon to handle it. Stuff is on the frog's skin to keep it from being eaten by its enemies. It only takes a few grains to kill a human."

"What the hell?" Lynn said. "Where'd the poison dart frog come from?"

"Probably someone imports exotic pets. So yeah, the poison must have been sprinkled on the doughnut Tom ate," Jim Cutler said.

Lynn shook her head while she gathered her composure. "After that, Gene and I tried to save Jimmy Deerinwater on the turnpike when he ran his car into a bridge abutment, but we couldn't. And let's not forget some asshole tried to run me down in a Denali."

"We talked about the Saudi bodyguard. Neither of us witnessed it, though," Mark told Jim.

"You know Preston Li is in rehab, right?" Lynn asked Jim.

He nodded. "Seems to be a personal issue, but I'll bear it in mind."

"He said he had a cousin who died in the Murrah bombing in Oklahoma City, so being in Oklahoma reminded him of it. The casinos seemed to rope him in, more than most people. Somehow, he got an unlimited line of credit. But Preston's gambling never screwed him up like that before."

"Seen it many times. It was only a question of when, not if," Cutler said. "What else?"

Mark interjected. "Gene told me he's missing a man, his distillation foreman. He might have gone AWOL over a girlfriend, but it looks suspicious."

Lynn nodded. "If Gene's worried, so am I. You heard about the crazy man at the river?"

Cutler nodded. "Carla reported it to the tribal police and they loop us in on most things. They seem to believe it was either a meth head, or someone defending a lab. Lot of that around there, out in the sticks. But yes, awfully coincidental and again, involves your group of people."

"Someone threw a Molotov cocktail at me in Los Angeles. Stuff like that has happened before—they always think they're making a point because they use gasoline."

"It may not be connected to everything else," Jim said, "but I'm sorry you were the target. We've learned there was some sort of flash mob. The thrower was caught and is in jail, but it appears he was taking orders and wasn't the organizer."

"And that brings us back to Nordval, which looks professional," Mark said.

"Are you doing anything that would make TriCoast a particular target?" Cutler asked Lynn.

"No. The board wants me to sell the Tulsa refinery, so we're talking to people about that." Lynn described her meetings with the Cherokee Investment Group, the Saudi prince, North Seas Resources, and Dag Nordval. "Representatives from Sansei, the people who were rumored to be financing Robert Guillard, were supposed to meet us in Paris, too, but Mark here cancelled the meeting after the bodyguard was killed. Beyond that, we're making gasoline, diesel, and jet, like we always do. Upgrading to meet the new specs, so we have contractors in and out."

"You've started selling jet fuel to the Israelis. In the so-called brains of some crazies that would make you a target," Cutler said.

"Sure," she replied, "someone out there could have his shorts in a knot. When you're talking about oil or gasoline, people often do." She put down her coffee cup. "That's all I can remember. Gentlemen, I have a meeting downtown in half an hour. Keep me posted and I'll do the same for you."

"Cheryl should be accompanying you as much as possible when you travel. We're paying her to keep you safe," Mark said.

Lynn sighed. "Got it."

The sky outside the glass walls of Lynn's office was blue. She shot free throws at her basketball goals, making most of them. *Dirk Nowitzki against the LA Lakers in game 3 of the Western Conference semifinals.* On rebound the ball slapped against the hardwood floor, the part not covered by an Oriental rug. Mike wasn't around to object to the noise. *Wonder if he meant what he said about my candidacy for CEO.*

Since she had kept up from the road via phone and computer, she was surprised at the large number of reports piled on her desk, but most were annual reports for other companies, put together by the planning group for competitor analysis. Preston would have been heading up that research, too, she thought. She wondered when she would get to see him, or if he would even want to return to TriCoast.

She looked over project proposals that'd come in the last few days and compared them. The projects had already been approved by her refinery managers, so hers was a final review. Three were desulfurizers necessary for the tighter diesel fuel specifications. Some of her refineries were selling their diesel against natural gas to their large fleet customers and required the cleanest possible fuel.

She was surprised when Mark Shepherd stepped into the office. "A couple of questions and I wanted to confirm with you without bringing them up in front of Jim. They're on my mind. North Dakota. It was a professional hit." His tone was serious. "It was also a message, and it hasn't been the first. Who did you piss off?"

"No one. Why do you act as if Dag Nordval's death is my fault?"

"I'm not saying it is."

"Then don't jump on me for doing my job." The traveling of the last two weeks caught up with Lynn all at once and her eyelids felt like cotton had been glued on their insides.

"Lynn, is there anything you could have done differently?"

Guilt bolted through her. Her calves knotted with cramps. She stood up to stretch them. Shepherd's gaze followed her as she paced.

"No. "

"You're in a situation with a person, or people, who are ruthless."

"What do they want?"

He shrugged. "Beats me, but we have to find out before you're next in the morgue."

⬦

"You may have heard the board of Chestnut Oil, one of our competitors, replaced its CEO and CFO, who have resigned. The board calls it a comprehensive change to the company's business plan. So in other words, they fired the bastards and decided to start following the law." Sara Levin, TriCoast's CFO, had opened the executives' meeting. "You guys do your safety talks. This is my safety talk. I'm reminding you to keep me informed of material changes in your business at all times. I can't spring surprises on our investors. And if the SEC discovers there's something you haven't told us, well, neither Mike nor I look good in one of those orange prison jumpsuits."

"Tell us how you really feel, Sara," David Jenkins responded. Jenkins was TriCoast's EVP for domestic drilling. With the growth in onshore shale drilling, his status and his budget had doubled.

Lynn sat at a long table in TriCoast's headquarters building with Sara, Mike Emerson, Jenkins, and several others. Mike's face was still ruddy from their morning run.

The company's EVP of international exploration, Sid Walker, and the EVP of European refining, Henry Vandervoost, were on line by secure video link from Dubai and Rotterdam, respectively.

"These shale plays are your basic can of whoop-ass," Jenkins said, "they're so prolific."

"Done with your rock talk?" Sara asked.

"I have a show at the end of the meeting. It would be good for our investors to see it, too,"

"Our investors? Jenkins, I love it when you suck up to me." Sara winked at him.

"I'll go next," Lynn said. *Might as well get this over with while they're in a good mood.* "All our refineries are on track to meet the upcoming sulfur regulations. We've installed new hydrotreaters at Houston and New Jersey on schedule per the budget we talked about last time."

All the gazes directed at her were intense. "We're taking bids on the Tulsa refinery from several groups. It has become even more valuable as the oil production Jenkins talked about —both shale and non-shale—has increased. All those folks need nearby refining capacity."

"What happened in North Dakota?" Jenkins flipped a pen into the air. "Jeez, I heard you walked in on a dead guy."

"Yes, it really shook me up, to be honest. The Williston police are investigating." *No need to mention that the FBI and Interpol are also probing.*

"Wouldn't it be better if you auctioned the refinery off like a lease sale?" Jenkins asked.

"A simple auction would make us look desperate. We wouldn't get the full value our shareholders deserve. We have serious bidders and we're receiving solid offers."

Henry Vandervoost, still a prisoner of his old-fashioned haircut, said, "Well, any further discussions with the Saudi prince stopped when his bodyguard was killed."

*As usual, Henry's dropping a stinking mess into the middle of the discussion.* "This is a rumor-filled business. I haven't had any official communication but I'm hoping to re-engage with them soon." She looked at Mike, who nodded almost imperceptibly.

"Hey, you know, that nighttime dinner...they didn't want you or any other woman there. Maybe they're talking to Riley instead," Henry suggested.

"Henry, give it a rest," Sara said, in a tone everyone knew meant *fuck off.* "I'm positive if such communication occurred, Burl or Riley would immediately inform Lynn."

"I hope so," Lynn agreed. *Might as well play the card and up the pressure on Burl Travis.* "I understand Burl may be trying to get us another hearing with the Saudis. He says his connections in the kingdom are excellent, so we'll see."

"But Lynn, all this stuff happening around you. You're Typhoid Mary. I've actually had people ask me not to bring you to meetings," Jenkins said. "Especially the guys in North Dakota. They think you're poison."

"I've talked to Mark Shepherd about my own safety. All I can say is investigations are underway. I don't carry a gun, but I have a bodyguard at the appropriate times. Thank you for your concern." She smiled at Jenkins, because his comments had not been about her safety.

"So I hear your ex-husband is part of one of the companies bidding," Henry said.

*Wish I could shut Henry up.* "Yes, and I take it as a compliment to Gene's well-run operation at the Tulsa refinery."

"So will Keith add ten percent to the price because he still has the hots for you?" Sara asked.

Lynn's face burned. *Supports me one moment, turns on me the next.* "TriCoast's negotiating position won't be affected by my and Keith's former relationship. Although if he wants to add an extra fifteen or twenty percent bonus to the price I won't object."

"Lynn, if you're uncomfortable, Mike could assign someone else," Henry insisted.

"Meaning you?" Lynn said.

Mike laughed. "Lynn Dayton is the best person for the job. She's handling it just fine."

"Ready for the show?" Without waiting for an answer, Jenkins lowered screens on the walls, dimmed the lights and called up a program on his laptop. Suddenly the group was surrounded by three-dimensional bands of color. The bands were uneven, some intensely bright, most looking like peaks and valleys.

He smiled. "The small-screen version will be available as an app for your phones but I didn't want to bring the whole dog-and-pony. And no, Sara, I didn't blow my budget on a bunch of fancy animated graphics. But I do want to show you what it's like to be *inside* the Permian, the big West Texas play we're exploring and developing more intensely."

*Good trick*, Lynn thought. Jenkins' expenditures had pushed part of her own division's projects off the table.

He pointed to wider bands of black. "I've taken the liberty of highlighting the shale layers that have a larger oil density. We do the horizontal drilling and multi-stage fracturing similar to what we're doing in the Bakken. The Permian is more thoroughly delineated geology, though."

"How soon do you think this program will supply enough to feed our refineries at a minimum of thirty thousand barrels a day?" Lynn asked.

"Soon," Jenkins said, "if I don't go the way of ol' Dag Nordval."

He formed a pistol with his thumb and forefinger, put it to his ear, and dropped the hammer.

Lynn shook her head. "If you'd been the one to find him you'd know how much of a jerk you sound like."

"Yeah. Sorry." The dark figure of Jenkins moved to another wall and bands of color played across his jacket. "We have a seven-rig program running in the Permian. We'll be coming back to you and the board for more money because we'd like to do similar projects in the Ohio Utica and maybe the Colorado Niobrara."

"What are your proved reserves?" Sara asked. "That's all my bankers care about."

"Damn good. From this seven-rig program, I estimate we'll have between twenty and thirty million barrels in another eighteen months."

Mike and Sara nodded.

"Okay, Jenkins, to slop around a few clichés," Sara concluded, "as long as the price deck doesn't start sucking wind, you're in business for more iron."

⁂

While I waited, I checked options and futures prices, and plugged them into some formulas. I needed a few more months of the forward strip to go positive so I could clear my personal debts. Then I'd be free. But if I was honest with myself, I knew I'd never be free. I wasn't free of my memories.

The Oak Street Beach in Chicago was windy and cold. But like the Vancouver slum where I'd met the Chechen, beggar that I was right now, it wasn't my decision where, or if, to meet this man.

Lake Michigan's waves had rippled the beach's trucked-in sand. Its palm trees were gone, hauled off for the winter and hibernating in Chicago Parks' storage until next summer.

At the assigned place I saw an ordinary-looking man with wires from ear buds trailing to an iPod in his pocket. For some stupid reason I wondered what bands he liked. I heard strains of Penikel and Torpedo Boyz.

He appeared to recognize me. "Allo." His accent was crisp. I couldn't place it but I was reminded of workers at the German hospital where I'd been sent to recover.

"The Chechen told me I'd find you here." The rule was no names.

He motioned me to walk with him along the cement path. He looked comfortable in the weather, as if he did indeed come from someplace north. The wind bit through my thin jacket. Everyone around us was dressed as I was, in shorts and light jackets, perhaps fantasizing this 45-degree day was still summer.

"Chechen. Is that what he told you?"

I shrugged. "Yes. But it's not my business to care."

He sped up, just enough to keep the pace uncomfortable. "But it is your business to complete assignments. Or should we make your mistakes public?" Assignment was his word for hit. I was on call to complete them until I paid back the money they'd lent me. Talk about usury.

"Your contract is clear. Two more and potentially two more after that," he said. "Should I take the assignments away from you?"

He was smoother than the Chechen. The Chechen had flashes of emotion; this man had none.

"There's no difficulty."

The volleyball nets hadn't been taken down yet, but only a few people were using them. Their strings flapped forlornly.

"Perhaps you are too close to your assignments. You like them?" He shrugged in what appeared to be a learned gesture. "Doesn't matter. You don't meet the contract, you suffer, not me. The contract will be completed, even if I must be the one to do so."

Despite the chilly air, a small food-and-drink shack was still open. We went inside, out of the cold Lake Michigan wind. I bought two bottles of beer and we picked chairs against the wall. We must have looked like old friends sitting side-by-side, instead of the new acquaintances we were.

"So you must be someone who sees all glasses as half-empty," I said. It was a lame joke but I was tired of seriousness.

"What do you mean?" he asked, pouring beer into his glass.

"It means you only see the negative."

"Very well, I'll play this game. What do I think of your assessment? I'm someone who believes a glass is fragile and temporary." He stood up to leave and dropped the glass to the cement. It shattered into a hundred razor-sharp pieces.

# Twenty-Seven

*Dallas*
*Sunday*

"We've only got time for one. Wedding planner or state fair?"

"State Fair!" Marika and Matt shouted in unison, twisting and giggling.

"I thought so." Lynn turned to Cy. "If you get them ready, I'll do battle with Attila the Honey. You owe me, and you can't come back later and tell me you want to scale the wedding up again."

He hugged her.

When Lynn told the planner she needed to reschedule, the woman's predictions were not as sugarcoated as her accent. "Most weddings I do have a six-month lead. You have less than four weeks and this is the third time you've rescheduled. One more week and I can't help you. You'll be on your own. Honey, you're sounding awfully gummed-up. Sure you want to go through with this?"

"Please call me Lynn, not Honey. Am I sure I want to go through with what—having you plan?" But Lynn knew what she was asking.

"The wedding. The marriage. I've had clients delay, even after the invitations were printed and sent. It's always a good decision."

"You're supposed to help me, not make it more difficult."

"Skip the State Fair. You know what they say. When you're an adult time goes really fast, unless you're getting your kitchen remodeled or waiting for the dog to poop."

Lynn laughed. "We want our wedding simple and kid-friend-ly. No china, no poinsettias."

"See, now, those are the kinds of details I need to know, Hon-I mean, Lynn. It'll cost extra but I'll see what I can do. I can probably fit you in next week. How's Wednesday at 10 a.m.?"

*Smack in the middle of the work week. Has to be a test.* She finally got the Whippet to agree to meet the following Saturday.

Outside, Cy folded the stroller and adjusted Matt's car seat. He turned to her. "Wonder if his car seat fits in your Porsche."

"We'll find out soon."

"Not that I'd ask you to give it up for a car seat."

"I'm glad you're not even bringing up the issue." She sighed. "I'm sure Marika will enjoy driving the Porsche when she's six-teen."

"Now you're scaring me," Cy said.

"Let's go!" Marika said. "I'm hungry!"

Everything was drawn toward the Texas State Fair as if by gravity. The surrounding parking lots issued forth thousands of people, the trains hundreds more.

"What are we going to do first?" Marika asked. "I want to see the horses and the baby animals. And eat."

"How about the extreme rides? The bungee jump? The Fireball? The giant Ferris wheel?" Lynn knew what the answer would be.

Cy frowned and spoke before his kids could. "They're too young. Something could happen."

"Don't go on those rides by yourself, Lynn. We don't want anything to happen to you, either." Despite Marika's serious words, she hopped and jumped alongside.

The pang of guilt over stirring the girl's fears pierced Lynn. *Marika lost her mother at a much younger age than I did.*

Cy's wife, Matt's and Marika's mother, had been killed in a car accident with a drunk driver two years ago, not long after Matt had been born.

"How's your appetite for fried food on sticks?" Cy asked her as they pushed through the turnstiles and walked past barkers hawking all-purpose spot remover, phone cards, and plastic outdoor spas.

"Stick food like corny dogs?"

"And chocolate-covered key lime pie." He grabbed her arm, as excited as his kids. "I'm talking fried bananas, Tornado Taters, and fried salsa!" he exclaimed.

Lynn bought shaved ices for Marika and Matt, and Lemon Chills for Cy and herself. "First round's on me."

The crowd of people with whom they'd entered grew larger as they neared the animal barns. They stood in line at the children's zoo, and Marika shrieked happily when she petted the lambs and chicks.

Cy quietly said, "Don't let her spend too much time with the puppies. I'm not ready to get one."

"Cy, I have to tell you something."

"We're already married and I was asleep when it happened?"

"Keith's on the other side of this Tulsa refinery deal."

The name didn't register at first although the timing did. "So? Can't Mike give you a few weeks off to get married? Wait a minute. Your ex? Sure you're the best person to do it?"

He was voicing the same concerns she had faced from her fellow executives an hour ago. "Of course. In fact, I know him better than most so I can make a better deal. And it's my area of responsibility."

"Tell me, though. After all this time, have you thought of getting back together with him? Are you still attracted to him?" Cy was holding Matt against his chest, and the boy turned his face away from Lynn.

"No and no," she answered.

Cy's face reddened. "What if I don't believe you?"

She shrugged. "We had some fun times, and maybe he's a good person at heart. Just, by the end of the marriage every day was horrible. I couldn't trust him. So judge me by my actions. And call me anytime you're worried."

He nodded. "Where's Marika? Damn, where'd she go?"

They looked for her in the crowds of fairgoers for three of the longest panic-stricken minutes Lynn had ever lived. Finally, they found her in front of an awning-covered booth, watching the carnie ride the unrideable bicycle.

"You sounded like you were fighting with my dad, Lynn," the girl said. "I didn't want to hear it."

Lynn knelt and whispered in her ear, "Your dad is the best man in the whole world. I hope you know that, Marika."

She smiled and nodded.

The agricultural history of the fair was evident. So was its reputation as ground zero for fried food experiments. Lynn lingered over the ethanol-fueled tractors, comparing them with their diesel-powered cousins.

"You can call this market research instead of time off," Cy said to her, poking her in the ribs as he noticed her interest.

"Especially when we get to the auto show."

They made another stop for corn dogs and fried okra. Lynn wasn't surprised when Matt ate half a corny dog but pushed the vegetable onto the ground. She picked up the mush and threw it away.

In the next shed they saw hogs scrubbed pink, their big balls glistening.

Marika noticed them, too. "Oooh, gross."

Lynn whispered to Cy, "I know folks who think theirs are that size."

They sat on bleachers to watch the swine judging, pushing Matt's stroller back and forth.

"The hogs sound like garbage disposals," Cy said. The show ring was crowded with several big black and pink gelded swine that communicated their displeasure with insistent squeals and long, guttural grunts.

"But they're not," Lynn said, pointing out a line of slim, dog-like brown sows waiting for their turn in the ring.

Tapping the animals lightly with prods, rail-thin teen-agers guided sows and boars in front of an ever-pattering judge. Yellow-brown sawdust hid bits of meal the bigger hogs readily found. Each teenager took turns positioning his or her hog in front of a blue drape for a photo. One curried his pig with a brush and then applied the same brush to his own hair.

Back outside the swine judging shed, the smells of animal manure, sawdust, hot dogs, trash, turkey legs, and sweat permeated the air. The excitement of the country kids in the city was sweetly infectious as she listened to the raucous tunes of the midway rides, the jangly country bands, and the nonstop calls of the carnies and barkers.

They watched Frisbee-catching dogs, then escaped into icy air conditioning of the auto show. Lynn lingered over each display, noting gas mileage of the new models. She compared sports cars to her Porsche and decided she wasn't ready to trade.

Matt's squeals ended her reverie.

"More market research," she said to Cy, giving one of the sleekest cars a pat as he devoured the last stick of chocolate-covered key lime pie.

194

# Twenty-Eight

*Minneapolis*
*Sunday-Monday*

Gernot Insel didn't like multi-client projects. People usually came to him. But this time, he'd floated a proposal through his network to see whether his existing clients or new ones would sign on. Enough did to make the assignment worth his while.

Some in the consortium were overseas oil producers who wanted a tighter market for the gasoline their crude would make. A few figured a US ethanol shortage would mean refiners would have to buy more of their foreign-source ethanol. And, since corn was used to make ethanol, others wanted cheaper corn.

In the last few days he'd traveled between North Dakota and Chicago—he thought of the naïve fool he'd met on the Chicago lakefront—and now back to Minneapolis. Including a ride south into Iowa, he had located over a dozen ethanol plants. They were small. That was one reason he was charging so much, no economies of scale. But they were relatively unguarded.

He liked the elegant simplicity. He needed no dangerous chemicals. At each site, he disabled the cameras. Then he injected several gallons of water into the storage tanks. The water mixed into the ethanol, rendering it worthless for blending into gasoline. He made his rounds quickly, in two nights, to stay ahead of conversations the plant managers would have among themselves once they discovered the contamination.

Breaching the tanks had presented challenges, but those did not compare to the patience required to wait for the country's best ethanol engineers to meet at a conference. Between the hundred or so of them, they represented thousands of years of hard-to-replace experience. Reducing their numbers would stop new ethanol plants from being built and would halt maintenance on dozens of existing ones. Thus, more opportunities would arise for his international clients to sell their ethanol, or even their gasoline.

From websites he had tracked them to the Minneapolis suburb of Eden Prairie. The Americans did have their idyllic names, he thought. He was about to turn the suburb into less of a paradise.

He'd registered under an alias as the lone representative of a newly-incorporated European ethanol manufacturer and disguised himself with colored contacts, half-eye reading glasses, and a black toupee. He even sat through a tiresome day of presentations. That allowed him to find his targets and judge the most efficient approach. He got more pleasure than he expected when speakers at the conference repeatedly described new, surprise water contamination at their plants. His work.

After a day of observing the American engineers, the answer was simple. Even though they made ethanol and joked repeatedly about building "stills in the hills," they didn't drink much beer, wine, or liquor. However, they did drink coffee.

The hotel's camera placement was good, but not complete. Best of all, the food was put out in a dark, narrow hallway connecting the conference rooms.

In the evening, posing as one of the organizers, he called to confirm the next day's coffee delivery to the engineers' conference buffet.

In the morning, he changed toupees and added horn-rimmed glasses. When the giant silver urns were placed on the long table next to the croissants and bagels, he sat nearby, apparently just another tired businessman awaiting his morning caffeine fix in the half-dark. With forty minutes before the conference started, few people were around.

After the serving staff returned to the kitchen, he stumbled next to each urn, using his body to shield his movements from the hallway camera. Confident it would mix with the bitter coffee, he poured enough ricin concentrate into the urns to make the hot cups deadly.

He returned to his room to do what the Americans called "checking out." Unlike the engineers whose colleague he had pretended to be, his checkout would be temporary, not permanent.

# Twenty-Nine

*Tulsa*
*Monday*

On the flight to Tulsa Lynn used the airplane's wi-fi to read news and weather. A month of hurricane season remained before their dangers to her refineries and offshore oil supply would end.

She clicked through stories about major oil producing countries of Saudi Arabia, Iraq, and Nigeria. Gasoline consumption had bumped up over the Labor Day weekend, as usual. But when she read two related headlines, her blood chilled.

She reached Mark Shepherd on the first ring. "Two dead and five hospitalized at an engineering conference in Minneapolis this morning? What do you know about this?"

"My sources tell me it was ricin," Mark said. "No suspect, no known motive. Would have been much, much worse, but a hotel security guard somehow figured out the coffee was poisoned after the first man dropped. He cleared the area. He was heavily exposed, though, so he was the second casualty."

"They were in Minneapolis for a conference on blending ethanol into gasoline. Two dead is bad, but we could have lost most or all of the country's ethanol expertise."

"I talked to others in the hotel's security staff. They were shaken up to lose one of their best men. One of our TriCoast engineers was there. Fortunately he's not a coffee-drinker. They're reviewing the security tape now frame by frame. But because of the placement of the urn, there's nothing obvious. I've been on the phone with Cutler at the FBI and Tierney at Interpol and they're working it, too. Obviously the ricin makes us think of Amanda Parsifal's killer."

"Give me a call when you learn more." She puzzled over the news. The killings seemed related, and yet not. It was if someone was going down a list, checking boxes—except the boxes were coffins.

After touchdown, Lynn walked through the gray retro-modern airport terminal. Outside, she loaded her baggage into the BMW she had unexpectedly been able to rent.

The urge to drive was irresistible. She appreciated the geeky stitching of interstate highways that bound Chicago to San Antonio to Washington to Los Angeles. She found charm in the final, paved result of Dwight Eisenhower's long-ago fevered nightmare that the US wouldn't be able to move supplies or troops within its own borders.

Lynn felt free driving alone, especially knowing that tomorrow her bodyguard would rejoin her. She took pleasure in this car's quick acceleration, its slight hitch as it shifted through gears. She reveled in the music, the bubble of isolation, the smell of the leather, and even the choreographed dance with the other drivers. She'd been driving, sometimes too fast, since she was fifteen. Roads could take her anywhere, and had.

Like many Midwestern cities, Tulsa had grown up near a river. Unlike most, it had also grown up near oil fields. They had waned for decades but now were on the upswing again, so Tulsa traffic was heavier.

Lynn arrived at the Mayo to pick Helena up for a ride to the refinery. Its old-world luxury was something she had seen only from the outside when she was a girl.

"Nothing is close to anything in the States," the dark-haired Englishwoman said as she opened the passenger door. "And I find this city particularly landlocked. In England it always seems as if I can smell the sea and I'm never more than a few hundred miles from it, even in London. Here, I could be swept up in one of your dusty tornadoes. Oklahomans seem perversely proud of their violent weather."

"Good morning to you, too. Not *my* tornadoes, but I understand what you mean." Lynn had experienced enough hailstorms to be familiar with the variations from pea-sized to softball. As she drove I-244 toward the refinery she noticed again the heavier traffic. Old-fashioned short distances between signs and subsequent exits meant that when drivers missed a sign, or couldn't intuit what it so timidly indicated, within seconds they found themselves driving southwest to Oklahoma City instead of northeast to Missouri as they had intended.

"Yes, the wind has these Italian paces," Helena said, in a tone Lynn found momentarily irritating.

"Explain."

"Like opera." Helena began to conduct in the air. "Allegro. Presto. Crescendo."

Lynn laughed as if she agreed, but running five refineries had left little time for opera. She focused on the road. Extreme heat and cold had twisted the pavement into jarring bumps and potholes.

"Compared to London, I also find the lack of people oppressive. Worrisome."

"Safety in numbers?" Lynn asked.

"Yes. One of your men, Riley Stevens, took me out last night. He said he would show me what the pubs look like here. I can't say I was impressed, either with them or him. He couldn't give the bloody sex talk a rest."

Lynn sighed. Riley going out with Helena, one of the refinery's potential buyers, was wrong on so many levels.

"I know, we shouldn't have, but 'twas a bit of a break. He's not for me anyway." Helena's white china-doll complexion colored pink.

"What do you mean?" Lynn asked, surprised she found herself ready to defend Riley. Despite his faults, he was part of her team.

"His problem's in front of him," she said, patting her stomach to emphasize Riley's girth. "Still, he's much nicer than Toad Wold."

*Nigel Wold of North Seas?* "Your nickname for him?"

"Everyone's."

"What do *you* think of him?"

"Wold? I think he has a private life about which we know nothing."

Lynn began to laugh until she noticed Helena's serious expression. "Meaning?"

"Exactly that. We don't know if it's two jobs or two lovers, but he's always headed off for a secret meeting. But he's bonkers with the bankers, so that's primary."

They passed a billboard for a church reading *Set Sail with Jesus.* Helena nodded at it. "Yes, extreme religion makes sense here. The infinite is so much easier to find, isn't it? Infinity in land, in wind, and, I'm afraid, in boredom."

"Sounds like you're ready to return to England," Lynn said. They weren't far from the exit for the refinery. *Thank God.*

"Oh, brilliant! Look!"

Lynn glanced in the direction the other woman pointed. "The black Lamborghini Murcielago?"

"No, I mean who's driving it. He's wicked hot. Don't you always notice the driver first?"

"Nope. The car. Remember, my job is to make gasoline. And I like driving." She wouldn't tell Helena that the last time she'd focused on a good-looking man instead of his car, she'd wound up with her failed marriage to Keith. Worry flickered. *Will my second marriage be better, happier than my first?*

Helena's words brought her back. "So, if you had another job, you'd be a lorry driver?"

Lynn laughed. "Yes."

"Well. Most women, and I daresay the gentlemen, notice the drivers."

They pulled into the refinery's parking lot. Lynn was anxious to get out among the pumps and pipes, away from Helena. She ushered the woman inside to the grays and browns of the refinery's office, a neutralist's dream. Greg and Riley greeted her; Lynn noticed Riley's smirk. When she saw Gene Blahunka, she said, "Let's walk to the distillation control room. You can update me."

As they exited, Gene whispered, "You only spent twenty minutes with her, not the last week."

"She was nicer in London," Lynn said. "She's clearly uneasy here. What's going on?"

"We're treating her right but we've had to move her around in the offices a few times to keep her away from other buyer groups. Your ex and Pete and the Cherokees have stopped by twice."

"I thought you were only doing scheduled meetings with them. Tyree and Mark will be unhappy," she said, referring to TriCoast's general counsel and security chief.

"We cleared it with Tyree. They made appointments and gave us specific agendas. And we have complete documentation on what they saw and what we told them. But we didn't let them cross paths with Helena. And while she seems prickly, I've been impressed with her thoroughness. Either North Seas or the Cherokee Investment Group could be good owners, much as I hate the thought of TriCoast selling us off."

"She needs a few huevos rancheros."

Gene frowned at her.

"One of my first jobs was in west Texas," Lynn said. "Each morning a group of us got together and ate huevos rancheros. Cafe used lots of jalapeno peppers, but sometimes we'd ask for the hotter habaneros to be thrown in. One day a few of our overlords stop by. These guys show up wearing suits, so they're already sweating. They want to fit in with the rank-and-file, so they eat huevos rancheros with habaneros, too. Now they're red-faced and dripping. Maybe Helena needs the same experience."

"Must have been a hell of a conversation you two had this morning." Gene looked at his watch. "I have to cut out for a meeting with the EPA. Hell, they should move in with us, too. Maybe we could let 'em make the gasoline and jet fuel. They change the damn recipes every year. Next they'll want us to leave out all the hydrocarbons and use only water."

She punched his arm. "Sure, electric cars and hydroelectric dams. We're there."

He smiled. "Right. Different topic. One of our contractors has a guy missing. Said the man, name of Roberto Molina, was last seen at our refinery. Sure enough, looks like Molina logged in but no record of him logging out. We try to run a tight ship, but we don't exactly get the news cameras and protestors here either. Know what I mean?"

"Yes. Someone has unauthorized access to the refinery. Damn, Gene, that makes two guys, counting your distillation foreman. Three with Tom. Did the foreman ever show?"

"Nope. I've got Tulsa PD on both of them."

"Tell Shepherd. He needs to pass it along to the FBI."

"I'm worried about finding them, and I'm worried about everyone else. Folks are getting afraid to show up. We've already had to cut our volume. If our operations are worse this quarter, it will drive down the price buyers are willing to bid. That's not good for me *or* you."

She nodded. "God, I hope those men are okay. Could you have an outsider getting through the gate somehow?"

"One of my contractors has a badge missing, so it's possible. I hate running criminal checks on everyone, but I'll talk to Mark about it."

⁂

I'd heard they were looking for two men who'd disappeared but it would be a few more days before anyone would get serious. Even when they did, there'd be nothing to find of the first one except fear. Fear that it might happen again. Fear that would hasten the sale of the refinery, another step toward my freedom.

Ultimately, I'm not a forgive-and-forget person. I'm remember-and-revenge. That I care enough to want revenge is a weakness. That's what the Chechen and the man from Chicago would say. So what if they're right?

I drove past a pipe yard guarded by German shepherds. They

ran to the fence and snarled when I stopped to put on my jacket for the cooling weather.

Two miles farther down the road were a half-dozen mechanical horseheads, creaking loudly as they bobbed to pull a few barrels of oil from a decades-old field. I'd seen their hypnotic rocking many times. Today I pulled over and watched them. When it was time for another accident, a horsehead might serve me well.

# Thirty

> *"Everything is funny as long as it is happening to*
> *Somebody Else." —Will Rogers*

Lynn took Helena to the airport for her flight to London, picked up Cheryl, and then turned the driving over to her. Gene had arranged for the Cherokee Investment Group to meet at TriCoast's refinery so they could see more of its operations. They were led by Carla, and their checklists required several hours of inspections and explanations, something Lynn was anxious to finish so CIG could finalize its bid.

Afterwards, Jesse said, "We need a break, Lynn. Since you're headed west to Ponca City, why don't we go with you? We have business with several of the tribes around there, especially the Osage. We'll work our way back east from the Poncas. And we can play golf at Kah-Wah-C."

"What's that? One of your courses?" Riley asked.

"It's too long a drive," Pete complained. "Damn big counties, too. Osage County is bigger than Delaware or Rhode Island." He turned to Jesse. "It's a cow pasture course."

Lynn was dubious, too. "I play beginner golf and if I lose a ball, I'll never find it."

"We've got plenty of balls to go around," Riley said.

"Never heard that one before," Lynn said. *Only about a thousand times.* "Riley, Greg, and I have a meeting tomorrow in Ponca City. The Darby Oil folks reserved us rooms at a local hotel tonight."

"And we'll play best ball, so we don't lose too many," Jesse said, not giving up on his Kah-Wah-C offer. "Unless all of you can hit your age."

"I'd have to be about ninety years older," Lynn said.

As if it were an afterthought, Keith said, "I'll stay over, too."

Lynn urged Gene to join them. Although he was reluctant to leave the refinery, she considered it important for him to spend more time with TriCoast analyst Greg Sutton and especially with the Cherokee Investment Group. Even if they didn't buy the refinery outright, they would continue to be an important gasoline customer.

The day was clear and bright. Two foursomes gathered, and Cheryl accompanied Lynn. Lynn, Riley, Gene, and Greg represented TriCoast. Jesse and Carla were from CIG, with Pete and Keith from Adela.

Lynn was annoyed that her ex would be staying at the same hotel. Despite the presence of her bodyguard, it couldn't be anything but trouble. But if his and Pete's company could help CIG buy the refinery for the $1.3 billion price they were offering, she had to be patient.

She feigned nonchalance about the Ponca City meeting. However, it had taken weeks for Tyree Bickham to clear the anticompetitive hurdles. He'd been specific about what she could and could not discuss.

Lynn rode with Jesse, Gene, and Greg with Cheryl at the wheel. Keith drove the others in a second car.

After their divorce, she hadn't planned to see Keith again. She didn't expect to have feelings for him other than a sad weariness. But there he was. And there they were. His eyes still crinkled in a way that caused her to shiver as she remembered their nights together. She'd be a robot not to acknowledge her feelings, and a fool to do so. She chose robot mode.

⤜⤏

Simone Tierney pounded her desk in frustration. *Who is the assassin? And who is ordering the killing?* The MOs were different but the killings showed planning, not passion. So while it was no decompensating serial killer, the motives appeared inconsistent. How was Amanda Parsifal connected to Dag Nordval, and both of them to Tom Martin? This was not simply a Neapolitan Mafioso avenging a family member. These apparent assassins-for-hire were creating fear in many places.

She had made no progress on her original list of three dozen men and a handful of women suspects. If she knew the sponsor or sponsors, that too would help identify the assassins. Of course the sponsors could easily hire someone else, even if she or Cutler identified and caught the original assassins.

Certain groups used certain killers. *Kind of like the eBay trust ratings in Etats-Unis*, she mused. *Bodyguard assassination. Ricin. Ricin again. Mais mon dieu. What's the additional activity the FBI's Cutler mentioned? Batrachotoxin. A highway death. Missing people in a refinery. A man gambling too much. Lynn Dayton being chased by one of those too-large sports vehicles Americans favored.*

Simone rubbed her forehead with her hands. The threads formed no visible skein.

⤜⤏

High clouds were whipped thin, melting toward the horizon in the south.

One of Greg's tattoos showed as he gestured. "These town names, Whizbang and Smackover, suggest the 1920s boom. They seem played out, but they're not, not completely."

"Sorta like me," Gene said.

"Old but reliable," Lynn said. "So I suppose they are like you."

"But there's new drilling, just like up in North Dakota and West Texas," Gene said. "And all of it means more oil for our refinery."

Jesse looked at him speculatively. "Sounds good."

Thick, stubby artificial branches marked a cell phone tower in bloom, the sign for which Lynn had been searching. She asked Cheryl to pull off. "You have to see these! Some are TriCoast's original wells. It won't take long."

The second car followed them on the dusty gravel section roads.

"These formations have been producing for a hundred years. Stop here," Lynn said.

Everyone exited, blinked in the sun, and stretched. She pointed to the new drill site. "There's plenty of oil left under our feet, in formations like the Mississippi Lime. Ours has always been a drill-or-die endeavor. If we don't keep finding new oil, we can go out of business within a few years."

"Drill-or-die. Sounds like a genealogical term," Riley said.

"What do you mean?" Carla asked.

He shrugged. "Procreate or the family line gets wiped out."

Again, Lynn counted the number of weeks Riley had left on his severance contract. She wished he would focus on finance instead of lame jokes.

But Jesse nodded. "A little more bluntly than I would put it, but we want to preserve Cherokee heritage and traditions, too."

Jesse told them the story of Pawhuska, the capital of the Osage Nation named for an early chief. "It means White Hair. It was given to an Osage chief during the Washington administration when he fought American troops in Ohio. The chief tried to scalp an officer who'd fallen, only to see him escape when the man's white hair wig came off in the chief's hands. The chief thought the hair had great power. He kept the wig the rest of his life and took the name *Paw-hiu-skah*, Pawhuska, or 'White Hair.'"

"Now there's a story I like," Gene said, pointing to some of his own graying hair.

They got into their cars and returned to the main road. Farther on, it swerved and dipped, sometimes falling out of sight into brown valleys with a few bottom-dwelling cedars. No billboards, or even trees, distracted from the rolling hills.

"I've heard jokes about the loneliness of driving into the Osage, a sort of no-white-man's land," Gene said. "Now they don't seem like jokes."

"It's isolated," Greg agreed.

Lynn searched course stats on her phone. Kah-Wah-C was a regulation-length nine-hole course sodded with bermuda grass. It closed at dark. Nine holes of her beginner's golf wouldn't prove to Keith she'd changed from when they'd been married. Aloud, she said, "Says here the course was designed by Chief Yellow Horse in 1922."

"Full-blood Pawnee," Jesse answered. "Lived on a farm with his folks but still got sent to Chilocco, same Indian school I went to."

*Chilocco.* Lynn kept hearing its name. Jesse had told her it was in the middle of godforsaken nowhere on the Kansas border. It seemed to have a role in the culture of several tribes, despite having been shut down years ago.

"Tell us more about the course," Greg said.

"The front none is the back nine," Lynn told him. "Used to be the Osage Country Club. A lot of these courses were built during Oklahoma's 1920s boom."

Greg shook his head. "This is the most monotonous land-scape I've ever seen."

"It's soothing. Very Zen," Gene said. "Listen up. This county is soaked with oil and blood."

Greg said it sounded melodramatic, but Jesse nodded. "Sometimes the past is a heavy burden for the present."

"Too mystical for me," Greg replied.

Gene was reading ahead. "Do you have any idea what the Osage have been through?"

Jesse nodded. "Same as all of the tribes, except their problems had big dollar signs attached. White men and white women have always chased those twenty-two hundred-plus headrights with their accompanying oil royalties and bonuses. It's the first story I tell anyone working for me on the Cherokee Nation's projects."

"Bingo." Gene said. "In the 1920s the Osage were the richest people per-capita in the world. Alone among the Oklahoma tribes, the Osage had kept the mineral rights to their land. When oil was discovered, they became wealthy beyond belief. Between 1907 and 1928 Oklahoma was first or second in the country in oil production every year. A big portion of that was Osage County oil."

Lynn remembered stories her father had told her of grand pianos left out on lawns and new cars abandoned when they ran out of gas. Some of those stories must have come by way of his envious Cherokee relatives. *My relatives*, she thought with a jolt. "I heard there were murders and suspicious deaths over headrights."

Jesse nodded. "Headrights got to be worth twelve thousand dollars, which is like several hundred thousand dollars today. Every kind of lawbreaking you can imagine occurred. Theft, merchants overcharging the Indians, banks charging them high interest rates. Guardians stealing money. Men married solely for their Osage wives' headrights. Everyone had a hand out, or a knife. Plus there was all the normal crime you get in a boomtown. One field hand said a man who flashed a roll wouldn't likely be eating his breakfast with the boys next morning."

"Sounds like  Chicago and a dozen other places in the 1920s," Gene replied.

As they drove west, clouds darkened and rain spattered their car for several minutes.

Jesse directed Cheryl through the small town of Fairfax, and the second car followed them. "At the football stadium, go east.

Follow the blacktop road through two cattle guards, and you'll be there."

"Just like Augusta or Pinehurst," Greg said, his sarcasm barely masked.

"So if we hit in the rough we'll be face to face with a bull," Lynn added as their cars clanked over the metal bars of the cattle guards.

Gene looked up from his cell phone. "According to this history, Fairfax has the grave of the last Osage chief to be provided a traditional tribal burial ceremony, in 1923. The ceremony required a fresh human scalp."

As if cued, all touched their heads.

"A Wichita chief was selected for the honor," Gene said. "Then the feds banned scalp-taking."

"Those federales. Always getting in the middle of a good thing," Greg said with a snort.

"That's what my ancestors thought, too," Jesse said.

The complex, bloody history of the Osage echoed in Lynn's head as she looked at the isolated countryside. *Where would I go for help if someone gets hurt?*

Once they'd all arrived at the modest pro shop, Lynn noted Riley's smile sizzling at Carla. She leaned close to him and whispered, "I heard about Helena's date with you. Should I tell Carla?"

He shrugged. "Sure. Helena's gone now."

She spoke aloud so others could hear and, she hoped, notice Riley's behavior. "Riley, take it easy with the ladies. I think Helena has a crush on you."

Carla cut her eyes to him.

He turned. "Aren't you part Osage, too?"

"Nope. All Cherokee," Carla said. "Well, just a little more than Pete. His daddy was a full-blood. As traditionalist a Keetoowah as comes around."

"So I hear the Keetoowahs are some weird parallel world, a small nation inside the big Cherokee Nation?" Riley asked.

"No," Carla explained. "They have sovereignty, even though their tribe is a twentieth the size of ours."

On the second green, Keith put a bite on the ball, and it stopped only a foot from the hole. *As usual,* Lynn thought, *he's lucky with everything.*

She made an awkward chip shot out of the rough and laughed. Her putt was short of the hole by only a few inches.

"Hey Lynn, you gonna hit your bra size on this nine-hole course? What, about a 36?" No one but Riley.

Lynn walked up and whispered to him. "Riley, you forget who's signing your checks for the next few months? Or do you already have a new job lined up?"

He rolled his eyes. "Yeah, I get it."

Clouds had cleared away and it was cool, although it was still windy. But then, the wind never stopped in Oklahoma. Lynn forced herself to relax. The rough for the fourth hole really was cow pasture.

⁓

Dayton had been right about her beginner golf. But to the extent I still felt anything, I was grateful to her for smoothing my path, as the business books say, to a few more targets.

I had been in this area before and knew something the others hadn't realized in their giddiness to play golf. This far out, there's no cell phone reception.

Except for the large size of the group, that would have fit my plans.

The constant, cleansing wind blew away memories of everything but itself.

# Thirty-One

*West Sussex, England*
*Tuesday afternoon-Wednesday night*

Gernot Insel's return from the States, from Minnesota, had been more difficult than he'd expected. He'd used another of his precious identifications.

Although he didn't discount his fees, female targets were always easy. So easy that amateurs carried out honor killings of young women constantly.

He studied her picture. This one, another young London woman who had done her research too thoroughly, was even more beautiful than Amanda Parsifal had been. Helena Farber's skin was porcelain, her dark hair severely pulled back, her skirts a few inches longer than fashionable. Her silk blouses were lustrous. But she put North Seas Resources at an advantage in competing with his client, and the client needed advantages eliminated.

She'd arrived in London from overseas this morning. He followed her on a train south about seventy kilometers to Amberley and picked up his waiting black Mercedes. Helena got into a private car. He followed the car at a distance to nearby Amberley Castle but decided not to try breaching its remote-controlled security gate. On the other side of the gate, he could see a helicopter arriving at the castle's vast green lawn-made-helipad.

Amberley Castle had been a manor house in the twelfth

century. With the construction of curtain walls, towers, and a gatehouse it was converted into a fort for the bishop of Chichester in 1377. The castle had since been turned into a small luxury hotel, complete with dry moat and working portcullis, lowered nightly. Pictures of the castle showed white doves squabbling for the best perches in what had been archers' arrow slits.

Judging by the traffic, the castle staff was preparing for one of the many weddings it hosted. Helena had revealed nothing in her online postings, but the women who were his targets seldom did.

He found an inexpensive hotel twenty miles away in Chichester, and began his watch amid the River Arun's pastoral villages. On a few short drives he noticed that, similar to other European countries, the roads had no shoulders. It would be easy to hit a pedestrian.

To those who asked, he was Frank Woolridge, another Englishman out for holiday rambles.

The first afternoon, he followed Helena with a group of similarly-aged men and women on a five-mile walk through forests to Amberley Mount, in South Downs. He slowed as the group marveled over sheep being sheared.

A herding dog, off-task for the moment, kept watch from a truck's window while two men in a big farm pen handled each animal. A man grabbed a sheep, flipped it onto its back, held its head between his legs, and sliced with generator-powered electric shears. He cut wool off in swaths as big as a blanket—close to the skin but apparently not nicking it, precision Insel appreciated. Once the shearer finished, he flipped the sheep upright and it ran away, bleating.

Insel was concerned Helena would notice him. But she and her group were too taken with their bucolic discovery.

Later, he followed the path along the River Arun. It became a bridle path, evidenced by its near-paving with horse manure. The final section of the path led across an open field blocked at one end by milling cattle and land-mined with their excrement.

Insel judged Helena would be jet-lagged, maybe saddened that she herself was still unmarried, and so even more off-guard.

On Wednesday, when he tailed her to a pub, he didn't expect her to stay long. Judging from the conversation, she was drinking with friends from the wedding party and would return to London by train the following day.

"How was Tulsa? Oklahoma, was it?" one asked.

"Dry, boring. Some of the men were attractive, others too forward. But overall it seemed locked into time, mostly the 1920s."

One man clapped his hands. "Bonnie and Clyde!"

When Helena rose to leave, another woman said, "It's too dark for you to walk."

"Oh, nonsense. It's not far. I'll be fine."

After she left, Insel signaled for his bill.

He'd determined the car itself was too blunt an instrument. Worse, it would hold evidence if he merely ran her over. Instead, when he saw her walking on the verge, he drove by as quickly and as close as he could without hitting her.

She stumbled off, further away from the road.

He stopped, putting the garrote in his back pocket before he got out.

"I didn't hurt you, did I?" he asked.

"Bloody near. What the bloody hell were you thinking?" Her face gleamed white in the dark.

"These village roads. There's no space." His statement had the deceptive merit of being true. Two feet of asphalt was all that separated cars from the walls of buildings lining the road. "Could I give you a lift?" He didn't expect her to agree.

Her expression softened. "Thank you, but no." She turned away and began walking.

He slipped the garrote out of his pocket, crept behind her, and draped it over her white neck. He pulled it tight before she could scream. "I must insist you come with me."

Her eyes bulged and she tried to vomit. She struggled to slip her fingers under the wire.

He pulled tighter.

She went limp and fell. His Mercedes concealed her from the view of passers-by. The air smelled foul as her body evacuated its contents. Once her pulse stopped, he opened the boot of his car and hoisted her body onto a layer of plastic sheeting.

An automobile passed after he closed the boot. The driver slowed and pulled over. Insel did not want to kill inefficiently, but he would if necessary.

The driver, another from the pub, said, "You all right, there?"

Insel smiled, thinking of a phrase he'd learned from the engineers in Minnesota. "Just stopped to squeeze my sponge."

The driver laughed. "Then I'll be on my way."

Insel drove to one of the dirt roads he'd found during a long ramble. Like many, it led to the River Arun. A steady rain began. He donned boots and vinyl gloves. If he was quick, his tracks and those of the Mercedes would be washed away.

He took two large, heavy-duty bags he'd purchased at Sainsbury's. Opening the boot, he wrapped the plastic liner around Helena's body and then fit the bags over her head and feet so the bags met in the middle. He pressed the air out and tied them together.

Insel lifted the body from the trunk. Pleased that she was light, he threw her body over his shoulder and walked to the river. His waders were already starting to stick in the mud.

He put Helena's body on the bank, then rolled it into the river.

The bags and body sank from view.

The current was slow. By his calculations, Helena Farber's body would stay under water for a few days. When it rose, it would float down the river, obscuring its discovery and the discovery of this initial submersion point.

# Thirty-Two

*Northern Oklahoma*
*Tuesday*

*"My hand is not the color of yours, but if I pierce it, I shall feel pain. If you pierce your hand, you also feel pain. The blood that will flow from mine will be the same color as yours. I am a man. The same God made us both."--Standing Bear, Ponca Indian chief, successfully arguing in 1879 before Elmer Dundy, US District Judge for Nebraska, that Indians were persons who deserved the protection of the 14th amendment: no state shall deprive any person of life, liberty or property without due process of law.*

"Are those real buffalo?" Greg asked.

"No. They're statues," Lynn said.

He looked at her so incredulously she smiled. "They're real."

The buffaloes' shaggy, black coats twitched but their massive heads barely moved when the two cars passed.

Gene said, "Companies say they use all parts of the oil the way Indians used all parts of the buffalo. Shows the business originated around here."

They looked at the rolling hills. "This is boring," Greg said. "Man, even the Tulsa airport was empty, like the people had all been raptured. I saw a dead armadillo back there, still in one piece. As in, no traffic."

Rumble strip grooves carved into the highway's shoulder

growled as they moved right on the two-lane road to let a speeding truck pass.

Lush grassland fell away from the side of the road. In the distance, hills yielded to flat draws, stock ponds, and an occasional tree. To Lynn, the sere grace of the land, with sightlines to the horizon, was calming.

Greg's opinion was different. "Where are the trees? They blow away in the twisters?"

"Never were many trees. Just grass," Jesse answered. "What you see is indiangrass, bluestem, and switchgrass."

"All that detail reminds me of Preston," Greg said. "How's he doing?"

"I hope he's back at work soon," Lynn said. She blinked rapidly as she thought about him. *Can he recover and somehow keep the gambling addiction at bay?* Her stomach fell as she thought about the odds of recidivism. *Odds. He'd like that word.*

Gesturing toward a small storefront with bright lights, Greg said, "Indian casinos are a big business out here in the big empty. The state will be returned to the Native Americans, to whom it was promised originally anyway."

"I've heard the jokes about casinos taking back from the whites everything we lost," Jesse said. "We're the most successful people on this continent at assimilating into the European invasion, and have been for three hundred years. We don't need pity or handouts or white man's guilt."

Greg saluted. "Got it, Jesse."

As they crossed another upstream bend in the Arkansas River, sun glared through the windshield. Hawks rode thermals far above the telephone lines. When they arrived on the southeast side of Ponca City, they stopped and exchanged Riley for Jesse. The other group—now Pete, Keith, Jesse, and Carla—left to check into the hotel.

After a few blocks of bone-rattling travel over brick streets, a dark-haired young woman in a navy suit met them at Refinery Gate C. Amy Hamilton explained she'd been drafted to show them around. She laughed. "I was a history and engineering double major in college, so I always pull this duty."

Riley pulled his gaze away from the guide's even, affable face and straightened a collar still damp from their golf game. Lynn shook her head enough for him to notice and made a show of twisting her own engagement ring. *Surely Riley won't hit on a married woman.* But such concerns had never stopped him before.

Hamilton explained that Pennsylvanian E.W. Marland had started his eponymous company when he discovered oil near- by. "Imitating Rockefeller, Marland decided he needed to turn the crude oil into gasoline and other fuels rather than getting a low price by selling it as crude. Soon, the Ponca City refinery's gasoline was being shipped to Chicago in the pipelines Marland also had built."

She indicated a white van with a sweep of her arm. "Suspension isn't the best but there's room to spread out."

"So who was this guy, Marland?" Riley asked.

"Town's benefactor. Once he struck oil, he built a company, stayed around, and spent his money here. He was elected to Congress in 1932 and governor in 1934. His first lease was on Ponca lands, allowed with Chief White Eagle's reluctant permission. The well was named for its section holder, the Willie-Cries-for-War #1. He had several successes, as you'll see. Also, Candy Loving, the twenty-fifth anniversary Playmate, grew up here. Many older men have that issue."

Gene got a goofy look on his face. Lynn punched Riley in the arm.

They motored up a long driveway and parked near a stone mansion set amid several acres of land and ponds. "Marland built this before he was governor. He modeled it after the Davanzati Palace in Florence, Italy. He held picnics here, fox hunts, invited neighbors to swim. But it broke him."

Under the porte-cochere an official Marland Mansion guide took over, a charming, cheerful white-haired woman.

From its nine bedrooms to its hunt kitchen and lime wood paneling, the mansion foreshadowed newer palazzos. The guide pointed out tiles in the game room floor next to the hunt kitchen. They were illustrated with pictures of buffalo, but the "buffalo" were half-pig, half-horse creatures, the Italian tile-maker's mental image of a buffalo. The last panel of the game room ceiling history showed Osage tribal members attending a party at the Marland Mansion.

The guide saved the scandalous narrative until the end. She spoke so nonchalantly that at first Lynn didn't register what she was saying.

E. W. and his first wife, Mary Virginia, had had no children of their own. They adopted his wife's nephew and niece, George and Lyde, aged eighteen and sixteen, respectively. Mary Virginia developed what was believed to be cancer. Increasingly, Lyde began assuming her mother's hostess duties at the mansion.

When Mary Virginia died, 56-year-old E. W., who with George had already scared away several of his daughter's suitors, had 28-year-old Lyde's adoption set aside so he could marry her.

Greg said, "Whoa! Didn't people think that was weird?"

"Like the movie Chinatown," Gene said.

Riley grinned. "Puts the euwww in E.W."

The cheerful, white-haired guide was accustomed to responding to the old scandal. "Many people did question his judgment," the guide said, "first about this monstrously expensive home he was building and then about the marriage to his niece. Guidebooks say E. W.'s marriage to Lyde 'shocked the conservative town,' but the person it really shocked was Marland's conservative banker. Not long after E.W. married Lyde, that banker called his note. When Marland couldn't pay, the banker took over his company and combined it with another small oil company. It ultimately became Darby Oil. The banker was J.P. Morgan."

"What happened to Lyde?" Lynn asked.

"After E.W. died, she became a recluse."

"Another wild story behind another big fortune," Lynn said.

When they'd arrived back at the refinery and their car, Amy smiled. "I'd be remiss if I didn't mention there are six or seven Indian-owned casinos within a thirty-mile radius. The tribes want you to spread your money around."

<hr/>

I'd heard about the lure of Anglophilia this little town found so exotic. But in the case of the humorless colleague I'd been forced to meet in Chicago, he must have been Anglophobic because he was two for two on his English assignments, though he wasn't emotional enough to love or hate. I'd heard it in his voice when he called me briefly, not to boast, or even really challenge me, only to remind me again of my own assignments.

Nor should I be emotional about my next assignment. But I was reluctant. My brutal debt was forcing me to become a brutal man.

Then I thought again of my mother, with her wheedling tone. She'd borrowed, then simply took, the twenties and tens I'd earned with my first jobs.

I thought of how she'd taken my money without thanks. Lately she'd blogged about her ungrateful, too-emotional child. When she received sympathetic clicks from fellow whiners, she forwarded them to me.

I thought of the putdowns, the large and small slights, even from those I initially trusted. Not that I allowed close relationships. Like those with my mother, relationships were a reason for someone to take advantage. I made sure I was the someone. So it never surprised me when others acted the same way. With those who appeared kind, I waited them out. Their treachery eventually emerged. In that respect, the Chechen had been easy. I knew where I stood with him before he opened his mouth.

I thought of people at whom I smiled, in whom I pretended interest. Of slights I'd experienced in dealing with wealthy fucks, like the woman who invited the club to her mansion and left her butler there to host, abandoning any pretense of hospitality. She'd explained later she had an Aspen-bound plane she simply could not miss. Or the time I was invited to a mini-mansion and then was asked to enter through the back door used by the cook and the gardener.

So I'd almost made my nut. I'd been within a few trades. Not so I could live like them but so I could live without them. I would do whatever it took to be free.

When everyone was back at the hotel, Jesse offered to show the others the site of Chilocco Indian School. "It's twenty miles away. I was sent to school there. I want to see what it looks like now."

Keith, Greg and Riley begged off the forty-mile round trip to instead try their luck at the nearby 7 Clans Casino.

After Pete, Carla, Cheryl and Lynn were loaded in the car, Jesse drove the straight road north to Chilocco. A drilling rig fronted the two-lane highway, more evidence of the area's renewed oil production. An unintentionally ironic stack of three billboards appeared along the highway. On top was one about saving for a college education. It showed a young girl, with the tagline *What's your plan for her?* The billboard beneath it advertised bingo at the Southwind casino. The bottom billboard headlined a seminar taking place at yet another casino. It was labeled *Getting Control of Your Finances.*

Lynn hoped Keith, Greg, and Riley weren't as gambling-crazy as Preston. She wondered again about him, wishing she could ignore treatment rules to call. She hadn't heard from Preston since she'd taken him to catch his plane. She missed his calm. *But he would have been exposed to even more temptation here.*

Pete said, "I've always wondered about Chilocco."

Jesse glanced at Lynn, then back to the road. "Pete and I have a history. His daddy and I were at Chilocco together, then served in the same unit in Vietnam."

"So where's your father now?" Lynn asked.

"He died," Pete said. Pete and Jesse exchanged looks Lynn couldn't read.

She thought of her ill father, and his and her remote blood relationship to Jesse. *Would helping Jesse help her father live longer?* It was irrational to hope so, but she did. "So what was Chilocco?"

Carla shook her head. "When whites thought they should *civilize* the tribes they built Indian boarding schools and sent children there."

Lynn winced at the thought of the children separated from their parents.

Jesse saw her glance in his rearview mirror. "Not as bad as you think. Not here, anyway. We were like a family."

They passed another casino. Its neon lights overwhelmed the meager scrub and dwarfish hills around it. A nearby gas station was the Kum and Go.

"Do ya think they thought about that name for more than five seconds?" Carla asked.

"Yes, probably." Lynn laughed.

"It's right there with the casinos advertising the hot slots of summer," Carla said.

Lynn continued looking out the window. "Hey, have you noticed every casino has at least one nearby gas station?"

Jesse told them about several Chilocco alumni. One, Joe Thornton, was a military veteran of World War II, served in the Signal Corps and earned a presidential citation, broke three world records to win the gold medal in the Archery World Championships before it was an Olympic sport, married one of the world's top female archers, and then settled in Tahlequah and owned a television and appliance store.

"Is everyone in the tribe born with super DNA?" Lynn asked.

"Count on it," Jesse replied. "Just another overachieving Cherokee."

They passed two more brightly-lit casinos. Large metal sculptures on a hilly ridge behind one casino showed five life-sized Indians on horseback hunting nine buffalo.

They pulled up to Chilocco's red iron bars, now posted with off-limits signs. Jesse shook his head. "Looks like we don't get a special pass, even though we own part of it." When they got out of the car, Lynn was surprised at the remoteness and desolation of the former school's grounds.

"It's out in the middle of nowhere," Pete said. "No wonder you and my dad signed up to go to Vietnam."

"It was a drug rehab place for a while," Jesse said. "Someone told me they're using this for government bomb testing now. Very secret."

Jesse's head hurt with nostalgia.

This flat stretch of prairie rolling north and west was dense with thousands of years of history. The traces, like the tribes themselves, were light-footed, sparse, and hard to find.

Yet this much-lived land was crowded with ghosts of tribes first free and later, restricted. It had been overlaid heavily with white settlers and their peculiar laws.

The wind swept with ancient rhythms, often violent. Unprovoked, the skies threw down hail and tornadoes. Any building, no matter how sturdy, could become flimsy and temporary. The scoured prairie spoke of the wind's violence. Next to it, human violence seemed almost puny. Yet in many places, the land was so thinly populated that any act of human brutality seemed particularly awful to people who had survived the storms.

Despite Jesse's politic words, especially to the *agaya*, his feelings about Chilocco were mixed.

It had been more than forty years since he'd left, fifty since his aunt had driven him down its long road. His aunties had done their best for him after his father was killed and his mother had gone crazy. One of his aunts finally said, "Jesse, there's a place for you. You'll meet friends. You'll get meals, real ones, three times a day."

The school was far away, almost a day's drive.

"I miss Mama. Will I get to ride horses?"

"I hope so," his aunt said. Of course she had been wrong.

It was not as green as the hills, merely a flat old plain with big buildings sticking up in the middle of it. No trees to hide behind or creeks to explore or hills to climb and roll down.

He learned that kids from many tribes boarded there. Sometimes it was because they lived too far from a reservation school. Sometimes it was because their parents and relatives were too drunk to get them to school. If he squinted he could imagine the formal, two-story buildings at the end of the road, beyond the gate he could no longer pass.

The great contradiction: Chilocco was confined by openness, restricted by the wide blue sky.

A mind farm for reeducation. A place to "re-form" his mind. *My mind was fine, thank you.* No accident the place had been recycled—and failed—as a New Age drug rehab. What Chilocco had going for it was its utter isolation, far from an ocean, a river, an interstate, or even a state highway. They didn't call it a reformatory. They didn't have to.

His aunt had said, "I'll come back to visit next month. You'll be fine. A fine warrior, *a-ya-s-ti-gi.*"

They'd teach him to do a man's work, yessir, and then he'd be ready to leave the hidey hills of Oklahoma forever and see the world, do his nation proud.

Although his aunt never came back, he met the man who years later would be Pete's father. At least Pete's mother said he was. His mouth twisted at the bittersweet memory. They had pulled pranks together, enlisted together.

His death had been...awful, *u-yo-i. And it was my fault...*

When they returned to the motel, Greg, Riley and Keith were waiting in the lobby.

"Tired of losing?" Gene asked.

"We figured we'd play poker here. Then at least one of us will win instead of all of us losing," Greg said.

Rain fell outside, spattering the pavement.

"Think I'll skip it," Lynn said. "See you in the morning."

Cheryl went ahead to the room next to Lynn's. Lynn returned to their car and retrieved her e-reader to continue the book, *The Vanishing of Katharina Linden*. When she walked back in, the lobby was empty except for Keith.

"You lose your shadow?" he asked, referring to Cheryl. "I'll ride up in the elevator with you."

Warning sirens blared in her mind.

"Gusty rain outside," Lynn said.

"Lusty rain," Keith whispered.

"Stop," Lynn said, momentarily captive to a wave of longing so deep it was a physical hurt.

"Always need to be in control, Lynn?" He softened his barb with a grin. She drew in a sharp breath. She remembered those nights. And the last night they'd been together, too.

"I got you alone because I have concerns about this deal. You need to come see me tonight."

She shook her head. "By myself? Are you kidding? First, I'm engaged to be married. And second, I'm supposed to have Cheryl with me when I'm awake."

"Don't you think I know that? And don't you think I've kicked myself every day for the way things turned out? But Lynn, this is business."

When he moved in close, it didn't feel like business at all. "We could talk. We need to. And yes, you could spend the night if you wanted. One last time before I lose you. No one would know."

"Not only would Cheryl know, but every single person at TriCoast will know by tomorrow," she replied briskly, unable to ignore his heat and the temptation she felt. "Keith, I've been there with you, done that, and I know the end of the story."

The elevator door opened. He nodded at her and walked away. The air cooled, and he was as gone as the last breath.

Much later that night, she wasn't surprised to recognize Keith's number on her cell phone's caller ID.

She expected he would ask her to spend the night with him, one more time, "for old times' sake." Then he'd say again about how no one else would know and how they were hundreds of miles away from her fiancée.

She took her time. Later, she regretted she'd let the phone ring so much before answering.

What Keith said wasn't what she expected.

"Lynn. Come to my room! Please! You're the only one I can trust! I've been poisoned!"

"Poisoned? Keith? Are you sure? What's your room number?"

His phone hit the floor.

"Keith?"

# Thirty-Three

*Northern Oklahoma*
*Late Tuesday night-Wednesday*

Lynn called 911, told the dispatcher she believed Keith had been poisoned and gave the name of the hotel.

"What room is he in?"

"I don't know. I'll meet the medics in the lobby."

She woke up Cheryl. They ran down the stairs and arrived breathless at the front desk. "Keith McConaugh, what room is he in?" *Damn! If I'd gone with him to his room I'd know.*

The underfed clerk eyed them warily. "I'm sorry. I can't tell you." The man spoke as if he knew Keith's net worth and figured the two of them for gold-digging groupies.

"This is a medical emergency! Keith McConaugh has been poisoned!" Cheryl said.

The ambulance wailed as it rolled up to the front door.

"What's his room number? Get us a cardkey!" Several four-letter words were rising to her lips but she realized saying them would cause the clerk to slow down, not speed up.

"Hold on," he said. "You're Ms. Dayton in 331 and Ms. Wilkins in 332?"

"Yes, and Keith McConaugh is with our group," Cheryl said.

"I was told to protect his identity," the clerk insisted.

"I don't know who told you but right now his life's in danger!" Lynn shouted.

Two EMTs, a man and a woman, pushed their way through the door. "We got a call about a poisoning."

"Keith McConaugh," Lynn said. "If this man will tell us where he is."

"I can't give you that information," the clerk looked at them stubbornly. "Ladies, if you wait here and watch the desk for me, I'll take these medics to Mr. McConaugh's room. I'll call my brother and he can take over from you."

Lynn ran behind the desk and shoved him. "Go!" *And remind me never to get in a lifeboat with you. You'd be too busy counting rivets to paddle.*

Within a few minutes, the clerk's brother arrived. She suspected he'd been drinking and had no interest in the situation. "They went to room 243," he told them, and sat down.

Lynn hit the stairs two steps at a time, Cheryl right behind her. She wondered whether Keith had been the one worried about stalking or if someone else had left a warning with the clerk to prevent him from being discovered.

The door to room 243 was propped open. Lynn rushed in, ignoring the tangy odor of vomit. Cheryl stood beside her.

"Haven't been drinking," Keith said. "Not much, anyway." The slur in his voice belied his words. The two EMTs had him propped up in his bed. "Lynn, don't come close! See you got your shadow again." He tried to smile, then leaned over and vomited into a trashcan. The underfed clerk was nowhere to be seen. Keith began panting.

"Sir, why do you think you've been poisoned?" the first medic asked.

"Feel like shit. Been throwing up for an hour."

"Have you been drinking?" the first medic asked, running a small flashlight across his eyes.

Keith gasped. "Like I said, not much."

"Have you done any drugs?"

"Hell, no."

The second EMT started an IV. "Who was with you?" she wanted to know.

"Everybody but them," Keith said, indicating Lynn and Cheryl. "We came back from the casinos and were playing poker."

"What did you drink?"

*Mixing beer and whiskey, if I remember his habits correctly.*

"Somebody went to the liquor store and got Coke and rum." He couldn't seem to stop panting. His voice sounded more panicked than Lynn had ever heard.

The female medic asked Lynn, "You his girlfriend?"

"Ex-wife."

"But you weren't drinking with him."

*Not this time.* "No."

"You're familiar with his habits?"

"I used to be. We divorced five years ago."

Keith slumped over on the bed.

The first medic opened Keith's eyes. "Pupils aren't dilated. Keep the IV drip and put him on a cardiac monitor."

"Does he drink a lot?" the female medic asked as she assembled some equipment.

Lynn nodded. "He used to, but he never got sick like this. He told me he'd stopped way back."

"So this could be alcohol poisoning, especially if his tolerance is lower than it used to be."

"I suppose."

"Is he diabetic, too? On any cardiac medicines? Other medicines you remember?"

Lynn shook her head. "He wasn't." A flicker of sadness went through her about how little of his life she understood now.

The male medic looked through Keith's suitcases and in the bathroom. "I don't see anything but ibuprofen."

The second medic said, "I'm going to intubate so his breathing doesn't collapse." After she did, she said, "For as drunk as he appears, I don't smell much alcohol."

The first medic said, "Let's transport him. The hyperventilation doesn't fit either."

"You're taking him to the hospital?" Lynn asked.

"Yeah. He's not responding. That's implied consent to treat and transport." He glanced at Lynn. "Meet us there? It's right down the street. The doctor will want to talk to you."

"I'll drive you," Cheryl said.

At the hospital, the emergency room doctor debriefed the medics. While she waited, Lynn called Pete Whitehawk. As his business partner, Pete would know more about Keith than anyone else.

Pete sounded groggy, no surprise at 2 a.m. "We played cards. We drank. Rum and soda, mostly. We all took turns mixing."

"Who was there?"

"Riley, Gene, Carla, Jesse, me, Greg . . . Everyone but you and Cheryl. He seemed depressed you weren't around."

In the examining room, the doctor asked her questions similar to those of the medics but more about his mental state and whether he had been suicidal. Then he said, "I'm running additional tests, but I've seen this before. I've had plenty of customers who drink cologne or antifreeze."

"What?"

"Just chasing the drunk. One woman had multiple admissions for being crazy. She had hallucinations, and was hyperventilating. Turned out she was being slowly poisoned by her husband. In routine blood work I noticed her electrolytes were way out of balance. She had metabolic acidosis: her $CO_2$ content was too low. Here, either Keith or someone else was trying to do a faster job.

"In Keith's case, the rest of the blood work doesn't support the usual causes like diabetes, kidney failure, insufficient oxygen, lactic acid generation. I ordered additional tests, including one for methanol and one for ethylene glycol. We found calcium oxalate crystals in his urine, so ethylene glycol, antifreeze, looks like the culprit. The acidosis leads to hyperventilation and the person becomes hysterical. Hyperventilation is the body's attempt to get rid of the acid. Eventually all of the body systems shut down. It's lucky he called you and you got help. You saved his life."

"I had no idea," Lynn said.

"It's hard to believe, but the rum he drank may have helped too. We're giving him one of the best treatments we can right now which, paradoxically, is straight ethanol. Nothing mixed in this time."

The doctor turned away, leaving Lynn with her thoughts. *What if Keith dies? If I'd gone with him tonight, he wouldn't be in the ICU right now.*

She realized there would be rumors and innuendoes. *I have to call Cy. What will I tell him? The truth. If he can't trust me, I should rethink marrying him.*

⁂

Keith stirred a few times after Pete Whitehawk joined them in the hospital room. Lynn, Cheryl, and Pete agreed that when Keith was ready in a day or so, Pete would arrange to transport him back home. "We'll get him a white wig," Lynn said. She explained to Pete the story of Chief Pawhuska's wonder when he tried to scalp a white-haired officer and instead wound up with his magical wig.

Lynn and Cheryl talked to a Ponca City police officer. He told them it was likely the physical evidence would show the presence of Keith, Lynn, the medics, room service, housekeeping, and the last hundred guests prior to Keith.

"In other words, nothing useful," Lynn said.

He nodded.

Cheryl drove Lynn back to the hotel at 5 a.m. Lynn's head felt as heavy as a bowling ball. She answered e-mails from her refinery managers, then pulled on running clothes. "I hate to bother you again," she said when Cheryl answered the door. "But I have to run."

"No problem. I'll join you."

Lynn was glad the woman was good-humored, but worried

how close she'd have to stay once Lynn got married.

Outside, the immense lake of sky opened like an infinite bowl above their heads, the fading moon its pale spotlight. They ran east on a road called Prospect and north on a street called Pecan, which eventually turned into a county section road. Lynn could see the grain elevator in the next town, but concluded its distance of ten to fifteen miles was too far for this morning. They ran for an hour, up and down asphalt hills worthy of any roller coaster. She asked Cheryl about her personal history. The woman didn't say much about her time in Iraq but told stories of her Coast Guard work. Wild turkeys and fawns roamed fields near the road. Bois d'arc trees—their wood as hard as steel, and what the Cherokees used to make blow gun darts, Lynn remembered—lined a creek.

Cool air spoke of the coming winter. When they returned to the hotel, Lynn gathered the five remaining in her group— Gene, Greg, Jesse, Carla, and Riley—in the downstairs breakfast room.

"Maybe you heard the ambulance last night. Keith was poisoned. Does everyone else feel okay?"

Some shrugged, some nodded. Their faces showed disbelief.

"My hangover was worse than usual," Riley offered. No one laughed.

"What happened?" Gene asked.

"He phoned me late last night. He was really sick," Lynn said. "I called 911. Cheryl and I went to the hospital to be sure he was okay. Pete showed up later and is going to follow through and get him home."

"You weren't with him," Riley said. A sly expression played on his face.

"No. We used to be married and he's a great guy, but I resent that insinuation." Lynn stared at him until he averted his eyes.

"Sorry," he said softly.

Their expressions gave no hint which of them had poisoned Keith.

⁂

Jesse and Carla departed for their meetings with the Ponca, Osage, and other tribes. Jesse said he particularly wanted to learn the status of the Chilocco school site.

Lynn, Gene, Greg, Cheryl, and Riley agreed to reconvene in an hour for their meeting at the Darby refinery.

Sitting in her hotel room, Lynn felt as if a fifty-pound weight had dropped onto her shoulders. She tried to decide what approach to take, how much or how little she should say, and whether she should just cancel the meeting and return to Tulsa. *But I can't go into hiding.*

She called Cy. "I want you to tell you something."

He sounded cheerful. "To what do I owe this early-morning pleasure?"

Guilt over last night's feelings about Keith— even though she hadn't acted on them—flashed through her. "Cy, I told you we'd be up in northern Oklahoma. We finished in Tulsa yesterday, drove west, played some golf, toured this little town, had dinner, and I saw an old Indian school. Today I have a meeting with Darby Oil. Cheryl's with me, of course."

"Sounds like your usual schedule, though I'm amazed you found time for golf. Marika, I see you. Don't hit your brother."

She paused, missing Matt and Marika, even their fights. "Keith decided to come along."

Cy's tone was darker. "And?"

"Nothing. Nothing happened. Except, somehow he was poisoned and he called me and I had to call 911 but then I got Cheryl and he's in the hospital and I don't know who did it or what to do." She caught her breath.

"Because he's your ex-husband."

"No one's here to take care of him."

"No one?"

"Well, his business partner."

"So, Pete's taking care of him, right?"

"You're right. I should relax. Keith's conscious, and he's being treated by doctors and nurses at the hospital."

She called Mark Shepherd, but refused his demand that she cancel her meeting and leave northern Oklahoma at once. "Then the person or people who tried to kill Keith win. And they shouldn't. The best way to smoke them out is to keep moving forward."

"You could be moving forward into even worse problems."

"But if the target was Keith, and Keith is out of commission, there's no reason to be afraid. And Cheryl's here with me."

Mark asked her to recount what she remembered.

"Six people had been drinking with Keith, or so I've been told." She gave him the rest of the story.

"Is Riley trying to get back at you for telling him he's gone in a few months?"

"He strikes me as sly rather than hotheaded. Why kill the ex-husband of the woman who is one of your references for your next job?"

"But he could have been trying to set you up when he asked if you'd been with Keith. What about Gene? Maybe he's making sure Pete and Keith back away from buying his refinery?"

"I hate suspecting everyone. Gene was with me when we tried to save Jimmy Deerinwater. He's never given me a reason not to trust him."

"Jesse, Carla, or Greg? Are Jesse and Carla hiding something together or separately about CIG's finances? And Greg is young. I don't trust anyone with tattoos."

"I don't know Jesse and Carla that well, so maybe their stories won't check out. As for Greg's tattoos, you're messing with me. Half the people who work for you—people who would walk through fire for you—have tattoos."

"Yeah, true. I've run the normal security checks on Jesse and Carla. Nothing besides a few traffic tickets comes up, not even as many as you've gotten for speeding."

"You're keeping track?"

"It's part of your security profile."

"Do Jesse or Carla have any financial problems?" Lynn asked.

"No, not them personally. And CIG is well-regarded among all the tribes and with the BIA for their clean audits."

⬿

Oklahoma is a state in which people are experienced in negotiating mineral rights. In its small-town families, every generation educates at least one geologist.

It was rare for Lynn to visit another company's facilities. She and her team had signed non-competes and confidentiality agreements, but Tyree Bickham still expressed reluctance. She reminded herself not to stray off the prescribed topics and reviewed notes as Cheryl drove her and the others over bumpy brick streets to the south side of town. The last few sentences of history she read didn't lift her spirits. According to local historian Ruth Knowles, when Marland first requested permission to drill, Ponca Chief White Eagle had been reluctant. "You are making bad medicine for the Ponca and bad medicine for yourself." *As well he might,* Lynn thought. *Marland drilled on the Ponca tribe's burial ground. Yow.*

Had Keith, like Marland, fallen victim to White Eagle's curse?

Before she saw its small metropolis of towers and pipes, the rounded, comforting smell of hydrocarbons told Lynn they were near the refinery.

When she turned to look at Riley, Greg, and Gene in the back seat, she saw wary expressions. A chill descended as Lynn realized they were all wondering whom to trust. *If only there had been a camera on Keith last night.*

She shook her head to clear the fatigue and said, "Tyree is allowing us to discuss only three subjects with Darby. The one I'm most interested in is buying more of the chemical they make called drag reducer."

"Sounds like a name for an indie band," Greg said.

"Drag reducer is a chemical Darby invented that cuts the frictional loss of liquid in pipes. It enables more to flow faster, using less energy. They've made billions on it."

"Billion is one of my favorite words," Riley said.

As Cheryl parked the car, a freight train horn blared from the tracks about a mile away. Its howl rose in intensity, as if to wake any sluggards who dared sleep past eight-thirty a.m. The clacking and hammering of its wheels echoed through the cool morning air.

"I heard trains all night," Gene said.

"Sure it wasn't your snoring?" Greg asked.

The five TriCoast visitors were buzzed through Darby's security. They met the refinery manager and his engineering chief, a woman whose precise appearance reminded Lynn of Preston Li. She introduced Cheryl, Greg, Gene, and Riley. Cheryl stepped down the hall to get coffee for all of them. *Probably a good thing that she's mixing in the cream and sugar for us herself after what happened to Keith.*

They were shown to a low-ceilinged conference room. Greg looked at her and winked, indicating the room's eight-foot height with a lift of his eyebrows. One of the tattooed analyst's favorite theories was that high ceilings encouraged conceptual, long-range planning, while low ceilings indicated a place for detailed work, like accounting. So maybe this low ceiling meant Darby expected to complete a deal with TriCoast today. *Or maybe not*, Lynn decided, after the refinery manager's first remarks.

He pulled at one of the buttons on his shirt. "I heard what happened in North Dakota. You don't have any guns on you, do you? Not your bodyguard or assistant or whoever she is?"

She laughed to cover her concern and changed subjects. "No. None of us are carrying, including Cheryl. And our security chief tells me the Williston police are all over the case. Now, we wrestled with our general counsel, who's quite the wrestler, for permission to talk about three ideas. First, I want to mention that our board has requested we sell TriCoast's Tulsa refinery. You may have heard we've enhanced efficiency by bundling two

Houston refineries together. You could get the same efficiencies by combining operations and purchasing for your refinery and the one in Tulsa."

The trim engineering manager took over with one shake of her glossy black hair. "When we dialed in our estimates, we concluded the extra labor cost from managers keeping tabs on both places outweighed the savings."

The refinery manager worked another button on his shirt. "Hell, it's been in the news so I can tell you. It's likely we'll be asking TriCoast to buy this place."

"I wish we could consider that." *One down, two to go.* The second issue had been raised by Darby Oil. "You mentioned Darby's excess ethanol plant capacity."

The refinery manager sat up straighter. "Can we sell you a couple? We have a few here and several in Minnesota, more than enough for the volume of gasoline we're making. It's already about pure enough to drink. Folks think we ought to open a bottling line and sell the stuff in package stores."

They laughed, but Lynn was wistful they were competing to sell plants rather than build them. She worried again about Keith and the fact that it was alcohol—ethanol—that snatched him away from her during her marriage and threatened to do so again last night, and yet had ultimately saved him.

The manager looked at Gene. "You're from the Midwest. You could run these. You have enough ethanol for your Tulsa refinery?"

Gene nodded. "Our main issue is keeping security tight. Every alky in town wants to tour the refinery for free samples. I direct them to the St. Louis breweries. And I hate the weeks we have to use tank trucks when water gets in the pipeline. One day someone will get the bright idea to hijack one, open the tap, and kill the people he sells it to. We're also having trouble getting enough real ethanol engineers. Brewery operators have a different experience, I've learned."

"Well, a few dozen more of those engineers were almost wiped out in Minnesota last week. You didn't bring any of Marland's bad medicine with you?" the refinery manager asked, looking anxious. "You heard the story?"

"Yes, we heard the story, and no, we didn't," Lynn said.

"Our production research people have a new program they're marketing. Maybe you'd be interested," Darby's engineering manager said. "For rod-pumped wells this program increases a well's production rate by optimizing the rod pump's speed, stroke length, and size."

Riley's response was instantaneous. "Got one in a strap-on? I'll take it for my bedroom."

The engineering manager looked confused.

"Hey, it could help my performance," Riley said.

Lynn felt like she was only a few deep breaths away from breaking Riley's nose. She looked at Gene and waved her hand.

He read her signal. "Riley, I forgot you need to call our inventory manager." He walked Riley outside.

Darby's refinery manager said, "Did I miss something?"

Lynn responded with emphasis, "No, our temporary consultant Riley did. His sensitivity training. Gene will straighten him out."

Darby's engineering manager shrugged off Riley's lame joke. "We typically only deal with companies who have billion-dollar or more capital budgets. We consider individual consultants like Riley as hangers-on at best, crackpots, or even enemy tangos at worst."

"Got it," Lynn said. "Let me change the subject. We'd like to talk about buying more drag reducer from you. We've seen about sixty percent reduction in turbulent flow from what we've been using. We hear you also have formulations for very heavy oil and extreme cold. Since we're looking at very cold, very heavy oil from some of our Canadian production, can you mix us a special blend?"

# Thirty-Four

*Florence, Italy*
*Wednesday-Thursday*

The TriCoast group returned to Tulsa and left Lynn at the airport. When she spoke to Mike Emerson, he surprised her. "Fly here to Dallas and get a change of clothes. I want you to go on to Florence."

"Florence, Italy?"

"Yes, the prince has given us another chance."

"So Burl delivered. Good for him. Riley's not being sent along this time, right?"

His answer couldn't have been sweeter. "Nope."

"Then I'm on it. With luck, Reese can go with me. Fresh start."

The Saudi prince was on a private tour to Florence, Venice, and Milan with his wives and entourage. The wives were to be fitted for couture from Gucci, Armani, and other designers near the Via dei Tornabuoni, which Claude explained was the Florentine street of high fashion. Claude was TriCoast's French-born communications vice president and informal chief of protocol.

When he met her at Dallas' Love Field airport to review the schedule, he looked at her appraisingly. "It would do you good to shop there, also."

"Am I getting a bonus I don't know about?"

He shrugged.

Claude had heard the prince himself was hunting a rare 11<sup>th</sup> century Fatimid rock crystal ewer.

Lynn said, "The prince's emissary said the prince had new ideas on how he might assist with supplying TriCoast, so that's the treasure we hope to find."

Reese Spencer, her former mentor from her days in New Orleans, was wrapping up an assignment similar to Gene's as manager of TriCoast's Centennial refinery. Lynn's assistant re-arranged their meetings in Dallas and Houston, then booked the most convenient flights to Pisa, the nearest major airport to Florence.

"Your bodyguard and driver will be the same man, David," Claude said.

"David? You're kidding, right?" Lynn said.

Claude's smile suggested he agreed with her about the alias. "That's the name the security firm gave me."

Later that day Mark spoke to Lynn. "You can't go. Cheryl is assigned elsewhere. Your ex-husband was just poisoned, and I don't like the news I'm hearing from Interpol. I know Claude arranged a combo bodyguard and driver, but he didn't go through me, so I haven't vetted the guy."

"But if I don't go, my career at TriCoast will be dead. This is the Saudi prince who can assure our company a continued oil supply. It's a critical meeting that Burl cashed in all his chips to arrange."

"Florence is not a safe place," Mark said.

Lynn took a deep breath. "No place in the world is completely safe. And I'll be traveling with Reese Spencer. He's a former Navy pilot."

"You're not flying any planes."

"Again, Claude has arranged a driver with security credentials."

"Okay, but I'm on record as being against this trip."

"Got it," Lynn said.

After transferring through JFK, sleeping a few hours on the transatlantic flight, and stumbling through passport control, they were met at the small Pisa airport by a man holding a sign.

"David?" Lynn asked.

The man smiled warmly. "Ms. Lynn Dayton? Mr. Reese Spencer? I will take your baggage."

He drove them an hour through ancient, scrubby countryside featuring occasional hills and stone outcroppings.

They exited for Florence. Lynn liked its Italian name, Firenze. They wound through tiny streets toward the hotel in the Centro Storico, or historical center of the city. After checking into rooms at the Palazzo Niccolini al Duomo they met to walk off jet lag at the thirteenth-century green and white marble cathedral for which the hotel had been named. Unwilling to wait until the traditional seven-thirty opening for restaurants, Reese and Lynn ate calzones and drank wine at a small trattoria, finishing with gelato from one of the stands near the Ponte Vecchio bridge.

The next morning Lynn and Reese confirmed dinner with the prince and an evening pick-up time with their driver.

David met them at the hotel at seven-twenty that night. The prince had reserved one of his favorite Oltrano, 'other side' of the river, restaurants. Lynn was surprised to see David program the car's Garmin to get directions. "Maybe he spends most of his time in Rome," she mouthed to Reese.

Without the twin annoyances of Riley Stevens and Burl Travis, Lynn expected the dinner with the prince to proceed much more smoothly than their Paris meeting.

Constricted streets and impulsive drivers made Lynn glad she wasn't driving. It was seldom clear who had the right of way, so all took it simultaneously.

When they arrived, the prince had already ordered for them: seafood antipasto, minestrone, bruschetta with local Tuscan olive oil, and bistecca alla fiorentina.

"Glad to see the man likes steak," Reese whispered to her.

The restaurant had more waiters than guests. Lynn found the absence of a crowd eerie.

After pleasant conversation lasting through dessert, the prince said, "We are reducing our sales to buyers because we need more production ourselves. The Chinese, our largest customers, are especially insistent. At our last meeting, we discussed a contract for a percentage of Zuluf production. What can you offer?"

"Standard pricing, but we also have a refinery in the middle of the country for sale," Lynn said.

"A possibility, although our money is being spent now on a Texas refinery upgrade. Will this refinery run our sour crude and make gasoline that meets US requirements?"

"Yes."

They talked about a long-term sale of crude, although the stipulations were so hazy it seemed like aimless discussion. But negotiations with the Saudis and the Asians were always slow and indirect.

The prince and his entourage left after midnight. Following protocol, she waited until he was gone to call their driver. No answer. David should have been nearby, waiting for them to exit the restaurant. She called a few more times. Fifteen minutes passed.

"We could walk. We'll keep calling him and have him meet us en route," Reese said. "It's not too far, even with your heels."

At first Lynn enjoyed the clear night air. But when she didn't recognize the streets, she realized they were lost. The residential neighborhood was dark. "I see a busier street. Surely it will take us toward the river and our hotel." She tried calling David to give him their new location. Still no answer.

"We'll be there soon." Despite her reassurance to Reese, the unending roar of traffic worried her. She turned around several times. It was too dark to see much. Finally, she could glimpse small tiles. *Via Romana.* They continued toward the river and the lights of busier streets.

"Look at this wall. It's massive!"

A sturdy, primitive wall loomed above on their right. David had described the fortification that encircled the old city. But contrary to what he'd said, this wall stretched several hundred meters. *It's unscalable*, Lynn thought. The wall had corners, but no openings or street intersections.

"We're near Boboli, not far from the river." Reese sounded anxious.

A microsecond after she heard the shot, the wall exploded in front of her. A cloud of old dust billowed out.

She grabbed his arm. "Reese, down!"

Another shot punched the stone above them.

They were trapped between the wall and the busy street, as if in a tunnel. The wall was blocks-long both ways and impenetrable. If they ran into the street, the fast-moving traffic would be lethal. There was no escape.

Lynn risked a look over her shoulder but couldn't find the source of the shots. She pushed Reese. "Crawl back the way we came."

They crawled next to a parked Mini. The car with the gunman pulled over a half-block ahead while she and Reese continued crawling back along the parked cars.

Behind them in the traffic she saw a police car.

Suddenly, a second car rear-ended the gunman's vehicle.

At the sound of the collision, the police car's lights and siren came on. Lynn gripped Reese's hand and they stood and ran toward the polizia, zigzagging close to other cars that were squealing and braking.

The police car pulled into the right lane and stopped.

When the driver of the second car got out, the gunman's vehicle screeched away. It u-turned and Lynn worried that the gunman might strafe them again.

In a hurry to get off the deadly sidewalk, she tried to open the police car's door but it was locked.

The policeman got out. "You are looking for drugs?"

"No. Someone is shooting at us! There!"

"In!"

After they got in and crouched down in the back seat, the officer flashed bright lights at the oncoming cars, turned on his light bar, and said, "Why is someone shooting at you?"

Gernot Insel's window of opportunity was small, but he was a professional, with perfect timing. He had paid off the driver TriCoast hired and replaced him with one of his colleagues. When the TriCoast-hired driver showed up to meet Insel for his bonus, Insel had killed him and disposed of the body. No reason to leave a witness.

The replacement driver was an experienced Mafia enforcer and had reported to Insel, somewhat sullenly, on Lynn's and Reese's destinations. After he took them to the restaurant and parked nearby, Insel exchanged cars with him.

By the time the prince and his bodyguards were a few blocks away from the restaurant, Insel noted the guard he'd killed in Paris had been replaced. Using his .45 with exceptional marksmanship, he shot the replacement in the head.

He slipped away before anyone in the group realized the bodyguard had done more than stumble.

He hadn't shot the prince, but he'd shown he could have. He'd proven that the prince, despite all the latitude given his excesses by governments and hoteliers around the world, was not immune to bullets. He also demonstarted to the Saudis the danger of continuing to do business with TriCoast.

Two hours later, the hired professional reported he'd fired at Dayton and Spencer, careful not to hit them. When the man took his money and turned away, Insel drew the .45 and shot him once, careful to avoid the back splatter of blood and brains.

The other half of this particular project was complete. With perfect symmetry, he'd also shown TriCoast the danger of doing business with the Saudis.

The police brought a translator to the hotel. The translator asked Lynn and Reese about the death of the Prince's second bodyguard.

"What?" Lynn was shocked.

"He's dead? We just saw them," Reese said.

"Yes, you were the last to see them," the translator said, as the police stared hard at them. "You didn't hear the shots?"

"Stop." Lynn called Tyree, TriCoast's general counsel. Despite the late hour in Florence, Tyree called local and federal lawyers. They soon arrived, rubbing their eyes.

It was clear the police wanted to arrest Lynn and Reese, but nothing linked the two executives to the crime. And when their local lawyer switched into his native Italian, Lynn concluded it was just as well she didn't speak the language. The only word she could understand was "jihadi."

After several more hours, she and Reese were finally allowed to return to their rooms. In the hotel lobby, she hugged him and said, "We survived!"

"I need a drink. You?"

"I need three," she said. "I'd sure as hell like to have a day go by when I didn't have a target on my back. I'd bet everything I own both shootings are related to everything else that's been happening. It sure seemed they were going to kill us."

"Maybe not," Reese said. "I have the feeling that whoever was shooting at us had good enough aim to hit us if he'd wanted."

After the third drink, they exchanged another hug of relief and agreed to meet late the following morning.

# Thirty-Five

*France/Czech Republic/Washington, DC*
*Friday*

> *"There's no trick to being a humorist when you have the whole government working for you." —Will Rogers*

Simone Tierney regretted the news of the second bodyguard's death, and the attack in Florence on the two TriCoast executives. However, the discovery of the mafia hit man's body gave her a kernel of satisfaction. It was not so much for the death of a man himself responsible for killing dozens, although she appreciated that, but for what it meant. Her group of three-dozen suspects had been halved. Many of those on her original list didn't have the contacts and ability to hire or work with the hit man. Fewer still had the ability to take him out afterward.

She called FBI agent Jim Cutler.

It wasn't Gernot Insel's mountain, so he was surprised he cared. On the public path at the top of Zugspritze near the border between Germany and Austria, a young boy whispered to a burka-draped woman whom Insel surmised was Turkish. After her one-word reply, he ran several meters away. He opened his pants and a yellow stream of urine arced out into the snow, staining it like a dog would. He laughed when he finished and rejoined the woman.

Expecting she didn't speak German—many immigrants and visitors did not—Insel got her attention and pointed to the sign on the building for restrooms. She shrugged and turned away.

Resentment knifed through him, and he tamped it down as he thought of how he preferred Berlin to Munich, and his native Austria to both. Munich shared the mountains with Austria, and was near his beloved Vienna. But Berlin had fewer veiled women with urchins like this one. His fellow Austrians knew how to deal with the Turkish invasion. The Germans were too hands-off.

Enough. Insel had to be focused through the ordeals of the border crossings. The man he was meeting in the Czech Republic wouldn't hesitate to torture or kill him. It was mutual. But they needed one another. Insel expected violence only if he didn't deliver the money.

There was the problem of getting the material to the destination. Cargo planes flying directly to the US were too closely inspected. He would contract to fly the material from Prague to Mexico, where it would be "inspected" by a guard twenty miles from the landing strip. Mexican drug cartel members he'd dealt with would finalize its importation into the US. Jumpers would transport it to a pre-arranged location. The cartels had the merit of being faster than any normal delivery service.

Insel wanted to keep his distance. Set foot in the wrong territory and his head would wind up on someone's doorstep. He remembered the evening at a Mexican nightclub when one of his contacts had stepped onto the dance floor with a burlap bag and turned it upside down. Everyone screamed as dozens of severed human heads rolled out, some fresh enough to slick the floor.

The United States had too many subcultures. And it was easy to offend many of them. After the Czech Republic and a second destination, he would travel to a remote outpost there, province of Oklahoma, city of Tulsa. He would have to remember to smile. The Americans could forgive almost any transgression except a lack of humor.

At the urinal in the Munich airport, he aimed at the fly baked into the porcelain and hit it. Where the Turks were crude, like the boy and mother he'd seen at Zugspritze, the Germans had a sense of humor.

The airport was packed with families coming and going from their governmentally-scheduled six weeks of vacation that occurred between August and mid-September. They would be back in time to plan for Oktoberfest.

In Prague, his supplier told him the C4 price had increased. Since Insel had expected negotiations to take this course, he'd started low. His supplier bargained on everything except money transfer safety, and was quick to point out he was being pressed by al-Qaeda, the Taliban, and others for the same supplies.

Logistics concluded and money transfers verified, each texted their contacts on throwaway phones. Insel caught the next flight to London. He wished briefly for that which his supplier could never provide—an afternoon shopping the thousand types of sausage at Munich's KaDeWe.

⸎

Once Tyree Bickham had arrived with Mark Shepherd and a few well-connected Italian functionaries, Reese was willing to stay behind in Florence to answer questions about the death of the prince's second bodyguard. Mark's military bearing showed the smallest droop when they talked about the apparent replacement of "David" with a hit man. "And the thing of it is, no one's located the guy. No one's seen him for several days. That's the last time I let Claude make security arrangements."

By the time her plane finally arrived in Washington, D.C. Lynn was mute with exhaustion.

Only a moon stripe of light shone above L'Enfant Plaza Hotel. She met her bodyguard, Cheryl Wilkins, and checked in. Cheryl debriefed her in preparation for their following morning with the FBI.

Lynn fell asleep before she could read even a paragraph of her book.

She called Cy when she awoke. After catching up on Marika and Matt, she told him about Florence.

"You should come home, take a break," he said. "Somebody is trying to kill you. And hey, I've even met with the Whippet a few times myself, so you don't have to."

Echoing Reese's earlier words, she said, "If the shooter had wanted to kill us, we'd be dead. So I need to find out who it was."

"You know, we're supposed to get married. Instead, you're taking chances with your life. Are you even thinking about Matt and Marika?"

"First, Cy, I'm not inviting it. I don't know the source of the attacks, but the negotiations come with the job. And second, this isn't normal. Most weeks, hell, most *years*, are not like this one."

"Lynn, please just take care of yourself. We all miss you." His voice broke. "I love you."

"I love you, Cy. I wish I was there to hug all three of you." She felt a post-traumatic stab of fear that she might not see him again and mentally put it aside to consider later. The pain of being apart was so intense she had to sit down a while.

Later, Cheryl and Lynn met a TriCoast deputy counsel who appeared to have stepped out of an Abercrombie and Fitch advertisement. They walked a half-mile to the J. Edgar Hoover Building.

Inside the plain white room, she was relieved to see a second, younger agent, as well as Jim Cutler, the FBI agent with whom she'd eaten Barbec's biscuits. But Cutler nodded at her coolly, as if they'd never met.

They had reassuringly-detailed information about the Florence attack, but they dodged her questions. *The famous one-way street.* It seemed harder than being interrogated in Italian since there was no waiting for a translation.

"What is your opinion of the prince? Do the hits on his body-guards benefit you or TriCoast? Do you have a reason to kill them?

Were you involved? Was there an arrangement to kill them?" Jim asked. "Do you have knowledge of who arranged the second assassination?"

TriCoast's deputy counsel held up his hand. "You have everything in front of you."

Lynn added,"We need your help, and Interpol's."

"I can't help you if you don't answer the questions."

Lynn glanced at the deputy counsel, who nodded reluctantly. She said, "No, I was not involved. No, there was not an arrangement to kill either of the bodyguards. More to the point, do you think I'm crazy to scare one of our biggest suppliers?"

Both agents stared, as if they didn't believe her. "The deal TriCoast might have had in mind with the Saudis is off the table. The Saudi ambassador has conveyed his concern about doing business with you."

"We have legal contracts with the Saudis," Lynn insisted.

The deputy counsel held up one freckled hand again. "No discussion of contracts."

"Do the bodyguards' deaths benefit you in any way?"

"No, of course not." Lynn's neck was hot.

"Nonetheless, you can understand that the Saudis are reluctant to have any further discussions," Cutler said. "While it's obvious you have the least to gain by having the bodyguards killed, they seem to have become superstitious about TriCoast."

*Damn. How is it I've wound up with the exact opposite of what I wanted? Less supply instead of more.* "Look, besides the tragic loss of life, there's fear. That fear has a dollar value to TriCoast, our board, and our shareholders. Multiply three hundred thousand barrels a day by the cost of oil and you have a huge number by anyone's standards." One of Lynn's legs started to cramp, always an indicator of stress.

"You can get other supply."

"Not that much, and not fast."

But she understood the Saudis' reluctance. She was not afraid, but angry at whoever had killed the prince's two bodyguards and thrown the suspicion onto her and her company.

She counted the number of people who knew about the trip. It was a small group—Burl, Mike, and of course Reese. She trusted Reese and Mike. As little as she liked Burl, she couldn't see his motivation, particularly not when they'd pressured him to reopen the discussions.

*Apparently, it's important to someone to keep TriCoast apart from the Saudis, so important they'd kill. Is it a competitor? Someone who doesn't want the Saudi billions buying the Tulsa refinery? Who could be so interested in, as Riley called it, 'a collection of ancient metal?'* The Cherokee Investment Group had made a large bid for the refinery, and North Seas was rumored to be considering one. *Did I miss a cache of gold buried under its distillation columns and heat exchangers?*

※

Mapping software didn't show Insel much of his US target, but he hadn't expected it would. That's why his contact existed. He hoped the contact would be calmer than in Chicago.

※

Across town, Jesse chatted amiably with Pete, Keith, and Billy Perry, the head of economic development for the BIA.

Jesse explained the differences between the three Cherokee bands. "Keetoowah has the same words we do, right Pete?"

"If you say so," Pete said. "I haven't had much time to study the language. Goldman Sachs wasn't big on any lingo besides cursing. But I do remember Cherokee citizenship comes from the Dawes Rolls. It's not racial."

Billy said, "You took in over a half-billion in revenue last year, mainly from the casinos. Why do you need Pete and Keith's company to back you to buy this refinery?"

"They see assets like this all the time. They have financial expertise."

"And Pete's a friend of yours," Billy said.

"Yes," Jesse said, glancing at Pete.

"If you need their help, why buy the refinery at all? Why not buy stock in oil companies, or a mutual fund?"

Jesse pulled at his tie. If Billy was going to big-time him, he'd reply in kind. "I don't have to tell you the Cherokees are a sovereign nation of almost three hundred thousand people, two-thirds of whom live in Oklahoma. We've been running casinos for a while now. If we can handle a bunch of crazy gamblers, we can handle a refinery."

⁓

In a kinder voice than she expected, FBI agent Jim Cutler said, "I've told folks about your good instincts the last time you called me in. That's why I didn't hesitate to get involved when Mark called us this time."

"It was more than good instinct, and I note that this time you were responding to Mark, not me." A few months ago, Lynn had described her concerns about Houston Ship Channel accidents being deliberate. Although her CEO had backed her, FBI agent Jim Cutler hadn't agreed. Only later, after the sabotage had spread to other refineries, and Lynn had been ambushed by the French saboteur, was she taken seriously. She'd proven herself to Jim Cutler.

"Point taken. Let me change the subject." Cutler turned on a computer and flicked a switch to lower a projector screen.

Pictures flashed on the screen of Saudi port Ras Tanura, the Houston Ship Channel packed with refineries including two of her own, seas of tanks at Cushing, Oklahoma and Perth Amboy, New Jersey, the little group of refineries on the Arkansas River in Tulsa including TriCoast's, drilling offshore Brazil, and several other oil and gas installations.

"Most of this is standard introductory material we show corporate security groups."

A picture of an arch came up on the screen. It was made of pipelines topped by a valve wheel and labeled, *Welcome to Cushing. Pipeline Crossroads of the World.*

As she looked at the pictures of Cushing, Lynn explained to

Cheryl, the agents, and the TriCoast deputy counsel, "People are always buying and selling storage there. Now that it's about eighty million barrels total, it doesn't fill up."

She thought about the Darby refinery they had just visited. The manager had told them he shipped in 130,000 barrels a day of crude from Cushing. Millions of dollars of crude and gasoline moved underground. Oil moved by rail, too.

Aerial photos of Cushing showed the small, thousand-square-foot houses and scraggly, scrappy buildings that surrounded industrial areas the world over. Trees flanked straight gray asphalt highways and the town's standard Midwestern grid of concrete streets.

Another photo showed the acres and acres of gigantic storage tanks, with a close-up of pipe and valve arrays.

Then, Jim continued with pictures that stunned her. They were of her, Jesse, and the others, taken a few days ago at the gates of Chilocco. A thirty-second video showed their car arriving and leaving.

"What the hell?" Lynn said.

"Just because we had Barbec's biscuits together doesn't mean you weren't being watched. What were you doing there?" Jim asked.

"Nostalgia. Jesse's." She choked with surprise, then recovered. "Jesse Drum, the head of CIG, went to school there. We're negotiating with him, as I'm sure you know, too. He'd told us much about Chilocco. As you can see," she heard acid rising in her voice, "we couldn't get in."

"You got too close to a sensitive area. I can tell you what the locals know. If you had the security clearance and the reason to go in, you'd have seen bomb craters. Those grounds are now used to test sensing devices for IEDs."

"What do the tribes who own the place think?"

"They're the ones who get paid. They're the ones with whom the government contracted."

Lynn wondered what Jesse thought about the destruction of Chilocco, or if he even knew.

As if he read her mind, the agent said, "We sure as hell weren't going to turn it back into an Indian boarding school." He turned off the projector. "We'll be in touch with you again."

They left the building and said good-bye to the deputy counsel, Lynn noticed her bodyguard's eyes followed the attractive man for several seconds. Then Cheryl turned to her. "You're surprised they know so much?"

"I shouldn't be," Lynn said. But she felt violated.

"He wanted to shake you up," Cheryl said.

"Mission accomplished. But I still have to do my job, which includes selling the refinery, whether he approves or not. I answer to TriCoast's board of directors."

When she turned her phone back on, she saw Josh Rosen, a trader at Kodiak Securities, had phoned. He rarely called during trading hours, and his message was short. "ASAP."

She stepped out of the wind into the shelter of a nearby building while Cheryl waited.

"How well do you know your ex-husband?" Rosen said, once she was put through.

"Josh, cut the crap. What do you want?"

"Have you seen him much since the divorce? Talked about his business?"

"Not until a couple weeks ago. I wouldn't waste your time, Josh. Don't waste mine. What's going on?"

"I'll just say don't hang around your ex-husband and his partner too long. A lot of the people they buy businesses from wind up in the morgue."

"You called me to tell me that blindingly obvious fact? Of course they do."

"Right, to be blunt, Keith and Pete get options to buy businesses from old farts whose bratty children don't want to run them. The guys are pretty decrepit, so they usually die."

*Josh Rosen, you haven't just been targeted in Italy by an unknown assassin and had the FBI messing with your business as a result. Get to the freaking point.* "Then Pete and Keith pay the estate so the children get the money. They get the business, turn it around, and sell it for a profit. No big deal."

"Are you aware that these owners always die before Keith's and Pete's options expire?"

"They're older people. Of course they die." She winced when she thought of her own father, struggling each moment to breathe. She didn't, couldn't, let him go, no matter what her sister said.

"If I were you, I'd tell Mark Shepherd about it fast. And keep your bodyguard next to you."

"Josh, I thought you traded on more than hunches."

"My best trades have been on hunches. We're not talking money, here. We're talking about your life."

# Thirty-Six

*Dallas/San Antonio*
*Friday-Saturday*

On the TriCoast corporate jet to Dallas, Lynn opened her e-reader again to *The Vanishing of Katharina Linden*. She nodded between words. Finally she tilted her seat back and slept.

When she arrived in Dallas, she drove toward her father's house. Despite the nap, she was jet-lagged after the days in Washington and Florence. As she drove, she remembered her father's longtime pulmonologist saying there was nothing more he could do.

She had taken her father to other pulmonologists, some who would not give up so easily, but hadn't found one who would accept him as a patient. The fourth one had said, "Once you've been advised to get a hospice doctor for him, you can't expect to sign him up as a new patient with me. The best thing you can do for him is get him under the care of a hospice doctor."

"But that means I've given up, that he won't improve," she said.

"I wish I could offer you a different answer."

Lynn had reluctantly contracted with a hospice service, and they had started a few days ago. But she continued to pay nurses to stay with her father around the clock. Hermosa had taken care of him for several years and Lynn was glad to pay her wages also. *I wish I could be with him all the time myself.*

Her father had said that he preferred Lynn work and tell him about it, rather than hover at his house.

His afternoon nurse updated her, saying the doctor had increased her father's morphine, and that his antidepressant seemed to help him relax and breathe more easily. With a jolt, Lynn realized drug addiction was no longer a concern. He'd never go off his drugs as long as he was alive.

The nurse confirmed he was using oxygen tanks more quickly. He'd shrunk since the last time she'd seen him. His cuticles were still blue, a symptom of insufficient oxygen, despite what was delivered through a tube in his nose.

At her first visit, the hospice doctor said he had eight to ten weeks left. "So say everything to him that you need to," she suggested.

"His doctors told me he could live up to eight months."

"I'm sorry. No."

So this night, after her several days away, she held his hand and talked to him until he fell asleep. His breath whispered through the plastic tubing.

The next morning, Lynn let herself into Cy's house to find Matt power coloring, his two hands gripping nine crayons. He dropped them and ran to her to show off his Batman cape. After she admired it, he insisted, "Want brektiss," wrapping chubby arms around one of Lynn's legs.

She lifted him up and kissed him. "Let's see what we can find."

"I had to get up at seven-like-thirty. My legs are burning. I need to run," Marika said. She kicked over a pyramid of Matt's plastic blocks, then looked at her brother to see if he'd noticed. He had, and screamed.

"Sounds like this soccer game is just in time." Lynn bounced the two-year-old on her hip, wiping tears from his extra-long, baby-fine eyelashes.

"And it seems like everything in this house is either a bat or a ball," Cy said, kissing her. "We missed you. It's great to see you. How's your dad?"

Lynn shook her head and freed one hand to wipe away her own tears.

Cy nodded.

Lynn strapped the boy into a booster chair while Cy toasted bread and poured fruit juice for both children.

"Dad, can you put this juice in a parent glass, not a baby glass like Matt's?" Marika asked.

"Not a baby!" Matt said, and started to cry.

Cy shook his head wearily at Marika.

An hour later, standing on the sidelines of the girl's soccer game, Lynn raised her hands to the fall wind. Though only a few degrees cooler than the last five months of summer heat, the sweet breeze was a harbinger of more civilized temperatures. Even Matt seemed to feel better, looking less flushed than he had the past few weeks.

At a neighboring field, two high-school girls' teams resumed their lacrosse game. It reminded Lynn of the stickball game she'd seen in Tahlequah. Same ball, same netted rackets. Though in some nations girls were not allowed to play lacrosse. If they even touched a player's stick, a purification ritual was required.

*Men's fetishes . . . same the world over.*

Lynn recognized about a half-dozen of the soccer players' parents from industry groups in which she participated. But all adult conversation was drowned by a roar from Marika's team and their supporters when Marika scored a goal.

The teams changed sides for half time. Cy was rolling a ball back and forth to Matt. He motioned Lynn aside and hugged her. "You're working too hard. Maybe you should downscale, especially after what happened in Florence. And Jesus, northern Oklahoma . . . were you with Keith when he was poisoned?"

"No. He called me from his room because he was so sick." She paused, seeing the dubious look on his face. "Cy, I didn't even know his room number. The first thing I did was call 911. I was the third or fourth person in the room." She realized Cy didn't know any of the others, that he might not believe her.

"We've always been honest with one another," he said, slowly.

"Is there anything you need to tell me?" The noise of the crowd covered his words so that only she could hear them.

"Our divorce was so bad that after five years of holding a grudge I'd try to poison him? No," she said.

"It's interesting you were the one he called," Cy said.

"Old habits die hard. When we were married I was always the one who was called, no matter which bar he'd passed out in," Lynn said.

"So he's drinking again?"

"Like I said, it was no accident. Someone poisoned him. I've been racking my brains trying to figure out whom without accusing the wrong person. So has Mark Shepherd. Keith is still at home, recovering. He almost didn't make it."

As they watched Marika's team, Cy said, "Well, maybe now isn't the time to tell you I've been hearing from the wedding planner nonstop."

Lynn looked at him and shook her head. The list the Whippet had sent to Lynn's phone rattled through her mind. She was supposed to be checking off each one. Color scheme, guest list with addresses, gift registry, florist, photographer, music, parking valets, reception food, mementoes for the guests, bridesmaids' dresses, childhood video montages, dance lessons for the bridesmaids and groomsmen, DJ or band, corsages, honeymoon trip, bar bill, punch server, greenery rental. Even though she had tried to simplify, it was hard to do so at an event in which one was both host and honoree.

She sighed. "I can't do this. We can't do this."

"Get married?"

She smiled so she wouldn't cry. "Stage a wedding according to the Whippet when I'm about to lose my father."

He nodded.

"Can I call her off? Can we say vows in a back yard with a few friends and not the huge, entire family? Serve lemonade and cookies? Something that doesn't require the planning of World War Three? I know you and your family want something big, but I just can't manage it."

Cy frowned, but then pulled her close in a hug. "My huge, entire family would be just fine with lemonade and cookies. Do you want me to call her?"

"I will." Lynn pulled out her cell phone and hit a speed dial number.

"This is Lynn. I'm sorry to spring this on you, but we've decided to radically simplify our ceremony."

"But honey, we've been doing that."

Lynn detected a slight wail in the Whippet's voice. She sighed. "We'll pay what we owe so far, but that's it. My father doesn't have long to live. And I can't devote time away from work to make wedding arrangements. Any spare time I have, I need to spend with my father, or Cy."

The Whippet was, finally, kinder than Lynn expected. "Honey, I saw this coming. Even though it hurts me, you're doing the right thing."

Lynn gave Cy a thumbs-up as the last whistle of the game sounded.

Marika was dispatched to a friend's house for a post-game play date. Lynn and Cy returned to his house with Matt. She lifted the two-year-old into a small bed a few inches off the floor. He'd begun climbing out of his crib a few months ago so Cy had moved him to a low bed. "Naptime, sweet boy."

One little foot stuck out from the covers. "Don't kiss me."

"Kissing you is my favorite part." She covered the exposed foot.

"Okay, you can kiss me."

When Matt's eyes finally shut, she and Cy checked the monitor and closed the door.

"How do you figure this out? How do you parent two kids and keep a full-time pace at your law firm?" she whispered, concerned she might wake the boy.

"Never as well as I'd like," he whispered back. "I swear I wasn't ADHD until we had kids. There's so much my wife did. Before she died I wanted to split myself three ways, between her, them, and work. Now, it's between them, work, and you."

"I guess we have as much chance of doing that as Marika

finding the potion to turn herself into a horse at will."

He smiled and nodded. "You can kiss me, too."

"Happily. How long will his nap be?" She wrapped her arms around his back.

"Long enough," he murmured.

It was.

I knew I would kill her someday. I didn't expect it to give me full satisfaction, but still, it was a pleasure I had reserved for myself. I'd pick a time when her seed cap farmer "friends" weren't around.

Like jewelry on layaway, her killing was something I promised myself in the future.

I didn't expect she would understand why I was killing her. Glib and stupid, she'd never understood anything else. Sometimes I hated her with every fiber of my identity; sometimes she was just another twitchy bitch and hating took too much energy.

Jesse Drum was in Dallas. He had offered to meet Lynn. Lynn welcomed the chance to talk to him further, although she wondered if he was the one who'd poisoned Keith. So for their lunch she chose a public, sun-lit place, the cafe inside the Nasher Sculpture Garden.

As she walked from her office to the sculpture garden, she called her sister, Ceil, in Paris. "Dad's hospice doctor says he has eight to ten weeks. I'm telling you so you can get ready."

The phone was silent, then Ceil sniffled. "Jesus, despite what I told you, I really did hope he would have longer. Stupid to say, because we saw how Mom struggled."

Lynn's eyes were wet. "I don't want to believe it either."

"Well, tell me when you need me there. If I don't hear from you, I'll plan on returning in a month or six weeks. How are you doing otherwise? How's wedding planning with the Whippet?"

"The Whippet's gone. I told her with Dad's condition, I'd be doing well to manage beer and pretzels in his back yard."

"You fired her?"

"It was mutual." As Lynn turned off her phone, she realized with relief she had received no new exclamation-filled texts in the last few hours about color-matching the napkins to the floral arrangements.

She greeted Jesse at the Nasher's barrel-vault entrance. TriCoast's name was somewhere high up on the wall of donors, so they were waved through. Jesse strolled past the Miros faster than she expected, saying, "Not my taste. We sponsor our nation's artists in a show later this fall. You should come and see it."

He explained he met regularly with Dallas banks, venture capitalists, and investment firms. "Plus, I stopped by our competition." He meant the Chickasaw Nation's WinStar casino seventy-five miles north of Dallas, a mile across the border in Oklahoma. A prime location, it had doubled in size and employed several thousand people, many bussed from Dallas' northern suburbs. Other dedicated buses carried customers to and from the casino from suburbs like Richardson and Plano. The casino's billboards were all around town; it was so big it had its own exit from I-35.

Jesse ordered a rare roast beef sandwich and red potato salad while she picked a farmers' market salad and a grilled cheese sandwich. The grilled cheese resembled the toast-and-cheese-food-slices she'd eaten while growing up in name only. Provolone, cheddar, and mozzarella crowded slices of sourdough bread.

When they sat outside, he looked around with more interest than he'd shown for the pieces inside.

"So, tell me why CIG wants to buy this refinery," Lynn said.

His voice was soothing, with the right level of new-age toughness. "Simple. Backward integration. Our casino business is expanding at," he smiled briefly, "more than a double-digit rate each year. All those people drive cars, most of which still use gasoline." He explained CIG already owned nearly a hundred service stations. "We have several sources for gasoline, but your refinery is the best." He smiled again. "So owning it is a good fit for us."

He described how the concept of individual ownership was

still hard for some of the nation's elders to understand. "They don't really believe anyone owns anything, which is hell on property disputes. They don't think we actually own land. They think dirt is dirt and we're to use what we need. That's why all the tribes ceded so much land to whites. First the whites shoved us off the land we were using, then they assigned us other land in the treaties. After a while they needed more land, so they offered us a lose-lose deal. They would either come and take the land or we could cede most of it for a small payment, reserving some for ourselves. Hence, reservations."

"It's a painful history," Lynn said.

"Well, now that we have money, when we spend it, we have to be careful. And I have the whole Cherokee Nation to worry about. Everything from the rising number of diabetes cases to K12 education to translating our newspaper stories into the Cherokee language."

They finished eating and walked around the garden. Lynn pointed to Quantum Cloud XX. "If you stand back, you can see the man inside all the stainless steel bars."

"Like a fog of knives. I know the feeling," Jesse said. "Budget week at the council."

She nodded toward two pieces. "They remind me I need to get back to work."

He frowned.

"The Richard Serra fifty-ton plates? Oil tankers. The Hammering Man—"

"—yes, I see. Sucker-rod pumps. Like the horsehead pumps all over Oklahoma. This guy's even the same size." The giant sculpture loomed about twenty feet high.

Her cell phone rang and the display showed Mark Shepherd's number. He asked, "Can you get to the office now?"

"Why?"

"Are you with someone?"

"Yes."

He hesitated. "Jesse Drum?"

"Yes."

"I'll explain when you get here."

Her head buzzing with unanswered questions, she fought impatience. She wanted a calm, upbeat end to the meeting with Jesse, the man who represented the most promising buyer for TriCoast's Tulsa refinery.

As they parted, he said, "Effective soft sell. But I get it often."

Mark Shepherd was waiting for her when she entered her office in the headquarters building. "I want Cheryl with you all the time."

"We were outside in the Nasher Sculpture Garden in the middle of the day. He's my father's age, not a young man. Cheryl is only supposed to be with me in situations we consider risky." She wouldn't add that Jesse was a relative, too, and so that she was even less inclined to suspect him.

"You can't make that judgment. One mistake and you could be a goner."

"What are you trying to tell me?"

"You should already have heard it from Gene."

"What?"

"Remember the missing men at his refinery?"

She nodded.

"One of them has been found."

Lynn knew the worst was true. "He's dead?"

"Yes. They started to recommission one of the storage tanks they'd mothballed. Remember the contractor, Roberto Molina? His body was at the bottom in two pieces. One of his legs had been severed at the hip. He'd bled to death."

"How horrible! I'm so sorry."

"From the angle of the cut, it looks like someone used a high pressure water hose on him."

Lynn had heard of similar deaths, but always as accidents. Water spraying at several hundred pounds of pressure was deadlier than a machete.

"Has Gene talked to Roberto's family?"

"He and Roberto's boss at the contracting company are on the way now," Mark said, and left.

Lynn called Gene. "I'm so sorry about this. And I'm sorry you have to tell his family."

"Yeah. It's bad. The guys who found him, well, after they finish talking to Tulsa PD they'll have to take a few days' leave, at least."

"Whatever they need, they get. Whatever his family needs, same thing. Any cameras, any evidence? What does Tulsa PD say?"

"Mark's coming up to talk to Tulsa PD with me. I think some outsider is using the missing contractor badge to get in. Fuck. We have so many contractors, to say nothing of all the bozos you've brought through to buy it." Gene's swearing and his angry tone was new.

She softened her voice as much as possible. "Bozos, Gene? Look, we have our orders to sell this refinery. Why don't you take a few days off? You've been through a lot yourself."

"It's a signal we shouldn't be selling," he said.

*I wish I could convince these guys,* Lynn thought, as she was waved into the boardroom to present an update on the sale.

There was no avoiding it. After she described her meetings with potential buyers, she said, "I've just been notified a missing contractor was found onsite, dead. It appears his death wasn't accidental."

Several people in the room frowned. Burl Travis, whom she had not seen since the disastrous trip to Paris with Riley, said, "You got your ex-husband poisoned, too, I hear."

*You asshole!* Her face flushed with the anger she couldn't hide. "Our divorce wasn't that acrimonious." After the laughter stopped, Lynn continued. "But frankly, I wouldn't go after someone who said he's ready to help buy the Tulsa refinery for $1.3 billion. At any rate, the investigation is in the hands of the police. They'll let us know their results." *Dammit, Riley's been telling Burl everything. Maybe to deflect attention away from himself. Is Riley the one?*

"What other good news do you have for us?" Burl asked, in an acid voice.

*You weren't the one to find Dag Nordval's body, you jerkwad. Oh damn. He would have also heard about...*"And you got the news about the prince's second bodyguard?"

"Damn shame. You and Mike were the last ones to see the prince and his entourage," Burl said. "I arranged that meeting for you, you know. You screwed it up."

"No, whoever killed him was the last person to see him, *and* the one who screwed it up." Lynn's leg started to cramp, so she flexed her foot to stretch it out. The cramp would get worse until she left the meeting.

"Lynn, maybe it's time you step down and let Riley, Henry Vandervoost, or someone else take the reins until this all blows over," Burl said.

Lynn thought her head would explode. She pushed her hands into the table so she wouldn't knock Burl out of his seat. She kept her voice even, dropping it to a low whisper. "I don't like your proposal or what you are implying about my presumed culpability. I seriously question whether you have the best interests of TriCoast in mind."

His expression, like a turtle's, didn't change. "If you are unable to sell this refinery, we should get someone who can. Someone who can travel to the Middle East and meet with people there without worrying about politically-correct diplomacy."

*Someone with a penis*, she thought.

"Lynn's doing a superb job. TriCoast has over three billion in refining assets, Burl," Mike said. "Too many refineries spread across too many continents for one person. Henry and Lynn need to continue splitting the responsibility. We need our US refining chief in the US, and it will remain Lynn."

TriCoast's CFO, Sara Levin, said, "Burl, you and this board are the bosses. But my responsibility to TriCoast shareholders leads me to suggest you are not doing your fiduciary duty when you suggest replacing Lynn with a pair of balls."

*I love this woman.* Lynn almost said it aloud.

Mike Emerson coughed. "And with that, it's time to move on to the next agenda item. Thank you for your time, Lynn."

⁊

After an eight-mile run to relieve her frustration, Lynn packed a suitcase and drove to Love Field. Within two and a half hours she was in San Antonio introducing herself to executives from several small companies at a pre-conference cocktail meet 'n greet. All were producing gas, light liquids, and oil from the nearby Eagle Ford field. She hoped in the room full of black suits her green one stood out; she had chosen her colors to attract attention.

Lynn needed to speak with as many people as possible. She kept her tone light. However, the Saudis had indeed stopped doing additional business with her after the death of the prince's second bodyguard, and many seemed to know it, knowledge they leveraged to drive harder bargains.

Despite the clink of glasses inside and the well-lit, placid Riverwalk outside, she shuddered when she remembered finding Dag Nordval's body. Tom. Roberto. Jimmy. Almost Keith. She had been invited to speak to the attendees about changes TriCoast made in its refinery configurations to meet the newest gasoline and diesel specs. She would also listen to the panel on security and terrorism.

People around her spoke in the peculiar, familiar oilfield patois. "Bolt a set of leases onto the side of it…time is the enemy…stacked pay, nothing's better no way no how…our Aggies are smarter than their Aggies…gut check…key takeaway…land rig utilization."

The voices were as intense as those on a trading floor. Lynn noticed most around her were young men, chock full of testosterone, all sharp elbows and emphatic curses. None heard or all ignored double entendres in phrases like, "payback," or "we had to clean out a deviated hole," or "rate of penetration."

One of the youngest men, about Greg Sutton's age, sidled up to her and said, "Feels like I'm pinging a dark pool around here."

"What do you mean?"

"Feeling people out. No one discusses the identity of his trading partners until the deal is signed. Right now everyone's making small offers to see what's thumping."

"Like bats."

"More like sharks. We're all looking for big prey from small blotches of blood."

# Thirty-Seven

*London/Oklahoma*
*Sunday evening-Monday*

The shade was mud-colored, although there was no mud in paved Burroughs market. Insel ducked into the warren of stalls to get out of the insistently gentle rain that made England both green and depressing.

Stall after stall was packed with cheese, pastries, ducks, wheat-free brownies, chorizo, and cake. Insel bought a large roast, which was wrapped and secured with heavy plastic twine. Once he paid, he went into a nearby restroom, donned latex gloves and unwrapped the meat. He pocketed the twine and threw the meat and paper away.

Gernot Insel wasn't partial to religions. They were organizations with peculiarities. They could incite fervor, but the simple truth was they didn't pay enough.

However, religious services had their uses.

It was certain he would be photographed by the omnipresent cameras, so he had altered his appearance as much as possible with an inexpensive gray jacket from H&M, brown-colored contacts, hair dye, a lift in one shoe, and a hat. His biggest advantage would be, as always, surprise.

His instructions hadn't been specific as to why Nigel Wold of North Seas Resources was to be killed, but he calculated Wold's deals had soured and he'd made noise about one particular asset he controlled, an asset Insel's current employer found of special interest.

His reconnaissance showed him the best place to find Wold. The man was careful in his daily commute to the massive, anonymous green glass building. But he attended evensong services at Southwark Cathedral, across the Thames. Gernot had followed him there enough to learn the boys sang different hymns twice on Sunday, and once each evening except Wednesday, which they called "a dumb day."

The location surprised Insel because the service was routinely drowned by roaring trains.

High voices of the youngest boys rang out in rituals focused more on singing than sermonizing. *Nunc Dimitis* was followed by the priest's homily about sacrifice, followed by another choral response. One boy soprano wielded his voice like a weapon. Deeper voices, also male, set the bass foundation.

Choristers' robes flashed red and their surplices white. The organ's chords slid and pierced and thundered into every corner of the vast cathedral. Gernot preferred Viennese opera, but he understood why Wold had made attending this service a habit.

His target was near the front, in a pew with several others.

When evensong ended, Insel moved close enough to hear Nigel exchange pleasantries. "Thank you. Please. Sorry."

He drifted further back as Wold commenced a walk that would eventually take him to his favorite pub. They strode through a narrow, dark passage on the bishop's grounds. To the left was the Clink, one of London's first prisons.

Wold pulled out his phone and pressed a button, a call to his wife, Insel surmised.

At the pub, he took a small table not far from Wold's perch. Insel drank seltzer water as Wold downed two pints of Boddingtons Pub Ale.

Insel paid his bill and went to the men's loo, locking himself into a stall. After a few minutes he heard Wold enter and unzip his pants. No one else was around.

Insel double-looped the twine and quietly opened the stall. He secured the restroom door with a metal wedge-shaped doorstop.

Wold twisted a quarter turn as he urinated. "I say, what are you doing?"

In one motion, Insel looped the twine tight over Wold's head and pulled it into his neck, snapping his head back. Wold's eyes bulged. His face turned red, then purple. His hands scrabbled at the twine. Insel pulled tighter, his knee in Wold's back, until the man stopped struggling.

Is perfect memory a blessing or a curse?

I remember living with my mother. After the age of five, I lived with my uncle.

I recall my mother's dogs, those two scrawny poodles. She combed their hair, not mine. "Yours is too long, too tangled," she'd say to me. I was always washing their poop—"Poop, dear, not shit"—from between my toes in the big, mildewed claw-foot tub. The poodles had "oh, little accidents," as she called them, all over the house when I didn't get them outside fast enough, and sometimes even when I did. When she told me to let them outside, my diaper, especially when it was wet, got in the way of four-year-old legs trying to move fast. Sometimes a rash on my bottom slowed me down, but by the time I was five, I learned to bring my mother a diaper and powder so she could change me. Sometimes she did, if it wasn't in the middle of a show.

I wished I could diaper the dogs, and tried once or twice.

My mother smelled of the yappy dogs, and most wonderfully, of chocolate, which she often shared with me. She couldn't walk much, telling everyone who stopped by, "I got the sugar." Her pale white legs had become little sticks barely supporting the heft of her big, droopy trunk, mounds of breasts eclipsed by the bigger mound of stomach.

I remembered the dogs, and the bare mattress and the bugs skittering late at night. Once in a while I'd wake to find one on my face.

People I didn't know visited once, twice, three times. When they saw the house, and me, their faces drew tight and they looked scared, or angry. Then one day they took me in the car as my soft mother wailed, "Who will take care of me?"

I heard one of the big people sigh. "She thinks a five-year-old should take care of her?"

They sent me to live with my uncle up in the hills east of town where there were so many more rules about taking baths, and using the toilet, and going to school. My cousins punched me when they thought no one was watching, and teased me about my skin's pallor. Or they'd steal my pillow, with which I was finally learning to sleep. At school my teacher looked at me with concern—"you don't know how to count?"—but she didn't realize I'd learned to button my shirt the week before, or just learned how to use the bathroom, most of the time.

⁂

Insel looked at the destinations on the signs at Heathrow: Abu Dhabi, Mumbai, Helsinki, Lisbon. His destination was even more exotic.

This time his route into the United States was roundabout. A changed identity, a dark maroon Reisepass in the new name, and bribed officials of friendly countries hastened his progress.

On one of the flights, the clouds raced past the moon like players running past a stationary football. The States, he recalled from his trip to North Dakota, where football was "soccer" and "football" was a sport of apes moving a ball that wouldn't bounce back and forth in nine-meter intervals.

He delayed a day for a total of five flight segments before a private plane ferried him to a small airport outside of Tulsa, Oklahoma.

Before this assignment, all he knew about Oklahoma was that a long-ago Austro-German relative had moved to the western town of Shattuck and nearly been wiped out by the Dust Bowl. But it had been easy to learn what he needed. Geography and history didn't concern him as much as the arrival of the materials he had purchased in the Czech Republic. They had been shipped to a Mexican drug gang, who likely had stolen some for themselves, then trucked into the US near Organ Pipe Monument close to Yuma, Arizona and finally transported northeast to Oklahoma.

Upon landing he changed into khakis and a blue striped polo shirt. He smoothed gray tint into his hair. His cover was of a European fund executive ready to invest in the lucrative fracturing projects that pulled oil from old fields.

His actual base for the next few days would be an abandoned barn. Several locations were too well-patrolled, even in seemingly empty Osage County. He'd finally found a place twenty kilometers southwest of Tulsa. Miles, he had to remember. Twelve miles.

A private car, arranged through a third party who would never know any of his names, waited for him. This dry region contrasted with London's dampness in a way he found pleasing. The constant wind was a zephyr, a caress. Flags flapped. Women's hair blew around their faces.

He slowed his car. Like North Dakota and unlike the German autobahn, he reminded himself that the highways here had speed limits.

He bought a supply of bottled water. Drinking tap water was barbaric, a custom he would never adopt. And ice cubes were unsanitary and wasteful.

He picked up the packages that had been dropped off for him at a storage unit.

After settling into the remote house, he drove into downtown Tulsa. To him it was small, but none of the buildings was signed with graffiti. He hadn't expected to find an evensong here, nor to be reminded of his most recent project, but he slipped into a back pew at Trinity Episcopal Church. This time there was no target, so he merely listened to the service. Nothing ever shocked him, but when he examined the stained glass panels he was surprised to see an image of Adolf Hitler, apparently in a section depicting evil.

As he walked around the city after the service, he noticed the wind again, and the omnipresent No Smoking signs. Signs on buildings showed him the city's history filled in joyously, carelessly, including all the years between 1930 and 1989. It was unlike his beloved Berlin, where references to World War II were rare and the gap in history books routine.

Throughout the day the temperature range was extreme. Insel found himself looking for the car's heater controls in the morning, air conditioning in the afternoon.

He was due to meet his American contact in the next few days. He hoped the contact had been more productive since their last meeting and had completed more of his assignments.

Finally, he returned to his rented house southwest of the small city. He began shaping the C-4 charges.

"I think one of my dogs is sick. It's Huck, not Hooper," I told my mother.

"Bring me a soda," she said. "My legs hurt." My mother had never become any less vicious. Maybe she did feel guilt about giving me up. Maybe she was angry at me for seeing her poor, obese, and hung over when she had once been none of those things.

"Your legs would hurt less if you got out of your chair and walked." Usually I didn't offer advice. My gut tightened with worry over Huck. He hadn't been eating much. "You used to have dogs. What happened?" I felt desperate, but vowed I wouldn't plead.

"County took 'em. Bring me the soda and a sandwich. I'm starving."

"Mom, you haven't missed any meals. How did you feel when the county took your dogs?" Why was I asking after all this time?

"Bad. Really bad."

"As bad as when they took me?"

"Worse. You were a whiny kid. You needed too much." No surprise. She'd told me so before. "You should have been able to take care of yourself."

"For Christ's sake, I was five."

"Fine. Whatever. Get me the sandwich."

She would never change, a prickly burr whose only meaning was to remind me I was alive. "Get it yourself," I told her.

"Look, I got a friend coming over later. I have to save my energy for him. They tell me you're bright. So you understand what that means." She chortled, then stared coolly at me for a minute before returning her attention to the computer monitor. Another reality show clip. And why should I care? I'd bought the computer for her.

I wanted her to feel remorse. I wanted her to understand how deeply she'd failed me. I wanted her to be tortured by guilt. Before I said a word, I knew she'd never have those feelings. But I spoke anyway. "What did you do with my things after the county took me?"

"They handed me all kinds of cleaning solutions. They wanted me to clean the place up before they would bring you back. But I had the sugar even then. Told 'em I couldn't. Needed someone to do it for me. They said they couldn't pay for that."

"So what did you do with my things?"

"I cleaned up." She grinned vacantly. "You didn't have much but I started by throwing out your clothes and toys. They weren't going to do me any good."

For some reason I thought of Huck's scent, of his loyalty. I didn't want him to die. But he hadn't jumped up with his usual verve this morning. I needed to take him to his veterinarian, but there wouldn't be time until later.

"Could I bring Huck over here? Could you watch him this once? I have a vet on call that'll come and pick him up if he gets worse."

"I can't. Why would you think I would? Come on, get me the sandwich. Do I have to say sit up and beg?" She turned in her chair to face me, a big concession.

I stood in front her.

Her shapeless breasts sagged nearly to her waist. Irritation flashed in her eyes. "What do you need?" she asked. "You always need something. You always have."

"Not any more." I planted myself, equal weight on both feet. I leaned over and locked my hands against her neck. I stared into her eyes and pressed her head against the back of her chair. I pressed harder until her white stick-like legs stopped thrashing.

Her stink was as unmistakable, and familiar, as that of the yappy dogs she had loved.

Then I made an enormous sandwich. It was the most delicious meal I've ever eaten.

# Thirty-Eight

*Tulsa/Tahlequah*
*Monday*

I needed more time. I didn't want her found by her latest beau. A group of small-time thieves had been stealing from businesses around Tulsa recently. That and one of the Osage stories gave me an idea.

The hardest part was getting her heavy, stinky, floppy body into the trunk. I stopped and bought thick rope at a hardware store. I had another assignment so I would finish later.

I didn't like killing women. My mother, or the body in the trunk, didn't count. She hadn't been a woman for a long time. The older women among our clients, well, they'd lived long lives.

But it can be a deadly mistake to be sexist. It was in Iraq. And it was now. I particularly respected the abilities of one woman.

In the late afternoon I took my supplies and rented a room on the same floor Lynn had said they were staying, putting out a 'do not disturb' hang-tag. No one else was on the floor, and the housekeeping staff was finished for the day. I could see the parking lot and saw them return. I prepared my supplies, and hoped I could rely on Cheryl's few regular habits. She was strong, tough, a deadly shot. She only had one weakness that I'd spotted.

The ice machine and some laundry machines were located in a big alcove between their rooms and mine. I dipped the dart in the frog poison and stood just inside my room. When Cheryl's door opened and then fell closed, I waited a few seconds. There would be a very brief time when she had her back to me as she took a bucket of ice from the machine.

When the ice machine door opened, I slipped out of my room, ran down the hall. As she was turning, I stabbed the dart into her neck, as close to her carotid artery as I could get, clapped my hand over her mouth, and dragged her back to my room. She struggled and landed a few elbows to my stomach, but only the first one hurt. Within a few seconds, her muscles were paralyzed, including the ones that allowed her to breathe.

I opened my door and pulled her inside. Her face had turned purple, and she couldn't speak.

"Yes, it's me," I said.

I tied her up, just in case the poison took longer than usual to work, although it appeared she only had a minute or so left. I found her cell phone. It was locked, so my plan to use it to text Lynn wasn't going to work. And Lynn would be checking for Cheryl in a few minutes.

Lynn could sign contracts. I needed Lynn alive for at least a few days longer. I packed up, left the tag on the door, and headed downstairs. No one would check the room until late tomorrow morning, and by then I'd be long gone.

I left a message in an envelope at the front desk for Lynn supposedly from Cheryl, saying I thought I might have food poisoning and had gone to the hospital. I tipped the front desk clerk a hundred dollars to forget what I looked like, explaining I was here with a woman who wasn't my wife.

Well, that part was true.

⁂

Carla thought about Keith McConaugh and Pete Whitehawk's Adela fund. They acquired struggling companies from elderly owners, rebuilt the companies, and sold them.

Pete Whitehawk, a half-blood Keetoowah and full-blood financial genius seemed to make sure their company cut good deals. Carla trusted Pete because his father had been a member of the United Keetoowah Band of Cherokees, a fifteen thousand-member group with its headquarters in Tahlequah, near that of her own, three hundred-thousand-member Cherokee Nation.

Since they were preparing to back her tribe's investment in the refinery, she was seeing even more of handsome, dark-haired Keith—until he was poisoned—and nine-fingered Pete Whitehawk. They disagreed with her over the refinery's income potential. Her numbers were more conservative, at one hundred and fifty million dollars a year, than theirs of three hundred million a year. Despite that, Keith had taken time to answer all her questions. *Who poisoned him? His ex-wife? Does she hate him that much?*

Her dark hair spread on the back of the chair. At first, Cherokee Council members and the Adela investors challenged her ability to step into Jimmy's role, making her wish she lived in the old days when Cherokee women owned all the assets. Then she could have simply assumed control and made decisions without having to prove herself. What a fantasy.

Right now, it felt more like a burden. The tribe had moved on from printing their own license plates and running tax-free smoke shops to managing casinos, overseeing road funding, raising lower-fat buffalo for tribal consumption to combat diabetes, and dozens of other projects.

Her cell phone chimed. She hesitated before answering it. Then she rebuffed Riley's question. "Every man coming through my office thinks if he sweet-talks me enough, he'll get Cherokee casino money to go spend on his boat and his girlfriend. Sorry."

He didn't appear to have heard her. "I've got friends, just like Pete and Keith, who also want to invest with the Cherokee Nation. You'd like them."

"Heard it all. Jesse and I make sure money is invested right so we can take good care of our people, down to their dentures and eyeglasses. Anything you suggest, I've already heard." Carla clicked off her phone. But it wouldn't hurt to go out with the guy.

*What am I doing otherwise? Jesse sure isn't ringing me up.*

She called Riley back and said they could have dinner, but only at one of the Cherokee casinos. She figured she might as well make the man flip his cash, or more likely TriCoast's cash, to the tribe.

Riley would probably turn out to be another of the unfortunate experiments she had been trying after waiting too long for Jesse Drum to make a move. She was Wolf Clan, through her mother. Yes, she'd learned Jesse's mother had been *Ani-Sahoni* or Panther Clan, or she wouldn't even have allowed herself to think about him. As if clans mattered. They weren't supposed to any more. Just a group to sit with at powwows. Usually she didn't know her friends' clans, unless they posted them on Facebook. Her fingertips brushed the acne pits on her cheeks. Well, maybe he was too old for her. He obviously thought so. And technically he was her boss, which made him really off-limits.

Anyway, he was probably still mourning his wife. It was out of harmony to consider him in ways other than as a bereaved widower.

Riley Stevens, Special Projects Manager for TriCoast, showed up at her Tulsa office with sweaty palms and a generous smile.

The Ramona Casino was twenty miles away. Riley talked as she drove; she would return him to her office later to retrieve his car. That would at least give the evening the flavor of a business meeting and not just a date. Riley told her he was recently divorced with kids he saw on weekends and that he lived in a forgettable Houston neighborhood. "By the way, I do have a great investment opportunity you ought to look at."

She waved a hand. "Later."

They were leaving behind the tawny yellow grasshoppers and the hard heat of summer. Fall was underway. She could tell it by the mashes of too-slow squirrels on the highway.

They trailed behind a manure-smelly cattle truck for a few miles. A sign reminded her of her competition: *Osage Million Dollar Elm Casino*. It was a reference not only to the Osage casino in the next county, but also to the tree under which the Osages had signed a million-dollar deal with an oilman nearly a century ago.

When oil was discovered in Indian Territory, one of the first needs was storage. So during 1901, an eleven-million-barrel tank farm, one of the world's largest at the time, was built just east of Osage County. As production grew during the teens and 1920s, Oklahoma became the world's largest oil-producing area. Storage needs grew in tandem, and ground was broken for tanks at Cushing, southwest of Ramona.

As they neared the small town, Carla explained the history and pointed at earthen mounds marking the tank farm's former location off Highway 75.

Riley said, "So now Ramona gathers casino dollars for you instead of oil for others."

She laughed at his analogy. The man had possibilities.

When she parked, dust clouded up from an unpaved outer rim of the lot, the only open place she could find. "Accountants don't have parking privileges," she explained to Riley. "The upfront spots are saved for the best customers, those who lose the most."

Located next to US Highway 75, fifteen miles south of Bartlesville, the ten thousand-square-foot Ramona Cherokee Casino had cost six and a half million dollars to build and was the tribe's eighth. Its target market for both employees and customers was the forty-mile north-south leg of US 75 between Tulsa and Bartlesville, as well as smaller towns like Skiatook and Nowata.

Carla ran through numbers in her head, one of her favorite activities on or off the job. The casino operated 24/7 with a staff of a hundred and a monthly payroll of four hundred thousand dollars, mostly going to local workers. It featured two hundred electronic games, free soft drinks and coffee, full-bar service, and was themed after a significant period in Cherokee history, a time of strength between 1881 and 1906.

"You ain't one of them friggin' eyelash vegetarians, are you?" Riley chuckled at his own joke.

"You'll have to explain that one."

"Eyelash vegetarians won't eat meat from animals with eye-lashes, like cows, sheep. But they eat chicken and fish."

"If I don't have a steak from time to time, I go nuts," she said. He nodded.

Still, she wished she had picked another place tonight, one with more familiar food on the menu, like fried hominy or eggs and onions. Then she wished the hour afterward with Riley Stevens had ended on a more promising note, or at least made her laugh more.

She'd enjoyed the first part of their talk when he intimated that as a former CFO himself he understood her accounting woes. He sympathized when she talked about how much time she was putting into her day job. Together with after-hours work for the Cherokee Nation's accounting and its investments, it barely left her time to sleep.

I'm 62.5 percent Cherokee, she thought, reveling in exactness. Her workdays consisted of matching payments to accounts receiv-able, but she was even learning to speak and write the Cherokee language, using a marked-up syllabary from Jesse. It was good to better understand the first language, one she'd heard all her life.

After he'd had a few drinks, Riley began complaining about his dementia-ridden father, his harridan ex-wife, and his uptight boss at TriCoast, Lynn Dayton, who'd put him on this special project while he looked for a new job. Carla pegged him as an-other man who found therapy in a glass.

"And worst of all, it's so hot here I'm sleeping at sperm-kill-ing temperatures," he said.

Still, they'd had a surprisingly good conversation about issues she could seldom share with anyone, like getting CEOs to report honestly and managing earnings-per-share expectations with elephant-memory analysts. She asked him about oil and gas reserves accounting and he'd said he'd be setting up a consulting business, but gave her all the information she needed, for free.

Well, not completely free. Then it was on to jokes about spreadsheets and spreading between the sheets.

Face flushed, he'd moved his bulk closer to her. His round stomach rested against her arm. The grin changed to a leer as he finished a joke. "Drill deep and as often as possible. That's what I always say."

*Is it my Cherokee heritage in assimilating or am I just too nice to this guy?* Carla wondered. She was startled by what he said next.

"What do you think really happened to Jimmy?"

"Traffic accident." She thought, *Since Jimmy died in September, his family can't go to a powwow for the next twelve months, according to the rules.*

Riley interrupted her thoughts. "You know, he was fine when he left that night."

"You think there's more to it?"

"Isn't that always the way? Kill the messenger? Or in this case the accountant?"

"Are you suggesting I'm in danger, too? Are you threatening me?"

He shook his head. "You did time on auditing projects, right?"

"Everyone does."

"What are the signals for management fraud?"

She answered, as if seeing the tests, "Circumstances which indicate unusual pressures on management like a lack of working capital, a lack of internal auditors in a large client, or evidence of reckless or dishonest act."

"Adela has plenty of working capital," he said. "They're not large or public, so they don't need internal auditors."

"Which leaves a reckless or dishonest act."

He lowered his voice. "Don't you think it's strange their company owners keep dying?"

"No. They're old. Old people die."

"But I looked it up. Every one of them had rapidly-accelerated dementia. They might not have been in perfect health before, but suddenly they were talking nonsense, running onto highways, jumping out of moving cars."

"Damn." She remembered the next dictum. *The auditor should first inform the appropriate client personnel of the illegal act.* Her breathing came faster. "Are you saying we should call Pete and Keith?"

"Keith's still in treatment, so yeah, we should call Pete."

"But why? If they're doing something, they'll turn on us."

"And if not, they'll have a good explanation."

"Let's find an office," she said.

They moved away from the smoke and busy machines. Carla explained what she needed to an attentive manager, and he showed them into a quiet, paneled office walled in with security camera screens.

"Pete, this is Carla. You're at a basketball game with Lynn and Jesse? I need to talk to you for a few minutes. It's important." She looked at Riley and nodded.

"Pete, we've been very pleased with our relationship with Adela, and we appreciate your backing on buying this refinery. But I'm here with Riley talking auditing, and we have to make sure you and Keith are good to go. I'll put you on speaker."

"Of course," Pete's voice echoed. "I understand. You have statements from our banks and we gave you financial statements. Not audited, but they don't have to be since we're private. Our businesses are illiquid—there's no market for them—so we use our best guess. It's possible we may value them incorrectly, but usually we sell for what we expect."

"About that. We see your typical turnover for a company is six months. Seems awfully quick."

"I guess we're simply lucky. We find owners who are ready to sell and whose heirs don't want to run their companies," Pete said.

"Pete. Riley here. What about hedging? When they're selling grain, metals, or oil do you hedge to prevent losses?"

"Absolutely. Wouldn't think of doing otherwise."

"How is Keith doing?" Carla asked.

"He'll be back in a week, if he follows his treatment proto-col," Pete said.

"Well, I hate to disturb him," Riley interrupted. "And Pete, don't mention this call to Lynn either, since she's my boss and his ex. I'd guess they still talk to one another pretty freely. She'll defend him, I know. You're sure there's nothing he's doing on the side, something you don't know about. You think he's drink-ing again?"

"Since you mention it, he's been absent more often than I'd like—says he's skiing and snowboarding. I take him at his word," Pete said. "And what happened in Ponca City, I've heard it wasn't really from drinking. Maybe one of the room cups wasn't clean."

After they hung up, Carla said, "Pete sounds honest to me, but I have my doubts about Keith."

"We'll watch him," Riley agreed and they returned to the ca-sino floor. They walked around for a couple of hours, tried dollar games, and sat in for several hands of poker.

After his fourth drink, Riley stopped talking and stared at her chest. "You need to eat the miracle fruit."

"What?"

"Afterwards, everything you eat, even sour stuff, tastes sweet."

"Riley, my eyes are up here."

He pinched her upper arm. "You're really the little corn-fed heifer, aren't you?"

She jerked back. "What do you mean?"

"The extra weight. It's cute."

"My name is Carla Fourkiller. Make another crack like that, it'll be Fivekiller." She was ready to dump him now, but his car was at her office. Worse, he was too drunk to drive. She knew the hotel on the premises was already booked—she'd seen the schedule. She needed to escape Riley but didn't want to call Jesse Drum.

She left the table and called Pete again. "It's Carla, alone this time. I could really use a favor. Could you give Riley a ride home? Do you mind? We're at the Ramona casino. I could drive him back to his car, which is at my office building, but he's too drunk to drive on to his hotel and I don't want to walk him to his room."

"Could he stay there? Isn't there a hotel on the property?"

"Yeah, but it's booked."

"Why don't we just meet at the casino's front door instead of you trying to get him into your car? It will take me about a half-hour to get there. Can you put up with him for that long?"

"If I have to, I will. Pete, I really appreciate it."

Carla returned to Riley and persuaded him to try a few more dollar games. After thirty minutes and two more rounds of beer, she said, "Riley, it's time for us to leave. I called Pete and he's going to give you a ride back to your hotel."

"Can't you?"

"He lives closer to where you're staying. It's easier for him to drive you back."

⁂

Jesse rubbed the eyeglass indentations on each side of his nose and rose to shout support for the team. "*Osda!* Way to go!"

Lynn, Pete, and Jesse were crammed together in a large crowd at Sequoyah High School's basketball gym, *Tsu-Na-Ne-Lo-Di,* or Place Where They Play. Shouts in Cherokee and English surrounded them as the Sequoyah team pulled ahead.

Jesse related news from Cherokee Link about how Nike had studied the feet of Native Americans from seventy different tribes and determined they had wider, taller feet than the average American. Nike had then designed the Air Native N7 with a wider, larger toe box, fewer seams, and thicker sock liner. "Looks like the whole team is wearing N7s."

Gene had been unable to join them, pleading a piping failure at the refinery requiring his immediate attention.

*Which it does,* Lynn thought.

She tried to compartmentalize the concern she felt. She had called Nigel Wold's office earlier in the day. When someone finally answered, the British-accented voice delivered disturbing news. "Oh, so you're Ms. Dayton. What kind of bad-luck charms do you Yanks give out? Both Mr. Wold and Ms. Farber are dead."

She immediately called TriCoast's security chief, Mark Shepherd, and asked him to look into the deaths further.

That evening Mark had returned the call. "Lynn, Scotland Yard and Interpol are investigating both deaths as homicides. And I've told Jim Cutler with the FBI. The deaths were in different locations at different times but the killings don't appear to be random. Weren't Nigel and Helena evaluating the Tulsa refinery for North Seas Resources?"

"Yes."

"Are you okay?"

"Yes." But she was lying. She felt confused, bone-weary, and uncertain of where to turn. "Mark, should we stop the sale?"

"Yes. And is Cheryl with you?"

"She was this afternoon. When we got back to the hotel, she left me a note at the front desk saying she was feeling sick and was going to a clinic, and that I shouldn't wait for her. I'm at a basketball game. I tried her cell phone, but there was no answer."

"It's odd that she didn't text, call, or even just knock on your door to tell you. I'll find her. You should get back to the hotel. You shouldn't be out without her."

"I can take of myself."

"I don't like it, Lynn."

Lynn dreaded her calls to Sara and Mike. During their last conversation, TriCoast CFO Sara Levin had lost patience, telling Lynn she wanted to include the news of the sale in her analyst update next week. "Which means you have to have a buyer contracted for the refinery. So get on it. There's nothing more important to the company right now, and you have a ready buyer."

But tonight, when she explained the news of Wold's and Farber's apparent murders, both Sara and her boss Mike Emerson were immediately sympathetic. Mike said, "There's no need to rush a deal. Find a stopping point in the next few days and pull everyone back to Dallas. Let's take a breather. Let the FBI and Interpol investigate."

Sara's tone was similar. "Mark Shepherd called me, too. He's anxious that Cheryl isn't with you. He said Cutler will be there tomorrow to talk to you and Gene. They'll patch in Simone Tierney. Forget everything I said earlier about this sale. We want you, and everyone, safe and sound."

Pete excused himself to take a call. When he returned, he leaned toward them amid the noise and said, "Riley and Carla asked me a few questions. No problems." Despite his calm report, Pete's eyes flickered with an emotion Lynn could not name. Jesse was more direct. "What's she doing out with Riley? I thought she didn't like him."

Pete shrugged.

The Sequoyah team won by twenty points. In the parking lot filled with cars and trucks bearing blue-on-white Cherokee Nation license plates, Pete handed them each cups of iced soda. "Little caffeine for the trip, so you stay awake. Lot better than the low-alcohol beer."

"Thanks," Lynn said. "This wind is blowing so hard, I'll be fighting to stay on the road."

"Yeah," Jesse replied, "we don't want to get blown into a bridge abutment. And watch the low-lying areas. We had a flash flood kill a family of six last year. You sure don't want to be upside down in a creek."

Pete nodded. "Snakes come out when it rains."

⌘

I drove for a while and remembered. There had been naming ceremonies and clan ceremonies I wasn't allowed to attend. "You are the clan of white women, that's all you know," my cousins told me, since clans are determined by the mother's clan. "But my dad's same clan as your dad," I'd say.

"Don't matter. Clan's a mother thing and she ain't Keetoowah, so you ain't part of any Keetoowah clan. Hey, maybe they could make up a new one for you, the white bitch clan."

I'd run and cry and hide. Eventually my darkest-skinned girl cousin would feel sorry for me and come find me, usually right before the dinners that had gotten skimpier. My aunt made fry-bread and my uncle would supplement the meager meal with potato chips.

When I arrived at the site, I hoisted the body from the trunk and slipped a rope around her neck. She was heavy so I had to rest as I dragged her body to the bobbing horsehead.

I made a loop and a knot with the other end of the rope. It had been years since I'd thrown a lasso. But the pump wasn't running away, like cattle did. On the third try, the loop caught on the walking arm and tightened. The motors took over and her body rose up and down in the arc of the horsehead. The extra weight slowed the motion but didn't stop it.

When I returned home, the dogs sniffed my shoes attentively, identifying where I had been. Huck looked a little better than before.

Then I got a call from Carla Fourkiller asking me to drive Riley back to his hotel. If I helped her now, her guard would be down. It would be easier to kill her later, maybe even later this evening. I liked her, but ultimately she was just another assignment I had to complete quickly. It was already clear that, like Jimmy Deerinwater, she knew too much.

⌘

Out at an old, remote well location in Osage County, the scene resembled that from the county's lawless days almost a century earlier. The sucker-rod, or horsehead, pump clanged, pulling more barrels from the ground. It squealed and clanked, slowed by the weight of the old woman hanging from it.

# Thirty-Nine

*Tahlequah/Tulsa area*
*Monday night*

After watching the Sequoyah High School boys win their basketball game, Jesse stopped by his office. Lynn had asked for changes to Cherokee Investment Group's final bid before she presented it to her board. Although she had been circumspect, he understood theirs might be the winner. She'd said something an hour ago about slowing the pace of the deal, and he worried that her new hesitation was because she had other, better bids.

Jesse was hungry, craving pretzels and a candy bar, but he could hear his doctor's voice. The combination would send his blood sugar into orbit. *How'd I go from red warrior to old white wise man so fast?* He drank some of the soda.

He pored through spreadsheets, rubbed the back of his neck, and tried to remember what time the stomp dance started tomorrow. He wondered if Carla was planning to attend. *Probably not, especially if she's going out with Riley. Shouldn't think of her anyway; she's too young for me.* He drank again.

The stomp dance was a precursor to the powwow. Agaya didn't understand. They made jokes, then, eyes wide, covered their silly white mouths with smug grins, and said, "Oops. You know what I meant."

*No, the powwow is not some day-spa spiritual renewal crap.*

Jesse's head ached. *My ancestors didn't endure the Removal for me to drop the ball on my responsibilities.* He turned back to the diagrams and contract terms.

The casinos were supporting the tribe now. Their goofy flashing lights and the ever-helpful operations men meant all he had to do was sit back and count money. Maybe Billy Perry at the BIA was right. Why think about anything else? *Because the tribe needs to diversify,* Jesse silently answered.

He needed Pete here now. Maybe he could persuade him to help, or at least advise him occasionally. Even though Pete Whitehawk was a rich fund manager Jesse hadn't seen for years until recently, he still thought of him as the son of his old friend. *Don't think about Pete. Don't remember what happened. Don't think about the grub and grime and neglect from which I rescued him. I did rescue him,* Jesse thought. *I don't know if he did any better living with his uncle. Still, I had to do something. It was my fault his father died.*

And Pete had succeeded. The boy, now the man, had the heart of a warrior and an intellect as fine as Sequoyah's. It was odd; he was missing a finger, just like his father, Jack. Pete had lost his finger to a drill pipe smash the same day he'd learned from his mother about his Keetoowah heritage, and how they had been shunned after Jack broke tradition to marry her. His father had lost a finger to a claymore mine in Vietnam when he and Jesse served there together, a pact they'd made after going to Chilocco. Chilocco, where they'd been friends and, at least in private, every student had been allowed to speak his or her native language, unlike other Indian boarding schools. He was pleased Pete had said he wanted to learn more Cherokee as well.

But after Vietnam came San Francisco. No, he wouldn't think about that night again. And once he finally met her, Pete's mother hadn't been sure whether or not Jack was even Pete's biological father.

Jesse turned back to the refinery proposal to reread why TriCoast was selling it. In the end, he trusted Lynn and Gene.

◦⁊◦

When Carla told me she was with Riley, and needed him taken off her hands, the images of all of my mother's boyfriends returned. "Uncles," she called them as she shut me out of her bedroom when they arrived.

Fury rose in my throat. I would contain it. That would make it easier to kill Riley, and eventually, Carla.

When I arrived at the casino, Riley looked loose but wasn't falling over. Perfect. "Hey Pete. How's it hanging? Whatcha doing here?"

"Thought maybe you and me could do a little fish-gigging before I take you back to your hotel. You can pick up your car at Carla's office tomorrow."

"Isn't Carla coming with us?"

Even in the dark I could see how fast Carla was shaking her head. "No." She knew how much she owed me for dealing with Riley.

"So what is this fish-gigging? You do it at night?" Riley asked.

Carla helped me. "Usually it's in the spring, but yes, it's at night. Pete knows all the honey holes."

Riley grinned at Carla. "Are you one of them?"

I kept my jaw clamped against how much I wanted to hurt him. Maim him. Punish him.

"Sure, why not? Let's go." Riley hopped into my car. Carla gave me a grateful look, one I would collect on later. "Where we going?"

"Lake Skiatook. It's near here."

Once in the car, Riley couldn't stop talking. It was making my job easier. "All the evaluation in the world doesn't matter on the trading floor when the oil price goes against you. Have you ever had a problem like that?"

*Does he know? If he does, it doesn't matter now.* "So, we'll go after carp and red horse. The gigs have fourteen-foot handles. A buddy of mine has a boat with the floodlights."

"I thought you were a New York hot shot who didn't have friends here," he said.

"You thought wrong," I said. "We get points based on the weight and the species."

The marina was dark. Riley lumbered out to pee. "Hey, Carla's some piece of ass, isn't she?"

When he returned, I got a flashlight and pointed him toward the lake, him in front of me. I slid the tire iron from my waistband. When we were two feet away, I swung the iron with everything I had.

"What the—"

I crushed his ear and jaw and stood over him when he went down. I drove the sharp end through his throat, pinning him to the ground and watching his arms flail.

He never had a chance.

"Riley, don't you know that pain is just your body expelling weakness? You're expelling all your weakness now."

I pulled a skinning knife from my trunk. I used the tire iron to break his sternum and carve out his warm, still heart. I threw it in the lake. The catfish would feed well tonight.

Anyone who saw the body would know the Raven Mocker had made a visit. The only person who'd seen me with Riley was Carla, and I would soon make sure she couldn't tell. Unlike on the canoe trip, this time I'd be successful.

❧

On the part of I-40 that ran through tribal land there were no billboards to distract Lynn or break up the monotony, so she welcomed the phone ringing. It was Mark Shepherd, TriCoast's security chief. "Are you with anyone?"

"No," she said.

"Where are you?"

"Driving from Tahlequah to Tulsa."

"Pull over."

Lynn did as he asked.

"Did you see Pete Whitehawk?"

"Sure. Jesse and I just went to a basketball game with him."

"Did he get near your car? Give you anything?"

"No, why?"

"A few minutes ago I got word from the police Jimmy's brake fluid had been mostly drained. And they've gone back and looked over Pete's and Keith's previous clients, all those deaths from supposedly accelerated dementia. Then they tested the blood of three of Adela's current clients. Each shows abnormally high byproducts associated with ethylene glycol. Antifreeze. Stay away from Pete and from your ex-husband."

"Oh my God! Not Keith! He wouldn't! Besides, he's not even here. He's still in Houston, recovering."

"You don't know him now."

"They were able to figure it out?" Lynn looked over at the cup of soda. She'd had a sip and then put it aside while she drove. "Mark, at the end of the game Pete gave me a cup of soda for the road."

"Don't drink it!"

"I've already had a sip."

"Did you see the cup when he bought it at the concession stand until the time he gave it to you?"

"No. He gave me and Jesse some for the road. He said it would help keep us awake."

"There's a good chance it's poisoned, Lynn."

*The first swallow tasted too sweet.* "I just had one sip." She reached over to the cup and started to pull it from the car's cup holder.

As if he read her mind, Mark said, "Don't throw it out. Save it and we'll test it."

"He gave Jesse a cup, too. I'd better call Jesse right now."

"If he drank it, he should go to the hospital."

"If Pete's involved, someone he trusts has to talk him down. The only person who can do that is Jesse. Maybe we'll get lucky and Pete will tell Jesse everything."

Mark was curt. "Maybe the moon is polka-dotted. You have to get Jesse to an emergency room if he's been drinking antifreeze."

"Why, to get tested? I know from chemistry that ethanol's the antidote," Lynn said.

"Not self-administered. You don't know how much you need. Going to a liquor store won't solve the problem. You're driving and you're poisoned. I'm calling the highway patrol now," Mark said.

"Okay. I'll phone Jesse and go to an emergency room." She hung up. *The only reason I'm alive is because Jesse saved my father. I owe it to him to keep him safe however I can.*

When Jesse answered his phone, Lynn said, "Pete may have tried to poison us. Did you drink any of the soda he gave us?"

"Lynn, are you okay? That's crazy."

"I can't go into it now, but did you drink any?"

"Yeah, about a quarter of it."

"My security chief has told me we both need to go to the hospital. The antidote is alcohol."

"I've heard about cases like this before but it's hard to believe I'm one now. The hospital, when they come to me for funding, told us about antifreeze poisoning from people trying to get high, and that that's how they justify pure ethanol in their budget. So Lynn, do what you want. I'm going to buy PGA."

"PGA?"

"Pure grain alcohol. Beer won't work, at least not the stuff they sell in this state. If you didn't drink much you could counteract with just a few shots of grain alcohol. Then I'm going to Pete's and make him tell me the truth. Pete is the son of one of my best friends. I can't believe what you're telling me about him."

Mark had doubted Keith, but had Pete poisoned Keith, too? And what about Preston? Had Keith arranged his suspiciously unlimited casino credit line?

They needed to find and stop Pete now before he hurt anyone else. Carla probably wasn't safe. They'd explain to the police and the sheriff, but it would be complicated. "Where's Pete's house? I'll meet you there."

Lightning forked nearby. She punched in her ex-husband's cell number, hoping he wasn't still so weak he couldn't answer the phone, and was relieved when he picked up. "Keith, listen. We need your help. I think it's Pete."

"Love the guy. He's not afraid to take risks and seems to have a real knack for finding clients."

"Well, more about that later. Two things. Pete said a lot of your clients happen to be teetotalers. As you seem to be now. Mostly."

"Sure."

*Bingo! Since Pete's quickly-deceased clients and his partner, my ex-husband, don't normally drink the antidote to ethylene glycol—ethanol in any form, from beer to hard liquor—it would have been even easier to poison them.*

"Second question. Has Pete had any kind of problem lately? Financial or otherwise? Has his behavior changed?"

"He's cursing the oil futures and options markets more than usual. I think he's got really serious money in them. Our company doesn't. I don't know what he's done on his own."

"Has he lost a lot of money, maybe?"

"Doesn't act like it. But I've seen him studying volatility tables and charts. He said something about being long in the market when he should have been short. And every so often he takes a day to go somewhere. I think it was Vancouver a few weeks ago. We give each other space and privacy. That's how the partnership works."

"Who else would know about his investments?"

"What, now you're a cybercop?"

"I don't have time to explain it. Let's just say your clients haven't been dying from natural causes."

⁓

I wanted to see Huck and Hooper before I met Insel. I knew he'd arrived. He told me he'd been testing explosives and finalizing his plan...our plan...the plan to which I had mortgaged my life. Once it was completed, the Chechen had told me my debts would be erased. My life could begin again.

I was worried about Huck. He'd been bred as a hunting dog and was only eight years old. Yet he'd begun having trouble seeing and sometimes he wheezed. Last week he'd bumped into a chair, then tripped over his food bowl. One night I'd let him outside and he didn't return. When I heard a noise, I went outside and found him stuck between a water pipe and the house. The vet had prescribed pain pills but nothing else.

Hooper seemed to sense the problem because he stayed closer to Huck than ever.

I couldn't believe my mother never cared about Huck and Hooper when she had cared about her own dogs more than me. Well, her time had come. And gone. Someone would eventually find her body.

When I opened the door to my house, my heart stopped. In the next second it felt as if someone had scooped out my insides and thrown them on the floor.

Huck and Hooper were motionless on the porch. A few half-gnawed rib bones nearby were soaked in yellow-green liquid. I screamed once and buried my head against their bodies, first Huck, and then Hooper.

I stroked both of them, but through their thick, soft fur I felt cold skin. Their paws were icy.

Huck would never wait at the door for me. Hooper would not bound and bark, his eyes dancing as he begged me to give him a slab of meat. Pure, naked grief. Grief for a lifetime of memories. Grief because they would never get better. I loved them and they had loved me back, the only creatures on the planet that did. They were more faithful, more loyal, and kinder, than any human I had ever known.

My family was dead, and it was my fault. I stared hard at their bodies, as if staring could make them jump up again.

I stumbled from the house. Their house. Now a mausoleum. I closed the door, stunned by silence in the space where their joyous barking should have been.

In a flash it was clear. In my hurry to leave earlier, I'd dropped the plastic bottle of antifreeze on the kitchen table as I often had. They'd never been able to get to it before, but they must have been hungrier than usual, gotten up, and knocked it over. It was sweet, so Huck and Hooper must have lapped it up. It was like I'd killed them myself.

I was due to meet him in an hour. Hot grief forged from my love for Huck and Hooper sharpened my mind to a diamond point as I gathered my supplies. I would complete the job, then return and decide whether I wanted to join Huck and Hooper in death immediately, leave town and disappear, or wait to be picked up by the county sheriff.

# Forty

*Northeastern Oklahoma*
*Monday night*

> *"Heroing is one of the shortest-lived professions there is."* —*Will Rogers*

"We have to find Pete!" Lynn said. She'd gotten Greg Sutton to drive her and to pick up Jesse, in case they were more poisoned than they felt.

Jesse called Pete's cell phone, then shook his head. "No answer."

Greg floored the car and held their speed just above the limit. Lynn and Jesse flung on seat belts as they raced through downtown Tulsa hills.

"He'll vamoose as soon as he sees us," Jesse said.

"Not if you're the one to talk to him," Lynn replied.

Greg pulled up one final hill, blocking Pete's driveway. "That big truck of his—he could bowl us over if he's in the back, though this might slow him down."

Jesse got out of the car and walked with an old man's shuffle to Pete's front door. The closer he got the more he seemed to slow.

"Faster," Lynn said under her breath. *Is Jesse giving Pete time to slip out the back door, or is he feeling ill from the antifreeze? Am I risking his life on what could be a fruitless search to find Pete and coax answers from him? But finding Pete could mean saving the lives of many other people.*

Jesse turned and waved them forward. She and Greg ran up the hilly front yard.

"We'll have to break down the door," Jesse said.

"I say we leave and look for him somewhere else," Greg suggested.

"You don't understand." Jesse's voice betrayed impatience.

"You're right," Lynn said.

"Right about what?" Greg said. "You two are speaking in riddles."

"What's missing here? What does he talk about most?" Lynn asked.

"Oh shit," Greg said. "No dogs. No dogs barking."

"Those dogs always bark," Jesse said.

"Does he keep a key under the mat?" Lynn asked.

"No," Jesse said.

"We have to get inside!" Lynn returned to the car, popped its trunk, and retrieved two golf clubs, a fat-headed driver and a narrower 5-iron. "Let's break the windows."

She took the driver and handed the iron to Greg, who tossed it to Jesse as if it was hot. "Not me. I'm a hipster with tats. People think breaking windows is what I do for a living."

Lynn and Jesse bashed the glass together. Another surprise. No alarm.

*Maybe Pete didn't set his alarm because he's waiting inside for us,* Lynn thought.

"Pete, let's talk. We can straighten things out," Jesse shouted. Silence.

Lynn remembered the powerful strokes with which Pete had propelled their canoe. "No splitting up. Stay together."

The house was not big, but even to Lynn's untrained eye, it appeared someone had left in a hurry. Boxes had been knocked over and there was still no sign of the dogs.

They crept onto the glassed-in porch.

"Oh no!" Lynn said when her flashlight beamed across furry ears.

Jesse found a light switch and turned it on.

The dogs lay still on the porch, head to head. Between them was the attraction and the source of death. A yellowish-green liquid dripped from the spout of a white plastic container on its side. The liquid curled in a lethal ribbon around half-gnawed bones, still oozing into the porch's wooden floorboards.

"You think it was…" Greg started.

"An accident?" Lynn said. "Yes. And Pete blames himself." She guessed that, intrigued by the smell, one of the dogs had jumped up and knocked over a gallon container of antifreeze. They'd licked the sweet-tasting poison until their kidneys failed.

"Antifreeze?" Greg said.

"Two ounces can be enough to kill someone," Lynn said. "Antifreeze! That's what killed Pete and Keith's clients."

"So he had a homemade murder shop," Greg said.

"Not Pete. It must've been an accident," Jesse said.

"What? No! He tried to do the same thing to us!" Lynn was astonished at the older man's stubbornness.

"A dead frog!" Greg yelled, poking his head out of the kitchen.

They circled around a bluish bundle on the counter that looked like twisted leather.

"Don't touch it! It's a poison dart frog," Greg said. "Only takes a few grains of poison to kill you."

"Oh my God! That's probably what killed Tom Martin, the crane operator," Lynn said. Another brain circuit connected. "So *that's* what bothered me!"

Greg looked at her. "What do you mean?"

"When we were canoeing. The crazy man who came out waving a gun. Something bugged me more than his unexpected appearance, but I was too concerned with rescuing Carla to figure it out. Unlike the rest of us, Pete wasn't surprised to see him."

"You think he arranged the attack?"

"Yes. And Carla *was* the target, but Cheryl scared him off."

"Like Jimmy. The tribal accountant she replaced. She must know something he's afraid of."

"Jesse, call Carla and make sure she doesn't open her door to anyone, especially Pete."

She heard his urgent call. "When? Where did they go? Skiatook Lake?"

"Carla was so pissed at Riley she actually called Pete and asked him to take Riley back to the hotel," Jesse said. "Pete said they were going fish-gigging at Skiatook Lake. But this isn't the season for it."

"Do you know how to get there?" Lynn asked.

"Sure, let's go," Jesse said.

"And if all else fails, there's always GPS," Greg said sardonically.

Lynn tried Riley's cell phone but got no answer. *Not like Riley.* She felt a chill that didn't come from the evening autumn air. She also tried Cheryl's phone with the same result, but she figured Cheryl was still in the hospital as her note had said.

Greg covered the dogs with blankets. "Hey!" A piece of paper was anchored by the toppled antifreeze container. None of the chartreuse liquid had seeped onto it. The note was written in the same script Lynn had seen on the Tahlequah street signs.

RⱨꞀ OˀꬵꞀR
DႱ0ᴸV
—Riley

OˀⴑꬵꞀ4Ꙩ OˀAꙀ ᏟWy DVꝒꙩS OˀAꙀ
—Cushing

ႱꙨ AT OˀyꙩWꙀ ꙀႱꝊꝊ ꝒꙩꙨ DꙩႱGꙄꙄ
DB OˀꙈWyDႱꙄꝒ4Ꙁ hꝊ. OˀnꙈWyDႱꙄꝒ4Ꙁ DB

Lynn handed the paper to Jesse.

He studied it. With a pensive look, he said, "Pete never told me he could really write Cherokee, though he's sent me a couple of email messages using the syllabary, which suggested he was starting to learn. It's not the Keetoowah dialect, which is what I would have expected him to use."

"There's a difference?" Greg asked.

"Some."

"So he clearly wrote it for you," Lynn said.

"I can read it, but I don't understand all of it."

"How much of it can you read?" Lynn asked.

"The first line is *e-tsi u-yo-hu-sv*, my mother dead," Jesse replied.

"Oh, shit," Greg said.

Jesse surprised them by shrugging. "There's a lot of bad history there. It was only a question of when."

"Should we send police to her house?" Greg asked.

"She's dead. Past tense. We can't help her and the rest of the note worries me. We'd better deal with it first," Jesse answered.

"Does it say where he is now?" Lynn asked.

"*A-da-nv-do*. Heart. Riley."

"He hearts Riley?" Greg asked.

"No. We'd better find Riley as soon as possible," Jesse said.

"So Jesse, Carla told you Pete was talking to Riley about fish-gigging at Skiatook Lake?" Greg asked.

"Let's go," Lynn said. "Read the rest of the note to us on the way."

They ran to the car and jumped in, Jesse moving more quickly now despite his age. Greg floored the accelerator and headed to Skiatook Lake, a thirty-minute drive northwest of Tulsa that Greg seemed determined to cover in twenty minutes.

Lynn called Riley. Still no answer. She tried Gene, who picked up. "We think Riley's with Pete, and is in danger. Carla told us they were going to Skiatook Lake. Can you meet us there?"

"Um, yeah. Sure. It's a big lake. Where?" Gene asked.

Lynn punched a button and turned to Jesse. "Gene, I just put this phone on conference so you and Jesse can hear one another.

If you were going fish-gigging, where would you go?"

"Did he have a boat?" Jesse responded.

"Carla didn't mention one," Lynn said.

"Maybe he has one docked," Gene suggested. "There are two marinas: Cross Timbers and Crystal Bay."

"Best guess?"

"Cross Timbers is newer. He's probably more familiar with Crystal Bay," Jesse answered.

"Gene, we'll meet you at Crystal Bay," Lynn said.

After she hung up, Jesse said, "You trust Gene, but he's been nearby when at least two of victims have been discovered. And a body turned up in his refinery."

"You're right. I trust him. A killer wouldn't have risked his own life running to a burning car to try to rescue Jimmy, *your* accountant," Lynn said.

"You don't know what his intent was. He doesn't want the refinery sold," Greg said.

"But he's not going to kill to keep it," Lynn countered.

"I served with Pete's father in Vietnam," Jesse said, and stopped.

"You've said you go way back with him."

"But you don't know why..." Jesse paused for a long time. They were on a smooth stretch of road. Lynn willed Greg to drive even faster.

Jesse continued. "I...I'm responsible for his father's death."

Lynn turned to stare at him in the back seat. At first, she'd only heard the word 'father,' and thought of her own.

Jesse had his head down. "I'm the reason he had to grow up with only that poor excuse of a mother, until finally I reported the situation and he got moved to his uncle's. Later, he seemed okay. But the damage must have been done."

Lynn thought she hadn't heard him correctly. "Wait. What? You caused Pete's father's death?"

They whizzed through a red light in the small town of Sperry. Their luck was holding.

"Pete's father and I grew up together, even though he was

Keetoowah and I was part of the main tribe. We served in the same platoon in Vietnam. It was hell. Any soldier in any war will tell you."

"So he died in Vietnam?"

"It would have been easier if he had. We came back home through San Francisco. Bad time. Just say we weren't welcome. We got drunk, started running down a hill. I teased him, pushed him. He fell right into a speeding car. Killed instantly. After everything we'd been through in Vietnam. It was my fault."

"I'm sure…" Lynn started, but Jesse interrupted her. "It *was* my fault. Let me finish. Before we'd left for Vietnam, my friend had married a trashy, crazy white woman who said she was pregnant with his kid. I'm not so sure, but he was convinced it was his."

"The child was Pete," Lynn said.

"Yeah. The woman sent pictures of the boy, but my friend, Jack, had never seen him. So Pete's own father, and I have to assume Jack was Pete's father, didn't even get to see him before he died. I'm not proud of what I did. I came back and avoided her, tried to forget it all. But then I ran into her in a bar, we started dating, and I saw the little boy Pete was becoming and how his mother neglected him."

"What do you mean?"

"Bitch doesn't even begin to describe her. Needy, selfish, unwilling to lift a finger, wouldn't change his diaper, drank all day, stayed high. No feeling for her son except to scold him. When she wasn't abusive, she forgot about him. I'd grown up in similar circumstances. Going to Chilocco saved me. Chilocco wasn't around for Pete. But I finally got one of his uncles to take him. Still, his mother messed with his mind, called crying, lied, you name it. He's always been real smart, but he didn't trust anyone. Well, you can imagine."

"Surely, things improved with his uncle." Greg squinted at the sign for Lake Skiatook, then followed the arrow.

"Not really. Pete's father and his uncle were Keetoowah."

"So his uncle took Pete and Pete didn't see his mother again?"

"No and yes. The Keetoowahs are based in Tahlequah, and she stayed in Tulsa. She wasn't far away, but she never visited him. And, to the Keetoowahs, being full-blood is important, so Pete took a lot of teasing and shunning around the time of certain ceremonies.

"Keetoowah requirements for tribal membership are strict, so I doubt he was ever completely accepted as a member of the tribe. And they're isolated, hard to get to know. Many of them live up in the hills near the eastern Oklahoma-Arkansas border."

Lynn understood. "So maybe bringing Pete's company in as a backer for this Cherokee deal was, at least in a small way, a gesture toward making up the years and distance?"

Jesse nodded. "But it's been a horrible mistake."

*Damn.* "What about this. Since Pete's quickly-deceased teetotaler clients and his partner, my now-dried-out ex-husband, didn't normally drink alcohol in any form—from beer to hard liquor—it was even easier to poison them with ethylene glycol." Thinking of her father and wishing she could be with him, she said, "Since most of the victims were old, their sense of smell and taste wasn't sharp to begin with."

"So they would be less likely to pick up the EG poisoning," Greg said, driving through another stop sign.

"Speaking of which, you and I should have more shots of this PGA to counteract the ethylene glycol," Jesse said.

Lynn drank what she estimated to be two ounces of the pure grain alcohol. It felt like a lava flow all the way to her stomach. "Remember what the emergency room doctor told us? That's what made Keith so sick! So Pete was the one who tried to kill him. But why? They're partners."

Greg said, "And why'd he leave a note instead of sending a text? Why in Cherokee?"

Lynn said, "For exactly the result he's getting. To slow us finding him, and to be sure Jesse's involved, because he's one of the few who can translate it. Can I see the note again?"

Jesse handed it to her.

"So if I understand, you've explained the first two lines. What does the rest of the note say?" She handed the paper back to Jesse.

They flew past hills and stoplights.

"*U-da-yo-hu-se-di u-go-di Tsa-la-gi a-do-li-s-ga u-go-di*. Lose much Cherokee borrow much," Jesse said.

"So he says he lost much and borrowed much. What does the word 'Cherokee' have to do with anything?" Greg asked, not taking his eyes from the road.

"Keith told me Pete said the oil futures market had gone against him. It's easy to lose money on options and futures, even when you're an experienced trader. And Pete targeted the tribe's accountants, so he must have lost some of the tribe's money, along with his own. That's why 'Cherokee,'" Lynn said.

"Keith figured out some of what Jimmy, Riley, and Carla must have learned about Pete's losses. Pete defrauded the tribe to pay off his losses and started killing anyone who suspected it," Greg said.

Greg drove faster and Lynn closed her eyes when the speed-ometer reached a hundred and ten. Jesse muttered something that sounded like Cherokee curses. The car flew around curves and bottomed out on hills.

"Can you read the next line?" Lynn asked.

"Cushing, you see it on the note. Then, *da-na go-i u-gi-s-ta-ti di-da-hi-hi he-s-di a-s-da-wa-de-ga*. Roughly, 'Meeting oil pay murderer don't follow,' Jesse answered.

"Jesse, what's the last line of the note say?"

Jesse frowned. "It doesn't make sense."

"Just read it," Greg said.

Jesse didn't reply directly. Instead, he shook his head and said, "Forget it. Let's talk about the line I just read. Pete is somehow paying off what he owes by meeting someone else, a murderer? in Cushing. He doesn't want us to follow him. I don't understand the 'oil' part."

"Gene's car is ahead of us," Lynn said.

"I'd follow him, but he's going too slowly," Greg replied.

He passed Gene and raced down the winding asphalt road to the marina.

No other vehicles were in the lot. Gene pulled up behind them and they went to his car.

"You got flashlights?" he asked.

"A couple," Greg said.

"Pair off. They may still be here."

Lynn punched in Riley's number. When it rang, she heard his ring tone. "The Stripper."

"It's over there," Greg said, running in the direction of the music.

"Oh my God!"

"Looks like a cougar got him," Gene said.

Bile rose in her throat. She stepped aside and vomited in the grass while the song played on.

"It was Pete, not a cougar. Gene, call the highway patrol," Lynn said. "We have to find Pete. And somebody stop that goddamned ring tone."

In the grass in front of them, Riley's body lay spread-eagled. His neck had been broken. The bloody hole in his chest was visible in the moonlight.

"His heart?" Gene said, shining his flashlight at the body.

"His heart's been cut out," Jesse answered. "As if he were attacked by a Raven Mocker."

# Forty–One

*Cushing, Oklahoma*
*Monday night*

> "The current energy economy (oil wells, pipelines, tankers, refineries, power plants, transmission lines) is worth an estimated ten trillion dollars."—Alex Schmid, "Terrorism and Energy Security" for the Memorial Institute for Prevention of Terrorism

The cool, fishy wash of air from the lake made Lynn sick again. "We need to drive to Cushing to find Pete and whoever he's meeting." She looked over at Gene and paused to collect her emotions. "Will you stay with Riley's body?"

He nodded.

When she reached the highway patrol, the dispatcher interrupted her. "Lynn Dayton? We're looking for you. Where are you? Mark Shepherd told us you'd been poisoned."

*Damn him.* "I'm at Crystal Bay Marina and I'm fine. But my colleague, Riley Stevens is dead. He's been murdered."

"We're sending units to your location."

Lynn ended the call. She didn't want to lose Pete by waiting for the highway patrol. It sounded as if he was planning something at Cushing, one of the biggest nerve centers of the oil universe. He had killed already. A big disruption to oil could kill millions more indirectly. If tanks ran dry, food couldn't be delivered, ambulances couldn't run, and people would panic.

She, Greg, and Jesse got into Greg's car. She called Cheryl, but there was still no answer. She tried the Payne County sheriff and the Cushing police. Dispatchers at both said units had been sent to the giant tank farm. Then she called Jim Cutler with the FBI and told him the situation.

"Just turn around and go home. This isn't for amateurs."

"We're almost there. Jesse Drum is with us," she said. "I think he can talk to Pete."

"Just because they share a history doesn't help. It might make things worse."

"Jim, we have to try."

Greg backtracked a few miles on the marina road while Lynn programmed the car's GPS. West of the marina, they saw an Oklahoma highway patrol car, overheads flashing, headed toward Skiatook Lake.

She was surprised by a strange feeling of loneliness. Riley had been relentlessly annoying and had preyed on women, but he wasn't guilty of behavior warranting his violent death.

"What's so special about Cushing?" Jesse asked, interrupting her thoughts.

Lynn kept an eye on the GPS display as she answered. "Hub of the oil business, at least in the US. Billions of dollars of oil is stored there. Comes from everywhere, goes to everywhere. Incredibly strategic."

"If Cushing is a just bunch of tanks in the middle of nowhere, who cares?"

"Cushing's the nucleus of a major oil storage and distribution system," Lynn said. "It took on even more importance when the New York Mercantile Exchange made Cushing the point of physical delivery for the crude oil futures contract. Prices at Cushing and at Brent, in Europe, set oil prices for the world. So assuring everything in Cushing is copasetic is like people knowing that the gold we store in Fort Knox is safe."

"I still don't get why Cushing is such a big deal," Greg objected. "The oil price everyone talks about is Brent."

"NYMEX oil pricing is the most transparent in the world. And, as our own production has been increasing again, storing oil is even more important. The inventory at Cushing determines whether prices will move up or down. And it's vital to our national security," Lynn said. "So, Pete and his associate must think they can bust the defenses and do damage. But who's his associate? And who are they working for?"

"I'll speed up," Greg said.

"Who owns the Cushing storage?" Jesse asked.

"Half a dozen companies," Lynn said. "Each tank is mammoth, from fifty thousand barrels to almost six hundred thousand barrels. Total capacity is about eighty million barrels, so that's a lot of tanks." After she said it, Lynn found an overhead shot of the Cushing tank farms on her cell phone and showed it to Jesse. The number of places Pete and his associate could hide appeared infinite.

When I found Huck and Hooper, it was all over for me. I didn't want to run away or be picked up by the county sheriff, after all. I figured the best way to kill myself was to keep the appointment with the assassin. He wouldn't want any witnesses when we finished with the operation. If I played it right, I could take him with me.

We'd blow up some tanks, screw up the operations software, and the Chechens Insel and I were working for would make back what they'd loaned me a thousand-fold. I'd leave this world debt-free.

I met the Austrian on the side road. He had guns, armor, C-4, blasting caps, detonators, and if needed, RPGs.

Killing the first two guards was easier than I expected. Then we were able to surprise the sheriff and the Cushing police officer, so that made four. Though I'd never seen it explained in business school, assassination was the hammer in our toolbox of skills.

"We're in the middle of nowhere," Greg said.

The car's headlights showed the road to be a steep, burned-out stretch of gray asphalt ribbonning up and down the hills. Its shoulders were narrow and disappeared entirely at some points. In those places the roadbed fell vertically toward a ditch or was crowded by a dense thicket of knobby blackjack.

Greg was driving ninety. Lynn felt every bump.

A strong south wind rushed over them, rocking the car and shearing a layer of dust off the paint. The storm was pulling in winds from all directions. Ominous western clouds illuminated by nonstop lightning looked as if they were ready to drop swinging elephant trunks of tornadoes at any time.

Lightning flashed more fiercely inside the big thunderheads. As they turned south, rain started. Soon it felt and sounded like they had driven into a waterfall. Sheets of rain came down so hard Lynn could barely see past the car's hood. Greg slowed.

She hadn't been to the giant Cushing terminal in a long time. Never at night, never in the rain, never to find a murderer.

The car began to hydroplane. Greg tapped the brakes and steered away from the narrow shoulder. They had not seen another vehicle for miles, hardly a surprise with so little visibility.

Finally, the rain slackened, its brief intensity spent. A cell tower winked its height. A triangular stock pond on their right had filled to overflowing. A pump jack labored, no doubt filling the two storage tanks on a small cement pad nearby. Lynn thought of how Jesse had saved her father. She turned to look at him. He was quiet in the back seat, staring out the window.

"Maybe Keith has more information," Lynn said. However, when she called, a nurse answered the telephone. "I'm sorry. He's not to be disturbed."

"He has information that could save someone's life," Lynn insisted.

"There's no way I can verify your identity."

"Then put him on. He'll tell you I'm his ex-wife, and I wouldn't call him without a reason."

Lynn heard the phone being shifted to Keith. When she spoke, Keith told the nurse, "It's her. It's okay."

"Keith, Pete's meeting someone in Cushing. Do you know who it is? Pete's in danger."

"Let me think. He knows some rough people. He's mentioned a Chechen who threatened him in Vancouver, but nothing came of it. We get all kinds of weird calls and propositions, you wouldn't believe. Some people are offended just because we make money. And he had tickets to Chicago not long ago—I know it wasn't for Adela business. But like I said, we try to give each other privacy since we're together a lot."

"Yet you think he owed someone a bunch of money. We have a note suggesting the same thing."

"This deal, where we back the Cherokees for the refinery, it was more important to him than anything else. We're buying in with some of our own money, too. I never questioned where he got his five million, but they may be putting pressure on him."

"So he not only had futures and options investments that probably went sour, but he needed cash to partner with the Cherokees." She looked at Jesse, who was nodding.

In the background, the nurse said, "Mr. McConaugh, that's long enough."

Lynn thought fast. "Have you seen any loan documents, anything that would tell us who he owes? This Cushing trip seems to be part of his payback."

The next voice she heard was the nurse's. "I'm sorry, he's exhausted. You can call back in the morning."

"Give me a bois d'arc tree any day," Jesse said.

"What?" Lynn asked as she ended the call.

"Wood like iron. It's what we use to...damn!" Jesse said.

"What?"

"Pete wanted to know how to make them."

"Make what?" Lynn asked.

"Blowgun darts. We use bois d'arc wood because it's so strong."

"Remember the dead frogs?" Lynn said. "He's got poison, too. This is not good."

"A traditionalist's weapon for a history-bound traditionalist half-Keetoowah," Jesse surmised.

Lynn called Mark Shepherd. "Mark, I've already called the Cushing police, the county sheriff, and Jim Cutler, but we need you to call any law enforcement, FBI, or Homeland Security people you know in this area. We need help. This is going to sound crazy, but I think Pete Whitehawk and maybe another man are going to attack the Cushing oil terminal. If they succeed, we're all screwed. Everyone in the country."

"Go on."

"As best I can tell, Pete had an options position that went sour. He'd lost some of the Cherokees' money along with his own. He's been killing elderly business owners in the companies he buys so he could turn around and sell the companies, but that wasn't enough. He must have connected with some vicious people to get money to make up his losses. On top of that, he promised to come up with five million dollars to buy his share of the Tulsa refinery. So he's in deep trouble with whoever lent him the money. He's been going after everyone who figures it out, like Jimmy. He tried to get Carla when we were on the river, and it looks like he killed Riley. I left Gene with the body and called the highway patrol. We're headed to Cushing now. We have to stop him."

"Whoa. Who's with you? Is Cheryl there?"

"She got sick this afternoon and was going to the hospital. The front desk gave me a note. I've been trying to call her, but she hasn't answered. Greg is driving and we have Jesse with us.

Jesse wants to reason with Pete, tell him not to worry about the tribal money, that they'll figure a way to make good on it."

"Lynn Dayton, listen to me. The best thing you can do is go back to Tulsa and let the trained professionals take over. I'm calling the Cushing police and the Payne County sheriff's office to follow up on your calls, and then the OBI, and FBI. You've already talked to Jim so the FBI will take the lead. I'll call the Sac and Fox tribal police to let them know what's going on since it's near their jurisdiction. And I'll phone Simone Tierney at Interpol in case she knows anything about this other person."

"Mark, we have a chance to save lives and save the country a bunch of trouble if we can get Jesse there to reason with Pete."

Mark's military background came through. "Doesn't sound like Pete's reasonable, and I don't want civilians in the way."

"I know what's at stake, and I would never forgive myself for chickening out if we can save some people. We missed the boat on Riley, and now he's dead. Besides, we're almost there."

"Lynn, you're walking into a trap."

"So help me, Mark. Tell me what we should do."

"I'm patching in Jim Cutler and we'll figure it out."

After Jim and Mark talked her through the few things they could do before law enforcement officials arrived, Mark said, "I'd still prefer you back out."

"Mark, Pete killed Riley Stevens. No matter what I thought of Riley, I can't just turn around and walk away."

She hung up and told Greg and Jesse the plan.

⁂

Greg plugged his iPod into the car's sound system. When a song in German launched, Lynn turned to him, trying to stay calm. "You speak German?"

"No, but I like this song, and it's appropriate. 'Durch Den Monsun,' which means 'Through the Monsoon.' Remember, I played it before we went canoeing?"

Lynn barely heard Greg, wondering if she had misjudged him. If so, it was too late now.

He snapped his fingers. "Someone else likes this song, and another one I have." He switched to a woman warbling in English, "All the Things You Said." He waved toward the speakers, "It's in English, but it's a Russian band. The other person who shares these songs on his playlist is Pete Whitehawk."

"Which means exactly zero," Jesse responded.

"Oh, yeah? There's a line about staring at a broken door," Greg said. "Maybe it means more than we think. Anyway, Pete said a friend had recommended the songs. Now how many people know German and Russian indie bands?"

"More than you think and that thread's so thin I can already see it fraying," Lynn said.

"Just saying, it's not a coincidence. I don't believe in 'em," Greg replied.

Lynn's phone rang. Mark was calling her back. "Dispatchers repeated to me what they told you. The sheriff and the police are already on site but they haven't reported back. I'm not raising the Sac and Fox officials."

They drove through a small town with steep brick streets and downhill angle parking.

Signs announced they were leaving the Pawnee Nation and entering the Sac & Fox Nation.

As they neared Cushing, Highway 33 widened. "Where are all the tanks?" Jesse asked. "I don't see them."

"Other side of town," Lynn answered.

"Okay, we're in the right place," he said. A pipe arch was topped by a valve wheel and painted white: *Welcome to Cushing-Pipeline Crossroads of the World*. Spotlights showed the reality of the picture she'd seen at the FBI in Washington. She hoped they wouldn't be too late.

The highway turned into a literally-named Main Street, with small-town staples Mazzio's Pizza and Dollar General.

Lynn smelled fast food and sulfurous oil. The bridge across a now-overflowing Skull Creek was not far from Saints Peter & Paul Catholic Church.

Old stone cottages lined the streets. Lynn directed them to the first group of tanks. The lights of the car flashed on a red sign: *Vehicles subject to stop and search.*

They drove past the sign.

⁂

Gernot Insel liked the irony of meeting Pete at the gasoline station. They changed into contractor's uniforms; Pete looked calm. His voice was toneless as he explained what had happened to his dogs.

The Austrian was disturbed that there would be no easy way to dispose of the bodies. The Germans had mastered it once, burning millions of the dead. And he only had four.

He stopped at one of the tanks on the periphery. He and Pete took the bodies out of the truck and placed them near the tank, then covered them with a tarp. That tank would be one of their targets on the way out.

Without the distraction of any more interference from law officials, Insel and Pete stopped at several pumps and control stations. At each, Insel provided thermite and potassium permanganate. Pete pulled out his supply of antifreeze. They put thermite powder at the base of each pump and station, then mixed potassium permanganate with antifreeze and quickly backed away. The mixture produced so much heat that the thermite ignited to over twenty-five hundred degrees. The big, heavy-duty pumps melted before their eyes.

Insel knew from his aerial survey that destroying the more than four hundred Cushing tanks would not be possible in the time they were likely to have, but if he breached several, the disruption would satisfy his client. Although the tanks weren't at capacity, each one held between twenty million and fifty million dollars of crude oil. The breaches would send prices skyrocketing as the NYMEX price of crude oil—which depended on safe operations at Cushing—spiked.

The Chechens had already arranged leaks about Russian responsibility for terrorism at Cushing, with the objective of drawing United States' ire and might against its former cold war enemy.

"Now for the tanks," Insel said. They laid C-4 charges and detonators out in a quadrant around giant 400,000- and 500,000-barrel oil tanks, setting off each to breach the tank before moving on to the next. Oil gushed out, and they ignited it. Each tank was surrounded by a large dike, so they were too far apart to ignite one another. Instead the oil formed individual, huge burning pools.

⊛

When Greg pulled up to the first security gate, they expected to be stopped. Doors were open, but no one answered their calls. A nearby pick-up truck was empty, but Lynn didn't see the Payne County sheriff's truck.

The next road, Harmony, turned into a dirt track that the rain had made impassable. There was no central control, nor many above-ground pipes. Batteries of colossal tanks loomed behind cyclone fencing topped with barbed wire, each tank surrounded by a gigantic spill moat.

Outside the second guardhouse they saw a spatter of blood and two bois d'arc darts.

When Greg reached for them, Jesse grabbed his arm. "Don't touch those! They're evidence. Besides, I'm sure they're poisonous. A trace would be enough to kill you."

"Maybe they killed the guards and took the bodies," Greg said.

*My blood is the same color as yours.* Lynn remembered White Eagle's court case plea and wondered where the guards and the sheriff were. She shoved open the door to the tiny gatehouse. A computer was on a table near the door.

She jostled the mouse and the screensaver broke to the computerized logbook. "The guards recorded an entry at 10:19 p.m.: 'Two contractors from Tankwash return. Asked them why so late. Were they here to continue tank cleaning from yesterday?'"

"Then?" Greg said.

She shook her head. "Nothing else."

They got back in the car and drove along a dark asphalt road, following signs to another control room. A Cushing police cruiser was there, empty.

Lynn texted the information to Jim, including the locations of the two empty cruisers. Their phones were on to enable the FBI to track them, but they wanted to make as little noise as possible, so all but Greg's phone were in vibrate mode.

At the next control room, they flung open the door and found a pool of blood. Torn clumps of red-gold hair were caught under the legs of a chair.

Greg tugged her over to a bank of video monitors and pointed. "There they are!" In the far corner of the tank farm, two figures were crouched along the side of the white tank, pulling a tarp over something big.

"Zoom in."

She found the lever and moved it forward. "I can't see what's under the tarp. Jesus. Do you think it's bodies? And the two men moving around have something on their faces."

"Night vision goggles, maybe infrared, like Mark said they would," Jesse answered. "They've got guns. Pete's carrying the blowgun tube, too. And they have a bunch of other supplies."

"Where are they relative to us?" Lynn asked.

"Southeast side, almost the corner," Greg answered.

"What are they doing?" Jesse asked, peering at the monitor.

"Oh my God!" Lynn put her hand to her mouth as a huge flash whitened the screen, followed by a quiet boom.

"They're burning up the pumps and control stations! Would you look at that!" Greg said. The three of them stared, shocked, at another screen. "What could do that?"

"Thermite," Lynn answered. "Does anyone see the guards and the sheriff?" She texted Jim Cutler and asked how the fires changed their plans.

Jim texted back, *Noted, but no change. Stay away.*

"Where are they now?" Lynn asked.

"They're out of range of the monitors here," Greg said.

"If anyone is tied up or hurt, we need to find them. There may be other people working here too that we should warn. Do either of you want to stay here and wait for the FBI?" Lynn asked. "That would be safest."

"I'm with you," Greg replied.

"That plan you made with Mark. If we can get Pete on our side, we have a chance," Jesse said.

"Okay. Do you see a number on the tank with the tarp?" Lynn asked.

"Yes . . . C-232. And this map shows its location relative to where we are," Greg said.

They ran to Greg's car and climbed in, slamming the doors as he started it.

"There's C-132!" Jesse said. "So the one we want must be nearby."

Greg fought to keep the car on the road. The floodlights that lit other sectors were dark, and Greg had his own headlights off to avoid detection.

Lynn pointed. "There's the tank, and there's the tarp!"

Greg rolled the car to a stop. They got out and ran up the concrete wall of the dike that surrounded C-232, then stepped sideways down the other side and sprinted over to where heavy plastic sheeting was flapping in the breeze.

Lynn pulled back the tarp. Greg shined a flashlight. Four bodies in uniforms were sprawled in unnatural positions. They tested each man for a pulse, but could find none.

"Dammit. I wish we'd been earlier," Greg said. He took a gun from one body and stuck it in his waistband. Lynn did the same, but Jesse shook his head.

Hot tears of fear and anger welled in Lynn's eyes. "Let's move the bodies away from the tank. We can't leave them behind."

They formed a short break line, with Jesse dragging each body to Lynn, Lynn dragging it several dozen feet to the foot of the cement dike, and Greg dragging each body up and over the dike wall.

Lynn transferred the last body to Greg, moving awkwardly with the gun at her waist, just as an explosion rocked the air. An enormous wall of fire sprang up about a half-mile away.

Greg started. "What the fuck?!"

Lynn stumbled as she climbed the fifteen-foot slope of the dike. She shined her flashlight on the ground and saw what looked like a small plastic brick. She picked it up. "Jesse, look at this."

Jesse took the brick from her. "Hell! That's a quarter-pound block of C-4 . . . plastic explosive. They must've dropped it. That's how they're breaching the tanks, probably using a fourth of this on each tank, maybe on a hatch. I'll bet this tank is wired to blow. Shine your light around and . . . no, never mind. We don't have time to find the charges."

"Damn. Okay. Now we know where they are, and what their plan is," Lynn said.

A second explosion  thundered, and another  massive wall of flame roared up to the sky.

Even though the tanks were surrounded by dikes large enough to hold their thousands of barrels of oil in a pond, the heat and the fires could spark or jump and spread throughout the entire hundreds of acres of the terminal. The dikes had been designed to prevent just such an occurence, but they'd never been tested by this kind of situation. It wouldn't take much of the ever-present Oklahoma wind for the flames to spread beyond the dikes and combine.

"They're blowing these up one by one!" Greg's voice held a note of terror. "We need to get out of here!"

"We have to stop them before they hurt anyone else. Are you ready for me to call him?" Jesse said.

"Are you sure you want to be the bait?" Lynn asked.

"We can't let this chance go by."

Lynn nodded. Jesse punched in a number. To her surprise, Pete answered.

Jesse spoke in Cherokee, as they had planned with Mark and Jim Cutler. "Pete, it's Jesse. Your father was my best friend and I'm sorry he died. I know what you're doing but you have to stop and get help. I'm sorry about your dogs. Will you meet me?"

Another surprise. Pete agreed.

Jesse said, "He asked where we were. He told me to go about a quarter-mile straight on this road, make a right, and park behind the Payne County Sheriff's truck. He'll be out in the open."

"So they took the sheriff's truck. Let's change this up," Lynn said. "I'll drive and get out with Jesse to cover him. Greg, you crouch down in the back seat. If we're lucky neither of them will know we have a third."

Lynn hoped the highway patrol and FBI were closing in.

She pulled the car behind the sheriff's truck, parking about five feet away. "Greg, ready?" she whispered. Greg had programmed his phone to play the German and Russian songs they had heard earlier as a distraction.

"Why do I feel like I'm taking a cell phone to a gunfight?"

Pete was standing about twenty feet away from Jesse's passenger side door. They couldn't see the second man. Jesse opened his door. Lynn scooted across the seat and got out of Jesse's door behind him. She was carrying her gun loosely, walking to Jesse's left. Both were about five feet away from the car now.

The driver's side car door creaked slightly as Greg eased it open.

Pete stepped closer to them, his night vision goggles glinting menacingly.

Jesse said gently, "You cover yourself with the blanket of heritage and risk not coming out, being stuck in the past. I can help you."

"I'm not some trauma survivor and I'm not a victim," Pete said, evenly.

"But you have done so much good," Jesse said.

Lynn listened, hoping Greg was now at the back bumper of their car and still out of Pete's sight.

"Since when is murdering old people doing good?" He glanced to Lynn's left.

"There's a way to make amends, Pete, I'm sure of it," Jesse said. "We all need closure on your father's death."

"Don't tell me about closure. I fucking *hate* that word!" Pete shouted. He raised a pistol and aimed it at Jesse.

Lynn raised her gun and stepped between them. "Don't shoot him."

"No!" Jesse said.

Lynn felt an arm around her throat and she was yanked away. She remembered when Cy's daughter Marika had covered Lynn's eyes in the pool and almost drowned her that Marika said she could identify people by how their hands felt. The second man must have been hidden in front of the sheriff's truck and come up behind her. That's what Pete had been seeing, maybe even signaling. Now the accomplice had her.

The man behind her growled," Continue, Pete. Kill him or I will. Then we'll deal with her. Women are easy to kill." His voice could not have been clearer or colder.

Pete stepped closer to Jesse and took aim.

The German monsoon song blasted. In the fraction of a second distraction, Pete threw himself in front of Jesse to protect the older man from the accomplice.

Lynn hammer-fisted her attacker's groin, but it was protected by body armor.

Greg stepped from behind the car, his gun aimed at the second man's head.

Lynn half-turned, kicked back into his knee and fired at his ankle. Despite his scream, she wasn't sure she had hit him.

The accomplice, dark-haired and fair-skinned, lifted his leg to take the weight off the ankle. He held his arms up as if surrendering.

Greg waved the gun at Pete. "Drop it."

Pete did and Lynn kicked it away.

Then Pete grabbed one of his darts.

Jesse shouted, "No!"

Pete jammed the dart into his own neck and reached toward Jesse, who held him as he collapsed.

The accomplice broke and ran to the sheriff's truck.

Lynn chased him, her anger accelerating her pace.

He jumped in and roared away before she could reach him. She fired a couple of rounds in the direction of the fleeing pickup.

Lightning flashed. She heard the first sirens and the long, low rumble of helicopters.

⚜

I saw Huck and Hooper at the bottom of a clear lake. They were trapped but alive. Their tails were wagging and they were looking up at me from under the water. I dove in to save them or join them. It didn't matter which. I would be with them.

⚜

Jesse heard helicopters above. They were a welcome sound now, just as they had been in Vietnam.

# Forty-Two

*Dallas*
*A few weeks later*

Tyree Bickham and Cy found lawyers for Lynn, Keith, and the others. For ten days they were questioned by the FBI, Interpol, and the US attorney.

One afternoon Lynn went to Cheryl's funeral, where, as an Iraqi war veteran and former Coast Guard officer, she was given full military honors. Neliah Jefferson told her Cheryl had been poisoned with batrachotoxin, or BTX. Tom Martin had died from the same poison and she'd seen Pete kill himself with it. Other evidence also linked Pete to Tom's and Cheryl's deaths, as well as Riley's. Evidence also showed he'd accelerated the deaths of several elderly business owners by poisoning them with ethylene glycol.

They'd been questioned separately and together about the murder of the Saudi prince's two bodyguards, the sabotage they'd disrupted at Cushing, the murders of Riley Stevens, the security guards, the county sheriff, and the Cushing police officer. With the FBI and US attorney, they traced the Minnesota deaths and injuries, the murders of Nigel Wold, Helena Farber, Amanda Parsifal, Dag Nordval, Roberto Molina, Cheryl Wilkins, and Pete's mother, as well as the suspicious deaths of Tom Martin and Jimmy Deerinwater. Simone Tierney, of Interpol, had been especially relentless in her interrogations.

After putting a name to the second man, Gernot Insel, they

wouldn't answer Lynn's questions except to explain he was a wealthy foreign consultant whose business services were believed to extend to assassination. But until this time, his involvement had never been proven.

The law enforcement officials were skeptical Keith hadn't known about his partner's penchant for hastening their clients' demise with antifreeze. "I couldn't monitor all his phone calls or what he did when he wasn't with me," Keith insisted. "I noticed the owners would get confused a few weeks after we met them, but I thought it was dementia."

Lynn was exhausted but continued answering the questions as thoroughly as her lawyer allowed. Each day she reminded her questioners about her father's fragile health. She quickened the pace of the wedding planning, and returned to work in her Dallas office, or to see her father and Cy, when she wasn't being interviewed.

Together with Jim Cutler of the FBI and Simone Tierney from Interpol, she and Keith constructed flow charts and added to the link analysis programs.

One Saturday morning, Lynn sat at Mike Emerson's glass-topped table in the TriCoast CEO's office. "I still can't believe my ex-husband's partner tried to ambush me with an Austrian assassin in the middle of the Cushing tank farm."

"And Pete was responsible for killing not only his own mother, but several of their clients? Working for Chechens, whose real goal was to blow up Cushing, and then blame Russians for the resulting sky-high oil prices?"

Lynn nodded. "The FBI didn't tell us much, but they surmised the Chechens had some way to put the blame on their arch-enemies, the Russians. Russia could then have been drawn into conflict with the US, and the Chechens would have us doing their dirty work for them."

Mike shook his head. "There's a grudge match I don't want to get in the middle of."

Lynn nodded. "And that ethylene glycol was nasty stuff. Not only did Keith and Pete's older clients have trouble tasting it, but because they were generally teetotalers, it was unlikely they'd be drinking the natural antidote in their nightly toddies. Instead of getting to them all at once, like he did with Keith and tried to do with me and Jesse, he poisoned them gradually, over weeks or sometimes months."

"Tyree told me they found Pete's mother hanging from a pump jack in Osage County," Mike said. "Pete's were the only fingerprints. The coroner determined she was already dead by the time he put her there."

Lynn was astonished at the destruction Pete Whitehawk and Gernot Insel had wrought. When she named all of it for Mike, he shook his head.

"And those are the ones the FBI knows about. They wouldn't tell me much, but they did say this guy Gernot Insel moves easily, has several passports, and appears to have cover in high places in several countries. It's a shame he got away from us in Cushing," Lynn said.

"Are others involved with him?"

"I gathered they think Insel is a mercenary. A very good, very expensive one. They didn't tell me much except the obvious. His client, which seemed to be the Chechens, wanted the Cushing oil terminal blown up so they could blame the Russians. But there's a long list of countries that would benefit, either directly through oil prices or from the symbolism as a jihadi action. They're still narrowing it down. The Chechens had gotten to Pete, offered him the loan in exchange for his help. Maybe he intended to exert power once Adela bought into the refinery with the Cherokees."

"So, when it wasn't certain that would occur, even after they kept knocking off the other potential buyers, they went for the more direct choice of attacking Cushing." Mike shook his head. "Amazing."

"Well, we were lucky lightning didn't hit Insel's truck," Lynn said. "The back was apparently loaded with RPGs and even more explosives. I'll take luck any day. Of course, I'll need that same level of luck to ever get in the room again with the Saudis."

"Keep your hopes up. Burl may come through again for you. Tyree also told me that with the help of Neliah Jefferson, it looks like the shoeprints near Riley's body came from Pete's shoes, a pair of Air Natives."

"Yes," Lynn said, "Neliah and I talked basketball, and Jesse told me about the bigger-than-normal Air Natives the night we went to the game. I should have guessed Pete owned a pair. He got in trouble when he had to pay up on oil options that went against him. You know from TriCoast's hedging program about strike prices, right?"

Mike nodded. "Sure, it's the price at which an option is exercised."

"He had a bundle of options that hit their strike price. He owed millions he didn't have. And, he'd borrowed five million more to pay for his share of the refinery.

❧

One day, after a meeting preparing CIG to take over the Tulsa refinery's operations, Jesse finally translated for Lynn the last line of Pete's note.

"*A-yv u-ne-la-gi-a-da-de-li-se-di ni-hi. Un-ne-la-gi-a-da-de-li-se-di A-yv.* I forgive you. Forgive me."

"You did everything you could for him," Lynn said. "And Jesse, you saved my father's life."

He shrugged. "*Howa.*" Okay.

❧

When she suggested to Cy they move up the wedding because of her father's poor health, he agreed immediately. Seeing Keith had helped her overcome doubts from her failed first marriage. She felt only joy about marrying Cy.

The minister altered his schedule for the accelerated date. At one last, long afternoon of counseling, Lynn and Cy found no major areas of disagreement. They had concluded weeks earlier Cy would keep the parental on-call responsibility for Marika and Matt.

They picked up the children at Cy's sister's house. At dinner, Matt was even willing to try a few bites of pad thai once Lynn assured him it contained peanut butter. Marika savored her noodles and declared she, too, would like to grow up and own a restaurant. "Then I could eat anytime I want and I wouldn't have to pay, right, Dad?"

"We need to talk about how that works," Cy said.

After delaying their honeymoon and promising their families and friends a large reception in a few months, Lynn was relieved to focus on their immediate families. Her father's cheer broadcast his approval of the marriage.

Ceil arrived from Paris mid-week. The family reunion completed Lynn's elation. She arose at 5:00 a.m. and talked to a wide-awake Ceil the next few mornings as Ceil adjusted to the time change.

One morning Ceil looked at Lynn with tears in her eyes. "There are nights when I dream of Mom and how she was always there. Then I wake up and realize she's dead."

Lynn cried with her. "I miss her too. . . . so much."

Often, Ceil entertained their father with stories of her new life in France, telling him, "I couldn't put everything in my e-mails."

A few days later, Lynn and Cy married in the garden at her father's house. The afternoon was clear and cool.

Cy's parents and his sister's family attended. A niece played keyboard preludes influenced more by Fall Out Boy than Johann Sebastian Bach. Yet at Lynn's nod, the young keyboardist's version of the wedding march could not have been more traditional.

Ceil pushed their father's wheelchair so he could hold Lynn's hand. He gripped it with a strength that made her hope, despite the complications, despite the oxygen tube he required, despite everything, he would recover. His cheerfully robust grip was the best wedding present she received.

Jesse Drum sent a box shaped like a 7, with both the design of the seven and the material—cedar wood—representing the highest levels of sacredness and purity.

The minister first addressed Cy's children. "Do you promise to honor your father's new partner as your step-mother?"

"We do!" they said.

"And do you, Lynn, promise to love and cherish Matt and Marika?"

She smiled at them. "Yes, I do. I sure do."

After Lynn's and Cy's own vows and a long kiss as husband and wife, Matt and Marika yelled, "Time for bubbles!" Together the children cranked the handle of a big bubble machine. Soft, wet bubbles flew and sparkled in the sun.

◦◦◦

The Cherokee Investment Group reported its highest-ever casino revenue, allowing it to increase tribal employment and to venture into a new business, oil refining. They described technical assistance from Gene Blahunka and several other TriCoast Energy engineers. CIG was soon supplying gasoline and diesel not only to all of the tribe's own stations, but to dozens more in Kansas, Missouri, Arkansas, and southern Oklahoma. The contracts were finalized in Tahlequah the day the Lady Indians basketball team won another state girls' championship.

Jesse Drum's Cherokee language classes filled to capacity. Profits from the Cherokees' refining business allowed him to add more courses and more teachers.

A week after the wedding, Lynn put her house on the market and moved her furniture and clothes to Cy's house. They again discussed buying a larger house but decided to wait until Matt and Marika were comfortable with Lynn's constant new presence in their lives.

She returned to work. Together with Sara Levin, she requested a company-wide review of all risk exposures, financial and physical. She chose Dallas-area projects and meetings so she could be near her father.

⟨≫⟩

When she met with the same minister to discuss the austere service she would need, the minister said, "A phrase you might think about is that your father will be entering into rest. Maybe he wants to stop fighting the pain, even though you don't want him to."

The minister's words were not enough. But they came back to her when she visited her father that night and heard him gasp for each breath.

Although Hermosa's care of her father had been joined by round-the-clock nurses and daily hospice visits, Lynn agreed with Mike to handle work from her father's home for a few months. She returned to Cy's house—*our house*, she thought—at night. Ceil got a leave of absence. She divided her time between their father and playing with Matt and Marika.

Despite the preparations, Lynn wasn't ready when Hermosa called.

Cy rolled over and looked at the clock's glare. *11:37 p.m.* He stroked her back as she hunched over her cell phone.

"Of course. I'll be right there." She hugged Cy, then dressed in the dark and drove quickly to her father's house. When she entered, what she saw first was Hermosa's tear-streaked face.

"He can't eat, three days. It all comes back up."

Lynn's father had instructed no resuscitation.

She went to him, held his hands and cried. "Go if you're ready. You've lived a good life. We've repaid your debt to Jesse, and now he's even part of the family. We want you to be happy, and free of your pain. You have grandchildren now, Dad. And we all love you."

He opened his eyes. One of his fingers curled against hers.

"I love you, Dad."

"Love you…will…your mom."

She covered her face with her hands and sobbed.

His oxygen tube bounced when he used all of his strength to take a big breath. It was the freest sound he'd made in months. His jaw dropped open and he didn't breathe again. Pain-etched lines on his face softened. He looked younger.

༄

In the remote, gently-rolling hills of eastern Oklahoma, it appeared as if nothing much happened, or would. But when visitors topped a hill to see a slow, rusty pump jack, they realized that for over a century, all the action started underground. And ended there, too.

ᎤᎵᏍᏛ (*U li s dv*)

# Acknowledgments

My first thanks go to fellow author and former law enforcement officer Gary Vineyard, my critique partner. Gary edited a key draft, offered encouragement many times, and powered me through doubts about writing my second book.

Lisa Smith and Linda Houle of L&L Dreamspell: you were the best. You focused on quality and on publishing innovation. Lisa, we share your grief over the loss of Linda.

It was a pleasure to work with editors Patrick LoBrutto and Cindy Davis. Both made such nice catches they belong on a pro baseball team.

Thank you to the experts at CrimeSceneWriter. Just a few of the many include Adam Firestone, Joe Collins, Orblover, Doug Lyle, MD, Wally Linds, Steve Brown, CJ Lyons, Robin Burcell, Allison Brennan, Joe Prentis, and moderators Wally and Donnell.

Danny James Cassidy, MD at St. Joseph's Regional Hospital in Ponca City, Oklahoma, has diagnosed gradual-exposure ethylene glycol poisoning. He answered several questions at the end of a long night's shift at the emergency room. I have owed him these thanks for a long time.

Kim Brumley's and Edward Lucas' excellent books were re-sources, as were family members and historians such as Charles and Virginia Starks, Ann Champeau, and Bessie Rivers. Ann also gave me a style rule I use every time I edit.

I appreciated Alex Schmid's article on energy security for the Memorial Institute for the Prevention of Terrorism (MIPT), in Oklahoma City. At MIPT I was fortunate to speak with William Cox, Training Director. He described the Institute's work and the path from William Pierce to Timothy McVeigh.

Thanks to Kay for the music and Bill for the electronics expertise. Toni Hennike and Bill Dannenmaier each provided background stories.

Teacher Ed Fields, a Cherokee language coordinator for the Cherokee Nation awakened my interest in the language. Donna Flood's history archives the unique place that was Chilocco Indian School.

The **Cherokee Phoenix** is a comprehensive, well-written source for news and culture of the Cherokee Nation.

Thanks to Ron Nelson, lawyer and traveler, for the discussion of Oklahoma Native American law and life in Bahrain.

What first seemed like bad luck—dropping a driver's license in Tulsa's River Park—became fortune when it led to meeting refining structural designer Tom Trimble, Sr. Tom returned the license, along with useful advice about pressure vessels.

Public relations expert Diane Feffer focused me on the end game. The several opportunities to discuss energy economics and writing she found kept me going as I finished revisions.

Thanks to critique group members Art Bauer, Helen Holmes, and Carol McCoy for their assistance with early drafts. Half-Price Books generously hosted us. When I first began writing scenes for this book, Carol gave such strong praise to one particular scene that I was boosted by it as I wrote other scenes. Thanks, Carol.

Tulsa-area natives Ruth and George Ratliff and Bonnie and Dave Simms provided background. And one classically windy Oklahoma morning, I toured the University of Tulsa, courtesy of its chemical engineering department, and met its appealingly energetic students.

I couldn't have progressed without the Cooper track rats. Thanks to Emily, Julie, Sam, Diane F, Irving, Arnie, Marcia, John, and Maurice.

Several fellow authors were encouraging in different ways and at different times, sometimes just with a word or two: Vince Flynn, Ben Fountain, Twist Phelan, Jordan Dane, Karna Bodman, and Jim Fusilli.

Thanks to readers for your impatience to read the next installment.

I appreciate my family and friends for your patience. Joe, always.

Words don't exist to sufficiently thank the innumerable people who helped my sister in her last months. In particular, I thank Karen and Jim Deakins for giving my sister two special days.

Linda's husband and sons were treasures throughout her illness and remain so today.

## Historical Notes and References

Oklahoma's history began with the forced resettlement of dozens of Native American tribes. It entered statehood in 1907. Shortly thereafter, an oil boom began that, at one point, made Oklahoma the world's biggest oil producer.

Fourteen years later, in one of the worst rampages in the country's history, as many as three hundred African-Americans died in the 1921 Tulsa riot. In the 1930s, the Dust Bowl further decimated western Oklahoma.

The Murrah bombing in 1995 was a sorrowful, punctuating note.

Overall, the history of Oklahoma is rich with the contributions of its Native American tribes. It has also been marked by, and built back from, catastrophes. The following notes refer to some of its tribes and three seminal events: the discovery of oil and the Tulsa riot of 1921, the Dust Bowl, and the Murrah bombing of 1995.

### Four of Oklahoma's Native American Nations

Federal recognition establishes a government-to-government relationship between a Native American tribe and the US government. It also allows tribes access to health funds for clinics, culture, and education. Achieving federal recognition status is difficult, requiring extensive documentation. Of the more than 560 federally-recognized tribes, including nearly 230 in Alaska, fewer than fifty have attained this status since 1960.

Thirty-eight federally-recognized tribes are headquartered in Oklahoma. Most were forcibly moved to what was "Indian Territory" during the 1800s.

Four tribes mentioned in this book are the Cherokee Nation, the United Keetoowah Band of Cherokee Indians, the Osage Tribe, and the Ponca Tribe.

**Cherokee Nation and United Keetoowah Band of Cherokees (UKB)**

There are three federally-recognized Cherokee tribes: the Cherokee Nation, the United Keetoowah Band of Cherokees (UKB), and the Eastern Band of Cherokees. All originally lived in North Carolina; the Eastern Band still does. The eastern "mother town" of the Cherokees is Kituwha. The Oklahoma town of Fort Gibson, near Tahlequah, was also once named Keetoowah.

The Cherokee language is Southern Iroquoian. It became the first written Native American language when Sequoyah created the Cherokee syllabary in the early 1800s. A living language, Cherokee is believed to be spoken today by about ten thousand people in North Carolina and Oklahoma. Numerous programs build and support its use.

Per Cherokee.org, the Nation's official website, "The Cherokee alphabet is technically not an alphabet, but a syllabary. Each Cherokee symbol represents a syllable, not just a consonant or a vowel. For example, in the English alphabet, *ama* ("water" in Cherokee) is written with three letters: **a**, **m**, and **a**. Using the Cherokee syllabary, the same word is written with only two characters, pronounced 'a' and 'ma.' For this reason, Cherokee symbols are usually arranged in chart form, with one column for each Cherokee vowel and one row for each Cherokee consonant."

| | A | E | I | O | U | V |
|---|---|---|---|---|---|---|
| | Ꭰ a | Ꭱ e | Ꭲ i | Ꭳ o | Ꭴ u | Ꭵ v |
| G/K | Ꭶ ga Ꭷ ka | Ꭸ ge | Ꭹ gi | Ꭺ go | Ꭻ gu | Ꭼ gv |
| H | Ꭽ ha | Ꭾ he | Ꭿ hi | Ꮀ ho | Ꮁ hu | Ꮂ hv |
| L | Ꮃ la | Ꮄ le | Ꮅ li | Ꮆ lo | Ꮇ lu | Ꮈ lv |
| M | Ꮉ ma | Ꮊ me | Ꮋ mi | Ꮌ mo | Ꮍ mu | |
| N | Ꮎ na Ꮏ hna Ꮐ nah | Ꮑ ne | Ꮒ ni | Ꮓ no | Ꮔ nu | Ꮕ nv |
| QU/KW | Ꮖ qua | Ꮗ que | Ꮘ qui | Ꮙ quo | Ꮚ quu | Ꮛ quv |
| S | Ꮜ sa Ꮝ s | Ꮞ se | Ꮟ si | Ꮠ so | Ꮡ su | Ꮢ sv |
| D/T | Ꮣ da Ꮤ ta | Ꮥ de Ꮦ te | Ꮧ di Ꮨ ti | Ꮩ do | Ꮪ du | Ꮫ dv |
| DL/TL | Ꮬ dla Ꮭ tla | Ꮮ tle | Ꮯ tli | Ꮰ tlo | Ꮱ tlu | Ꮲ tlv |
| TS/J | Ꮳ tsa | Ꮴ tse | Ꮵ tsi | Ꮶ tso | Ꮷ tsu | Ꮸ tsv |
| W | Ꮹ wa | Ꮺ we | Ꮻ wi | Ꮼ wo | Ꮽ wu | Ꮾ wv |
| Y | Ꮿ ya | Ᏸ ye | Ᏹ yi | Ᏺ yo | Ᏻ yu | Ᏼ yv |

The rapidity of Cherokee assimilation can be seen in the names reported in the early-1900s Dawes Rolls, and farther back in other records, even to the 1700s. In the Dawes Rolls, surnames like Thompson and Robinson outnumber vivid names sometimes considered more "truly" Native American, such as Fox or Roastingear. There are more Proctors than Pumpkins, more Parkers than Panthers.

A complete history of the Cherokees is beyond the scope of these notes. Those interested are referred to sources such as Angie LeBeau's history of the Trail of Tears and resettlement, **And Still the Waters Run**. The following is drawn from general sources, the Dawes Roll, oral histories, and **Cherokee Phoenix** issues.

Cherokee society was matrilineal. Women owned the property and passed their clan identification to their children. The seven clans—originally fourteen—function as large families within the tribe. They are the Bird, Wild Potato, Deer, Wolf, Blue, Paint, and Long Hair. They originally governed marriage and retaliation for killing.

Children could marry into any of the clans except those of their mother and father. A mother's clan members were considered sisters and brothers to a child. The father's clan members were considered fathers and aunts to the child. At one time, marrying into a parental, or forbidden, clan was punishable by death. Similarly, clans originally operated by a blood law system: if you murdered a person, any member of your clan could be killed in retaliation.

The Cherokee had "red" and "white" governments. The red government ruled during wartime. During peacetime the white government and priests presided.

According to Cherokee history, in 1540 it was Spanish explorer Hernando de Soto and his party who were discovered by the Cherokees in their homeland.

In 1721, before the United States existed, the Cherokees entered into their first treaty, with England. In it the Cherokees ceded 2600 square miles near Charleston, South Carolina, then the trade center for the new world.

In 1822 the Cherokee Supreme Court was established.

It's believed one reason the Cherokee were open to the establishment of missions was so their children could learn to read and write. Between 1810 and 1820 Sequoyah invented the Cherokee syllabary, and in 1828 the *Cherokee Phoenix*, the first Native American newspaper and the first bilingual newspaper in the Americas (Cherokee and English) was published. It is still published today.

By this time, the Cherokees had established themselves as farmers in the southeastern United States. An economic reason for the subsequent conflict was white settlers' desire for the Cherokees' easy-to-cultivate land.

Changes came quickly. In 1832, U.S. Supreme Court decision in *Worcester vs. Georgia* established tribal sovereignty and protected Cherokees from Georgia laws. However, President Andrew Jackson would not enforce the decision, and Georgia held a lottery for Cherokee lands.

The Cherokees were never conquered in war by the United States. All land cessions were made by treaty. In 1835, a minority of the Cherokee tribe, about a hundred men, signed the infamous Treaty of New Echota, which led to the Trail of Tears. The treaty, which was decided in the US Senate by one vote, gave title to all Cherokee lands in the southeast to the United States in exchange for land in Indian Territory (later, Oklahoma.) According to Chad Smith, former Principal Chief of the Cherokee Nation, "In the 1830s, the Cherokee Nation won court cases, but Congress and the President ignored the rulings and instead forcibly removed the Cherokee Nation from our eastern homelands on the Trail of Tears, killing more than a quarter of our tribe's population."

So in 1838-1839, the Trail of Tears, also called The Removal, and by some, The American Holocaust, originated in Chattanooga, Tennessee. In preparation, thirty-one forts were built, eleven of which served as internment camps. Fifteen thousand Cherokee Indians walked twelve hundred miles and at least four thousand died in stockades or on the trail.

Author's note: One family story is that my five-generations-back grandmother, a Cherokee baby, was supposed to make the arduous Trail of Tears journey. However, she was so sick that her parents must not have expected her to survive the trip. Instead, she was literally left on the doorstep and raised with the other children of a Kentucky family. While I don't have documentation, in view of the large number of casualties during the Removal, one can imagine a mother leaving a baby with a Kentucky family instead of carrying her to near-certain death on the Trail.

In 1859 the original Keetoowah Society organized to maintain Cherokee traditions and fight slavery. But in 1861 Cherokee Chief Ross sided with the Confederacy after Union troops pulled out of Indian Territory.

In 1887 Congress approved the Dawes Act to break up communally-held tribal lands into single lots to give to individual Indians.

In 1903 William C. Rogers, (not the well-known humorist, Will Rogers), became the last elected Cherokee chief for sixty-eight years and in 1905, land allotment began after the Dawes Commission Roll was taken of the Cherokees.

Not until 1924 did Cherokees and all Native Americans became U.S. citizens and get the right to vote through the Indian Citizen Act. In July 1947, literally tons of records, including those of the Cherokee Nation, were burned in Muskogee by the BIA.

The first Cherokee National Holiday was held in 1953. It commemorates the signing of the 1839 Cherokee Constitution.

In 1970 a U.S. Supreme Court ruling confirmed Cherokee, Choctaw, and Chickasaw Nation's ownership of a 96-mile segment of Arkansas Riverbed. In 1991 Wilma Mankiller won her second term as principal chief with a landslide 82 percent of the votes cast.

Members of the Cherokee Nation are renowned for their athleticism and their military service as well as for their adaptability, interest in education, and business acumen. Oklahoma's governor signed legislation to name a stretch of highway in Oklahoma City after Cherokee Nation citizen and military hero, Billy Walkabout.

During his military career, Walkabout, a full-blood Cherokee from Oklahoma, received a Purple Heart, five Silver Stars, five Bronze Stars and the Distinguished Service Cross, the second-highest U.S. commendation for gallantry in combat.

Casinos built as a result of the Indian Gaming Regulatory Act of 1988 gave Cherokees, and many other tribes, economic self-determination. Revenues typically are budgeted for tribal social, medical, and cultural needs. For example, casino income funds preservation and teaching of the Cherokee syllabary and language. Now, like other languages, Cherokee is available as a computer font, is taught in online classes and is available through Google as a G-mail language.

While it's easy to see the Eastern Band of Cherokees arose from those who escaped the Removal, or the Trail of Tears, development of a separate United Keetoowah Band of Cherokees resulted from intertribal politics dating back to different sides of the Civil War.

The UKB, like the CNO, is headquartered in Tahlequah. Its membership totals over fourteen thousand, compared to nearly three hundred thousand for the larger Cherokee Nation. Its shared history with the Cherokee Nation of Oklahoma (CNO) includes uneasiness exacerbated by changing decisions from the US courts and the BIA. For example, in June 2009, a federal appeals court rejected the UKB's claims of treaty rights and jurisdiction within the Cherokee Nation. However, in June 2010, US Assistant Secretary for Indian Affairs Larry EchoHawk ruled the CNO and the UKB were equals in jurisdiction in their 14-county area. The particular focus of concern is a 76-acre property for gaming.

Similar to the Cherokee National Holiday on Labor Day weekend, a UKB celebration at the beginning of October commemorates the history of the Keetoowah people. The celebration included a volleyball tournament, blowgun competition, gospel singing, stomp dance, fishing derby, 5K run and walk, downtown parade, arts and crafts, and a powwow.

## Osage Nation

The Osage tribe was the only one to retain its mineral rights, a fortunate decision made by Chief James Bigheart.

According to Jenk Jones, Jr., "Bigheart was the greatest of a line of strong Osage chiefs. He spoke English, French, Osage, Cherokee, Ponca, and Sioux and had a reading knowledge of Latin. A full-blood, he favored the developmental policies more associated with mixed-bloods, believing his people would prosper through capitalism. He presided over the committee that drew up the Osage constitution and was responsible for the tribe keeping control over subsurface mineral rights, so that all members who had headright shares would benefit from mineral riches (i.e. oil) no matter where found within the Osage Nation."

This was not the first good deal the Osage had struck. In 1870, they sold their Kansas land to the US government for $1.25 an acre and bought 1.5 million acres in Oklahoma from their old enemies, the Cherokees, at seventy cents an acre. They banked the difference and earned interest on it. They also earned fees from ranchers for allowing their land to be used for grazing. Later they sold some of the land to a related tribe, the Kaw, and some back to the government.

However, during this time the Osage lost as much as half the tribe to diseases such as cholera and tuberculosis. The survivors faced hunger since the buffalo on which they relied were hunted almost to extinction.

When oil was discovered under their land in the early twentieth century, the Osage became, for a time, the richest people on earth. For example, in 1900, six thousand barrels of oil were produced from the area that is now Osage County. By 1914 the same area produced eleven million barrels. Altogether, Osage County fields have produced over 1.3 billion barrels of oil and 165 billion cubic feet of natural gas since their discovery. New production techniques are boosting these totals further.

The Osage Allotment Act of 1906 established headrights for

each of the 2,229 tribal members, including children born before July 1, 1907. Those born later could become tribal members but did not have headrights. Since they could only get them through inheritance or marriage, this provision became extremely important.

Between 1919 and 1928, over two hundred million dollars was paid to the Osage tribe in royalties, bonuses, interest, and land rentals, at a time when the highest price for oil was $3.50 per barrel and the dollar had considerably more purchasing power. Osage headrights grew proportionately in value, from $385 a person in 1916 to $12,400 a person in 1923.

Extraordinary wealth brought extraordinary predation. Alcoholism surged. Merchants and doctors overcharged the Osage. Criminals robbed them. Outsiders married into the tribe and killed their new spouses to obtain allotments. For protection, most Osage had to have court-appointed guardians until they proved themselves "competent," but the guardians swindled, stole, and killed. Dennis McAuliffe, a reporter with the *Washington Post*, wrote in the early 1990s about one such case involving his grandmother in *Bloodland: A Family Story of Oil, Greed, and Murder on the Osage Reservation*.

So many Osage were killed during the 1920s—estimates vary between two and five dozen—the Osage Tribal Council brought in a then-new agency, the Federal Bureau of Investigation. The numbers vary because some of the early deaths were not described as suspicious, but as "wasting," or "unknown."

The FBI was successful in finding and prosecuting a ring leader, William K. Hale, who was killing for headrights. He and some of his accomplices were convicted, received life imprisonment sentences, and went to jail. Despite Osage protests, Hale was paroled in 1947. In 1925, Congress passed a law prohibiting non-Osage from inheriting headrights from people who were half or more Osage Indian.

Violence in Osage County wasn't limited to tribal members and wannabes. According to Jenk Jones, Jr., "Pistol Hill between Whizbang and Shidler was an especially dangerous place. Outlaws would emerge from roadside brush as autos slowed for the steep climb and rob motorists. Bridges also could be bad, with armed men suddenly blocking both ends and trapping drivers in between. The most infamous was the community best known as Whizbang. Located near Shidler, Whizbang was a wide-open place where slayings were common. Nor did holdup men spare oil rigs; many working crews were held up and relieved of money, watches and rings. In retaliation, workers at one rig surprised would-be robbers and hanged them from the well's walking beam. The sheriff asked no questions."

Today, the Osage tribe still resides in Osage County, the largest county in Oklahoma, about the size of the state of Delaware. Notable Osages include nationally-recognized ballerinas Maria and Marjorie Tallchief. Clark Gable worked as a roustabout in the Osage oil fields before heading to Hollywood. The first American Boy Scout troop was headquartered at the Osage County seat of Pawhuska.

A key reference for Osage history is Lawrence J. Hogan's book, *The Osage Indian Murders*. Jenk Jones, Jr. has also written an Osage County history.

### Ponca Tribe

The Ponca Nation is first noted in the 1700s living near the Niobrara River in Nebraska's border with South Dakota. They were closest to the Omaha, and spoke the Omaha language. In 1868, the federal government mistakenly assigned Ponca lands to the Sioux, subjecting the agrarian Poncas to frequent, fierce raids from the Sioux tribe.

The federal government took the Poncas' possessions, including their farming tools, and forcibly removed them from Nebraska to land in northern Oklahoma.

With a harsh trip, disease, and no way to make a living, about a fourth of tribe died within a year, including Chief Standing Bear's son. As he was dying, Chief Standing Bear promised his son a burial at the Poncas' traditional burial ground in Nebraska. He, his wife, and a group of tribal members took his son's body to Nebraska, on foot, five hundred miles, leaving without permission. Standing Bear was arrested for violating the removal.

Supported by many in the local and national community, particularly **Omaha Herald** editor Henry Tribble, Chief Standing Bear successfully argued a breakthrough case before the US District Court for Nebraska. The most famous part of his plea to Judge Elmer Dundy is: "This hand is not the same color as yours, but if I pierce it, I shall feel pain. The blood that will flow from mine will be the same color as yours. I am a man. The same God made us both." In his 1879 decision in favor of Chief Standing Bear, Judge Dundy affirmed Native Americans were persons, as defined by the Fourteenth Amendment, with the same legal and Constitutional rights as other US citizens.

Chief Standing Bear is honored with a statue and park in his name on the south side of Ponca City. The park recognizes six area tribes—Kaw, Tonkawa, Ponca, Otoe-Missouria, Osage, and Pawnee—as well as the eight patrilineal clans of the Ponca.

A few tribal members did not move and others soon returned to Nebraska. So, similar to the Eastern Band of Cherokee, there is also a Ponca Tribe of Nebraska. Indeed, there is still a town of Ponca, Nebraska.

E. W. Marland, the founder of Marland Oil Company and the major benefactor of Ponca City, scouted one of his first well sites on the Willie-Cries-for-War allotment of the 101 Ranch west of Ponca City. Unfortunately, the site was atop a traditional Ponca burial site; Chief White Eagle was understandably reluctant to lease it. With the intercession of a trusted friend, George Miller, White Eagle eventually permitted the well to be drilled, but not before labeling it bad medicine. This is the origin of the so-called Marland curse. It must not have seemed a curse initially: the *Willie Cries for War No. 1*, Marland's ninth well, was his first oil producer.

The tribe for which Ponca City was named now lives largely

south of Ponca City in White Eagle, named for the last war chief of the Poncas.

References for Ponca history include the official websites of the Oklahoma and Nebraska Poncas, **Standing Bear and the Ponca Chiefs** by Henry Tribble, and **Ponca City and Kay County Boom Towns** by Clyda R. Franks. **Prairie Light** gives a history of Chilocco, the former BIA-run tribal school near Ponca City.

## The Tulsa Riot of 1921

A Tulsa incident in which a part-white, part-Cherokee, angry about his father's killing, randomly wounded two and killed three African-Americans, chosen only for their race, was an unhappy reminder of vicious history. But unlike the history, Tulsa police, the FBI, and the ATF found and caught the killer, Jacob Carl England, and his accomplice, Alvin Watts.

In 1921, Tulsa city's population was 73,000, of whom 11,000 were African-American. That year it joined several major cities as a site of mass violence against blacks by whites. The Tulsa race riot of 1921 rivaled the East St. Louis riot in number of deaths— around three hundred. The entire 35-block black Greenwood neighborhood was looted and burned.

The first African-Americans came to Oklahoma as slaves of the Native Americans who were themselves forcibly relocated from other parts of the country. After the Civil War, US-Indian treaties provided land allotments for the freed slaves. Because Oklahoma welcomed African-Americans, by the late 1800s it had more all-black towns than any other state in the country.

Oil was discovered near Tulsa at Red Fork in 1901. Not coincidentally, Oklahoma became a state in 1907. The Osage killings, carried out by non-Osage trying to accumulate valuable oil-royalty headrights from their tribal owners, were occurring one county west, and peaked between 1921 and 1925.

In the early 1900s, Tulsa's population boomed from an influx of roughnecks, treasure-seekers, and Americans looking to make a fresh start. The secretive Ku Klux Klan, targeting blacks, Jews, Catholics, Asians, Republicans, Congressional radicals, and union members, had many members and sympathizers in Tulsa. After the Civil War, lynching resurged across the country. According to Tuskegee University records, in every year between 1883 and 1922 between fifty to more than one hundred and fifty African-Americans were lynched. In 1921 alone fifty-nine African-Americans were killed, "without legal sanction."

After World War I, African-American soldiers returning home met racism. Fresh from the battlefield, they had little patience for Jim Crow laws.

Inconsistent and absent policing by the Tulsa Police Department was another factor in the riot. Four years prior, in 1917, Tulsa oilman J. Edgar Pew's home had been bombed. Pew and his family were not hurt. However, one of the local newspapers, the *Tulsa World*, implicated the Industrial Workers of the World (IWW). Twelve men were arrested at the IWW union hall. Judge T. D. Evans sentenced them—*and the five witnesses for their defense*—to jail. The *World* ran an editorial called "Get Out the Hemp." That night, the police allowed about forty armed men to take the seventeen out of town, whip, and tar and feather them.

In 1919, a white accused murderer, Roy Belton, was taken from his Tulsa jail cell and lynched.

Still, the African-American community had formed a strong, prosperous neighborhood in north Tulsa. Early Greenwood business leaders patterned their district after Durham, North Carolina. Because of segregation, blacks were only allowed to live, work, and shop in this 35-block area. According to Dr. Leroy Vaughn in his book, **Black People and Their Place in World History**, "The business district, beginning at the intersection of Greenwood Avenue and Archer Street, became so successful and vibrant that Booker T. Washington...bestowed the moniker: "Negro Wall Street." By 1921, Tulsa's African-American population of 11,000 had its own bus line, two high schools, one hospital, two newspapers, two theaters, three drug stores, four hotels, a public library, and thirteen churches. In addition, there were over 150…commercial buildings that housed clothing and grocery stores, cafes, rooming houses, nightclubs, and a large number of professional offices…Tulsa's progressive African American community boasted some of the city's most elegant brick homes, well furnished with china, fine linens, beautiful furniture, and grand pianos."

On May 31, 1921, a minor incident occurred in which black 19-year-old Dick Rowland, a former high school football player who had become a shoeshine operator, stumbled against a young white elevator operator, Sarah Page. Page claimed she had been attacked. Rowland was arrested the next day.

The incident was reported as a rape in the *Tulsa Tribune*, a newspaper published by Richard Lloyd Jones. One story was headlined "Nab Negro for Attacking Girl in Elevator." In addition, an inflammatory back-page editorial ran that allegedly called for lynching Rowland. "Allegedly" because no records or copies of this issue can now be found.

Eventually, Page would drop all charges and the incident would be deemed a misunderstanding.

But that afternoon, the damage from the article and the alleged editorial was done. Several hundred whites gathered in front of the courthouse, a frequent prelude to lynching. Sheriff Willard McCullough refused to turn Rowland over and telephoned an African-American newspaper in Greenwood to warn them of the mob.

Black leaders convened to discuss protecting Rowland. Twenty-five of them went through the mob to the jail but Sheriff McCullough persuaded them to return to Greenwood. Determined to protect Rowland from lynching, fifty to seventy-five armed blacks returned to the courthouse.

In the meantime, the white mob grew even bigger, to about two thousand.

An older white man insulted a younger black war veteran, a shot was fired and the scuffle turned into a sixteen-hour battle.

The white mob swelled to ten thousand. Any store that sold

guns was ransacked by whites. Throughout the night groups of whites and blacks fired at each other.

The following morning, at five a.m., the much larger group of whites moved north to Greenwood, looting, burning, and leveling everything. Airplanes flew overhead, raining gunfire.

Ultimately, in one of the worst race riots in American history, about three hundred Tulsans were killed. Most of the casualties were black; some whites were killed when blacks defended their families and property against them.

Because hundreds of black families fled, there is not an exact count of the number of deaths.

When the National Guard arrived, they "restored order" by arresting between four and six thousand African-Americans and holding them for three days at the baseball park and the convention center.

The entire Greenwood District was destroyed, including twelve hundred homes. Ten thousand people were left homeless. The district's thirty-one restaurants, twenty-four groceries, two black newspapers and its library were burned to the ground. White mobs also destroyed six churches, including the new Mount Zion Baptist Church dedicated six weeks earlier, as well as Dunbar Elementary School and the offices of more than a dozen professionals. The black-owned roller skating rink was burned. Hundreds of black families left Tulsa for good.

Richard Lloyd Jones followed up with stories blaming blacks for the riot. White Tulsa city officials refused offers of help from around the country, saying publicly the city would help blacks build back Greenwood. Privately, they did nothing except pass an ordinance prohibiting rebuilding in the original neighborhood. Four months later, courts overruled the ordinance.

Greenwood homeowners refused to sell their land. They lived in tents donated by the Red Cross. Without help from the city, they began rebuilding.

Author's note: Although I grew up in Oklahoma, attended Oklahoma schools, and graduated from an Oklahoma high school, I never heard this history mentioned by anyone privately or publicly. Even in my state-required Oklahoma history class, the Tulsa riot was not described.

Tulsa representative Don Ross first heard the whispered stories as a teen-ager when his history teacher and riot survivor, Bill Williams, introduced him to several other survivors. In 1996, on the 75th anniversary of the riot, Ross organized a Tulsa coalition to mark the anniversary and dedicated a "Black Wall Street of America" monument at the Greenwood Cultural Center. In 1997 as a Tulsa state representative, Ross was instrumental in leading the Oklahoma Legislature to authorize the Tulsa Race Riot Commission. Commissioners interviewed survivors and researched sources to determine the truth of one of the country's worst race riots.

According to commissioner and author Eddie Faye Gates in her book, **Riot on Greenwood: The Total Destruction of Black Wall Street**, "After three and a half years of intensive research, the commission found what had been hinted at for four decades. There had been a pattern of deliberate distortion of facts regarding the riot and even the destruction of vital documents and a subsequent cover-up."

Another comprehensive history written by Tim Madigan published in 2001 is **The Burning: Massacre, Destruction, and the Tulsa Race Riot of 1921**. An authoritative source on the Tulsa Police Department is **History of the Tulsa Police Department, 1882-1990** by retired Tulsa police officer Ronald Trekell.

### The Dust Bowl, 1930s

The Dust Bowl scarred western Oklahoma and Kansas, southeastern Colorado, and the Texas Panhandle. Its effect on the western part of the young Oklahoma was profound, not least as the source for the xenophobic epithet, "Okies," used to describe poverty-stricken refugees from its towering black storms.

World War I-induced government price supports, the lure

of the last cheap land, and abnormally good rainfall gave farmers reason to bust the sod of the High Plains in the early 1900s. They plowed under deep-rooted prairie grass and planted wheat in its stead.

One farming subculture to which **Strike Price** refers is the Volga Germans. The *Russlanddeutchen* were lured to Russia from Germany by Catherine the Great in the mid-1700s. A century later, Czar Nicholas was less accommodating. When agents for the American railroads proffered German-language brochures and pitched places like Nebraska and western Kansas to be as suitable for growing hard winter wheat as the Russian steppes, the *Russlanddeutchen* listened, and emigrated. They busted the sod as energetically as their longer-established American countrymen.

However, when normal dry weather returned in the 1930s, the loose soil was barely held by roots of the new crops. It shook loose and started blowing east. Successive dust storms buried farms, bankrupted towns, and choked adults and children to death. These storms, called "black rollers," plagued the High Plains from 1930 through the early 1940s. The nation-wide Great Depression compounded the regional misery.

Although the Dust Bowl affected western Oklahoma, not eastern Oklahoma where **Strike Price** is set, it shaped the history and culture of the entire state.

Readers can find a vivid, comprehensive narrative of the Dust Bowl in **The Worst Hard Time** by Timothy Egan.

### The Oklahoma City Bombing
### April 19, 1995, 9:02 AM

Timothy McVeigh's bombing of Oklahoma City's Murrah Building on April 19th, 1995 killed 168 people, including nineteen children. It injured another 850. Two hundred and nineteen children lost a parent, including thirty who were orphaned. The Oklahoma governor's office has estimated that a third of the state's population at the time, or nearly 400,000, knew someone who was killed or injured in the bombing.

McVeigh was executed for domestic terrorism on June 11, 2001. His co-conspirator, Terry Nichols, is serving life in prison.

The mass murder left a deep wound in the state. Every Oklahoman remembers where he or she was that day.

Author's note: I was in an airport terminal, traveling on business, my toddler at home with a babysitter. How easily I could have been a parent working at Murrah, thinking my child was safe in the downstairs day care. And one of my uncles had a late-morning appointment at Murrah on April 19th. By random good fortune, my always-prompt uncle didn't arrive early for his meeting that day.

What the Murrah bombing revealed about Oklahoma was the generous response of its people, first as they supported the work of firefighters and later in the design of the memorial, built and dedicated by then-president Bill Clinton in April, 2000.

Two gates, one marked 9:01 and the other marked 9:03, comprise the memorial. Each of 168 stone chairs is placed to represent where in the building a victim was found. Each chair represents a victim of the bombing. Nineteen of the chairs are child-sized.

# About Author L. A. Starks

If you liked STRIKE PRICE, try the first Lynn Dayton thriller, 13 DAYS: THE PYTHAGORAS CONSPIRACY.

L. A. Starks was born in Boston, Massachusetts, grew up in northern Oklahoma, and now lives in Texas. Awarded a full-tuition college scholarship, she earned a chemical engineering bachelor's degree, magna cum laude, from New Orleans' Tulane University, followed by a finance MBA from the University of Chicago. While at Chicago she made time to play for a celebrated women's intramural basketball team, the Efficient Mockettes.

Working more than a decade for well-known energy companies in engineering, marketing, and finance from refineries to corporate offices prepared Starks to write global energy thrillers. Since the release of her first book she has spoken at conferences, meetings, and bookstore signings.

She continues to research, write, and consult on energy economics and investing, often speaking to professional groups for their members' continuing education credit.

In addition to her Lynn Dayton thrillers, two of Starks' short stories have been published in Amazon Shorts. Her nonfiction has appeared in Mystery Readers Journal, The Dallas Morning News, The Houston Chronicle, The San Antonio Express-News, Sleuth Sayer (MWA-SW newsletter), Natural Gas, Oil and Gas Journal, and investor website *Seeking Alpha*. She is also co-inventor of a US patent.

Starks has run eight half-marathons. She serves as investment committee chair of the Board of the Friends of the Dallas Public Library, a fund-raising and advocacy group that supports Dallas' 29-branch civic library system.